DECEMBER

James Steel is a writer and journalist based in the UK.
To find out more about James visit www.jamessteel.info

JAMES STEEL

December

AVON

AVON

A division of HarperCollins*Publishers*
77–85 Fulham Palace Road,
London W6 8JB

www.harpercollins.co.uk

A Paperback Original 2009

2

The author gratefully acknowledges the following for permission to use extracts from books:

The Random House Group Ltd for:
Life and Fate, by Vasily Grossman, published by Harvill.
Reprinted by permission of The Random House Group Ltd.
Translation by Robert Chandler 2006.
Dr Zhivago by Boris Pasternak, published by Harvill.
Reprinted by permission of the Random House Group Ltd.

Wordsworth Editions Ltd, UK, for:
Anton Chekhov, Short Stories, published 1996,
as well as introduction and notes, copyright 2002 Joe Andrew.

AP Watt Ltd, UK. Permission is granted by AP Watt
on behalf of the Executor of the Estate of Constance Garnett for:
Constance Garnett, 1926 translation of Nikolai Gogol's story 'St John's Eve'
in the collection 'Evenings on a Farm Near Dikanka, Part I.'

James Steel asserts the moral right to be identified as the author of this work

A catalogue record for this book is available from the British Library

ISBN-13: 978-1-84756-162-6

Set in Minion by Palimpsest Book Production Limited, Grangemouth, Stirlingshire

Printed and bound in Great Britain by Clays Ltd, St Ives plc

Mixed Sources

Product group from well-managed
forests and other controlled sources
www.fsc.org Cert no. SW-COC-1806
© 1996 Forest Stewardship Council

FSC

FSC is a non-profit international organisation established to promote the responsible management of the world's forests. Products carrying the FSC label are independently certified to assure consumers that they come from forests that are managed to meet the social, economic and ecological needs of present and future generations.

Find out more about HarperCollins and the environment at
www.harpercollins.co.uk/green

Firstly for my family, and secondly for all Russian writers.

Chapter One

Alex Devereux knew something was wrong.

The man, on the other side of the street, was following him through the crowd of refugees streaming down the darkened King's Road. It was snowing and the streetlights had already been switched off.

He looked like a drug-dealer: cheap anorak, unshaven, long black curly hair. But there was something about his features that made Alex think there was more to him than that; a lean, athletic face with watchful eyes.

Alex stared at the man's reflection in the window of an expensive antiques dealer. He showed up in the headlights of the stationary traffic – the Tube was now shut as well, and the roads were gridlocked. One reason he stood out was that this was such an exclusive neighbourhood. Alex could still see the clear difference between him and the crowds struggling along the pavement and weaving in and out of the traffic.

They were all wealthy commuters, well dressed in tailored coats, expensive fur hats, pashminas round their necks – the unlucky ones who had stayed at work whilst the power was still on and then missed the five o'clock Tube curfew.

The drug-dealer had been tailing Alex ever since he had left his job interview with the private defence contractor in Victoria. He hadn't been a mercenary for many years not to do some basic fieldcraft checks, especially when he left one of those firms, and he had now seen him reflected in the windows of three shops when he had stopped to check.

Alex thought through his options as he pretended to take an interest in a chaise longue. Either the guy was an amateur or someone was in a big hurry to put a tail on him. Usually professionals would work with a team of three or four on a target if they didn't want to be seen.

Whatever the case, the question now was, what the hell was he going to do about him?

His immediate fear was that this was some sort of hit. He had been mixed up with enough unpleasant people since he'd left the army for that to be possible. His first instinct was to head for his house and get the illegal Glock 9mm pistol that he kept taped under his desk; out here on the street he felt exposed. He turned and set off again into the crowds; the man detached himself from the wall opposite and followed.

The freezing wind blew heavy flakes into Alex's eyes; they nestled in his black hair, making it curl. He hunched his shoulders and stuck his chin down into the collar of his overcoat; he was broad-shouldered and stood out by a head over most of the crowd around him. He had a strong, masculine face with fine cheekbones. His expression was habitually thoughtful, but now it was distinctly dangerous.

Apart from his current personal threat, the country was also in crisis. It was only early December but this was already the worst winter since 1947: deep snowdrifts, railway lines frozen, coal trucks stuck in sidings and then, to top it all, the Russians had turned off the gas.

Such political trouble was bound to follow the global recession. Oil and gas prices had tanked, taking the Russian economy with them. With the instability, faction fighting had erupted in the Kremlin. Putin had tried to return to his old post of President but Medvedev had opposed him. The Kremlin had been split and then Medvedev had been deposed in a palace coup. His replacement as President, Viktor Krymov, was supposed to be a bureaucratic nonentity acceptable to both sides but had become increasingly unstable and aggressive. He had suspended the constitution, declared himself President for life and banned opposition groups.

Other events had heightened the international conflict. Russia's annual energy blockade on Ukraine had backfired, uniting opposition to it within the country. Both Ukraine and Georgia had been fast-tracked into NATO, Krymov threatened military action and withdrew from the Intermediate Range Ballistic Missile Treaty. He then launched punitive bombing raids against Georgia, to punish it for joining NATO, destroying buildings and infrastructure in Tbilisi.

The EU reacted with outrage, imposing immediate economic sanctions on Russia. In response, Krymov called them fascist aggressors and cut off all gas supplies to Europe.

Around half of Europe's gas supply came from Russian fields, and so power rationing had had to be implemented. The UK was badly hit because it had the most deregulated energy market in Europe; it had only a few days' reserve storage.

No one could believe it was happening; it was like the 1979 Winter of Discontent all over again. Power was switched on from nine until five for business purposes but after that it was emergency services only. Petrol supplies were also running low as tankers struggled in the snow to get out from depots.

Predictably there had been a huge public outcry and angry scenes in Parliament. The PM was under a lot of pressure to do something: schools were shut and pensioners were freezing to death.

But there wasn't much he *could* do. Krymov had been

rearming Russia, and his campaign of suppression against the media and the few remaining pro-democracy organisations in the country meant that there was no internal opposition. Russia's vast nuclear arsenal meant that open war was just not an option.

Alex wasn't sure what to make of it all. Like most people, he thought Krymov was a lunatic but equally he didn't want the government to provoke a nuclear conflict over the issue. In the meantime a very Cold War had returned to Europe.

All Alex was focused on now, though, was getting his hands on the reassuring black grip of his Glock. He hurried past Wandsworth Bridge Road, casting a glance over his shoulder; the man was still following him on the opposite side of the street.

He carried on into well-heeled Fulham and finally turned left into Bradbourne Road, the quiet street where the Devereux family maintained their London residence when they were not in Herefordshire.

Well, that was how it was in the old days, anyway. Alex's alcoholic father had died recently and he had been having sporadic conversations with lawyers – when the phones worked – about whether he could pay the death duties and keep the old hulk of Akerly, where his ancestors had been in residence for nearly a thousand years.

He increased his stride, eager to get home. He scanned the tree-lined avenue ahead, with its smart Victorian houses. Nobody was visible on the pavements but there was a new Range Rover, with blacked-out windows, parked over the road from his house.

There wasn't anything unusual about that – it could just be a neighbour who had brought it up from the country to get about in the snow, but Alex hadn't seen it before and the tinted glass was worrying. He grasped his keys inside his coat pocket in readiness for a quick entry and eyed the vehicle warily as he came up to his front gate; he was now trapped between it and the threat behind him.

Two doors on the car popped open and two men moved out fast.

Fuck, it is a hit!

He frantically shoved open the gate and ran to his front door. The key seemed too big for the lock; he fumbled with it, his back exposed to the danger.

'Major Devereux!' The bark cut across the street like a shot.

Alex froze; he hadn't been in the army for years not to recognise the unmistakably commanding tones of Sandhurst English.

He stopped fumbling with the key and turned round.

A young man walked across the road. He was tall, his blond hair scraped into a short back and sides, and he had a beaky, aristocratic nose. He was wearing a full officer's uniform: green jacket, tie, Sam Browne belt and all.

'Lieutenant Grieve-Smith, sir, H Cav!'

The Household Cavalry – Alex's old division.

If he really was army, then that meant the guy who had been tailing him was as well. It clicked now – he knew where he had seen that sort of face before: Special Forces blokes, scruffy but highly disciplined at the same time.

He glanced back along the road. Yes, there he was, standing side on to them now and scanning the street, one hand inside the opening of his anorak. The other guy who had got out of the car looked equally dodgy, in a leather jacket, Millwall football shirt and ripped jeans, and had taken up a position on the far side of street.

If the SAS were involved in this, then that meant someone high up wanted a word.

The Establishment.

What the hell did they want with him?

Alex had parted company from his regiment, the Blues and Royals, on bitter terms. Equally, his years of combat in African wars hadn't increased his respect for the fresh-faced officer in front of him now. Someone wanted to be in touch with him rapidly and presumably they had pulled in this duty officer from Hyde Park barracks to make him feel reassured.

Alex recovered his composure and moved slowly back up the garden path towards him. Grieve-Smith walked across the road and they stood facing each other on the pavement. Alex's dark brows drew together, fixing him with a level stare.

'If you'd come with me, please, sir ...' The young officer seemed to think he had a right to command.

'And why would I want to do that?' Alex kept his voice calm.

Grieve-Smith looked uncomfortable. 'You've got to go and have "a chat" with someone.' He emphasised the word to indicate that it would be anything but pleasant social banter.

'And who would that be?'

The lieutenant looked even more pained. 'I don't know, sir.'

'What do you mean you don't know?'

The lieutenant dropped his gaze apologetically.

'Look, what the hell is going on?' Alex snapped.

Grieve-Smith shook his head, dropped his voice and leaned forward. 'Look, to be honest with you, sir, I have no idea what this is about. I was just pulled off the duty desk to come down and tell you to go with these men here.' He flicked his head to indicate the other two soldiers, then looked at Alex nervously, trying to share his disdain of the modern thugs behind him with another member of the old officer class.

Alex avoided his eye. He didn't belong to that tribe any more.

He glanced again at the shifty-looking men. He obviously wasn't going to get anything else from Grieve-Smith and he didn't fancy having to outrun two SAS blokes. He took a deep breath and sighed slowly as he thought what to do.

'OK.' He nodded. 'Maybe I'll get a nice hot cup of tea,' he added without humour.

Grieve-Smith looked relieved. 'This is as far as I go, sir. I'm afraid you're with that other lot now.' He glanced at the men anxiously and then quickly walked away down the road.

The drug-dealer walked past him towards Alex without saying a word.

'Bac'a the car, please, sir,' he said in a terse Geordie accent. It was an instruction, not a request.

Alex crossed the road and got into the back of the Range Rover with the trooper. The other man got in the front seat and muttered into a radio in his coat collar.

'Alpha, this is Charlie. ETA three minutes.'

The car drove slowly down the quiet road and then turned right and started winding its way around the backstreets of Fulham. Alex was thinking that they wouldn't be able to go far in the mass of traffic jamming the main roads, but then he saw that they were driving down the lane approaching the back gates of the Hurlingham Club.

What the hell are we doing here?

The Hurlingham was an exclusive sports club with huge grounds: cricket pitch, croquet lawns, tennis courts and pools. It was an old Victorian place with beautiful colonnaded buildings; Alex's family had been members for generations, but he hadn't actually paid his fees for a year now.

A security guard saw them approaching and muttered into his radio. The large back gate swung open. They were expected. Someone had obviously been pulling a lot of strings. They drove into the area used by the groundsmen, past the snow-covered rubbish bins and mowing machines, under the boughs of a huge cedar tree and round the back of the main club buildings to the cricket pitch.

A Sikorsky S-76 executive helicopter was winding up its

rotors, blowing a cloud of snow out towards them. It was painted an anonymous white with no company markings.

'Follow me, please, sir,' growled the Millwall fan in the front seat. He and the other trooper got out of the car with Alex and, bent double against the rotor-wash, ran over to the helicopter.

They clambered in, slammed the door shut and instantly lifted off in a cloud of snow.

They rose up across the river, southwest from the Hurlingham. Alex tried to work out where they were going. After a couple of minutes he couldn't tell anything as all power had been shut off so there were no lights on the ground and everything disappeared in the pitch-black and swirling snow outside.

The pilot muttered a few times into his headset, getting course alterations from someone, but over the noise of the engines Alex couldn't hear where to. He checked his watch to track their flight time; after fifteen minutes they began to descend.

The beam of the landing light showed glimpses of snow-clad pinewoods as they swung round to land. The aircraft veered and tilted in the wind but the pilot rode out the gusts expertly and brought them down with a slight bump on a football pitch, Alex could see some sagging wooden goal-posts in front of them with a high chain-link perimeter fence behind it, topped by razor wire.

'OK, sir, this way.' The drug-dealer opened the door. They both pulled their coat collars around their faces, huddled against the white fury whipped up by the rotors, and stumbled through the knee-deep snow. The snow got into Alex's black Oxfords and melted into his insteps.

Once he was able to stop squinting against the blizzard, he looked up and saw from the aircraft lights that the field was surrounded by dark trees on three sides but that they were heading towards a cluster of low buildings.

The man pulled a large yellow torch from his coat pocket and shone it along the side of the building: brick single-storey offices of the cheapest possible construction. The windows were dark, the place looked completely deserted.

He headed towards a door. Alex glanced at a plastic plaque screwed into the brick next to it: 'MoD Training Centre RG – 8894'.

The man unlocked the door and shone the powerful beam inside, illuminating a corridor with cheap brown pine doors leading off it, each with a little Civil Service number plate. The musty smell of bureaucracy filled the place.

'If you just go down the corridor to that door at the far end, sir …' He pointed to a closed door about forty feet from them with a faint rim of light around the edge of it. He handed Alex the torch and turned to go back to the helicopter.

'Well, who?' Alex blurted at him urgently. The darkened building and mysterious behaviour was beginning to get to him.

'I don't know, sir. Need-to-know only.' The man shrugged with indifference. 'If you just go down there …' he repeated more insistently, pointing.

Alex bridled. He didn't like taking orders. He glared at him, took the torch and stalked off down the corridor. The man shut the door. He was on his own.

What the fuck is all this creeping around?

He was now seriously alarmed. The operation had come from the top – the SAS and MoD connections seemed to bear that out – but the rushed nature of the contact, pulling him off the street and dumping him in this weird location, felt wrong.

Why was the Establishment being so secretive, so rushed? They were supposed to be the ones in charge.

He stood in the corridor for a moment, listening. Absolute

silence. The building was stone cold, his breath smoked in the reflected light from the torch. He flashed it around to get some bearings: worn brown carpet and scuffed beige walls.

He brushed the snow off his hair, stamped it from his feet, straightened his overcoat and walked down the corridor, the torch pushing a circle of light out in front of him. The anonymous-looking door at the end had a little blue plastic nameplate with 'C-492' on it. He paused, put his ear next to it and listened. Nothing.

He knocked and then opened it.

Inside was a windowless rectangular meeting room as bare and functional as the rest of the building, dimly lit by a battery-powered camping lantern on a brown veneer table. The lamp lit the table but the corners of the room were shadowy. A laptop lay open on the far side of it.

A tall man in a smart coat, worn over a dark pinstriped suit, was pacing back and forth across the far end of the room with his hands clasped behind him, his white hair scraped into a severe short-back-and-sides.

He flicked a tense look round as Alex came in.

Alex recognised his large, red, leathery face instantly: General Sir Nigel Harrington was a well-known military figure. Alex had served under him when the Blues and Royals had been in 5 Airborne Brigade, based at Aldershot. A former paratrooper and ex-head of the Joint Intelligence Committee, he had retired three years ago. He was now in his late sixties but still kept his back ramrod straight and had a character-istic combative jut to his jaw.

A tough, no-bullshit commander, he had been respected by his men but definitely not liked. All officers understood that command meant taking unpopular decisions, but Harrington had implemented them with an abrasive delight that bordered on the sadistic. 'Wanker' was his most frequent moniker amongst his HQ staff.

Alex realised the fact that the general was in the room raised the significance of what was going on by another order of magnitude. The government didn't drag major figures like him out of retirement for nothing. Alex involuntarily straightened his back.

'Ah, Devereux, glad you could make it. Take a seat.' The words were barked out as an instruction.

'Thank you,' Alex muttered, and sat down at the opposite end of the table. He managed to stop himself adding 'sir'; he wasn't in the army any more and neither was Harrington, at least officially.

'Now obviously you're wondering what the hell is going on.' Harrington was never one for subtlety and launched straight in; he grinned as if this was all a big joke, but there was definitely a nervousness about him as well.

'Well, first things first. This meeting is completely secret and deniable from Her Majesty's Government's point of view. The chaps who brought you don't know I'm here and I am retired and in no way a serving member of HMG. So, before I go any further, you're going to have to do your bit as well and sign the Official Secrets Act.' He nodded at some papers and a pen laid out on Alex's end of the table.

Alex was fed up with being railroaded, but managed to ask calmly: 'And what if I don't want to?'

'Don't be an arse, Devereux!' The bonhomie dropped away instantly. 'After your last operational activities in Central African Republic, HMG has got enough dirt on you to prevent you ever working in the security industry again if it so chooses.'

'I seem to think HMG had reason to be grateful at the time,' Alex replied with heavy irony.

11

'Grateful! What do you want – a bloody medal?' Harrington glared at him. 'Look, Devereux, you haven't got any work at the moment and this could be very lucrative for you. But if you don't sign the Act you're never going to find out what it is all about, so just sign it and stop playing silly buggers!'

Alex's jaw tightened as he stared back at the other man with a calculating gaze.

There was a pause before he slowly picked up the pen and carefully wrote 'Bollocks' on the bottom of the document.

Harrington couldn't see what he had written in the darkened room and breathed out in relief. He tried to get going again in a more positive tone.

'Right. Now, so that we're clear, I am representing HMG in an entirely unofficial capacity here – you have *never* discussed this issue with a serving member of the government – and this building is as near as you will come to any part of it. However, I have been authorised to communicate with you on their behalf, and obviously nothing we say goes outside these four walls or you will be in jug in no short order.' He nodded menacingly at the documents in front of Alex.

'Now, as you well know, the country is up shit creek at the moment with the Russian energy blockade. But what you don't know is just how worried HMG is about Krymov – and this is crucial to the whole operation.' He adopted a lecturing tone, jabbing his finger at Alex to emphasise points.

'Firstly, he gets appointed as a bureaucratic nonentity who is supposed to calm the faction fight. However, as Churchill said,' and here a note of deference crept into his voice at the mention of the master statesman, '"Trying to understand Kremlin factions is like watching bulldogs fight under a carpet." He outmanoeuvres everyone in the faction fighting, kicks Medvedev out and then becomes increasingly paranoid and aggressive.'

Harrington dropped the lecturing tone and became more candid. 'Our analysis of him is basically that he is just not up to coping with the pressure of the job. He's a working-class lad who made it to factory boss under the Soviets and then got promoted through the Party hierarchy mainly because he was so boring he wouldn't ever rock the boat.'

Alex's hostility eased. He folded his arms and leaned back in his chair to listen.

'Anyway, whatever the reason, we find ourselves dealing with a very aggressive operator who,' Harrington began ticking points off on his fingers, 'cuts off gas supplies to Ukraine when they get the NATO Membership Action Plan, starts harassing joint-venture oil companies until they all pull out, renews nuclear bomber flights into our airspace and ramps up arms spending from $35 billion to over $100 billion a year using up all his remaining Stabilisation Fund. He also starts moving troops up through Belarus to the Polish border over the missile shield, and finally we have the bombing raids on Georgia!

'Now, to put all this in context, you have to remember that Russians have a major persecution complex, so initially we thought that this was all just the usual manufactured hysterics, talking tough, playing to the domestic gallery and throwing his weight around to make the country feel good about itself.

'However, we now have good reason to think that Krymov actually believes his own propaganda. He genuinely thinks that the West is involved in a secret plot to undermine Russia,' he paused to consider the irony of his next point, 'so that has now become a reality.'

Alex's eyes narrowed. Harrington blinked self-consciously, disturbed by hearing himself actually admit the purpose of the meeting.

'Let me show you what I mean.' He twisted the laptop round so that Alex could see the screen. 'This footage was shot a couple of months ago by a journalist we have connections with. He was on a tour with Krymov in the town of Tver in the provinces. It was a sort of "meet the people" exercise. Krymov is a secretive, remote figure and some media adviser told him he needed to get out more and get some footage with the man in the street. So the local boss set up a tour of a street market with just a few hand-picked journalists covering it. That's why this footage hasn't ever been seen in public – if we revealed it they would guess our source and he'd be a goner. Anyway, see what you think.'

He peered at the laptop and tapped at the keys awkwardly.

An image flicked up on the screen, shot in daylight with a shoulder-held camera; it jostled about above the crowd but the scene was clear. In front of it was the familiar profile of Krymov, a nondescript, short man with a podgy grey face and glasses, wearing a fur hat and overcoat. He could have been a bank clerk but for the crowd of tall security agents and policemen in a protective ring around him. At the edge of the shot Alex caught glimpses of a daytime street market: red plastic buckets and cheap toys hung off the top frame of a market stall. It was snowing lightly and people's breath clouded around them.

The crowd moved down between the lines of stalls, and shoppers looked up nervously as the presidential entourage approached them. The camera managed to push slightly ahead of Krymov so that you could see he had a fixed smile on his face, as if he had been told to look friendly by his aides but wasn't sure how. A blonde PR lady in a white, fur-trimmed parka went in front, grabbed a woman shopper and dragged her over to meet him.

There was an awkward greeting with the terrified woman bowing her head in deference, not daring to look at Krymov, who continued looking around him, smiling inanely. The PR lady then stepped in and hosted an embarrassingly stilted exchange of questions: 'Tell the President how good your life is in Tver.' English subtitles had been added but Alex could follow the Russian without them. He had learned it on an army course, in search of an intellectual challenge to make up for the fact that he hadn't gone to university.

As the woman was mumbling about being very grateful for her government flat, Krymov paid no attention to her at all but continued to beam around him with a lack of engagement that was painful to watch. In the course of this an old man suddenly appeared at the woman's side and stared at Krymov. He was unshaven, gap-toothed, wearing a tattered old overcoat and carrying a walking stick. The PR lady looked at him in disgust.

'Ah! It's you!' he blurted out in a wheezy voice, jabbing a finger at Krymov. 'Yes, it's about time you came up here to answer some questions! Where's my pension?'

He waved his walking stick at the President and started shouting, 'We don't care what's happening in Moscow, give us our pensions! And what about all the corruption? Those sons of bitches in the town hall, they …'

Throughout the tirade Krymov's entourage stood paralysed with shock. It had the opposite effect on Krymov, though. From being frozen in the pose of a grinning idiot, he was suddenly galvanised into action by the presence of an enemy.

The false smile vanished and his face flamed red with anger. He jabbed a finger back at the man. 'Look here, Granddad! Fuck yer mother, you son of a bitch!' He yanked the old man's wooden stick from his hand. 'You don't know what you're talking about! I'm the master here! Do you get it? I'm the master here!'

Holding the stick halfway along the shaft, he struck the

old man across the bridge of his nose. He threw his hands up in defence but Krymov began beating him over the head and then grabbed his hair and struck him repeatedly across the face with the handle of the stick. Blood spattered over both of them as they continued to tussle.

The President's minders finally sprang out of their paralysis and dragged the man away from Krymov, who was now shouting at them: 'We've been infiltrated! He's a foreign saboteur! Shoot that son of a bitch! Shoot him!'

A large hand reached up towards the camera lens and covered it. The screen went black and the film cut off.

Alex sat back in his chair. He shook his head in disbelief, shocked to see a major world statesman behave in such a savage way. He now saw Krymov as completely off the scale of normal behaviour, in the same way he thought about Idi Amin or Hitler.

'He's lost it,' he muttered.

He realised that the country had a major problem on its hands and it wasn't something he could easily stand by and allow to continue. The Devereux family had been loyal servants of the Crown since Guy d'Evereux had fought for the Conqueror at Hastings. Alex's school, Wellington, had continued to drill the service ethic into him and there had been a family member in the Household Division every year since Waterloo until Alex had left it.

Despite his grievances against his regiment for passing him over for promotion, Alex still had much of this patriotic, patrician attitude; a sense of duty to the nation was woven into his being. Harrington had clearly been counting on that, he realised.

The general nodded now in rueful agreement with Alex's comment.

'Hmm, well, apparently the psychologists' analysis of that,' he nodded at the laptop, 'is that Krymov displays paranoid psychotic tendencies that are getting worse. We have already moved from a state of cold peace with Russia towards what is now cold war, and we fear that he may push us into hot war soon. Frankly he could start a war with himself, he's so paranoid. So … this is where *you* come in.'

He looked pointedly at Alex, who gazed back at him, trying to think how he could be involved.

'We have been approached by a contact within the Russian élite with a plan to overthrow Krymov. Although he is ostensibly a dictator, as I said, the Kremlin is in fact a hotbed of factional conflict – we saw that in action when Putin and Medvedev were deposed. The problem is that Krymov lacks the political skills to balance competing factions, so various people are not happy with the way he is leading the country. A lot of that is to do with the fact that they are not getting the slice of the financial pie that they wanted, but we can't help their motives.' He grimaced.

'Now, our faction's problem is that they are not strong enough to depose him outright and therefore need to repeat the sort of popular uprising that happened in 1991 when Yeltsin stood on that tank and was able to face down the KGB coup against Gorbachev. But in order to do that they need two things: one is control of the TV network to broadcast the revolt – and we are sure they can deliver that. The second is a popular figurehead to lead the rebellion. The guy running the faction is an oligarch who is resented by most people because of his money, so he couldn't do it and will therefore stay very much in the background.

'However, they do have the perfect candidate for the job: Roman Raskolnikov.' The general looked at Alex for a sign of recognition. 'Former national football captain, got involved in politics when he left sport and set up an opposition party, fell out with the government after protesting about human rights abuses. Has impeccable populist credentials: is widely trusted as an honourable man and has a lot of popular sympathy. The only problem is,' Harrington shrugged ruefully, 'the government got so pissed off with him that they sent him to prison in Siberia for fifteen years on trumped-up tax evasion charges.

'So, this is where we come in.' He paused, looking intently at Alex. 'We are going to indulge in what Sir Francis Walsingham used to refer to as "lighting fires in other men's houses". It's going to be your job to attack the prison camp, free Raskolnikov and then take him to Moscow to launch a coup against the government.'

Alex didn't blink but looked straight back at Harrington as he tried to take in the enormity of this task.

Harrington took his silence as assent.

'If you're wondering why we picked you, it's because you're ex-army and therefore trusted and have a proven track record of being able to pull off this sort of small-scale raid.' He gave a rare smile. 'You have the network of contacts that you can call on at short notice to do this, apart from which you apparently speak good Russian. However, you have been out of the Forces for a few years now and are well known on the international circuit as a mercenary, so I'm afraid that, if this does all go tits up, you will be completely deniable. As you can guess by the secretive nature of this meeting, the government is going to have no more contact with the op after this briefing. It will be over to you.

'Our contact can't organise the raid himself because he's a businessman, not a soldier. He approached us for help because he's based in London a lot and has links here, and it's more secure for you to organise it than anyone inside Russia – it would run the risk of leaks.

'Now, there is one final point. The oligarch has actually been talking to us about this for some time now but we ignored the idea as being too risky until this current energy crisis blew up. The reason this whole contact with you has been,' he paused apologetically, 'a bit rushed, is because our man now has intelligence from inside the regime that they may be making moves to kill Raskolnikov in a prison "accident" soon. If that happens then our last chance of bringing down this regime from inside will have gone and we could well be looking at a World War Three situation as Krymov goes increasingly crackers.'

Harrington looked at Alex grimly, but with the confidence that he would now have grasped the importance of the mission and do as he was ordered.

Alex unfolded his arms, leaned forward in his chair, looked straight at Harrington and said calmly, 'That is the maddest plan I have ever heard in my entire life. No way.' He shook his head and sat back.

He was not in a forgiving mood after his abrupt pick-up and the railroading at the start of the briefing. Quite apart from that, he was a sharp-minded, independent field commander, used to analysing the feasibility of operations and giving direct opinions on them.

He held out a hand in exasperation. 'It's as mad as …' he fished in his memory for a comparably risky venture, '… Suez!'

The word visibly stung Harrington. He was well aware of the risky nature of the operation and hated being reminded of the similarly secretive and half-baked foreign policy disaster that had brought about the end of the British Empire.

Alex pushed his chair back, stood up and leaned over the table, extending a hand again towards Harrington. 'This *will* start World War Three! I mean, we don't *know* that Krymov *will* start it himself but we sure know it will happen if we do this.'

Harrington wasn't used to having to persuade people to do things.

He jabbed a finger back at Alex, his face red. 'Look, Devereux!' he shouted. 'If you don't do what we say, you're fucked! We've got enough charges on you for launching illegal wars in your African adventures that you will never work again as a mercenary and will spend a long time at Her Majesty's pleasure if we really decide to kick you in the balls. And I don't give a *fuck* if you think you deserve a medal for saving the world! Do I make myself clear!'

The two were eyeball to eyeball over the table.

Alex was enraged but his mind was working fast. He knew that what Harrington said was true: if the government really wanted to get him they could; and from what he knew of Harrington he would enjoy grinding Alex into the dust. At the same time he could see that the country was in trouble and that this would be the opportunity to serve that he felt he had been denied.

Without breaking eye contact with Harrington, he said in an even tone: 'OK … I'll do it. With conditions.'

He paused. Harrington blinked.

'I want ten million quid, plus the same amount for my men.' He paused again. 'And, since I am putting my arse on the line for the good of the country, I *do* want a medal, actually. If I pull this one off, I want a VC. Gift of a grateful nation.' He raised an eyebrow.

Harrington huffed indignantly. 'You can't dictate that sort of—'

Alex interrupted calmly, 'Look, Harrington, you make the rules, so bend them. If you don't, you're fucked. Do I make myself clear?'

Chapter Two

THURSDAY 4 DECEMBER

Alex stumbled on an icy patch in the dark and cursed. He steadied himself and moved on more carefully. Getting around London now was like going for a walk in the countryside at night: there were no streetlights at all and he couldn't see his hand in front of his face.

The road was silent and knee-deep in snow; the stuff was falling slowly but heavily, his footsteps were muffled and he felt a soft resistance to each stride. A thick layer of snow had accreted on every horizontal surface, no matter how small: the tops of car wing mirrors parked along the street; between the uprights of the black metal railings screening the houses from the road.

He had met Harrington two days before and was now making his way from his house up the New King's Road to The Boltons in South Kensington – the exclusive street where he had been instructed to meet the oligarch. He hadn't even been given the man's name yet. Apparently he had just flown in from Moscow and was hosting a party, although Alex wasn't sure how the hell he was going to do that in the present circumstances: there was no power, and food stocks were beginning to run low.

Harrington had read out the invitation with a pained expression: 'It's to celebrate the Fixed Great Feast of the Russian Orthodox Church: Entry into the Temple of our Most Holy Lady Mother of God and Ever-Virgin Mary.'

He had then barked in irritation: 'Look, just turn up and introduce yourself as Alexander Grekov. Our contact will take it from there. I will sort the transfer of the money and I'll look into that other thing ...' He waved his hand in disgust at Alex's demand for a VC. 'Just pull this off and frankly you can ask for the bloody world. As far as you're concerned, though, this is your last contact with HMG. From now on we don't know who you are and we don't care if you get into any shit when you're on the op. You are *totally* deniable. You're on your own, Devereux!' he had added with relish.

Alex stopped to check his location with his torch. He shone the beam along a wall looking for a street name; familiar places suddenly became alien when they were plunged into pitch-darkness. The few passers-by he did meet seemed threatening and they huddled away from each other. He found a name and then brushed the snowflakes off the torch, stuck it back in his overcoat pocket, and walked on.

He was always struck by the huge scale of the houses in The Boltons neighbourhood: five floors plus basement. 'House' was an understatement; they were really white stucco palaces. Some of them had candlelight shining dimly from their windows but most were just black looming hulks.

Despite the ill-tempered meeting with Harrington, Alex was actually feeling a sense of excitement. He was committed to the operation now. The chance to serve his country again was irresistible once his anger against Harrington had died down and he was also galvanised by the huge sum of money that he stood to earn. This could be the restoration of the

Devereux family's fortunes that he had always dreamed of. Plans of how he could repair Akerly had already begun to circle in his mind.

He wasn't sure what to expect at the party. A Fixed Great Feast of the Russian Orthodox Church didn't sound like a bundle of laughs.

He was nearing the address now and thought he could hear a faint sound against the backdrop of the silent city. He walked cautiously on and detected a muffled beat coming through the night; there was also a faint glow from round the corner up ahead.

As he rounded it he saw a huge house lit up with strings of white fairy lights twisted around the bare branches of a pair of old beech trees, spreading a canopy of twirling lights over the driveway. A large mobile generator unit hummed under one of them. The place was lit up like a cruise liner gliding through a dark sea. Arc lights on the walls poured out a wasteful excess of light – almost obscene in the midst of all the darkness.

On the road outside stretched a line of cars with chauffeurs: huge, long-bonneted Rolls-Royces, Range Rovers and pumped-up 4x4s. A line of chattering guests filed up to the double gates of the drive; they looked like Eurotrash: twenty-somethings in expensively ripped jeans and blazers, and middle-aged businessmen in casual suits with trophy wives all wrapped up in expensive furs.

Alex walked up and stood awkwardly in line. He had been preparing to talk small-scale military operations rather than small talk. The house gates were open but blocked by two huge security men in black bomber jackets and a very attractive tall, slim girl from somewhere he couldn't place in central Asia – Mongolia? She wore high-heeled black boots and a long sable coat with a cowl-like hood. Standing in front of the two doormen, she was welcoming guests and checking them off on a clipboard.

She flashed a dazzling, friendly smile as Alex stepped forward, and said cheerfully: '*Dobry vecher!*'

Alex quickly replied: '*Dobry deetche.*'

'*Kak vasha familia?*' she continued, holding the pen poised over her clipboard.

'*Maya familia Grekov.*'

'Ah, Alexander!' She seemed to be expecting him and smiled as if she had found a long-lost friend, then ticked his name off.

She continued in Russian: 'Welcome to Sergey Shaposhnikov's house. My name is Bayarmaa.' She held out a delicate gloved hand. 'Please, follow me.' She handed the clipboard to one of the bouncers and led the way up the drive with a swirl of her long coat.

Shaposhnikov.

So that was who it was, thought Alex as he followed her. Sergey Shaposhnikov – he knew the name but couldn't think in what context he had come across it.

He followed Bayarmaa up the large front steps flanked by white columns and in through the open double doors. Heaters blew a curtain of warmth over them. There seemed to be no shortage of power here and the excess of heat felt luxurious after so many days of shivering.

The heat was just as well, thought Alex, as he was confronted by the sight of a scantily clad pole-dancer writhing on a platform as they walked into the hall ahead of the huge room that took up most of the raised ground floor of the house.

The Entry of the Ever-Virgin Mary, he thought wryly to himself as they walked past. Clearly Shaposhnikov didn't take his orthodoxy *that* seriously.

They handed their coats to a smartly dressed woman by the door and then a waitress with a tray of vodka shot glasses walked up to them. Bayarmaa handed Alex one with a smile that brooked no refusal. He nodded his thanks, threw the drink back and followed her through, savouring the burst of warmth in his stomach.

Beyond the pole-dancer, the high-ceilinged room was noisy and packed with a couple of hundred guests. A bar stretched all the way down one side with ten uniformed barmen running around frantically trying to supply the crowd of people.

A band at the far end of the room were enthusiastically belting out a Russian cover of a Stones song. After a few bars Alex worked it out as 'Brown Sugar'.

They looked an odd group, dressed in nylon imitation Russian peasant garb and fronted by a plump fifty-year-old woman with peroxide-blonde hair and heavy framed glasses in a long pink medieval robe and traditional Russian headdress. Behind her stood a tall, lugubrious-looking, bearded man in a green smock, tasselled cord belt, baggy Cossack pants and boots. He was playing bass on an enormous balalaika. The guests were too busy drinking and talking to listen to the band, though. No one was dancing yet.

Alex followed Bayarmaa's silky black hair as they pushed their way through the crowd to the bar.

A loud squawk of alarm came from the lead singer on the stage and the music crashed to a halt mid-song. Looking out over the press of heads Alex could see that a drunken businessman had clambered on stage and grabbed the microphone from her. Everyone turned to the stage and a chorus of angry shouts and boos broke out. The man with the microphone began shouting back at them in Russian: 'Shut the fuck up! Shut the fuck up!'

He was middle-aged, a bit above average height and well built, with a mop of straw-blond hair that shone in the stage lights and hung down over his eyes. He was wearing a crumpled suit and tie and had a large diamond stud that glittered in one ear. He stood at the front of the stage swaying and pointing at the crowd.

'You want to party, eh? I'll show you how to party! I am the Party Commissar!' He said this in English to get the double meaning and burst into a high-pitched giggle at his own joke. 'Yes, you're all miserable Russian fuckers! Your heads are full of dark forests with wolves running around in them and the Party Commissar has detected these anti-revolutionary sentiments, which have led to erroneous political judgements. *You're not dancing!*'

The crowd seemed to know that the man was just a good-natured buffoon and began laughing at his parody of Soviet political rhetoric.

'So as a good agent of the workers' state I will take all steps necessary to ensure the re-education of the proletariat. Unless you become party-Stakhanovites, I will have you all shot! I want over-fulfilment of your party quotas!'

The crowd had caught on and cheered loudly now.

Bayarmaa nudged Alex and said, her eyes sparkling with adoration, 'That's Sergey.'

Alex frowned. He was not at all what Alex had expected.

Sergey lurched round to look at the lead singer, who had recovered her composure.

'Lyuda, come on, enough of this Western shit. Let's have some *proper* dancing!'

The band hastily rearranged themselves and the lead balalaika player stepped forward.

Sergey spotted some friends in the audience. 'Grigory! Katya! Vera! Come on!' He jumped down into the crowd, who made a ring, whilst the four formed themselves into a quadrille and, when the music started, began a fast Russian dance. Sergey grinned and clapped along as the men waited for the women to complete their delicate shimmying moves – hands on hips and heads thrown back with narrowed eyes and pouting mouths.

However, when it came to Sergey's turn for a solo, his expression became deadly serious as he threw himself into the jumps and kicks – now squatting down, now springing up and whirling round.

The crowd roared in appreciation at his bravado and even more when his partner, Grigory, fell over. The dance ended with a storm of applause and much back-slapping.

Sergey blundered away through the crowd, saw Bayarmaa next to the bar and headed towards them.

'Hey, my little Artic fox!'

He embraced her with a huge bear hug, swinging her off her feet and around. She squealed with delight before kissing him on the lips when he dumped her back down again.

She collected herself and remembered Alex, standing next to her.

'Sergey, this is Mr Grekov.' She rested a light hand on Alex's arm and drew him towards Sergey.

'Eh? Grekov?'

Sergey looked confused and leered at him from under his shock of hair, now slicked flat over his ears with sweat. He had a broad-boned face with fleshy lips and pale skin. Laughter lines creased the corners of his eyes, which had a slight Slavic slant to them. The chaotic hair, rumpled suit and diamond earring gave him a piratical air.

'Yes, the geologist you said you wanted to talk to,' she prompted him.

'Ahh!' he slurred in recognition and stuck his hand out towards Alex. It was wet with sweat.

A man barged through the crowd and threw an arm around Sergey. He looked like an old-style Mafia don: in his fifties, black-suited and heavily built with steel-grey hair brushed straight back.

'Hey, you crazy fuck – "Party Commissar!"' he laughed at the joke again. Ignoring Alex, Sergey turned to the man, became animated again and roared along with him in an eager-to-please way.

'Vladimir Ilarionovich,' he said, using his patronymic as a sign of respect, and then saw that he had an empty glass, 'you've run out of magic party liquid! I'll send you to the camps for that!'

The man wheezed with laughter: 'Yes! Ten years with no rights of correspondence!' he said, repeating the euphemistic death sentence handed out in the 1930s purges.

Sergey giggled manically and mimed shooting someone in the head: 'That's right! Shoot the bastards!'

He turned to the bar. 'Hey, Ivan!' he shouted at the nearest barman. 'Three Litvinenkos!' He put a hot sweaty arm around both Alex and Vladimir and bent them over the bar.

'This is my favourite cocktail, in memory of that bastard.'

Vladimir nodded grimly. 'Yes – we fucked him up good and proper.'

Ivan the barman grinned as he lined up three highball glasses and poured lavish quantities of the ingredients, snapping off the stream of liquor with a flick of his wrists.

Sergey listed them as they went in: 'Vodka, crème de menthe, apple schnapps, melon liquor, a squirt of lemonade and then the final ingredient – not Polonium-210.' He winked at Vladimir as Ivan pulled a packet of Alka-Seltzer out of

28

his barman's apron and clunked two into each glass so that the bright green contents fizzed radioactively.

Sergey picked up his glass and clinked with the other two. 'See you under the table!'

Vladimir laughed and shook his head in admiration. 'Sergey Stepanovich ...'

Sergey smiled affectionately back and then threw his arm round Alex and said to Vladimir, 'Right, I've got to talk to this boring geologist. You can fuck off and find yourself something to do.' He pointed at the pole-dancer.

Vladimir looked at Alex and grunted, 'Geology, huh!' and then looked at the dancer and grinned at Sergey. 'I prefer biology ...' he grinned, and lurched off through the crowd towards her twisting figure.

Sergey grabbed Bayarmaa around the waist and steered her out of the room. 'Come on, let's go to my office,' he said over his shoulder to Alex, who followed, clutching his foaming, green drink.

By now he was seriously disturbed by what he had seen of Sergey. This is the man in charge of organising the most dangerous political coup ever? he thought as they threaded through the guests in the huge ground-floor room and made their way up the sweeping main staircase.

Alex had finally remembered where he had heard Sergey's name before – on the gossip page of *The Times*. There had been a paparazzi photo of him leaving a club late at night with some starlet. He couldn't remember what the salacious element of the story was but it didn't surprise him in the least after what he had just seen. The operation was risky enough without having a lunatic in charge of it.

They came to the top of the broad staircase where another pole-dancer was flexing herself in a large open room. A group of businessmen was gathered around her, admiring the show.

The atmosphere was calmer here: music played but guests were chatting, and canapés and champagne were circulated by yet more uniformed staff.

Set in an alcove on one side of the room were a large pair of polished wooden double doors. In front of it a small crowd of people was standing around with drinks, talking and evidently waiting for someone. Blocking them from the door was a large man in a dark suit with buzz-cut hair and an earpiece. His hands were clasped firmly in front of him and his eyes scanned the guests in a mechanical way.

Sergey detached himself from Bayarmaa and suddenly switched to hyperactive.

'Friends, friends, friends! Yes!' he shouted and then ran around the group embracing men and women alike, kissing everyone three times on the cheeks and making manic small talk with each of them.

'Yes! Yegor! Ah-ha! The new pipeline, great flow rates! Well done! Yes! I love it! ... Tatyana! Ah! I love the new store! Yes! We need to talk about the manager on the second floor, though; she's got to go! ... Misha! Great! We'll speak about Production Line Two. I have a new idea! Maybe we'll actually make some money out of it, heh? ... OK, please, talk, drink – I'll see you all in good time!'

Sergey gestured to Alex to take a seat on a large divan covered in oriental rugs along the wall opposite. He then pushed open the door to his inner sanctum and waved two men inside: one was Grigory, whom he had been dancing with – arty-looking with curly black hair and a crumpled Armani suit – and the other a pallid man in a formal dark suit and tie, whose eyes glittered quietly as he glanced round and slipped in through the open door.

Bayarmaa took up what seemed to be her usual position as charming hostess at the door, chatting to Sergey's employees.

Alex sat down, feeling annoyed at the chaotic way things were being handled. He took a slug of his strange drink – it was actually not bad. He sat back and quietly people-watched as guests came and went up and down the stairs.

After ten minutes, one panelled door opened and Grigory and the pale man came out, looking tense. They muttered goodbyes to Bayarmaa and walked off with their heads down. She turned to Alex and motioned him to come over.

He stood up and made to move towards her when something cut into the corner of his eye. His head flicked round.

The woman was tall with a lean silhouette mainly composed of long blonde hair, cheekbone and leg. She wore designer jeans, heels, and a white shirt with a high collar and large cuffs, sculpted to emphasise her generous cleavage – all very simple, very elegant, very impactful.

Despite all that was on his mind, Alex felt a systemic shock go through him. It wasn't just her figure, it was also the way she walked: head back, looking neither to left nor right. She was in her twenties but had the presence of a *grande dame*.

She moved from the top of the stairs and past the crowd admiring the semi-naked dancer in a few long strides; cutting through the sleazy atmosphere with the cold indifference of a Soviet icebreaker.

The woman fired a look like a bullet at Bayarmaa, who curled her lip in return but stepped back from the door. The guard also withdrew deferentially and the woman pushed open both doors at once, marched purposefully into the room and slammed them behind her. Alex sat back down, feeling a slight tremor from watching the episode.

It was five minutes before both doors were again wrenched open and she strode out. Sergey hurried after her: eyes wild, hair astray and hands outstretched imploringly. He put a hand on her elbow to stop her, but in one fluid movement she spun round and hit him hard with the back of her hand on his shoulder. He deflated instantly, ducking his head and hunching his shoulders. From this defensive posture he looked up at her with humble affection; his hands held meekly open in front of him as he mumbled some explanation. The woman listened to him with hands on her hips, mouth set firm, her gaze level and eerily calm.

Sergey finished speaking and looked at her imploringly. She held his gaze for a long moment, neither assenting nor dissenting, before turning her head away. He fumbled in his suit pocket, pulled out a small jewelled box and pressed it into the palm of her hand. She glanced at it wearily, sighed, and tucked it into a little handbag hooked over one shoulder before walked away from him.

As she moved past Alex, her head turned towards him and they looked at each other for a split second. The woman strode on and made her way down the stairs.

She walked out of the gate in her long fur coat and stepped into the back of one of Sergey's chauffeur-driven, black Range Rovers with tinted windows. As the driver moved off, she pulled the ornate box out of her handbag and turned it over in her hand, thoughtfully examining the gold whorls and the precious stones set into it.

After looking at it for a while she flipped the clasp open with her thumbnail and took out the single folded sheet of plain, white paper. On it were two lines of Sergey's appalling scratchy handwriting: cramped, unevenly spaced and with occasional spikes up and down.

She recognised the verse. It was Pushkin:

Past sorrow to me is like wine
Stronger with every passing year.

The woman closed her eyes for a moment in a look of pain. She folded the note, put it back in the box and looked out at the dark city sliding past.

Sergey suddenly switched on his normal, manic persona and threw his arms open towards Alex: 'Ah-ha! Grekov!' He gestured into his office.

Alex put his drink down and stalked through the open door, his dark brows knit in a frown of disapproval. He was not impressed by what he had seen of Sergey so far.

The room was a long rectangle, dimly lit with a large boardroom table down the middle and elegantly curtained windows along the left-hand side. On the opposite wall and between the windows were enormous bookshelves running up to the high ceiling. Alex glanced at the titles – both Russian and Western, mainly literature but also poetry, art, science and technical manuals, architecture and travel.

Sergey seemed oblivious to Alex's glowering and rushed ahead, flamboyantly waving him past the table – 'No, no, no!' – to a large oriental day bed set on top of a waist-high brick platform, in the Central Asian style, against the far end of the room. The bed was covered in expensive oriental carpets and pillows and surrounded by a low rail.

Portraits of various tsars, along with Lenin, Stalin, Trotsky, Tolstoy, and other bearded Russians that Alex didn't recognise, hung on the wall above the day bed.

Alex perched awkwardly on the edge of one side of it, whilst Sergey busied himself opening a cast-iron door to a stove built into the brick base and chucking a couple of logs into it from a wicker basket. He slid onto the opposite side of the platform from Alex, stretching his legs out and chuckling, 'I always like to warm up my butt a bit.'

The platform was covered in a clutter of books, newspapers, laptops and DVDs. Sergey wriggled his backside and then fidgeted and pulled a DVD out from under him. He looked at it and then showed the simple cartoon front cover to Alex. 'Vinni Puh?' he said quizzically.

Alex frowned. *What the hell was he on about now?*

'*Vinni* Puh?' Sergey said insistently. 'Ah! No, you say, "Winnie-the-Pooh"? This is the Soviet version from 1971. Used to watch them as a kid – much better, much deeper, complete with existentialist angst. Check it out on YouTube – *Vinni Puh Goes Visiting.*' He looked at the cover again, laughed and chucked it aside.

He ignored Alex's stony silence and proceeded to make tea in a small ornate copper pot by alternately spooning in tea leaves and pouring hot water from a kettle with a long thin spout. He muttered from under the shaggy fringe of hair hanging over his face, 'I like the Kalmyks' style with bay leaves,' and added some.

As he stirred the tea he looked up and said chirpily in English: 'So you are enjoying my party?'

Alex looked at him, startled, his anger disarmed by Sergey's sudden switch of language. He struggled to reply in a more civil manner in English than he had intended: 'Yes … you're the life and soul.'

Sergey stopped stirring the tea and stared at him. His smile cut out as if someone had switched off a light. He looked Alex gravely in the eye. 'And do you know why I am the life and soul?'

Alex looked straight back, again caught out by his change of tone.

Sergey said very slowly, 'Because in my soul I am alone.'

There was a long moment before he nodded, looked down at the pot and went back to stirring it and adding water.

The episode seemed to have brought a calmer mood on him. He started again in Russian: 'So you are fucked off and wondering what you are doing at a party, sitting on a bed with a crazy Russian who wants to send you on a suicide mission to Siberia?'

Alex couldn't have put it more succinctly himself so he just waited for Sergey to answer his own question.

'Well, you are at a party because I always do my business at parties. I love business, I love parties.' He held his hands out and smiled. 'For me they are one and the same. It also means that I can see everyone without suspicion.'

'Meaning?'

'Well, all of us oligarchs are powerful so Comrade Krymov likes to keep us all under surveillance. But me,' he gestured to himself, 'I invite the bastards to my parties. You have just been drinking Litvinenkos with Colonel Vladimir Ilarionovich Gorsky, the station chief of the SVR in London.'

Alex narrowed his eyes and looked more intently at Sergey. The SVR was the foreign intelligence arm of the FSB – the Federal Security Service – the successor to the KGB.

'We drink a lot of vodka together and he thinks he knows everything that goes on inside my head.' Sergey shrugged. 'He does know a lot of it but there are many rooms inside my head. So he tells me he thinks I am a clown who isn't worth wasting any of his men on.' Sergey nodded with satisfaction, seeming to take this as a compliment.

Alex began to unwind some of his early anger. Maybe Shaposhnikov wasn't such an idiot as he had first appeared.

'So Harrington says to me that we have you "by the short and curlies".' He pronounced the idiom with mock hesitancy and then grinned.

Alex replied curtly, 'It wouldn't be my first choice of operation.' He decided the time had come to press for more reassurance on it. 'I mean, what the hell chance does it have of succeeding? Krymov looks pretty well entrenched. He's an unshakeable dictator.'

Sergey seemed to ignore the question, put the lid on the pot, poured a little tea into an engraved silver thimble cup and sipped it. He made a face, lifted the lid and poured the cupful back into the pot and then replied, 'Hmm, well, from the outside, yes, but then nothing is as it seems in Russia. There are significant weaknesses in my country at both an élite and a popular level.' He made a horizontal slicing action with one hand high up and then lower down to indicate where the problems lay in Russian society.

He was sounding like he might actually have a point. Alex was prepared to listen and leaned back against the rail on the bed.

Sergey warmed to his theme. 'You see, Russia is not a state as you know it in the Western sense. The Soviets and then the Yeltsin anarchy undermined the rule of law. Everything was so inefficient and fucked up that people had to develop alternative currencies, and "informal practices",' he made speech marks with his finger, 'to make it work. It's what you call the favour system or patronage networks.'

He hurried on: 'Look, there used to be two ideologies in the USSR – communism and criminalism. Now there is only one.' He shrugged. 'I mean, we used to have a Communist Party that could actually control the KGB but now there is no Communist Party so the secret police have no limits on their power.' He paused to consider the irony and then smiled. 'Only in Russia would you get rid of communism and then bring back the secret police to run the country.'

He continued carefully, emphasising his points with slow

hand movements. 'So the combination of all these things means that the country is controlled not by the normal institutions of a Western state, but by factional networks controlled by the *siloviki*.' He looked enquiringly at Alex, who nodded in understanding – the bosses who ran the security services.

'But the point for our little expedition is that there are many different security services: FSB, GRU – military intelligence, MVD – Interior Ministry, OMON – riot police. They all have their own troops. Then there's the Spetsnaz – Special Forces – army, airforce, navy and marines. Each has its little networks of politicians and companies that it controls.

'Putin removed the constitutional checks and balances on the executive, and once you've done that you're back to the law of the jungle. I'm telling you, the factions in the Kremlin are like lions fighting over a kill. Putin and Medvedev divided power between themselves and then fell out, so Krymov was put in place supposedly because he was so boring that he wouldn't threaten anyone. But he was more cunning than they thought, was able to rally a faction behind him and spring a coup against both of them.

'So, we have gone back to a situation more like the court of a tsar, with competing factional groups of boyars – the nobles. The Tsar divided the assets of the country between them. That used to be land and serfs but now it's political parties, government ministries, oil and gas resources, mines and companies. Because of this, the leader of Russia appears to outsiders as an autocrat but only because of the support of élite factions behind him. They support him because he suits their interests. As soon as they are not getting what they want, then they'll turn on him.

'You can get a stable political system if you have an intelligent guy like Putin who can actually balance factions, but

37

Krymov is so stupid he can't write two words without making five mistakes. So now we have a fight between the various branches of the security services for the spoils of the economy.'

Alex nodded; he could see what Sergey was saying and how it would open up conflict at an élite level.

'OK, so who's on your faction?'

Sergey grinned. 'Well, officially I'm on no one's. Krymov thinks he's my best friend and,' he made an equivocating gesture with his hand, 'despite what I said, I like him. We're drinking buddies and he laughs at my jokes, so he doesn't take me seriously and just lets me drift around making money. I don't harm anyone. I'm safely neutral, you see, plus I am a businessman – I started out on a market stall – so I can actually run businesses, which the *siloviki* can't, so sometimes it's helpful for them to put a strategic sector in neutral hands. That's why I've got ownership of all the TV stations – it was easier to give them to a fool like me than start a huge fight between different groups.'

Alex saw a contradiction in Sergey's motivation and looked at him quizzically. 'But you're making a lot of money out of all this?'

'Yes, I am,' Sergey nodded, unashamed.

'So why are you starting a coup?'

'Because Russia deserves better than this,' he smiled, 'Alexander …' He frowned. 'What's your father's name?'

Alex was momentarily wrong-footed. 'Nicholas.'

Sergey started again in the correct respectful Russian manner. 'Alexander Nikolayevich,' he gave a self-deprecating smile and held up a hand, 'all in good time. I will explain my motives later and you'll meet our team tomorrow.'

He carried on along his former line of thought. 'So, anyway, as I was saying, that's the weakness at an élite level. On a popular level it's the same. Russia looks strong but in fact things are not so good if you look under the surface. Our main problem is the curse of abundant natural resources: we've got so much oil and gas that we don't have to go through the tiresome business of actually developing a functioning economy – we just dig a hole in the ground and the money pours out. Basically we're just a petro-state in the same way as any other Third World dictatorship. It leads to what I call the gangsterisation of the economy. You have an FSB man sitting on the board of all major companies. Now these guys are good at wiretaps, surveillance, hits – they can do that – but can they read a balance sheet? Do they have a feel for a market? Can they organise a supply chain? The fuck they can! They're hoods, spooks! And they have successfully screwed the economy as a result!'

Sergey grew more animated, jabbing his finger at Alex, his diamond earring flashing. 'Do we have a thriving industrial sector? Do we export any manufactured goods at all apart from weapons? No! Do we have a service sector? No! Can you name one fucking Russian company that isn't Gazprom, Lukoil or some other natural resources producer? A software company? A clothing brand? No! Because we are a fucking banana republic run by goons! Do I want that for my country? The fuck I do!'

Sergey was suddenly disturbed by how carried away he had got, and poured out two small teas to calm himself down. He did this with a thin stream of liquid from a height above the cups, and then neatly snapped off the stream with a flick of his wrist. He put the ornate pot down and continued.

'So, we are what you call a one-trick pony. Over half of all government revenue comes from oil taxes but they make money only when the price is over seventy bucks a barrel. When prices hit one forty-seven we were laughing, but now they've crashed we're screwed. We didn't share out the proceeds of the wealth when we did have it, so bastards like me are rich, but if you look at the provinces and the working class, they are desperately poor. I mean, the population is actually shrinking by seven hundred thousand people a year because of alcoholism, suicide, drugs and AIDS. We'll lose a third of our population in the next fifty years. *That's* not a healthy country! And those stupid fucking sheep signed all their freedoms away in the good times!'

Alex frowned, unsure whom Sergey was talking about.

'I mean the Russian people. Don't get me wrong, I'm one of them, but Russians have never had much respect for democracy. They call it shit-ocracy!'

Alex recognised the Russian pun on the words *demokratia* and *dermokratia*.

'So, they effectively signed a non-participation pact with the government that said: "You let us enjoy the material benefits of the oil price boom, and we'll turn a blind eye to whatever political violence you want to use." It's exactly like that thing about "When they came for the Jews, I did not protest because I was not a Jew", blah-blah-blah.' Sergey waved a hand to indicate the rest. 'So now that times are hard, there's no one left to protest for them.

'Now Krymov has spent all the Stabilisation Fund on re-armament so we have twenty per cent inflation – that has *really* pissed a lot of ordinary people off!'

Sergey was nearing the end of his tea ceremony now, adding salt in little dashes to the cups. He stopped to jab the tiny spoon at Alex.

'And the final issue that will help our operation the most is the way that they have driven out foreign companies. Those are the guys that actually do know how to run a factory, a refinery, whatever.'

He grinned lopsidedly. 'Have you heard my joke about foreign investment in Russia?'

Alex shook his head.

Sergey smiled. 'Well, at the beginning of the process the foreigners have all the money and the experience and the Russians have nothing.' He paused and looked at Alex with a twinkle in his eye. 'But by the end of the process the Russians have all the money and the foreigners have had an experience.'

Alex couldn't help grinning as Sergey bobbed his head about happily.

'It's good, yeah? So the *siloviki* get greedy and drive out ExxonMobil, Total, BP – all of them – so now there is no one left to run the oil refineries and we can't even produce enough petrol for ourselves, in the largest oil-producing country on Earth!' He was laughing now. 'I mean, it would be funny but …'

'You know, the same thing happened in Iran. We both had to introduce petrol rationing. Krymov used the OMON to suppress the riots when it was introduced but, believe me, with rationing and inflation, there are a lot of fucked-off ordinary people out there who want to see Krymov dead.'

He finished making the tea and put the spoon down.

'So, comrade, in answer to your question – do we have a chance of overthrowing Krymov? It will be tough, but yes, we do.'

He picked up a small cup of tea and stretched out his arm to give it to Alex.

Alex looked at him warily, thinking over what he had said and calculating the odds in his head. It tallied with what he had read in the papers and with what Harrington had said in his briefing.

He reached out, took the cup from Sergey and sipped the bitter tea.

Sergey smiled and drank.

'OK, good – you passed the interview.' He paused. 'So now you are Director of GeoScan.'

Alex frowned. What was the Russian on about now? His mind seemed to hop about everywhere.

'It's a UK-based international geo-survey firm. I have the details of your next survey mission.'

He jumped off the bed, took a large portrait of Karl Marx off the wall, opened a money safe behind it and pulled a black leather document wallet out. He passed Alex the bulky folder and sat on the bed again.

Alex put his tea down and took it hesitantly.

'Go on, have a look,' Sergey urged him. 'There's a lot of uranium ore in Chita province in Siberia and I want you to find the highest grade deposits.'

He reached over, pulled a map of Russia out of the wallet and spread it on the carpet between them. Alex quickly ran his eyes back and forth over it. He was amazed, looking at the Mercator projection map, how big the country was. The whole enormous mass of European Russia all the way east to Moscow only made up a tiny proportion of it.

Sergey pointed to a large highlighted area in the far east, three thousand miles from Moscow, near Lake Baikal and just north of the border where Mongolia and China met.

'Chita is the province in Siberia that I'm governor of – it's next to Abramovich's patch – and it's where Raskolnikov is in prison. Your cover for getting you and a team in there will be as geologists doing a survey. That'll also be a good excuse for you to have access to my mining company helicopters because it's a huge area to cover – four hundred and thirty-one thousand square kilometres.' He laughed self-indulgently. 'That's twice the size of the whole United Kingdom, and I am the sole, unelected ruler of it all – isn't that great!' He giggled at the thought.

'Total population is about one million, mainly Russians and Buryats – they're a Mongol tribe. Like Bayarmaa – she's gorgeous, yes? God, those cheekbones!'

He clapped his hands, looked dazed for a moment, and then suddenly switched into a focused mode, pulling sheets out of the folder, poring over them and pointing things out.

'This is the map of Krasnokamensk, the town near where Raskolnikov is in the prison labour camp. You will be able to base your team here.' He indicated an area on the edge of town. 'It's the transport depot for my mining company and will be a secure base for your operations. I have a Mil Mi-17 helicopter there in a hangar for you to use and a hostel for your men.'

Alex nodded. 'I know the Mil Mi-17 from my African operations.' It was a very popular, robust aircraft used all around the world.

Sergey nodded but wagged his finger at him. 'Hmm, but remember this isn't Africa. It's minus thirty out there at the moment.'

He pulled out more sheets. 'These are the plans of the camp, and as much detail on the guards and defences as I can get. I got them because I run the company that supplies the camp with food, but the prison itself is run by the MVD – that's the Interior Ministry – and they are *definitely not* on our side.' He raised his eyebrows warningly.

'OK, that is enough for you to start getting an initial plan together. I am giving you just twenty-four hours to do it because I know you're good,' he grinned encouragingly, 'and because I have a contact in the camp who gets messages out to me and I know that the bastards are planning to kill Raskolnikov soon, so we need to get going.'

'Why don't they just kill him straight out?'

Sergey screwed up his face. 'He's like a saint in my country. He's too popular for them to just go out and shoot him. There would have to be a state funeral and it really wouldn't do for his body to be on display with a big bullet hole in his head. No, it's a lot easier for them to just trump up some tax charges, lock him up for years and let his memory fade, and then bump him off in an accident.

'We'll meet back here with the other members of my team at eight o'clock tomorrow evening. OK?'

He smiled at Alex as if it was the simplest thing in the world.

Chapter Three

Prisoner D-504 squinted at the harsh electric light shining into his face.

Dogs barked, straining on leashes held by guards all around the parade ground.

Another morning roll call in the Yag 14/10 Krasnokamensk Penal Colony. Six a.m., sky pitch-black, ambient temperature, without wind chill, minus thirty-five degrees C.

His 868th roll call – the same every morning for over two years. He had calculated that he had 4,607 more to go in his fifteen-year stretch, although he knew that no one survived that long, so the figure was just hypothetical.

He pushed it out of his mind and stood rigidly to attention. Any movement would earn a beating from the guards, but his eyes still darted around. They were all that showed under his padded hat, his face wrapped up against frostbite in scraps of dirty cloth that he had managed to cadge. His eyelashes were rimed with ice, and crystals clung to the cloths where his breath streamed through.

Under the hostile acetylene light he watched a column of prisoners being led out of their overnight lock up in Barrack 7. That lot had it bad; he didn't envy them. Glazkov, their barrack sergeant, was a right bastard and hammered them whenever he could.

Like him, they all wore black padded jackets, hats with earflaps, padded trousers and mittens. All items were greasy and worn with age and had their inhabitant's prison number stitched on strips, front and back, so that guards could identify them when they were bent over at work. They moved with heads down and shoulders hunched against the cold like a bunch of apes shuffling through the snow onto the parade ground.

D-504 flicked his eyes up to the watchtowers astride the double fence of electrified razor wire. It gave no shelter from the wind that blew in from the North Pole and scoured along the rank of prisoners.

Wind, normally such a simple thing, became so much more in Siberia. It was not the gentle breeze that had stroked his hair in the hot summers of his childhood on the Volga. This was a slashing ghoul that cut through your clothes with its ice-hard claws, screaming around the barracks at night, baying for the warmth in your blood.

Warmth had become the centrality around which his life was lived. Just as an alcoholic craves drink, so he craved heat; hoarding pockets under his arms, trapping a morsel under his thin blanket at night.

Cold, though, was his ever-present companion during the day, sinking its little gremlin teeth into his nose, ears and fingers, nipping and gnawing at them. Then, at night, climbing into bed with him like an unwanted lover, wrapping its arms around him and pushing its freezing hands into his bones, grabbing them and shaking him with uncontrollable shivering fits.

He risked a sideways glance along the line of prisoners and then snapped his head back.

Sergeant Kuzembaev was coming.

Kuzembaev was a Kazakh, a flat-faced sadist with a horse-whip at his hip. It could rip through clothing and cut deep into the flesh if he really got some length on it. He was indifferent to the cold but seemed to take an icy pleasure in others' pain.

He worked his way down the line, shining his torch into each prisoner's face to check that the man fitted the number on his strips and had not been substituted by someone bribed or beaten into taking his place overnight.

Kuzembaev stopped in front of him; the thin slits of his eyes were implacable in the light shining up from his torch. He pulled D-504's hat off, revealing a badly shaved head – to reduce the lice. The prisoner felt the bones of his head contract as the wind got at it. Then the guard stabbed the beam of his torch into his face and yanked the cloths down.

The face that the sergeant scrutinised was the most famous in Russia. When he was captain of the national football team, the heavy brow, strong jaw and steady eyes had been idolised by millions as the embodiment of true Slav heroism – battered but unbowed.

He was the highest scoring player ever for his country. His heavy build and low centre of gravity had helped him ride out the roughest tackles as a centre forward, never fearing to stick his head into a flurry of raised boots looking for a goal, as the large scar across his right temple proved.

The face stared back at Kuzembaev impassively just as it had when the camera zoomed in on him as he'd lined up to kick off when they were 2–2 against Germany with just minutes to go. How the nation had prayed to that face as if to the icon of St George in the days of old – the warrior of a nation.

And he had not let them down.

The commentator was hoarse with shouting as the Russians threw everything forward. The Germans dug in and defended stoically until Raskolnikov intercepted a pass.

The commentator went mad: 'Raskolnikov intercepts! Past Shtrum! Past Weissman! Raskolnikov, our last hope!' His voice rose to a scream, 'Yeeess!'

That line – 'Raskolnikov, our last hope!' – became part of the Russian lexicon.

What made those moments of iconic glory even greater was the modest way that he had handled them afterwards. His quiet grin, with its self-effacing aversion of his eyes, had endeared him to millions of Russian women, but had made men trust him as well.

Two years in the camps had taken their toll, though. The bearded face was now pinched with hunger and his skin was grey and wrinkled like old newspaper.

Kuzembaev grinned mockingly. 'Ah, Captain, it's you! Who are we playing today then?' he chuckled, and moved off down the line, never tiring of that joke.

Roman Raskolnikov quickly pulled his hat back on and stared ahead, pushing his anger into the vast river of patience that flowed quietly through him like the Don.

He was forty-five now but had started playing aged eighteen in his hometown for Rotor Stalingrad. After stunning success as a striker there, he had transferred to Spartak Moscow and captained them and then Russia.

He stared at the white, blue and red of the Russian tricolour flying in front of him over the platform on which Commandant Bolkonsky stood with the machine-gunner next to him, squinting down the barrel of his belt-fed 7.62mm PKM, his finger on the trigger and itching to fire into the packed ranks of prisoners.

Raskolnikov had such mixed feelings about that flag now:

he used to look at it with tears in his eyes when the anthem played at the start of matches. He still loved his country but he hated the corrupt and tyrannical government that had sentenced him to this terrible place under Article 275 of the Criminal Code on trumped-up tax evasion charges.

The real reason for his sentence was his work for the United Civil Opposition party. Both his mother and father used to talk politics at home all the time. They had been true believers under communism – somehow managing to ignore the corruption and iniquity, and maintain a belief in the ideal of social justice that the system espoused.

He had ignored politics as a child and concentrated on his football, but some of their rigid morality stayed with him. When the anarchy of the Yeltsin era broke out, pensions went unpaid and healthcare and schooling collapsed, he felt he ought to use his fame to do his bit by setting up a football academy for street kids in Moscow. This brought him great respect amongst the city's working class, and for a time he did not take it further.

As a man of action he just wanted to do something practical to help, but gradually he was pulled into the political web. After he retired he became a sports ambassador for Russia, helping to win the hosting of the European Cup finals. He started working for Sergey Shaposhnikov's TV station as a commentator and every political party wanted a slice of the great Roman Raskolnikov, thinking that he would just be a meathead who would boost their popularity.

However, as Putin had eroded democracy and human rights, Roman felt himself more and more outraged by what was happening. The basic human decency that his parents had insisted on was being destroyed all around him. As a smart tactician he soon realised that, if he wanted to change the situation, he would have to do more than just run football academies, and get involved in politics properly.

The United Civil Opposition never really stood a chance in the era of media manipulation by the government; as independent newspapers and channels were gradually closed down, its activities had ceased to be reported in the press. But Roman was never one to bow to pressure. He dug deep and knew that what he was doing was right for his country. His wife, Ivana, and his two daughters, Masha and Irina, had suffered as well and that had been the hardest thing to bear. He had not heard from them directly in over two years, but his network of supporters told him that they were still alive and living in Moscow.

He tried not to think about them, it was too painful. He had to concentrate all his efforts on just staying alive in this place. It was a separate planet from the rest of humanity: oppressed by different laws of gravity, breathing harsh atmospheric gases, labouring under a different sun.

This strange world had been named 'Honolulu' by Commandant Bolkonsky. All the new 'enhanced regime' camps opened under Krymov's orders were nicknamed by the guards after famous holiday destinations: Honolulu, Marbella, Sharm el-Sheik and Yalta.

The camps provided labour for a range of activities: logging, mining and construction. Each of the nine hundred inmates was allocated to a work gang and their numbers were now being read out over the blaring Tannoy; Roman listened carefully for his. The day's arrangements depended on what his gang boss – Shubin – had been able to bribe the overseer with.

'The following teams will be on forest detail: 49th, 18th, 89th, 51st and 33rd.'

That was his then – the 33rd. A whole day out in the freezing cold, logging, but better than the mines.

'Better watch yourself out there today, Roman. Don't want to get a nasty sliding tackle, eh?' someone whispered to him from the rank behind and then made a strange creaking noise, which passed for a laugh.

It was Getmanov, a former FSB officer who had been sentenced for corruption and rape. He claimed he was a huge fan of Roman's but his interest in what he was doing verged on the obsessive. Roman found him a disturbing character. He had a wide mouth that he left hanging open most of the time; one of his front teeth had been broken in half, and the combination gave him an ugly, careless look.

Roman had seen him in muttered conversations with guards occasionally, huddled around the back of the kitchens. Whenever he saw him, Getmanov always stared back and then leered as if half-witted. Roman couldn't work out if he was just a fan, mad or something else.

Dannil Kozlov was sure he was bad news, though. Big Danni, in Roman's work gang, was a huge Moscow thug, an armed robber, whose shaved head showed the many scars of life in Moscow's poorest quarters.

One of the features of life in the camps was the mixture of criminals like Danni and political prisoners like Roman. The politicals were journalists, human rights lawyers and politicians who had fallen foul of the regime and been banged up for years on spurious charges, such as infringing health and safety regulations at work. Putin's 'Dictatorship of the Law' had certainly been used to good effect on them.

Generally, the criminals hated the politicals as lily-livered intellectuals, and harassed and exploited them. Danni, however, had spent some time as a boy in Roman's football academy and, although it hadn't kept him on the straight and narrow, he still regarded Roman as a saint, one of the few people in his hard life who had actually done something

51

unequivocally good for him. He was also a huge Spartak fan, with the club emblem tattooed across his chest, and the combination meant that he had taken it as his life's work to protect Roman.

Danni was standing next to Roman now and hissed back at Getmanov: 'Go sit on a dick, head-fucker!'

'Fuck yer mother!' Getmanov spat back.

'Shut up in there!' screamed Sergeant Kuzembaev from the edge of the crowd of prisoners, raising his whip. Guards quickly unslung their assault rifles and Kuzembaev waded into the ranks with the heavy butt of his whip raised. The machine-gunner on the platform swung the barrel towards them.

Kuzembaev lashed out at a few people but the noise died down so he returned to his post at the end of the line.

They didn't need to use much force on the prisoners. Even minor misdemeanours could be met with the threat of the *izbushka* or 'the little hut'. It was a small wooden building by the side of the parade ground. Prisoners were dragged off there after evening parade if they had committed any faults during the day.

Inside was a line of tiny bare cells with no windows. Each was set behind two doors, one behind the other. If a prisoner was deemed to have been particularly bad then both doors were shut so that absolutely no light penetrated the cell. This was known as 'getting the dark'. Prisoners who did days in the pitch-black soon became disorientated and unhinged.

More importantly, in winter the guards could also control the temperature in the cells by the amount of fuel fed into the stoves set in their walls at the back of the building. 'Getting the cold' meant little or no fuel was allowed to the prisoner, leading to hours of excruciating pain as the man was racked by shivers in an effort to stay alive.

Once the disturbance had settled down, Commandant Bolkonsky spoke into the microphone in front of him on the platform, his voice booming out over the parade ground, flexing in the wind.

'So, men, I hope you are continuing to enjoy your stay here. It's another beautiful day in Camp Honolulu. Whatever you're doing today – if you are at the beach, on the golf course or in the Jacuzzi – I want you to remember one thing: work hard or you'll get the cold and the dark!'

He chuckled heartily and the siren wailed, signalling the end of roll call.

Chapter Four

Sergey was entertaining again.

In the usual Russian manner everything was completely overdone. There was no way that everyone could possibly eat as much food as was laid out, but the display of generosity was what mattered.

This time the party was a more restrained buffet supper of *zakuski*: small, colourful dishes of food crowded onto side tables – smoked fish, caviar, cured meats, salads, cheeses, everything and anything pickled. About twenty people were milling around picking at the food in the large function room downstairs. Alex thought a number of the guests looked very jaded from the night before.

Sergey bounced up to him. 'Have some of my pickled mushrooms!' he said, and thrust one into his hand. 'I pick them myself on my estate outside Moscow! And here, have a shot of my raspberry liquor – my secret recipe!' He laid a finger alongside his nose, his blue eyes twinkling under his shaggy fringe.

Then he was off again glad-handing his guests and business partners. After making sure they were all catered for and drinking heavily, he winked at Alex and they made their way up the stairs to his office.

'So, you want to know who is on our faction?' Sergey

grinned as he swung open the door. 'Well, you will meet them,' he said as he swept into the room.

Two men were sitting on the far side of the large board-room table. Alex was not surprised that he had seen them the night before; he was beginning to understand the way Sergey worked. More food and a tray of vodka glasses were laid out on the table.

'This is Grigory Bezukhov, head of my TV stations in Moscow.'

Alex leaned over the table to shake hands with him. 'Alexander Devereux,' he said formally.

Grigory gave a friendly smile. 'Hello.'

He was in his forties, medium height, slightly tubby, with a few days' stubble and long curly black hair under a trendy Kangol flat cap worn backwards. He was dressed in a crumpled black Armani suit. A green Russian army surplus satchel sat on the table next to him with a laptop and his BlackBerry sticking out of it. His broad face had a trusting, open look.

Sergey turned to the next man. 'And this is Lieutenant-General of the Airforce, Fyodor Mostovskoy.'

Mostovskoy was also in his late forties but otherwise he and Bezukhov were chalk and cheese. He was thin, pale, like some deep-sea fish that lived away from the light. All colour had been leached out of him, his hair was fine and translucent and his skin had an unhealthy pallor. He was quite tall and stooped, with a thin nose that was crooked to one side. As a military man he had a more formal, reserved manner, and bowed his head slightly as he shook hands. Alex noticed that his hands were fine-boned but the grip was strong. His eyes had a watchful look that spoke of a greater intelligence than he would ever express openly.

'Fyodor is our key man,' said Sergey, coming around the table behind him and slapping him on the back. 'He is in charge of Moscow Military District air defences and has organised a lot of support for us in the airforce as well. The only problem is, he doesn't drink!' He opened his arms wide in astonishment. 'I sometimes wonder – is he Russian or a foreign spy?'

Fyodor's lips twisted a little in what passed for a smile.

'We are also waiting for one other person, who is helpfully late,' Sergey said sardonically and looked at his watch. 'This is as many of the team as I could safely get together in London at one time without arousing suspicion. There are a lot more backers in Moscow on the media side and others who will contribute financially, plus politicians who will declare for us when the time comes. A lot of people don't like Krymov's aggressive line against the West. We're all proud of the Motherland but we don't want to blow up the whole world in order to prove it!'

He picked up a small glass of vodka and proposed a toast. 'So, my friends! To the new *Dekabristi*!'

Alex dutifully slammed his drink back and winced at the kick. He would have to get used to starting meetings like this. He didn't, however, know the word in Russian and queried it with Sergey; Sergey hastened to fill in the blank. 'In English you would say "The Decembrists", you know, like Shaporin's opera?'

Alex was a confident enough character not to mind admitting that he didn't, and shook his head.

'They were a bunch of idealists back in 1825. They rebelled to try to liberate Russia from tsarist dictatorship. Funnily enough they ended up in the same labour camp as Raskolnikov is now in.'

Grigory and Fyodor both looked down at the table when he said this, and Sergey suddenly realised that this last point wasn't actually very funny at all.

'Well, you know,' he shrugged, 'let's be honest about the risks. Life is a fatal condition – no one has survived it yet. Anyway, this time we are trying to get someone out of Krasnokamensk and take them—'

The double doors burst open and everyone jumped.

'Sergey Stepanovich!'

The stunning woman from the party last night came sweeping in.

Alex sat bolt upright – what the hell was going on? Sergey's security could not be very tight if just anyone could burst in on them.

'I know! I'm late! I'm sorry.'

Sergey seemed very pleased to see her, though, and opened his arms to embrace her; she kissed him demurely on both cheeks instead.

'Ah! Now we are complete!' Sergey turned to Alex, puffed out his chest with pride and introduced them formally. 'Alexander Nikolayevich Devereux this is Lara Mikhailovna Maslova.'

Alex slowly rose from his seat; he was trying to get a grip on his conflicting feelings of shock that the woman was actually part of their faction, mixed with the physical impact of seeing her again. He did his best to cover it as he shook hands firmly and repeated, 'Alexander Devereux.'

She flashed a glance up at him; her blue eyes set above sweeping cheekbones to give her a look as wide and dazzling as the sky over the steppe.

As she moved away, Alex found himself watching the body language between her and Sergey; his hand rested lightly on the small of her back in a proprietorial manner as the two stepped past each other to sit down.

She sat next to Alex and looked at Sergey at the head of the table. 'OK, let's go!' She beamed at them all; she seemed to have resolved whatever issues she'd had the night before and leavened the previous sombre mood.

'OK.' Sergey looked at Alex. 'Lara and Grigory are the media side of this coup. Now, they are vital because in this game it's not about who *has* the real power, it's who *appears* to have the power. Krymov has many more soldiers than us, but when this all kicks off, people will sit on the fence and wait to see which way the wind is blowing. With the control of the TV stations we can get the images out there that can make it look like we have popular support on the streets of Moscow and then swing the army behind us.'

He looked at Grigory for comment, who spoke with the confident manner of someone who knew his job.

'Sergey is absolutely right, media coverage was where the KGB really fucked up in 1991 when they rebelled against Gorbachev. Everybody was watching TV to see what was happening and Yeltsin managed to get just a few minutes of airtime on the news of him standing on a tank. It broke their image of invincibility, someone had stood up to them and suddenly it was the emperor's new clothes time and everybody turned against them.

'Apart from that, Russia is the world's largest country, more than twice the size of the US.' He spread his hands across the table. 'It's nine thousand kilometres wide, over seven time zones. So to win, we will also need to get support from a majority of the eighty-eight regional governors and the politicians from those zones; as well as carrying business, the international community and the UN with us.

'We can't guarantee what will happen on the ground. It will be tough – Krymov is not going to give up without a fight – and a lot of people will wait and see, but with Sergey's TV channels we can at least make the wind *appear* to be blowing in our direction and that will be a big factor.'

Sergey broke in enthusiastically. 'Yes! And Lara will help us achieve it because she is the most popular TV presenter in Russia at the moment!' He glanced at her admiringly and she smiled and looked down modestly.

Sergey preened himself a little. 'Of course, I discovered her when she was ...' Lara looked up and interrupted him with a venomous glance; Sergey continued, '... doing other things. I put her on *Deal or No Deal*, everybody loved her and it all started from there. So now she fronts *Big Brother*, *Star Factory*, all the big national festivals ...' He gestured to her to continue.

She turned to Alex. 'I'm the nation's favourite girl-next-door, you know. I'm down to earth – I'm not a Muscovite; I have a provincial accent—'

Sergey leaned forward to interrupt her. 'Same hometown as me – Voronezh – only the best ...' he winked.

'Hmm.' Lara smiled graciously, taking the interruption in her stride. She seemed used to Sergey's manner. 'I do flash my boobs,' she gestured unselfconsciously to her sculpted cleavage, 'but I'm very sweet as well. All the dads fancy me and all the mums wish I would marry their boys.' She tilted her head on one side, looked up at Alex with her steppe-sky eyes and gave a coy smile.

To Alex it felt as if the earth had tilted slightly. He nodded as professionally as he could but in his head he shouted at himself: Get a grip, Devereux!

Lara switched the smile off and continued in her matter-of-fact way. 'I've also moved into doing some soft news; it's mainly interviewing celebrities, but I'm sure I can do a good job on reporting the news of the coup and fronting Raskolnikov.'

Sergey nodded approvingly and turned to Alex. 'So, that's the media side. In terms of troops we are confident of support from a key regiment.' He looked at Fyodor.

Fyodor cleared his throat. He spoke quietly, with his head down and his hands clasped on the table in front of him. 'Yes, the 568th Regiment is stationed in the northern suburbs of Moscow and is having some problems.' He coughed self-consciously before admitting, 'It's not an unknown fact that Russian army life is very brutal: bullying is a part of the conscription process and commanding officers refer to their men as "slaves". Far more men die from accidents and suicides every year than in combat.'

He glanced defensively at Alex, who couldn't tell if the lieutenant-general was just embarrassed to admit this to a former NATO officer or if he was just a cagey character.

Fyodor continued, 'Krymov has pushed for a return to what he calls "the old values" that made the Red Army great. What he means by that is an increase in brutality. He appointed a new commanding officer to the 568th last year – Colonel Karenin, a friend of his – and he has been so sadistic that his men have been pushed to the edge. Sergey has been in touch with junior officers in the regiment who say they are ready to rebel. We believe that they will come out for us.

'The 568th will be vital because they will help us hold on to the Ostankino TV tower – all the TV and radio stations in Moscow broadcast from there and then relay to the whole of Russia.'

Alex nodded but Fyodor could see that he needed some background. 'The tower, you know, it looks like the Telecom Tower in London but it's three times as high,' he stretched a hand up above the table, 'five hundred and forty metres. It used to be the tallest building in the world.'

Sergey interrupted him. 'Everything is bigger in Russia!' he said grandly with his arms spread wide, and then leaned towards Alex and said in a confidential tone, 'Although, did you know that Russian scientists have recently invented the world's *finest* microcomputer?' He looked at him with a raised eyebrow and nodded meaningfully.

This complete change of direction flummoxed Alex and he looked back at Sergey, unsure as to what he should say.

The Russian exploded, throwing his arms wide again and shouting, 'It's the biggest in the world!' He burst out laughing, looking round the table to see if they got the joke.

Lara and Fyodor both smirked and shook their heads, while Grigory bellowed with laughter.

An obsession with being the biggest in everything was all part of their country's general insecurity complex but some of the more intelligent Russians enjoyed poking fun at it. Sergey grinned, pleased to have made people laugh. 'It's good, yeah?'

Alex smiled and nodded appreciatively.

Sergey was finally satisfied and continued his former line of thought. 'So, the tower is about five miles north of the centre of Moscow but there was a lot of fighting there in the revolt against Yeltsin in 1994 – about thirty people got killed.'

Alex looked surprised. 'I didn't realise it was such a big fight.'

Fyodor seemed to take a gloomy pride in the event. 'Well, I was there as a junior staff officer. It was a big deal. We had six hundred armoured vehicles out in Moscow. Tanks shelled the presidential palace and burned it down.'

Sergey nodded. 'So, that's the plan. We get Raskolnikov to Ostankino, do the broadcast with him and Lara, call the crowds out onto the streets and win over the 568th Regiment – simple.'

Again he shrugged off the enormous risks with a smile. Alex was already thinking of a hell of a lot of things that could go wrong.

Sergey admitted some of them. 'What we don't know is what Krymov will do. The OMON riot police and the MVD troops will certainly support him, but the question is whether the other regiments around Moscow will support us. If they do respond to the broadcast then we win, but if they don't then we will have a hell of a fight.'

Alex nodded in agreement. 'Hmm, as von Moltke said: "When your enemy has only two options he invariably chooses the third."'

Sergey pondered it for a moment and smiled before he clapped his hands. 'Anyway, that's the Moscow end of things. Now explain your plan for the camp.'

Alex sat forward, pulled some maps out of his wallet, laid them on the table and talked them through his initial ideas for an attack. Fyodor leaned over and took a keen interest whilst Lara and Grigory sat back. Sergey listened carefully whilst Fyodor asked useful questions.

Alex wrapped up his presentation: 'I have been in touch with my usual team and they are interested in the job. Colin Thwaites is in the UK already, Arkady Voloshin and Yamba Douala are on their way back here from Africa, and I have contacted two more people.'

Sergey nodded with satisfaction. 'Hmm, very good, Major Devereux. Now, my only input on this is your call sign for the operation – it will be "Baba Yaga"!' he grinned.

Lara rolled her eyes. 'Sergey, is this necessary?'

Sergey looked at her with exasperation. 'Lara! Will you indulge me for once?'

She turned to Alex. 'His enthusiasm for Russian folk stories sometimes gets the better of him.'

Sergey's excitement was undeterred. 'It's a good name!' He too turned to Alex. 'She's a witch who flies around Russia doing harm to people – just like you! Although she has iron teeth and she eats children!' He grimaced, gnashed his teeth and made clawing gestures with his hands. 'Anyway, Alex should read some Russian literature if he wants to understand what this is all about! The struggle for the soul of the Motherland!' he declared grandly.

'Hmm ...' Lara sounded unimpressed; Alex had the idea that this was a well-worn argument between them but that she was happier just to let it go for now.

Sergey jabbed a finger at Alex. 'You see, you asked me last night – will we win? And I say, yes! We will win because we have the Russian soul!' He emphasised the words *Russkaya dusha*. 'All you Western bastards say we're all slaves but the Russian soul is not a slave soul!' He banged the table. 'Our free spirit will overcome this Krymov son of a bitch!' He tossed his head so that his thatch of blond hair flayed around.

Lara put a hand on his and smiled at him sweetly. 'Sergey, my little fish, can we get on with the briefing, please?'

Sergey harrumphed but she ignored him and looked at the others. 'So, now we have Raskolnikov, how are we going to get him back to Moscow?'

The airforce officer Fyodor came into his own here. He pulled a document wallet out of a briefcase; his eyes narrowed as he looked at the papers. 'Moscow has the best air defence system in the world but I have some ideas for getting around it.'

He talked them through, with Alex and the others chipping in suggestions. After a while they had finalised things as much as they could, and Sergey's attention began to wander.

'Right! I now want you all to piss off downstairs and eat and drink! I am going to explain to Alex why we are fighting for the soul of Russia!'

Chapter Five

The authoritarian side of the soul of Russia was making itself felt to Roman Raskolnikov that same evening.

He lay on his bunk in Barrack 9 and looked at the ceiling. He was at the top of the stack of four beds, shoved right under the planks. He slept there so that no one could get at him during the night – it was not unheard of for prisoners to be found with their throats slit in the morning. Two politicals who supported him and Big Danni slept in the three bunks below him to act as protection.

It was the half-hour after dinner when the men were allowed a few dingy electric lights so that they could get ready for bed and do their chores: darning socks and bartering for cigarettes with favours of one kind and another. He could hear the hundred other men in the hut moving around, muttering and cursing. They were only allowed a bath once a week and the place had the reek of old sweat.

He knew he should be using his time wisely – repairing boots and clothes, chatting to find out useful information, filing down a small knife to use or sell – but he was just too exhausted after his day dragging logs in the forest. The sinews in his shoulders and forearms felt like they had been pulled out of him.

His sawdust mattress was thin and conformed to his

hipbone so that it rested on the hard wooden bed boards. He lay still, staring at the cobwebs of hoar frost in the corner of the roof. It was below freezing in the hut and he slept fully clothed with his feet stuffed into the arms of his jacket and his head under an old blanket.

That had been his 868th day in the camp and he was still alive, so he had something to be grateful for. The slack-mouthed rapist, Getmanov, had watched him closely during the day but hadn't gone anywhere near him and none of the guards had beaten him up as they sometimes did when the mood took them. So, overall, it had been a good day.

There were only 4,607 more to go.

Chapter Six

In another world, in an opulent, warm mansion in South Kensington, Sergey peered at Alex through his fringe in a way that made him unsure if he was drunk or just being very searching. They were now alone in his office.

Sergey said slowly and emphatically, 'Sashenka, I can see from your face that you are not a man of no consequence, you are not a man who is blown here and there.' He flapped his right hand back and forth on the table. 'You are a man who understands the meaning of suffering.' He laid the hand, palm up, on the table between them in a gesture inviting assent.

Alex narrowed his eyes and looked back at him suspiciously. He didn't want to have a deep conversation with Sergey. The Russian's typical lack of personal boundaries was invading Alex's very well-defined English ones.

He could guess why he had said what he did; old girlfriends had always told him that he had a brooding look. His height, dark hair and the strong bones of his face gave him an air of authority that they said they liked. But Alex had never realised how his personal demons manifested themselves.

Sergey pressed on. 'Last night you questioned the integrity of my motives for this coup – that maybe I am in it just for the money. Well, a lot of people are!' he admitted. 'But to be me, and to take the lead in this, to risk everything,' he gestured around at the magnificent house, 'you need much more than that.

'And *you*,' he pointed at Alex, 'need to understand that I am *committed*.' He held a hand to his heart.

'OK,' Alex said calmly.

Sergey swept his hand out. 'We all look for something for meaning to coalesce around in our lives and for me this operation is the meaning of life!' He banged the table and then stood up, and began pacing around. 'I know we Russians are a bunch of miserable fuckers – "Today is worse than yesterday but better than tomorrow",' he repeated the expression with a tired wave of the hand as he walked around and then turned back to Alex. 'Comrade, forgive me, the lack of light eats away at the soul. But,' he held up a finger and looked at Alex, 'this Russian sadness is actually a truer appreciation of humanity. You see you can only be truly happy once you have been truly sad. A Russian understands this – that all emotions are just facets on the jewel of the human soul! In the west of Europe you have this obsession with happiness that demeans that jewel; you see only half of it, but the Russian soul has many sides.' He used that expression again: *Russkaya dusha*.

Alex was struggling to keep up with the way Sergey was flicking from one thing to another.

'The world of the soul touches our everyday world in the same way that the waves of the sea touch the shore. Sometimes it is a gentle lulling motion that calms our hearts.' He sighed with mock contentment, and rested his head on one side on his folded hands with closed eyes, as if asleep. Then he woke up suddenly. 'Often, when we are tired and spiritually dead, it is like when the tide is out, the sea seems a long way away, we cannot even see the water; the dry beach goes out for ever.' He stretched an arm out, looking across the room with a far-off gaze. Then he jabbed his finger insistently as he spoke. 'But at other times, like this, the sea is a crashing wave that pounds against us, forcing us to move! That is what it is like for me now. I cannot ignore it!' He clutched his head. 'The spirit has spoken to me at this time – and what must I reply with? I must reply with magnificence! A magnificent spirit, a great heart, *Russkaya dusha!*'

He calmed down and looked at Alex questioningly. 'Maybe every country has a soul – I don't know. What is the British soul?'

Alex shifted uncomfortably. 'Well … I hadn't really thought about it,' he said evasively. He was actually impressed with the fury of Sergey's feelings but he hated being pressed on his own thoughts. He had always found it safer to keep them to himself.

Sergey continued regardless, 'Well, Russia has a soul, a magnificent soul. If you could know the warmth of its people, the strength of its fathers, its mothers, its families … But, it has two sides to its soul. Just as it has a magnificence so it also has a subservience. Its governments …' He held up a hand in despair. 'I have to be honest with you, Alexander Nikolayevich. We have had the longest history of …' he paused to get the right words and then spat each one out, 'brutal, oppressive, corrupt, useless governments of any country!' He listed them on his fingers. 'Mongols – psychopaths! The Tsars – fucking idiots! Stalin – the second greatest mass murderer in history! Russia deserves better than this! Krymov wants to turn us back the way we came. Ever since the Mongols our freedom has been suppressed by these autocrat sons of bitches! But we were not meant for it! We are not born into slavery! You see …'

He had a sudden moment of inspiration, stopped and

69

then bounded over to one of the huge bookshelves lining the room. He hunted along the shelves, muttering to himself, 'Come on, you fucker, where are you?'

'Ah!' He pulled a large volume out. 'This is Chekhov, writing to his publisher.' He opened the book where a piece of paper was stuck in it. 'He was the same as me before all this bull-shit,' he waved a hand around to indicate the house and his riches, 'a humble provincial lad. So he's explaining how he developed from being a cowed boy to a freedom-loving adult.'

He paused as he hunted for the right passage and then carefully read out: '"Write about how this young man squeezes the slave out of himself drop by drop and how, waking up one fine morning, he finds that the blood coursing through his veins is no longer the blood of a slave, but that of a real human being."'

He nodded in agreement, put the book down, came back to the table and sat down at the head of it.

'So the question he is asking is the same one I am facing today: which part of the Russian soul will win? Its slave soul or its free soul? You see, this is why I love Russian literature! In Russia we explore our soul through our novels. Every one is an expedition into our unconscious and *you* must read them to know us! To do this mission!' he cried enthusiastically.

'And how many people share your enthusiasm for this mission?' Alex made a circular motion with his hand to indicate the people who had been in the room.

Sergey ticked them off on one hand. 'Well, I know Lara understands me, Grigory and all the TV people care about human rights and press freedom, Fyodor …' he made a tipping gesture with his hand and then sighed. 'Alexander, I may look like a lunatic but I am not naïve enough to believe that Lieutenant-General Fyodor Mostovskoy is doing this because of his love of the Russian soul or his humanitarian concern for the people of Russia. He couldn't give a fuck about them. All Fyodor cares about is himself and money. He hates Krymov because when they merged Mikoyan and Sukhoi and all the other Russian aircraft manufacturers into the United Aircraft Corporation, he and the airforce didn't get nearly the share of control on the board that he feels they deserved. That's why he is able to get us the support of the airforce as a whole, because they want the entire military–industrial complex restructured in their favour and away from Krymov's cronies.

'So I have promised him that when we win, he will be very well rewarded. So then he'll feel happy.' Sergey paused, then grinned and flicked an eyebrow. 'Until he decides he wants something else, but we'll deal with that later.'

His mood became very serious. He leaned close and laid a hand on Alex's forearm. 'Alexander, I am speaking to you alone for a reason. I have to tell you something that the others can't know at this stage ...' He looked down for a moment. 'I may require you to carry out another ... mission, when we get to Moscow.'

'Riiight,' said Alex warily. He withdrew from Sergey's grasp and folded his arms as the Russian outlined the extra requirements.

Sergey concluded with, 'I don't know what missions you have done before but this one is going to be a motherfucker! You will need a big heart to get through it.'

He clutched Alex's arm again with one hand and pointed at him with the other. '*You* are my man in this! *You* are leading the fight! Vasily Grossman said that when he was in Stalingrad only those with quiet at the bottom of their souls survived. You will have to find that quiet place in your soul – where the wolf drinks from the river at midnight – and then you will find your courage!'

Alex stared back at him, trying to take it all in.

By the time Sergey had finished his rambling explanation of the plan he had forced a lot of food and drink down Alex, so that he was feeling somewhat befuddled when he eventually left.

He stood on the pavement, swaying slightly as the large electronic gate clicked shut behind him. He shook his head and looked around the darkened street, trying to remember which way was home.

His senses were definitely not working well. After he stumbled away, a man in the patch of gloom across the street muttered into a lapel mike on his heavy parka, detached himself from the shadows and followed him.

Sergey continued pacing up and down his meeting room for some time after Alex had left.

He talked animatedly to himself, waved his arms around, pulled books off the shelf and flicked through them; lovingly reacquainting himself with favourite passages, nodding or frowning as he did so. His mobile phone rang several times and each time he glanced at the number, grunted and ignored it.

As he sat down on his day bed with a copy of Sholokov's *And Quiet Flows the Don*, it rang again.

He grimaced, looked at the screen and saw the word: '*Vozhd*'.

The Boss.

It was Stalin's old nickname and Sergey used it for the secret, secure communication channel that Krymov had insisted on having with him.

He hurriedly put his book down, stood up and became very animated as he answered the call.

'Yo, Comrade!' he began.

Chapter Seven

From: firstclassdrycleaning.com
To: Customer 39789G
Date: Saturday 6 December

Customer notice: First Class Dry-Cleaning regrets to inform you there has been a problem with your order. Please contact our Customer Service division immediately for details.

'Fuck,' Alex muttered to himself as he stuffed his BlackBerry back into his jacket pocket.

What the hell was going on now?

This project already had him on edge, without their emergency contact route being used already. It was only the morning after his last briefing with Sergey.

He replied to say he would collect his dry-cleaning in twenty minutes and then legged it out of the door of his house and up the Fulham Road to the upstairs room of the Fulham Tup pub, which they had agreed to use as a meeting point.

Sergey had an arrangement with the owner to use the room, which was normally let out for parties only in the evening, during the day. It wasn't perfect but they could both slip in via a back entrance and it was less obvious than Alex turning up at Sergey's house, or his offices in Mayfair, which he was pretty sure were under observation by the SVR.

Alex squeezed through the back door, stamped the snow off his feet and ran up the stairs into a room filled with empty tables, the noise of his footsteps echoing on the floorboards.

Sergey was already there, sitting at a table away from the window, wearing an Aquascutum overcoat, his hair as tousled as ever. He rose as Alex came in and strode over to shake his hand, offering profuse apologies.

'Alexander, I am so sorry to call you out of your house in this weather!'

Alex demurred and they sat down.

For once, Sergey seemed in a sombre mood. He looked at Alex in the wintry light from the window.

'I'm not sure what is going on ...' he started hesitantly.

Alex waited for him to continue. Could this whole fucking madhouse scheme be about to collapse? A sudden urge within him hoped it would.

'Krymov called me yesterday after you left; he wants me back in Moscow.' Sergey pursed his lips and looked across at the window.

Alex frowned. 'That doesn't sound good.'

Sergey nodded. 'They might know something. Gorsky, the SVR guy you met at the party, might have picked something up.' He narrowed his eyes in thought. 'No, it's too quick, we haven't done anything yet for them to pick up on.' He looked at Alex candidly. 'Krymov sometimes calls me in the middle of the night to discuss things. He trusts me.' Having voiced his concerns, he seemed to have come to a decision. 'No, he wouldn't have taken fright so quickly; it's nothing that I can't smooth over with him.' Having convinced himself that he was safe, he perked up again. 'So, I will fly to Moscow today and see what it is all about. For you, just ignore it.'

Alex spoke calmly: 'Well, I'll need a week to get the team sorted out in Herefordshire anyway, so I guess you will know for sure by then what it is about?'

'Yes, exactly! We'll know for sure by then. I'll keep sending you the all clear signal about the mail order,' he waved his BlackBerry at Alex, 'but if they do screw me over then it will stop and you will know to call off all the plans. If they start interrogating me then I have no illusions about my ability to resist the boys in the Lubyanka. They really know what they are doing in there,' he said with grudging respect, 'so I'll tell all and they'll just kill me quickly and the whole thing will be over anyway.'

Alex was disturbed by Sergey's clinical assessment of the possibility of his own brutal death. He suddenly had a sense of the ruthlessness that had built Sergey's vast business empire.

'So, Lara will have to fly down to your house to check up on you on her own, eh?' He cocked a knowing eyebrow at Alex, who responded with an innocent expression, even as he fought to control the surge of interest that this comment provoked inside him.

Alex had decided to assemble his team of mercenaries at Akerly. It still had a huge area of parkland around it and so was completely private. It was also snowbound, which would be good training for cross-country skiing and other drills he wanted to put the team through, plus it had sufficient accommodation and no outsiders need be involved. All in all, at short notice, it had seemed the perfect place.

The idea had been for both Sergey and Lara to fly down in Sergey's helicopter to inspect the team, but obviously that wasn't going to happen now.

Alex didn't rise to Sergey's bait. 'Well, I'm sure we'll manage without you.'

'Hmm,' Sergey mused. He didn't seem to have given up on his game entirely. 'Well, I brought you some Russian literature to read in the long dark nights by the fire.'

Alex groaned internally. He couldn't stand it when people pressed their favourite books on him.

'Oh, OK,' he said in an unconvincing display of enthusiasm.

'No, really, it's good stuff!' said Sergey defensively, as he pulled a slim paperback out of his overcoat pocket. 'I told you you needed to read more Russian stuff to know what this coup is all about.' He handed the book to Alex: *We* by Yevgeny Zamyatin.

'It's acknowledged by George Orwell as the basis for *1984*,' Sergey continued in a self-justificatory tone. 'The fucker ripped off the plot completely. Written in 1920, really ahead of its time.'

'What's it about?' Alex took an interest now, despite himself.

Sergey grinned a little too smugly for Alex's liking. 'It's a story about a straightforward guy who falls in love with a crazy girl who is trying to overthrow a totalitarian state.'

He looked at the Englishman meaningfully. Alex blanched. He was beginning to learn that it was typical of Sergey to mix apparently trivial and serious issues.

Sergey shrugged apologetically. 'Look, it's OK. Just be careful, huh?' He grinned. 'In Russia, we tell folktales about Brother Wolf and Sister Fox. Now, what you have to know is that Sister Fox is the smart one and she *always* wins. Watch out for her, she's a man-eater.'

Chapter Eight

Sergey settled back into his luxurious white leather chair and watched the lights go out across London.

His Gulfstream G550 intercontinental jet had got one of the last take-off slots of the day at London City airport. For once, the snow had stopped falling and it was a clear, dark evening, so he had a perfect view through the porthole as the aircraft banked over the East End and they shut off the electricity substations one by one.

A whole block of Dagenham suddenly winked out, the orange grid of street and house lights all went in an instant, leaving just a few car headlamps floundering in the murk.

Well, oppressed people of Britain! You won't have to put up with that for long if my plan works out! Sergey broadcast in his head.

As the plane levelled off, Bayarmaa sauntered in from the kitchen section at the front of the aircraft in a tight black cocktail dress with a tray of Sergey's homemade vodka, pickled mushrooms and meats. She knew him well enough to see that he wanted to be left alone so after stroking his hair and kissing his cheek she slunk back out again. Sergey followed her slim backside with a dangerous look in his eye. He hadn't yet got through the lust phase with her; he knew he would move on, but he was enjoying it at the moment.

Other things occupied his mind now, though; he took a shot of vodka and chewed on the food slowly as he thought. The softly lit cabin was a good brooding cocoon as they hurtled out over the North Sea towards Moscow. His face darkened and he pursed his lips, staring into the night and thinking hard.

Although he had been full of bravado with Alex he was actually deeply troubled about the forthcoming encounter with Krymov. He thought about what the summons could mean; it was hard to tell, as the President was such an erratic character.

Sergey wondered at his own capacity for duplicity. He was a good example of Soviet era 'double think' – the ability to think opposite thoughts at once. He had grown up with it as a boy: the ability to swear passionate allegiance to Marxist-Leninism at school and then go out and indulge in the raw, black-market capitalism that was necessary to survive it.

He remembered an Uzbek expression that one of his operations managers from a refinery there had told him: Uzbeks can say one thing, think another and do a third.

Sergey was a prime example of such flexibility. Sometimes he lived the part of a supporter of the regime and enjoyed the intellectual trickery of misleading them so much that he felt he had lost touch with what he really believed in. Only at odd moments of solitude, like this, would he call to mind the feelings that drove him. He suddenly felt the whole weight of the coup resting on his shoulders – he had a moment of self-consciousness like an out-of-body experience.

What the hell did he think he was doing?

He was trying to overthrow the government of Russia. No one had done that since the Bolsheviks in 1917. He could be on the brink of a major civil war. Even after the Bolshevik victory, it had taken two years of vicious fighting that had raged across the whole country and taken millions of lives. Was he about to inflict the same on his beloved Mother Russia?

Sergey had the capacity to dream great dreams, but the flipside of this was that he was prone to moments of black doubt, when the grand scale of his ideas seemed to crush him.

He was really just a small-town boy from Voronezh, a decaying industrial town, smack bang in the middle of the steppe. As a child he had a phenomenally high IQ and was very sensitive. He had watched everything intently, noticed things quickly and made connections unprompted. His mother felt unnerved by how closely he watched her when he was a baby, how fast he put two and two together.

He used to watch his father playing chess with mates from the steel mill in the kitchen of their tiny workers' flat. Once, as a two year old, he had been given jumbled up chess pieces in a box to play with whilst his mother peeled some potatoes. When she turned round she found that he had set all the pieces out accurately on the board and had begun moving them correctly: pawns forward and back, knights two forward, one to the side, and bishops diagonally. She stared at him, disconcerted. He had looked up, smiled at her sweetly and carried on as if it were the most natural thing in the world.

At primary school he ate up the curriculum. His teachers were very pleased with him, but then aged eight he became very frustrated; he would look at his classmates sitting quietly, looking around with vacant and content expressions or stumbling to learn things that he took in at a glance, and he would be suddenly filled with anger against them. They seemed such hateful dullards to him.

'Do you even think? Is there anything going on in your heads?' he would shout at them in his mind.

He fell into sudden rages and would rush at quiet, slow boys in his class and attack them for no reason, beating and kicking them. He was suspended from the nursery section of School 17 several times that year until he had had enough wallopings from his teachers and his father to know better.

After that he gave up trying to solve the problem of life and took to flippancy as a way of displacing the boredom and frustration in his head. He became the class clown, winding his teachers up, coasting through school, underachieving and driving his parents mad. But underneath his easy wit and idiotic banter, he felt the pressure of existence keenly; subconsciously he questioned why he existed and found no answers.

The lack of a solution distressed him. As a boy he would jump onto the slow-moving flatbed trains grinding through the points outside his family's concrete apartment block on the edge of town, and let himself be carried out onto the steppe. Then he would jump off and walk miles out into the endless, flat grassland, forgetting about how and when to get home and sleeping out under the stars.

He watched the sunset over the steppe, a painting of vast colours being shifted across the heavens by an unseen hand. The shades heaved and convulsed: yellow to orange to pink to red to purple to black.

The whole scene was watched by the earth in utter silence; it lay flat and quiescent, overawed by the majesty of the spectacle unfolding above it. And he too lay on his back on the warm summer earth, spreading out his arms and drawing breath up from the land under him, startled by the beauty of being alive.

To him, this landscape came together with the Russian character to form the Russian soul. It became for him the embodiment of great strength and yet, at the same time, great tenderness.

In reading *Life and Fate* – Vasily Grossman's epic of the Russian nation centred around the battle of Stalingrad – he experienced a moment of revelation: 'The earth was vast, even the great forests had both a beginning and an end, but the earth just stretched on for ever. And grief was something equally vast, equally eternal.'

He realised that the never-ending nature of the terrain was the same as the vastness of life, and this created both a sense of great freedom because it existed, but also of a great corresponding sadness because life will end and it will all be gone. He struggled to reconcile the tension between these forces.

He wondered at the wisdom that he could learn from observing natural phenomena: the flight of birds, the slow graceful gestures of trees and the stately progress of clouds across the sky. He felt that all these things were words in the conversation that nature was having with him in his life.

However, with such passionate experiences came the pain of unrequited love. He might love life but it did not feel the need to explain itself to him. He waited patiently, as a child waits on a parent to tell him how things work.

But all he got was silence.

He would go out onto the steppe and stare up angrily at the sky, but it just looked back at him with a gaze as empty and content as that of a Buddha and resolutely refused to answer his questions.

Sergey felt this absence of communication as a physical force, pressing in on his skull. It was the same as when he swam down deep in the local swimming pool, where the silence was heavy, and he could look up and see the surface shimmering a long way above his head.

He could feel the water pressing in on him from all sides; the walls of his head bulging in under it. He knew then that he had to swim desperately to the surface far above him to escape the pain. But the faster he swam the faster he ran out of breath and so the more desperately he kicked out. The feeling culminated in a fear of inactivity and created a terrified energy within him.

From his early teens onwards, this found an outlet in two ways. Literature was his first love. He discovered that other great human minds had confronted and wrestled with the same issues that he did and had left traces of their battles behind them. So he hunted meaning in literature furiously, frantically ripping through books like a starving man looking for food between the pages, all the while marvelling at the power of writing to gather and pin meaning onto a piece of paper. When he came across insights he shivered and thought to himself: This is black bread – black bread for my soul.

Books piled up in his room, all with significant passages underlined, pages folded and with thoughts that had spun off from the writing scribbled in the margins and on the blank pages at the back.

The second outlet for his skills was on his mother's market stall. She was a *chelnoki*, a market trader, who allowed people to survive both the incompetencies of the Soviet system and then the anarchy of its collapse in the 1990s. From her Sergey learned how to lie, to cheat and to bribe the police and other authorities that variously sought to regulate and profit from their activities. He started out by selling underwear off the back of a lorry, then graduated to buying second-hand Mercedes in West Germany, driving them back home through long days and nights, and then selling them on for a huge mark-up.

From this he went on to buying companies. He understood accounts instinctively and loved the challenge of ripping through a balance sheet, diagnosing faults and then taking on the cold-blooded risks necessary to win in the bare-knuckle capitalism of the Yeltsin era. From humble beginnings his business empire gradually expanded from automotive parts, to mines, to food preparation, and then into more glamorous sectors like media.

However, at times of inner crisis, like now, he had to turn back to literature to steady himself. He needed books as his touchstone.

He pulled the greatest book ever written out of the Louis Vuitton briefcase at his feet: *Life and Fate*. His battered copy had been heavily annotated.

He turned to the section where Sokolov and Madyarov were arguing about the true nature of what freedom meant in Russia. Sokolov was in full flood: 'Chekhov is the bearer of the greatest banner that has been raised in the thousand years of Russian history – the banner of a true, human, Russian democracy, of Russian freedom, of the dignity of the Russian man.'

The bearer of the banner of the dignity of the Russian man! That was what he was! That was what *Russkaya dusha* was all about!

He could see himself with a grand banner unfurled over his head expressing his love for the people of Russia. The great image stuck in his head, revivifying him.

He sat in his luxurious executive jet with the book in front of him, holding it and staring out of the window, lost in renewed dreams of glory as he swept on to meet President Krymov.

Chapter Nine

Sergey was ushered quietly into Krymov's office in the Kremlin.

Even though it was Saturday evening, the President was still hard at work. Being unable to let go was all part of his instability.

He followed the classic dictator-kitsch style of having a huge office with his desk set at the far end of it to intimidate anyone who had to take the long walk towards him.

Although, to be fair, this desk did have history. His particular office lay on the top floor of the Senate House, a triangular building around a central courtyard, along the eastern wall of the Kremlin, with Lenin's Mausoleum in Red Square just over the great outer wall to the east of it.

It had been the office of the Russian head of state since 1918 so the other occupants had included Lenin, Stalin, Khrushchev, Brezhnev, Andropov, Chernyenko, Gorbachev, Yeltsin, Putin and Medvedev.

Now Krymov sat at his huge desk with a green-shaded lamp illuminating the wall of paperwork that he liked to hide behind. It was ten o'clock at night and he was hunched over the desk, pen in one hand, signing documents. He looked up and glowered at Sergey like an angry pig.

Sergey walked nonchalantly across the deep pile carpet

towards him, wearing his crumpled suit and tie, his hair askew and his diamond earring glinting in the low lights.

Krymov wagged his finger at him threateningly.

'Shaposhnikov, what's this I hear about you meeting up with a man called Devereux in London?'

Sergey froze halfway across the carpet.

'You said he was a geologist you were flying out to Krasnokamensk but Gorsky has checked him out and tells me he is a well-known British mercenary. What's going on?' he barked. 'If you don't want to smell, then don't touch shit!'

Behind him stood Major Batyuk, the head of Echelon 25, Krymov's élite bodyguard unit. A tall, balding man with a hardened face, wearing a tight-fitting uniform, he had had his right ear sliced off years ago in a fight and the angry little stump of red cartilage stuck out of the side of his head, giving him a weird, lopsided look.

The major clenched his fists at his side, knowing that this was going to be another of those sessions when some poor subordinate was dragged into the office and shredded. Krymov would probe them to start off with; they would then be terrified, which encouraged him to bully them more so the whole thing would end with the President in a screaming fit and Batyuk having to beat someone senseless and then drag their battered body out of the office. He looked at Sergey now, waiting for him to sweat and start pleading for his life.

Sergey swaggered forward right up to the desk, looking straight at Krymov.

'I've hired him to go hunting elephants, comrade.'

Krymov sat up and frowned. 'Hunting elephants? What shit are you coming out with now, Shaposhnikov?' he shouted, unsure whether to be angry or confused.

'Yes, Devereux's worked in Africa a lot. He's an expert tracker to help me track down the Russian elephant.'

'What? The Russian elephant! Shaposhnikov, you're a head-fucker!'

'Ah! Comrade President, you know me.' Sergey waved a hand.

The overly familiar tone made Major Batyuk grind his teeth.

'Yes, you know, the Russian elephant. It has a trunk and two ears. Yes, like this, you see, it has one ear on one side of its head,' Sergey paused and pulled out the lining of his left-hand trouser pocket, 'and one ear on the other side of its head.' He pulled out the lining of his right-hand trouser pocket. 'And then it has a trunk. Yes, a trunk, like this.' Sergey paused again.

Krymov stared at him, not comprehending what was happening.

Sergey then unzipped his trousers.

Major Batyuk could not believe it. He knew that Shaposhnikov was a joker, but to come out with this in the face of an accusation of treason by the President was too much. He was going to have to shoot this guy here and now.

Sergey pulled his shirt tail out through his fly and started waving it around and laughing manically.

Krymov gave a weird sound, halfway between a scream and a wheeze. His face went bright red and he creased up, bent over his desk and banged it with his fist.

'Shaposhnikov!' he wheezed. 'I embrace you!' Tears of laughter streamed down his face. 'Russian elephant!' He staggered round the desk and embraced Sergey, both of them laughing hysterically now. 'Russian elephant!'

Krymov got hold of Sergey's shirt tail and pulled him around the office. 'Off to the circus!' he shouted, making trumpeting noises.

They pranced around Stalin's office until they collapsed on a pair of chairs to one side.

'Shaposhnikov, you make me laugh!' Krymov eventually wheezed. He looked with loathing at the pile of work on his desk. 'This job does my head in, I tell you. But you make me laugh. Come on! Batyuk, get the car! Fuck work! Let's go and drink vodka!'

The heavily armoured black Zil limousine swept west along Kutuzovskiy Prospekt. Using the central lane in the road reserved for government vehicles they were able to maintain a steady eighty miles an hour despite the snowy conditions.

The two Russian tricolours fluttered on its bonnet, another Zil followed behind with the nuclear launch codes and two large Ural military vehicles travelled in front and behind, loaded with Major Batyuk and two squads of heavily armed Echelon 25 troops.

In the back of the Zil, Sergey and Krymov sat facing each other, reclining in the black leather seats with their feet stretched out in front of them. They bantered and picked at a plate of pickled fish, mushrooms, salamis and other delicacies, occasionally breaking off to toast each other with shots of vodka when a good idea came to mind.

Krymov held up a pickled mushroom. 'That's the problem with the West, you know. Whenever I go there I can never get a good pickled mushroom.'

Sergey looked at him blankly. It wasn't one of the main issues he faced in London. He nodded sagely, though. 'Yes, that is the legacy of capitalism. You see,' he pointed a finger knowingly at the President, 'under capitalism, man exploits man.' He paused and they both nodded wisely. 'But under communism,' Sergey continued, 'it was the other way round.'

Krymov continued nodding and looked out of the tinted window. He then glanced back at Sergey, who was grinning at him. Krymov wheezed with laughter and slapped his leg. 'The other way round! Ah! Shaposhnikov!'

They continued eating, drinking and bantering and the MKAD, Moscow's main ring road, shot past unnoticed behind the black tinted glass.

After a while Sergey shouted, 'Here's to those British fuckers, to keep 'em warm tonight!'

'Yes! Fuck 'em! Do 'em good to get the cold up 'em!'

Soon they were heading down the long drive of Novo-Ogaryovo, the country estate that Krymov had taken over from Putin.

The President's official residence was an imposing nineteenth-century classical house set amidst snow-covered pine woods. Ice and gravel crunched as the convoy drew up outside the colonnaded porch. Golden light shone from carefully polished lanterns, and soldiers and uniformed servants stood at attention lining the steps up to the grand front door.

The convoy swept up and Krymov's limousine parked neatly in front of the steps. The Echelon 25 troops debussed and took up positions around the convoy to cover the President's movement up the steps.

There was a long pause as they all waited in the cold. After two minutes nothing had happened and eyes darted to and fro across the lines of attendants. Had something happened to His Excellency? Major Batyuk walked up to the Zil, anxiously trying to see in through the tinted glass.

The door burst open and Krymov fell out of the limo, laughing. Guards darted forward anxiously and then backed off. He rolled over in the snow and lay on his back shouting: 'The British are a bunch of pussies! Bunch of pussies!'

Sergey staggered out of the car, tripped over Krymov's outstretched foot and fell face down next to him. He shouted in anger and thrashed around trying to get the snow off his face.

Krymov hooted with laughter. He crawled over to him on his hands and knees and then staggered to his feet and helped Sergey up.

'Come on, comrade! You see, this is what living in Britain does to you! You can't take your vodka!'

Servants came forward to help but Krymov waved them away angrily and continued supporting Sergey on his shoulder up the steps.

Once inside they lurched down a series of long corridors to the banya complex overlooking the gardens at the back of the house. Saunas are to Russian male culture what the pub is in Britain: a place for men to be together and talk in private. Krymov's major-domo hurried along nervously behind them, fearing his boss's unpredictability in these sessions.

The President entered the changing room first, clapped his hands and ordered more vodka and food before stripping off his overcoat and suit and dumping them on the floor. The major-domo scurried about picking them up.

Sergey followed his example until both were stark naked facing each other. Krymov's body sagged with age: the bags under his eyes, and his flabby male breasts. His stomach hung down over his crotch and his skinny legs stuck out under the mass. Sergey was also rotund but slightly better built; his hair looked particularly dishevelled and ridiculous after his fall in the snow. The only thing he was wearing now was his diamond earring.

Krymov ignored the servant, thrust his chest out and looked Sergey straight in the eye. A moment of understanding passed between them before Krymov flung open the sauna door and they both strode into its swirling steam.

*   *   *

Krymov's sweating face leered up close to Sergey's.

Sergey could see that the pores in the President's vodka-raddled skin had opened up like moon craters. He was out of breath and his eyes were crinkled up with pleasure.

Sergey was retelling a scene from *Peculiarities of the National Hunt* – a cult Russian comedy film – in which the pilot of a nuclear bomber is trying to explain to his squadron leader why he has a smuggled cow strapped into the bomb bay of his aircraft.

'We've been infiltrated!' shouted Sergey with just the right note of defensive indignation in his voice.

Krymov screamed with laughter and fell off the bench that he was sitting on. Sergey lay back on his bench, snorting weakly with laughter. Both were exhausted by their humour-making and silence settled on the banya for a minute.

Eventually Krymov clambered off the floor, poured himself another shot of vodka and stretched his sweaty, white, flabby body out, face down on his front on his bench, with a joyful sigh.

The two lay still for a while before Krymov muttered, his chin tucked down by his shoulder, 'Come and whip me.'

Sergey heaved himself to his feet, pulled a bunch of birch twigs from a holder on the wall and began expertly to flutter them rapidly over Krymov's back, starting at his shoulders, drawing the blood to the surface and cooling it at the same time with the airflow. Krymov groaned at the sensation.

'Shaposhnikov, you are good to me,' the President muttered, incapacitated with pleasure.

There was a pause as Sergey continued his work; brow furrowed with concentration.

Krymov continued, 'Everyone needs someone close to them.'

Krymov's industrially proportioned wife was known as

'Mrs Stale Bread'. They slept in separate beds and hardly said a word to each other. He didn't seem to need intimacy and no one expected it from him, so Sergey's eyes flicked up in surprise from his work when the President returned to the subject in a slurred voice.

'It does get to me, you know, reviving Russia ... there's so much to do ... she needs such a great big kick up the arse ... get her going, up there again as a superpower.'

Sergey moved this gentle flagellation down past Krymov's shoulders, wondering where his train of thought was going. He was so absorbed in the challenge of misleading Krymov that it came as a distasteful shock when he really did open up, as if he was breaking the rules of the game.

'Hmm, they do say that everyone needs someone to trust ... but you see, you have to be careful who you trust.' Krymov pulled his chin away from his shoulder and rested his head on his hands so he could speak freely. Sergey continued his work.

'You see, I always think about Ivan the Terrible ...' Sergey knew Krymov admired him, '... how he was betrayed by Prince Kurbsky.'

Sergey tensed at the mention of his name. Kurbsky was the most famous traitor in Russian history, who had abandoned the Tsar and run away abroad to join the hated Polish enemies of the Motherland.

'His most trusted adviser!' continued Krymov, twisting round and resting on an elbow so he could look Sergey in the eye.

Sergey stopped flapping his twigs and stood looking down on Krymov, who became more animated as the idea gripped him.

'His closest adviser! A man as close as this!' He gestured to Sergey standing next to him. 'A traitor!' He sat up and swung his legs round onto the floor, staring accusingly at Sergey.

The sudden mood swing caught Sergey off guard. Was Krymov being serious? Was this an elaborate setup?

What he was saying was just too close to reality to be coincidence. Was this why Krymov had hauled him all the way back to Moscow: to spring this trap on him?

Sergey's normal bubble of bravado was punctured by the lance-like look of suspicion that Krymov now shot at him. He looked helplessly back like a boy caught with his hand in the sweet jar.

'Imagine! What a motherfucker!' Krymov stood up, outraged by Kurbsky's betrayal of trust.

Sergey felt suddenly washed out by the irony of what was happening and longed to get away.

Krymov looked at his defenceless stare and took it as helpless agreement with his sentiment. He was overcome with emotion.

'I could not wish for a better friend than you, Shaposhnikov! You are the embodiment of *Russkaya dusha*! Of real trustworthiness!' He opened his arms and, despite their nakedness, embraced Sergey with a bear hug.

Sergey returned it, not quite believing what was happening.

Chapter Ten

'Look, after this job you'll never have to work again!'

Alex opened both hands in a gesture inviting Colin Thwaites to think about the two million pounds that he stood to gain from the operation.

'Yeah, you're dead right, you'll never work again – because you'll be *fooking* dead, that's why!' said Colin emphatically in his harsh Lancashire accent.

Alex was struggling to make headway against a torrent of Northern scorn being poured on his bold new idea.

He was beginning to get exasperated; it was later the same day that he had met Sergey in the pub. He needed Col for the op; there wasn't anyone else he trusted as much to make the raid work as this tough former Para. He began to regret his confidence in front of Sergey about how quickly he could get his team together. It was true that they were assembling in London but he had not yet explained to them the details of the job – his emails had been very brief for security reasons – so as yet they had not fully signed up to it.

The two men were in Alex's living room in Fulham. Colin had made it down from Blackburn on one of the few trains that were still running and was now sitting on a sofa facing Alex.

He looked the epitome of a Northern hard man: short but with a strong, wiry build, tattoos of Blackburn Rovers on his right forearm and the Parachute Regiment on his left. He was in his mid-forties, balding on top, with grey hair shaved down to bristles, a coarse-boned face with gimlet eyes, small moustache stained brown from nicotine, and lean lines stretched down his cheeks from a fanatical exercise habit. He was an experienced marathon runner: 'Keeps yer fit, like – it's the only time I'm not fagging, yer know.'

He had worked with Alex through all his operations in Africa. Sharp, tough and a stickler for military professionalism, he was the mainstay of the team that Alex headed. He had been born on a council estate in Blackburn with a restless natural intellect that failed to achieve anything at school. Aged sixteen he was drifting into a life of glue sniffing and petty crime, but had signed up for 2 Para with a mate one day. They had been watching *The Professionals* the night before and knew that the lead hard man, whom they worshipped, was a TA Para.

As with many wastrels before him, the strictures of army discipline had provided the channel to focus his energies. He had seen action in Northern Ireland and Bosnia, had risen to sergeant major in the Pathfinders, the Para's élite reconnaissance unit, and had done stints all over the world training and advising Special Forces.

What he lacked in size he made up for with aggressive energy. Pithy comments and an endless stream of poor-taste jokes were delivered in his unattractive nasal accent.

His blunt nature meant he couldn't help but express his doubts now about the outline of the task facing them.

'OK, right, so let me get this straight. We rock up at this prison camp in Siberia or whatever and they say: "Yer, that's your bloke over there."' He mimicked casually pointing someone out. 'I mean, they don't shoot 'im or nowt. So we just get 'im and then booger off. *Then* we get on a plane to Moscow – and they don't shoot us down on the way, like – we land up in the middle of a fooking great revolution, and then just walk off, you know, come home, put our feet up and watch the telly, like?' He held his hands up and cocked his head on one side, looking at Alex in disbelief. 'I mean, it's bollocks, int'e?'

It was a testament to the trusting relationship between the two men that Colin could be so scathing to a superior officer.

The two were certainly an unlikely pairing. Public school officers from posh cavalry regiments were not usually respected by hardened former Paras; 'Ruperts' was the standard dismissive name they used for them.

Alex looked at him. Despite the huge social gulf between them, they shared a great deal of common ground that had allowed them to get through many differences of opinion.

They were both exiles from their social groups, who felt trapped by the conventions that they were supposed to observe and loved the adventure of escaping from them and discovering new things.

Colin hated the parochialism of people on his home council estate and had gone to great lengths to get away from it and broaden his worldview. He had learned to speak good French (with a heavy Lancashire accent) in order to explore West Africa and had become a huge fan of its music, travelling around to see bands play when he was on leave.

Similarly, Alex was supposed to be a county gentleman, but found the mental straitjacket that came with the class stereotype unbearable; he actually preferred the outspoken honesty of the Northern ex-Para.

He knew that Col's reaction to what he had proposed was

a fair one and that such plain speaking had saved him from some bad decisions in the past. He couldn't deny that the mission was risky and realised that it was pointless trying to reassure Colin that it would all be all right and everyone would come home safely, because it probably wouldn't be and some of them would almost certainly die.

Alex knew that a change of tack was needed.

'OK, you're right.' He held his hands up in acknowledgement. 'It's not your average job. Your average job would be the sort of thing we've being doing for years now in Africa. So, no, it's not another training mission; it's not another mine-clearance job, another close-protection job.'

He knew how much Col hated the latter task, nursemaiding arrogant African businessmen as they went around fleecing people. He sensed that goading Colin into the mission was the way forward because they both felt their lives were entering the long, slow glide path to mediocrity. Neither had really made it, and Alex knew that Col still shared his desire to get out there and face the challenges that made him feel alive, that stopped him feeling like he was living in the body of someone who had fallen asleep.

He was, therefore, able to turn the tables on Colin and continue with mounting fury: 'So, no, it's not just *another* job, it will be *fucking* risky and, yes, we probably will all get killed, but actually I don't give a *fuck*! *This* is the big one.' He jabbed an index finger at Col. '*This* is where we do get to save the *fucking* country! And if that's too much of a problem for you then I'll just have to fucking well do it on my own!' He stared at Col, challenging him to meet his gaze.

Col now had the uphill task of justifying his scepticism. With the boot on the other foot, he sat looking at the floor, rubbing his chin as Alex continued to glower at him.

Alex sensed he had won and changed tack again to give Col a face-saving way to climb down from his position.

He continued, the beginnings of laughter now softening his tone, 'I mean, if you don't want to then that's fine. I'll come and visit you in the care home and change your colostomy bag for you if you want.' He broke out into a sardonic guffaw, knowing that this was Colin's secret horror: of not being self-reliant, of dying a slow and pitiful death, and that he would prefer any sort of active, violent end to that.

Col accepted he had lost. 'Ah, fook off!' He tossed his head in disgust and then grinned at Alex knowingly. 'I tell you what, mate. I'm not a fooking granddad yet. How old's my new bird then, eh?'

'Dunno.'

'Twenty-seven, mate! Fooking tits like this.' He held both hands out in front of him. Alex roared with laughter.

Col grinned and then shrugged. 'Don't know what the fook she sees in me, though. I'm old enough to be her dad.' He looked baffled. Despite two divorces and numerous girlfriends, he never did understand why women liked his ferocious energy, and had always run away from them when they began to wrap their soft tentacles around him.

'She took me to Ikea the other day, and I were sitting on this sofa thinking to meself, what the bollocks am I doing here?'

Alex shrugged; he had never understood women either and was the last to feel he could offer another man advice on the subject. There had been enough of them over the years and they generally fell into two categories. When he was a young man there had been the good-looking county girls where the sheer physical urgency had shut out the fact that he couldn't stand their company. They had been raised scrupulously to

99

avoid discussing any controversial subject – politics, religion, even artistic preference in films, books – everything that his frustrated mind wanted to spend time exploring.

After he had realised that he could live without the sex, he had put a lot of effort into tracking down girls that he found interesting. With those few that he had then got close to, he was disturbed to find that something held him back. Although he could not articulate it, his greatest fear was that he might turn into his father. They both had the same good looks that seemed fatal to women but his philandering father had used them to crush and humiliate anyone who showed affection for him. The first time he beat his wife up was on their wedding night.

Alex had grown up with this intermittent domestic violence and somehow the image of his mother's bruised and tearful face had always overlaid that of his girlfriends in his thoughts. The fear that he might do the same had driven him to break off relationships before they even got started.

However, that was the past. Right now, all he cared about was that Col was onboard so he just laughed and said ruefully, 'Well, at least you're getting *some* fucking action.'

Chapter Eleven

SUNDAY 7 DECEMBER

Late on the following morning, Krymov and Sergey limped out onto the grand steps at the front of the residence, badly hung over. Both winced as the grey mid-morning light reflected off the snow on the drive and the lawns in front of them. Major Batyuk stood behind them as ever, looking tense. His ear stump tended to flame up when he was angry and it was vivid red now.

Krymov's face looked even more like grey, mottled salami than usual. Sergey had slept in his suit and his hair stuck out at all angles. Both of them could hardly speak but Krymov was able to embrace him and then tightened his grip as hard as he could. Sergey groaned and snarled in pain and tried to push him off but lost his grip and got his midriff crushed.

Krymov let go, laughed painfully and sagged against a pillar of the classical portico. Sergey stumbled over to the edge of it and retched down onto the lawn. He collapsed onto his knees, his head swimming with nausea, vomit and spittle dribbling out of his mouth.

Eventually, he lurched to his feet, muttered, 'Cunt,' scraped the filth off his face and wiped it onto a pillar. Krymov heaved himself onto his feet, staggered over to him and slapped him on the shoulder. Sergey grunted, acknowledging that there were no hard feelings, stumbled down the steps towards the waiting black Zil limo and fell into the door, held open by the uniformed chauffeur.

Krymov watched him drive away with an affectionate look in his eyes. He had meant what he said the night before about Sergey embodying *Russkaya dusha* – being so trustworthy – and because intellect is the plaything of emotion, this love blinded him to inconvenient facts, such as Gorsky's report from London that Sergey was arranging for British mercenaries to travel to Krasnokamensk.

However, although his love could protect Sergey from harm, it could not stop Krymov's peasant cunning from working. This told him that the mercenary could have only one target – there was just one thing of political value in that region – even though he couldn't think what Sergey wanted with him. Nevertheless, it had to be eliminated.

After he had watched Sergey's limo disappear around the bend in the drive, Krymov turned to Batyuk behind him.

'Get a message to Commandant Bolkonsky in Krasnokamensk. I want Raskolnikov dead – soon. Tell him to get on with it. We can't afford to fuck about anymore.'

Chapter Twelve

It was Sunday 7 December.

'Passport, please.'

The dumpy Asian woman sitting behind the immigration desk at Heathrow held out her hand to Yamba Douala across the counter. He had just flown in from Johannesburg. He handed over his South African passport and stared at her quietly.

She found the look intimidating.

He was dressed much like the other middle-aged African businessmen standing behind him in the queue – in a loose-cut, dark green suit worn without a tie – but his gaze was altogether different from theirs.

Yamba had an aquiline face that radiated suppressed anger. Tall and lean, he was in his early forties, with a finely shaped, shaved head. His face had prominent cheekbones and could have had an aristocratic look if it were not for his severe expression. His black eyes had an acute, cruel gaze, like a bird of prey.

The look came from the hard and disappointing life he had led. The drawn lines on his face and his muscled physique were the marks of ascetic, teetotal life.

Along with Colin, he was a mainstay of Alex's small team and had worked with them extensively on operations in

Africa. He had recruited and whipped into shape hundreds of soldiers in different countries and then led them into battle with brutal efficiency. They hated him during training but followed him like children when the bullets started flying.

He had been born in Angola and, as the brightest boy in his village, had been sent to a strict Jesuit mission school run by Portuguese colonialists. Despite the beatings, he had done well and became head boy. Academically gifted, he had been dead set on becoming a surgeon and using his talents to save the lives of his countrymen.

It didn't work out like that.

The country fell to the communists and his family were massacred. He was forced to flee into exile in the South African dependency of Namibia. Aged sixteen, he followed many other black Angolan refugees into the South African army to fight for his homeland.

His early manhood was thus spent in one of the most terrible wars in Africa. As a young soldier he had fought in the famous 32 Battalion, 'The Buffaloes', at the Battle of Cuito Cuanavale – the largest land battle in Africa since the Second World War, involving a hundred thousand men in total, over several months' of intense fighting, against a combined force of East German, Cuban and Angolan troops.

Neither side won, but simply by staying operational, Yamba's unit prevented the fall of Namibia. The action took its toll on him as well and his men often regarded him as a narrow-minded stickler. He could not care less; he understood that military victory required obsessive attention to detail in planning.

With the fall of apartheid, The Buffaloes were once again faced with rejection. They were regarded as race traitors by the new, black ANC government for having fought for the old white regime and were sent into internal exile in an old asbestos mining town and left to die – a situation that Yamba was not going to accept.

So here he was taking on another job for Alex Devereux. As a rootless man, all that anchored him now in the world was his sense of professionalism. His identity came from doing a good job at the one thing that he had known since he was a young man – war. He respected both Alex and Colin; they were also exiles in their own ways who found identity through their jobs. They were the only people he felt he could relax and laugh with because he knew they shared his high standards. Anyone else he regarded with suspicion.

So, as he took his passport back from the immigration official, he looked at her but neither smiled nor said anything and she felt a chill run through her.

Yamba turned away to collect his bags and made his way into London.

Chapter Thirteen

MONDAY 8 DECEMBER

Lara looked down from the front of the helicopter at the frozen landscape, and felt afraid.

The bare, twisted trees and endless fields of snow seemed barren and hostile. In her few trips to England she had never been outside the small world of Russian oligarchs in Chelsea, Kensington and Mayfair.

Now, as she flew out to Alex's country house to liaise with him, she was suddenly aware that there was so much more to the country. Under her beautiful, confident veneer she felt alone; exposed in a foreign land and very conscious of the risks involved in the operation.

Her discomfort was increased by the presence of the four men in the helicopter with her. She had never met any of them before. All she knew about them was that their main business involved killing people and consequently to her they all radiated a menacing air of suppressed violence.

They had been polite but taciturn when they met up at the heliport in London. Most of them hadn't met each other before either, but none seemed to feel the urge to make small talk. After a round of handshakes and grunted greetings they had loaded their kitbags and some crates into Sergey's executive helicopter, climbed onboard and then settled into watchful silence or fallen asleep once they were airborne.

The pilot sitting across from Lara had been the most forthcoming. He was also Russian and had grinned, with a cigarette sticking out of the corner of his mouth, as he shook her hand enthusiastically: 'Arkady Voloshin – pleased to meet you. I'm a big fan of your shows!'

She had smiled weakly at him. He seemed a typical, working-class Russian thug and she didn't want to encourage him. He was about thirty, stockily built, with a broad face, a gold tooth, pale crew-cut hair and stubble. He wore a chunky gold necklace and bracelet, smelled of stale cigarettes and body odour, and wore scruffy jeans, trainers and an old green sweatshirt under his heavy black parka.

Another of the men, also in his thirties, was tall and thin with a narrow face, neatly trimmed blond hair and blue eyes. He dropped his eyes when they shook hands. 'Magnus Løndahl,' he said in a quiet, precise voice.

The third man introduced himself with a nod of the head and grunted, 'I'm Pete,' in a strange accent. He looked younger than the others – mid-twenties, Lara thought – and had a strong physical presence about him: heavy jaw line and shaggy side-burns, six foot, with broad shoulders and neck muscles that showed at the loose opening of his snowboarder jacket. His brown, shoulder-length hair curled into ringlets and was tied back behind his head with a strip of ethnic-patterned cloth.

She found the last man the most intimidating, partly because, having lived her whole life in Russia, she had never personally met a black person before. He seemed to know Arkady and cackled with laughter as they shook hands like old friends. However, when he turned to face her he became stern, his black eyes cut into her and he spoke formally with a heavy African accent.

'I am Yamba Douala. How do you do?' His large hand felt leathery and tough when she shook it.

Once they were on their way, Arkady focused on flying and navigation, occasionally checking a map on his knees against a GPS system, so, with nothing to do and no one to talk to, Lara was left alone with her thoughts.

She had told Sergey before they left that she was worried about his recall to Moscow. He had been as blasé as usual, brushing her concern aside.

'Krymov just wants to go Christmas shopping with me. It'll be fine. You go and meet your nice Englishman,' he grinned, and cocked an eyebrow at her.

She flamed red, infuriated with herself that she had allowed her attraction to Alex to show, but doubly angry with Sergey for being so cruel as to mention it, especially at a time when she was so vulnerable. But then, he always liked playing emotional games. Why did she feel it was her duty to put up with it?

When she was scared like this she wanted to be with him again, like they had been before, when she was young and capable of trust. He had found her when she was at a low point in her life: beautiful but fragile, confident that she was meant for great things but unsure what they were.

Circumstances had conspired against her. In the madness of Yeltsin's Russia she had finished her degree but there were no jobs to go to. Like many young Russian women she had had to resort to virtual prostitution in Moscow, hanging around in hotel bars, trying to find a businessman with money to get her out of her dire straits.

Sergey had been on his way up in those days; the whole of Russia was a whirlwind that he'd seemed to be able to reap to his own advantage. He'd been even more erratic and compulsive then; he had spotted her in the bar of the Hotel

Ukraine and drunkenly lurched over to her. Something about the fine balance of strength and tenderness in her face had gripped him instantly: it seemed the embodiment of *Russkaya dusha*.

She was initially alarmed by his dishevelled appearance but she found that his stream of banter had a strangely compelling intensity about it and she listened to his ridiculous jokes with growing amusement. Apart from which, he was so rich she couldn't take it in. He recruited her to work in his TV station and launched her media career.

Their relationship burned with the white intensity of magnesium, the light so bright she couldn't see what was happening. She loved him dearly – his crazy, manic energy, but also his immense tenderness when they were alone together and he would whisper special words to her; each one flooded her with such meaning that she felt she had been carried away on a tide and ceased to exist. He told her about his love of *Russkaya dusha*, and how for him she personified it.

Lara caught herself remembering those times and forced herself to stop; she knew it was indulgent and unreal to think of them now. It had been hard enough living through the break-up without torturing herself again about it. Those special memories had been locked away deep inside her. She couldn't face the pain of loving Sergey again so she forced herself to look out of the helicopter window and away from them.

They were descending now. Arkady pointed down and to the left.

'Should be over there somewhere,' he said through her headphones over the noise of the rotors. She followed his finger and saw a rolling landscape of white forests and hills.

A red signal flare shot up from it, the colour burning

bright against the white background. She focused in on where it had come from and saw an area of parkland with huge old oak trees scattered across it.

Arkady banked the helicopter round and she made out a large, yellow stone country house at the bottom of a hill, with stables and outbuildings behind it. Two men were standing outside, waving and pointing to where an orange, day-glo landing zone indicator had been laid out on the lawn in front of them.

The helicopter flared as it came in to land and blew a storm of snow over the men. Lara felt it bump slightly but then experienced a different jolt go through her as she saw Alex make his way through the rotor wash towards her.

Alex had been waiting outside for them to arrive at Akerly for a while, his ear cocked for the sound of the rotors. He paced back and forth along the front terrace, partly to keep warm but also because of the sheer amount of nervous energy inside him.

One of Sergey's pilots had flown him and Colin and a load of supplies in the day before, and then returned to London. The two of them had been hard at it setting the house up, brainstorming ideas and preparing the planning meeting that they were going to hold shortly. As the commanding officer for the op, Alex knew he had to appear in charge of events at all times even if he was making it up as he went along.

There was so much that had to be done. His mind whirred. He not only had to come up with ideas for how to launch the attack, but then had to think through and organise the logistics of making it happen: payment, weapons, ammunition, rations, transport, medevac, communications and security issues all had yet to be thrashed out.

In addition, this was the first time he had been back to Akerly since his father's death and he felt like a stranger. The huge house smelled musty and deserted. His father had lived in it alone for years – apart from the odd prostitute he had hired when he had the money – since Alex's mother had died of stomach cancer when Alex was in his early teens.

Alex had wandered around, opening doors into long forgotten rooms, filled with dustsheets and the mixed-up memories of his childhood. Of coming back from glorious summer days rampaging around the estate with his friends, to find the furniture in the living room all knocked over and his father passed out drunk in the middle of the huge main hall, with his dogs curled up asleep around him. Mrs Repton, the cook, looking shaken in the kitchen: 'Your mother has a headache and has gone to bed.'

In the way that children do, he had blamed himself for it all. He wasn't conscious of this but he had internalised the conflict and assumed it was his fault. It had darkened his otherwise free-spirited character and made him intense in everything he did. He was driven to succeed in order to compensate for the failure around him.

He had been brought up to be dutiful and had followed his father into the Blues and Royals without going to university first, at his father's insistence, because he saw it as unnecessary and full of 'dangerous ideas'. This was partly the reason that Alex had not been promoted beyond major. The other reason was that the Household Cavalry Division is a very small and exclusive world, and his father's reputation as a disgraceful drunkard had hung over him like a storm cloud. 'Like father, like son' had never been said to his face but he knew from gossip that it had effectively finished off his prospects. This prejudice had added to his legacy of bitterness against the army and his class.

He had always argued with his father that they should sell the house. It was falling apart and they couldn't afford to keep it. That was what their last big argument had been about before Alex's father had died, before the Central African Republic operation.

However, now that his father was gone and he was the sole male heir to the Devereux title and estate, the responsibility for it had shifted onto his shoulders and he felt a strong affection for the place. It was a ramshackle dog's dinner of a house that had been cobbled together over the centuries by generations of his forebears, starting with the stone tower in the northeast corner, with its Saxon foundations.

As he waited around outside it, he found his mind switching from the operation to thinking about what he would do with the millions of pounds he stood to gain from it. The roof would need doing first of all; as soon as he got that fixed he would have some time to work out what to do next. This sort of calculation wasn't the sort of thing he had expected to be making when he went into the army as an idealistic young man, but it had a sort of grubby glory about it now.

His thoughts were interrupted as his ear caught the faint hum of distant rotors. He pulled the sailing flare from his coat pocket and fired it off.

'They're here!' he shouted to Colin, who was inside in the dining room tacking up maps for the planning session. He ran out and together they waved Arkady in.

As the machine settled in a blizzard of snow the two of them took shelter in the large Gothic porch of the house that a Victorian forebear had slapped on the Regency façade, completely ruining it.

Once the rotors died down, Alex ran out, bent double, sheltering his eyes from the snowstorm. He pulled open the

113

door and came face to face with Lara. She had the hood up on her thick white parka; it was fringed with fur and framed her pale face, emphasising its bleakly beautiful lines. He was once again startled by how blue her eyes were; set back inside the large hood they looked timid and even more alluring than before. He felt the same kick as when he had first seen her.

'Welcome to Akerly!' he shouted, and grinned and took her bags. He shook hands with the others as they climbed out, grinning and slapping Yamba's back – 'Good to see you, matey!'

The group walked in through the porch and along the grand, wood-panelled entrance corridor. It was hung with trophies and antlers from the deer park. In the presence of newcomers, Alex was suddenly conscious of how shabby it all looked: many of the antlers had cobwebs, the red Persian rug was threadbare in places and the Dervish shields and spears, collected from the battle of Omdurman by his great-great-grandfather, were covered in dust. He noticed for the first time in years the dents in the panelling at the end of the hall where he used to play cricket with friends during rainy holidays.

The visitors, though, were impressed. They walked through into the medieval hall behind the Regency rooms stuck along its side. The stone-flagged room was sixty feet long and twenty high, with a stained-glass window at one end over a massive fireplace with half a tree trunk burning in it. Huge portraits of Devereux ancestors peered down at them from the walls.

Alex walked over to the staircase on the other side to take them up to their rooms but the team ignored him and stood around looking at the portraits.

Pete put his rucksack down, folded his arms and stared

114

up at a picture of an arrogant-looking Elizabethan knight. '"Sir James Devereux, 1589,"' he read out loud in a thick Australian accent and nodded approvingly. 'Sweet.'

Lara pushed her hood back and looked around, wide-eyed. 'This is your house? Here you grow up?' she asked in heavily accented English.

'Erm, yes,' Alex replied with equally heavy English reserve.

She laughed. 'I grow up in Soviet apartment; we have four rooms for five people, so …' She gestured around her and laughed again delightfully.

Yamba was with Colin at the far end of the hall, looking up at a pompous Georgian portrait.

The Angolan clapped his hands and cackled with glee as Alex approached. 'We think you look like this fellow up here.' He pointed up at it and laughed again.

'Yeah, posh booger, in't 'e!' Col agreed.

Alex laughed; it was good to be working with them again.

When the team had dumped their gear in their rooms they assembled downstairs in the Regency dining room, over-looking the lawn where the helicopter was parked.

All seven of them seated themselves at one end of the long polished dining table.

Alex stood up at the head of the table with his hands on his hips and began his briefing.

'OK, so first of all, welcome to Team Devereux,' he grinned, enjoying being back in charge. 'Some of us have worked together a lot before, but for those of you who haven't, let me do the intros so we all know where we are coming from.'

He gestured first to the tall, slim man sitting at the edge of the group. 'This is Captain Magnus Løndahl, formerly of the Royal Norwegian Army.'

Magnus nodded to the others but his face remained immobile.

'I met Magnus years ago when I did an arctic warfare training course up in northern Norway. He was an NCO then, helping run NATO courses, and we ended up spending a lot of time together freezing our arses off in snow holes.'

The faintest flicker of a smile flitted across Magnus's face.

The two men had got on well and Alex had developed a huge respect for the Norwegian's quiet strength and integrity. His main memory was of trying to keep up with him on gruelling, day-long, cross-country ski marches. The lanky figure would always be ahead of him in white camouflage gear, his rifle on his back, sometimes lost in gusts of snow, but always re-emerging with arms and legs still gliding forwards in an easy rhythm. The more he had to endure, the quieter and more committed he became.

The understated exterior, however, belied an adventurous heart. Magnus had gone on to serve in the Forsvarets Spesialkommando, the Norwegian Special Forces, as a sniper, and had seen action in Bosnia, Kosovo and Afghanistan. Alex had stayed in touch with him over the years and helped him get some defence contractor work when he had left the Norwegian army two years previously. When a mission in the middle of a Siberian winter had come up, he was the first person who had come to Alex's mind as an arctic warfare specialist.

Alex moved on now to the man sitting next to Magnus, who looked like a cross between a surfer and a builder. Just as he was about to start his introduction, the man stood up and gave his own mock intro.

'Hi, my name's Peter Bridges and I'm an alcoholic,' he said, and then sat down again.

A worried look crossed Lara's face and she looked across anxiously at Alex.

The others laughed. As experienced mercenaries they were confident enough in their professional abilities not to care a great deal about military formalities; in fact they hated them.

Alex laughed and then continued the joke. 'Well, as you can see, Pete has some issues to deal with, but I hope we can all help him work through them on the op. He has been working on his problems with the Australian SAS on a rehab course in Iraq for a couple of years but finally became clean and serene and decided to join the mercenary fraternity.'

Colin, Yamba and Arkady cheered and Pete acknowledged them with a facetious nod. Alex had worked with him on only one previous operation, in Africa, but he had been impressed by the grit he displayed there.

With his heavy-boned face, shaggy sideburns and long hair tied back, Pete looked like a pirate, but he came from a rare group of men, such as racing drivers and extreme sports fanatics, who only responded to events that occur above a certain threshold of violence. Anything below this level didn't register with him as being significant enough to merit a response. However, once events did go over it he acted very fast indeed.

He had been born on a sheep farm near the small town of Dagaragu on the edge of the Tanami Desert. The life was hard there and had taught him self-reliance, but it had not been able to satisfy his thirst for danger and he had left for the army aged seventeen.

Alex continued, 'Pete also has a lot of experience of kicking in doors in Iraq so he will be advising us on the latest FIBUA tactics just in case events develop further.'

Fighting In Built Up Areas was something that Alex was conscious of not having much experience in. He knew the basics from a tour in Northern Ireland, but his more recent African work had been in savannah or jungle environments and he knew that if things did get messy in Moscow then they would need someone with more up-to-date knowledge.

He moved on. 'Now, Col and Yamba have already worked with Arkady a lot but for those who haven't, this is Captain Arkady Voloshin.'

The Russian grinned broadly at them, his slanted eyes creased up and the gold tooth winked in his mouth, which for once he didn't have a cigarette in.

'Formerly in the Russian airforce, then spent many years flying anything that moved – fixed-wing and rotary – for Viktor Bout in Africa, supplying various wars. Whatever you want, Arkady will fly it in or out for you: arms, drugs, diamonds, TVs, fags, hookers. You name it, he'll get it.'

Arkady took it as a compliment that he worked for a man labelled 'The Merchant of Death' and continued grinning in a shameless manner. Like a lot of Russian men he'd had any sense of morality removed by the experience of communism, and would do anything for money without asking questions.

However, over the years of working with Alex he had developed a strong personal loyalty to him. Through numerous combat operations he had come to respect the Englishman's leadership as intelligent but decisive.

When Alex had initially outlined the plan to him he had had a brief moment of doubt because of the massive political implications for his homeland, but, when the huge amount of money on offer was mentioned, any personal scruples died instantly.

Alex then faced the tricky task of what to say about Lara.

He didn't want to give any details of the political side of the operation. To emphasise this point he kept it very brief, introducing her quickly and adding, 'Lara is here to act as liaison with our political partners.'

She looked down at the table nervously as all eyes scrutinised her carefully. Alex could see a lot of thinking going on but no one said a word.

He quickly moved on to the final two regular members of his team, Colin and Yamba, who sat together and grinned back at everyone else.

'The two old-age pensioners over here are Colin Thwaites, formerly sergeant major in the Parachute Regiment, and Yamba Douala, of the South African Defence Force, 32 Battalion. Both of whom have been selected so we can make use of their free bus passes.'

This met with giggles from Yamba and, 'Ah, booger off,' from Colin.

Alex ignored them. 'Right, let's get on with planning then.' He motioned behind them and they all stood up and moved to the middle of the long table, which was covered in the maps and photos that Alex and Colin had spent much of yesterday laying out.

'OK, so first of all, Arkady will fly us out in a Gulfstream jet to Transdneister.'

The mercenaries were all familiar with the tiny breakaway republic between Moldova and Ukraine. It had declared independence from the USSR in 1991 but after a short war had been left with an ambiguous international status ever since, which made it a major transshipment point for drugs, weapons and people trafficking.

'Arkady is well connected in smuggling circles there and has already been in touch with his suppliers, so they will have our weapons and ammunition order ready for us to collect quickly and then fly straight on to our Forward Operating Base. The whole flight from here to Siberia will be eight hours and four thousand miles, so we are going to be a long way from home.'

There were a lot of serious expressions around the circle as the enormity of the distance sank in.

'OK, that's the big picture. So let's switch to the detail. We are going to assault the Yag 14/10 Krasnokamensk Penal Colony.'

He pointed to a regional map laid out in the middle of the table with the location marked on it.

'The camp itself is actually located fifty miles north of Krasnokamensk. There just isn't anything else nearer to name it after.' His finger looped over the empty terrain around the camp. 'That's because the camp is in a Closed Area roughly a third the size of England, where no one but the prisoners and their guards are allowed. Our FOB will be here on the outskirts of the town on the east side.' He pointed to some sparsely distributed huts and warehouses that petered out into the woods.

'Right, that's the background for you. From now on this is a planning session. It's not going to be an easy job so I want your suggestions.'

They all leaned in over the table around him, faces serious now, eyes darting back and forth, taking in the locations and distances on the maps. They were comparing what was in front of them with countless raids they had been on, balancing theories and practicalities, trying to envisage conditions on the ground: the terrain, the weather, infiltration and exfiltration routes, enemy positions and responses.

Alex continued to feed their busy minds with details.

'Our FOB is the operations base for a mining company in the region belonging to our political contact.' Again he didn't elaborate and no one asked.

'We will have access to a company helicopter.' His eyes flicked across to Arkady. 'Mil Mi-17 IV?'

The Russian shrugged and nodded. 'No problem.'

'We have access to a hangar and a repair shop for any military modifications we want to make on it, plus full refuelling facilities. We'll also have access to a Vityaz all-terrain vehicle for any cross-country movement.'

He pointed them back to the location of the penal colony itself.

'The camp is located on a flat, forested plain. They cut timber from it at the camp so we should find a clearing that will be big enough to act as an insertion landing zone.'

Arkady grunted. 'Rotor diameter on new Mil is twenty-one meters. It's a big fucker.'

Alex nodded and then moved along the table to the far end where a map of the camp was laid out. He had stuck a series of A3 sheets together to provide a detailed plan. Around the edge of these were a number of large format photos, each one with a piece of string Blu-Tacked to the point where it had been taken inside the camp. Alex and Colin had spent a lot of time getting them laid out and orientated correctly.

'Right, now, we are lucky to have some very detailed int on the inside of the camp. This plan is a copy of an official one so it's accurate and these photos were taken last winter so are pretty up to date.'

'Where does this int come from?' Yamba said abruptly, both looking and sounding fierce as he sought to confirm the accuracy of the details. Overconfident assessments by intelligence officers had caused many deaths on missions he had been on.

Alex was unruffled by his challenging tone, knowing that he was just being thorough.

'The photos come from our political contact. He runs a

company that supplies the site and is a big local player.' He didn't want to give the whole game away and say he was the regional governor. 'So he was able to get taken on a tour of it. He has been planning to get the prisoner out for a couple of years now so he used the visit to take covert photos. They were snapped from a camera hidden in his coat so they're not perfect but they give us a good idea.

'We are also lucky because we have some information on the prisoner – his name is Roman Raskolnikov, remember him?' – there were nods from around the table – 'from a source inside the camp.' He looked at Yamba. 'I can't say who, but the intelligence is good.'

Yamba refrained from questioning this.

Alex continued, 'Now, the approach to the camp is going to be tricky. They have got a two-hundred-metre-wide area cleared from the forest all around it, no tree stumps, no cover, no nothing.'

Colin gave a sharp intake of breath and there were pained expressions from the others. They could all see in their mind's eye the view from a watchtower out over a flat white expanse and then imagined trying to get across it without being seen. An infrared imager would make it impossible, even in the dark.

Alex saw their looks and held up a hand. 'OK, I know, but we'll work it out. Let me just show you the inside of the camp. It's made up of two rectangular areas, one set inside the other. The perimeter of the outer zone is a kilometre along its longest side, so it is a lengthy fence that they have to guard. It encloses all the support build-ings for the camp – like the garages, store sheds, oil tanks and the sawmill. The actual prison is inside the inner fence.' He circled the rectangle in the middle of the camp. 'This inner perimeter is made up of three fences of razor wire with a three-foot gap between each. The middle wire is lit by arc lamps and electrified so we can't even touch it without getting frazzled or being seen from the watch-towers. There are four gates in it, one in the middle of each side of the rectangle, and each has got a watchtower with a machine gun.

'Inside the wire there's a kitchen and canteen here, and the armoury here, but mainly it's these nine barrack huts. They're just numbered one, two, three, etc.' He ran his finger round the rectangle of long, single-storey buildings. 'Each one has about a hundred prisoners in it and its own lot of guards in a block on each end so that no one can get in or out without going through a guardroom. There are one hundred and ninety guards in total, armed with assault rifles, and there are machine guns in all the watchtowers.

'Apart from them, our other problem will be actually *finding* Raskolnikov. There are nine hundred guys in there and they all wear the same black uniforms so he will be hard to spot. We do know his prison number is D-504 and we think he is in Barrack 9 but we don't know exactly where he will be inside the hut. The only time we know where he will be is during morning parade. For security reasons he is always put right in front of the commandant's platform because they have a machine-gunner up there detailed to slot him at the first sign of any escape attempt.'

'Oh, great,' muttered Col.

'Hmm,' nodded Alex, 'so basically we have to get in there quietly and strike fast when we do go for him, or we will just have one dead opposition leader to fly to Moscow.'

He returned to his original track of describing the camp routines.

'As soon as the work parties for the day have been allo-cated, Raskolnikov could be dragged off to one of several locations – logging in the forests, construction sites, the sawmill, and so on – so we really won't have a clue where he will be.'

'Flippin' 'eck,' muttered Colin. 'I'm just wondering when you're going to give us the good news.'

Alex stood back and looked at them. 'Right, well, I did say it wasn't going to be easy. We've got six blokes and a helicopter against a hundred and ninety armed guards in a heavily fortified prison camp.' He paused. 'Suggestions, anyone?'

The discussion began with all the team members chipping in ideas, pacing around the table picking up photos and looking at them from different angles, trying to get new perspectives on the problem. Proposals were put forward and debated; some were chucked out, others kept in play.

Alex surveyed the room, pleased with the way it was going. Having laid the problem out in front of them they were now really stuck in to solving it.

He was feeling increasingly certain that they would come up with a plan to get Raskolnikov out.

Chapter Fourteen

Raskolnikov and the other nine men of the 33rd work team climbed up into the Vityaz.

They had just been through another roll call parade. Once he and the men were packed into the enclosed cab, a guard slammed the door shut and they were locked in.

They quickly huddled together on the floor over the vehicle's massive diesel engines. The metal plates were warm and they were out of the wind. This was the best part of the day.

The vehicle grunted and jerked, they were on their way. The DT-30 Vityaz was a huge beast with a wide body like the hull of a tank with a square cab covering the top. An all-terrain, tracked, amphibious vehicle the size of a large truck, it was the only thing that could withstand all the rigours of Siberian terrain from snowdrifts to forests and bogs. Behind them it dragged a separate, tracked, flatbed unit with a knuckle crane for the logs.

Shubin, the team leader, sat up front in the cab with the drivers, guards and crane operator, a 'trustie' or prisoner trusted to work on his own. Shubin was an experienced forester and used a remotely operated searchlight on top of the cab to spot stands of trees with the correct diameter for the Chinese timber merchants that they supplied. The team would then dismount, cut them down and load the trunks onto the flatbed unit.

The prison camp lay fifty miles north of Krasnokamensk on a plain covered in mixed woods of pine, larch and birch, but all the decent pine near the camp had already been cut so the teams had to be sent further and further out over the snowy wastes to find wood.

The prison was very remote; in winter the deep snow meant that they could only really be resupplied by helicopter, as it took at least ten hours by snowmobile. With the murderous December weather, very few precautions were taken to prevent escape; just leaving the shelter of the camp was a death sentence. Prisoners were transported there in the short summer when trucks could actually get through and then just dumped for years. Very few made the return journey.

The ATV belched black diesel smoke from the pipes on either side of the cab, like a pair of horns, and drove out through the inner prison gates of the camp and then on through the second pair of gates set in the perimeter fence of the whole site. Snow spewed out of the back of its tracks as the driver picked up speed and they flowed over the undulating terrain through the forest.

After half an hour, Shubin spotted a stand of correctly sized pine, up on a small hillock, and they stopped. The team was let out of the lockup and walked over to the trees with guards covering them with assault rifles.

Shubin revved up his chainsaw and began working away at a tree. When he had nearly cut through it, he stepped away and the snarl of the chainsaw halted. There followed a second's silence and then the heavy crack and soft crash of the tree falling. The rest of the team closed in on the fallen trunk like workers stripping the body of a whale and used axes to cut away the branches.

Roman became absorbed in the work, swinging his axe and enjoying the brief flood of warmth throughout his body. When the trunk was bare, each man got out a dragging tool with a spike on the end at right angles to the long handle. Roman swung his hard into the trunk and kicked it home with his heavy boot. All ten of them lined up either side of the trunk and did the same. Shubin looked down the line of black-clad figures in the half-light of early morning and shouted: 'One, two, three!'

They all hauled at once, dragging the two tons of wood through the snow a few feet at a time, out of the stand towards the crawler. Big Danni was opposite Roman, his huge shoulders bent as he strained at the load. Sweat broke out on Roman's body and he gasped at the raw air. He felt as if his arms were being pulled out of their sockets as he dug his heels in and tried to stop the log breaking away and sliding down into the crawler.

Finally, they got it down alongside the flatbed trailer unit. The trustie was sitting up on the little crane seat at one end, wrapped up in his hat and facecloths like the rest of them, but having spent the interim inside the warm cab. The team stepped back from the log and looked up at him with silent contempt.

He powered up the crane and the heavy arm unfolded itself. A huge pair of metal jaws on the end of it reached out and grasped the log firmly in the middle, the hydraulics whined as the crane lifted it high over their heads ready to swing it in over the large metal supports along the edge of the flatbed that held the logs in place.

The steady inbound movement stopped and the arm

jerked towards them. All ten men leaped backwards as the huge tree slammed into the ground right in front of them, sending a heavy jolt through the soles of their feet. Roman tripped and fell over on his back. The tree rose again in the air over his head, he frantically tried to push himself backwards with his heels and elbows but it moved with him, poised to strike again.

There was a shout and a heavy thud as the crane operator was pulled bodily off his seat and hit the ground. Danni smashed a fist into his face before one of the guards ran over and swung the butt of his rifle into the big robber's kidneys. He crumpled with an involuntary 'Oof!' as the air was forced out of him.

Getmanov rolled on the ground, put both hands to his face and held the cloths against it to stem the flow of blood.

The guard commander ran over and took in the failed murder attempt with one glance. He looked down at Danni squirming on the ground, trying to get breath back into his body.

'That'll be the cold and the dark for you, I-331.'

Chapter Fifteen

Once they had agreed a plan, Alex was able to get on with organising specialist equipment and training for it.

Magnus had brought two large crates of high-spec arctic kit with him. Alex had emailed him the men's boot and clothing sizes and he had picked it up from a supplier in Oslo on his way to London, along with a supply of winter rations.

The large medieval hall was used as a fitting room and equipment store for all the gear they were taking. As the crates were unloaded and divided up it became strewn with piles of heavy parkas, salopettes, boots, cross-country skis and poles, tents, sleeping bags, rucksacks and cooking equipment.

The weapons and ammunition would have to wait until they got to Transdneister. Arkady was constantly on his BlackBerry, haggling with his arms dealers to make sure they got the best assault rifles, machine guns, heavy weapons and explosives available.

Magnus then took them all out into the snowy grounds and got them practising cross-country skiing and some basic arctic survival drills.

He also came up with an idea for getting across the open ground to the camp perimeter.

As usual he started his sentence by clearing his throat quietly. 'Prevailing wind is northerly so I think maybe we have the ground blizzard on the north side?'

The others looked at him.

'Ground blizzard?' said Pete.

'Yes, it's when the wind picks up the snow and the ice and you have the fog effect on the ground, two feet high? Maybe it gives us the cover, but then,' he paused, 'we also have the frostbite risk as well. Ambient temperature is minus forty at night but for each mile per hour of windspeed you add a degree of freezing and so with average windspeed of thirty miles an hour you have minus seventy degrees.'

Col winced.

'At that temperature frostbite time is maybe,' he shrugged, 'five minutes. Even with the heavy clothing on, you will certainly be experiencing hypothermia by the time you get through the wire and that is not a good state to go to assault in.'

'Hmm.' Alex nodded; this sort of detailed knowledge was exactly why he had brought his old friend along.

'I take your point about the wind but I think we are on to something there.'

They began working on ways to reduce the wind exposure using Magnus's experience in snow camouflage and conceal-ment.

Pete also came into his own. He took over an isolated storage barn on the estate and quickly turned the huge, empty, metal shed into a FIBUA training centre. Using the rough-and-ready training techniques that they developed in Iraq, he drew chalk lines to the floor to simulate floor plans of buildings and used the stairs to the hayloft for all-impor-tant stairwell drills. He then took the team through a quick refresher course on urban warfare skills.

It wasn't perfect but in the limited time they had available Alex could see that they were beginning to function as a team: assessing threats quickly, communicating well and moving fluidly around obstacles.

Alex came back from a session in the FIBUA barn early one afternoon to check his emails, principally that the regular flow of mail order invites kept coming through from Sergey. So far, he was relieved to see that they had.

He entered the main house through the big porch, stamped the snow off his boots and headed in through to the medieval hall, paused to throw another huge log on the fire, before crossing to the other side into the kitchen to get a cup of tea.

This was a shabby modern room; last done up in the 1970s when some land had been sold off. His father had never updated the lurid orange cupboards and Alex retained a curious childhood affection for them.

He walked in and found Lara sitting at the table in front of the Aga, warming herself. The house still didn't have central heating so the kitchen always was the focal point in the winter.

They both looked startled and quickly scrambled for something to say.

She beat him to it, 'Ah, Sasha, how is your little winter training ground?' she said with a smile; he noticed that she had adopted the familiar 'ty' form of address in Russian with him now.

He hadn't seen her on her own since she'd arrived. She had listened in carefully to the planning discussions and had passed on a number of requests for special equipment to Sergey by email. She had also briefed the team on the Moscow end of the plans, when they hoped that events on the street would move their way and the team wouldn't have to be as directly involved as they were in the assault.

She had relaxed a lot since her uncomfortable journey here; the men were all focused on the job in hand and hardly paid any attention to her, apart from the odd covert glance at her figure as she walked past.

Alex adopted a similarly low-key manner with her now. 'Oh, it's going OK. The guys are out practising FIBUA in the barn.' He busied himself making tea. 'You want some?' he asked rather abruptly and she nodded.

He was normally pretty good at chitchat, he enjoyed the company of intelligent women, but he still found it hard to talk to Lara because at least half his brain was scrambled by the sheer physical hit of being with her; the sight of her long limbs, the curve of her cleavage, the thick snake of blonde hair twisted over one shoulder exposing the elegant arch of her neck. All these stimuli kept cutting into his normal thought processes like interference on the radio. It really didn't help this self-consciousness to have had Sergey's tactless quip about her being a man-eater.

He had no idea what Lara thought of him, but beneath her icy calm he suspected she was terrified. He had caught her once, when he turned away, out of the corner of his eye: her expression of intelligent interest in the briefing had fallen away and been replaced with a disconcerted, lost look.

He sorted out the tea and gave himself some time to restore control: *You're on a job, Devereux, stop fucking around! You do not have time for this.*

He turned back to her, prepared to be as chatty as possible, but she was quicker off the mark.

'Have you always done this?'

'What?

'Fighting.'

'Yes, I didn't go to university and joined the army straight

132

from school. Yes, I have always done this.' He sounded more defensive than he had intended to.

'Well, your Russian is very good.' She didn't mean it to but it sounded like a consolation comment.

'The army was keen for people to learn it and I discovered that I did actually want an intellectual challenge, after all, so I took a course.' He didn't add that it had been another way of sticking two fingers up to his father, who had been furious at him 'wasting his time on all that foreign crap!'

Alex continued, 'I also once had a Russian girlfriend in London.'

Oksana.

She had been so far removed from the sort of girl his father expected him to date that he had felt it was safe to go out with her. His main memory – apart from a lot of sex – was of the smell of her cheap hairspray and her mouth reeking of the strong Russian Prima cigarettes she favoured. She had been hard work but he had loved learning the language through her; even the most banal conversation – 'Pass the salt' – had become an adventure.

Lara nodded and there was a slight pause.

'And you? Have you always done TV?'

'Well, yes and no,' she said, recovering her poise. 'I did chemical engineering at Voronezh Institute of Technology.' She nodded, acknowledging his surprised look. 'Yes, I know. Everybody in the West always looks like that when I tell them, but technical education was always a lot bigger in Russia. Plus my father thought it would be a sensible thing for me to do.'

'And was it?'

'Well …' she paused to consider its merits and then said in a very direct manner, 'you have to work hard to get it right and I enjoy intense experiences. I mean, I like the rigour of engineering, it's very black or white; things are either right or wrong. Flow rates either go down a pipe or they don't. It teaches you to be very intolerant of bullshit.'

She looked at him straight, and now he had a moment of discomfort. He hadn't realised that she was that analytical about life. What was she making of *him*? He felt his previous remarks must have been scrutinised with a microscope.

He managed to nod sagely in response and then handed her a mug of tea.

'Thanks,' she muttered and sipped it thoughtfully.

He sat down opposite her at the table.

'So, after that, how did you get into TV?'

'Oh, Sergey "discovered" me.' She made speech marks in the air and laughed.

Alex smiled. 'Oh, right, was that a recruitment programme they ran or something?'

'Not exactly. He was drunk – can you believe it? – in a bar in Moscow and some instinct deep within him instantly recognised my journalistic potential.' She grinned a million-volt smile this time and then indicated her body with a downward sweep of her hand.

Alex was sent back to square one. He had been making some polite headway off that topic, but she had now, with disconcerting directness, brought him right back onto it.

She looked straight at him. 'Alexander, I am under no illusions as to why Sergey liked me: I have a fantastic ass and great tits. He always said they were a work of art, he thinks they should be in the Hermitage.' She laughed at the memory, folded her arms and squeezed her breasts together as she arched her back, pouted and cocked an eyebrow at him.

This was killing him.

She relaxed the pose, went back to sipping her tea and

continued, 'So, as you can see, after engineering I have subsequently done a degree in flirtation with a Masters in flashing my tits. I've done *a lot* of field work on my thesis.'

There was something rather disturbing in how coldly she was able to be honest about her attractions.

Alex nodded as he scrabbled to regain traction. 'Right ... So, you're very close to Sergey then?' he said with an intelligent frown on his face.

Lara's eyes lost their mischievous look; the blue suddenly seemed very cold.

Oh shit ... He felt he had just touched an electric fence around a no-go area and flinched under the intensity of her anger.

She dropped her eyes and turned away, realising that she had invited such a question by being so frank. She looked back at Alex in an evaluating way; he seemed a thoughtful man to her and she knew that they might well both be dead in a few days' time, so she felt an urge to tell him the truth about everything.

She said in a matter-of-fact tone, 'He took my soul,' then paused and shrugged. 'But you can live without one.'

His mind whirred. What did *that* mean?

There was an awkward pause before, with an effort, she regained her light-hearted tone and continued: 'But, unfortunately, Sergey has the emotional attention span of a five year old so it was never going to last. He is a very good businessman but he has still got to learn that women are not businesses – you can't invest in a diversified portfolio of them. I think he finds it easier to commit to grandiose ideas than a single real woman; somehow she might threaten the perfection of his idealism.' She shrugged again and concluded generously, 'We all make choices in life.'

Alex tried to move on. 'Sergey certainly seems very

passionate about the coup; he's a lot more profound when you get to know him.'

She rolled her eyes. 'Has Sergey been talking to you about literature again? About *Russkaya dusha*?'

Alex nodded and she tossed her head in annoyance. He realised that Sergey had not only favoured him with his thoughts on the matter.

'Don't get me wrong, I love Russian literature, it was one of the great things we shared, but he talks shit – all Russian men do. I wouldn't take it too seriously.' She shook her head dismissively and looked away.

Alex couldn't quite believe it was all nonsense; Sergey had seemed so passionate on the topic. 'You don't think so?'

She turned dangerously slanting eyes on him and a slight flush came over her high cheekbones.

'Believe me, it's all bullshit.'

'The Russian soul?'

She flared up and pointed at him. 'It's a romantic dream of his. Russian men like to get drunk together and talk about grand emotions to justify their boorishness by making out that they are profound underneath it. They're not, they're just ill-mannered louts. Look, Tolstoy once said, "Everybody thinks of changing the world but no one thinks of changing himself." Russian men are a prime example of that; I have had enough of them.'

She warmed to her theme. 'Sergey says he loves Russia but it's easy to love people from a distance. If he really loved the Russian people why does he spend most of his time living in London?'

This passionate speech completely steamrollered the attempts Alex had been making to calm his emotions; now he just stared openly at her.

It wasn't just Lara's beauty that made her so captivating

– her lucent hair, her figure, her finely etched features. It was the fact that such a keen spirit animated her, so that when she spoke she became almost iridescent: each word brightly illuminated by the arch of an eyebrow, a widening of the pupils, a pout of the lips or a tilt of her cheekbones. It all came together in a brilliant fusion of thought, expression and gesture, holding him helpless in its beam.

Chapter Sixteen

The next morning, Roman and the remaining eight members of the 33rd work team stood to attention as usual at roll call.

However, this time the eyes that showed over their iced-up facecloths were all fixed on the *izbushka* by the side of the parade ground.

All of them knew the hell that Big Danni would have gone through in there overnight: curled up alone in a tiny, pitch-black cell, racked by unstoppable shivering.

And Roman knew that he had done it all to save him.

His network of political supporters saw him as the figure-head of their efforts to bring freedom to Russia. But Big Danni was not a political; he was just an ordinary criminal. That was what made his sacrifice all the more telling for Roman.

He was worried as he looked at the hut. He couldn't see any smoke coming out of the chimney on top of it. Usually a little streamer of warmth hung from the metal pipe, bent over, away from the northerly gales.

The usual routine of roll call went ahead – Kuzembaev came down the line with his torch and made his joke – but

139

all eyes continued to be fixed on the hut as the morning guard squad opened it up and went inside.

A minute later the door banged open and a guard shouted to his sergeant on the edge of the parade ground to come over. He ran across, went inside and a few seconds later a guard ran out along the edge of the parade ground and into the infirmary block. He returned with a stretcher and then four men staggered out of the door carrying Danni's huge weight.

He was curled up in the foetal position, his feet and head sticking awkwardly over the sides of the stretcher. As the guards stumbled in the snow past the ranks of prisoners they stared at it. Roman could see that the body did not move at all. It was frozen solid.

Danni had fought all comers in his life but he could not fight the cold.

After they had gone, the sergeant ran over to Commandant Bolkonsky on the platform in front of them and spoke with him quietly. The commandant nodded and then returned to the microphone.

The Tannoy blared out over them; Commandant Bolkonsky sounded as cheerful as usual.

'So, good morning, guests, and welcome to another day in Camp Honolulu. As you can see we have had a, er, technical problem with the air conditioning in one of our guest suites and one of our visitors has overindulged on our wonderful climate. So watch yourselves out there or you'll get the same!'

Chapter Seventeen

THURSDAY 11 DECEMBER

The following evening, Roman took his place in the queue outside the canteen as usual, but he was hoping something different would happen.

The canteen only had room for ten work teams at a time and the men inside liked to sit for as long as possible after they had eaten, savouring the warmth and the feel of the food in their bellies, however poor it might be. Shubin and the deputy team leader went inside to drive a team out with shouts and cuffs in order to make room for the 33rd.

Eventually, the line of exhausted, frozen convicts was able to push its way through the double set of doors and into the low building. It was packed with men on benches or eating standing up when they couldn't find a place to sit. The sound of their shouting and arguing filled the space, along with the smell of fish and sweat. The temperature was just above freezing so the new arrivals steamed as the ice on their clothing and faces warmed up.

'Come on! Move yer fucking arses!' Shubin yelled at some scavengers who were hanging around the serving hatch hoping to cadge some extra helpings. He pushed a couple out of the way and the 33rd shuffled forward to the hatch.

Although there was a lot of shouting and pushing at the back of the queue, as the men approached the serving hatch they fell silent as if approaching the altar in a temple of food. Except for the numbers on their backs, the men in the queue were identical in their grubby black coats and hats, like some black-clad priesthood. They licked their lips nervously and each tried to look over the shoulder of the man in front to see if he would get a decent portion in his battered metal bowl. This was, after all, their lifeblood. If you missed out on a full complement of food in this climate it could mean you got a cough, caught pneumonia and died.

The dinner they awaited was fish skilly: porridge with bits of bones, scales and cabbage floating in it, with a measly bread ration.

Roman shuffled forward amongst them. He kept his spoon tucked into the top of his boot so he would have two hands free for carrying his bowl of precious food and fending off possible scavengers, or just pushing his way through the crowd. He felt exhausted, hungry and deeply troubled by Danni's death and stood with his head down. However, as they moved nearer the serving hatch he was careful to look up and see if his special contact was on the shift that evening.

He recognised the beefy hands and forearms doling out the food through the waist-height hatch.

Olga the cook was there.

She had been selected by Commandant Bolkonsky to be a worker at the camp from Governor Shaposhnikov's catering company, because he didn't like trouble over women and he thought that even in the years that the MVD guards worked at the camp, none of them would be tempted to indulge in her. She was heavy-set, with forearms like hams sticking out of the sleeves of her stained, brown uniform dress, wore a hairnet over her greasy hair and stank of body odour.

Despite this she was the most important woman in Roman's life. Only her substantial midriff, shoulders and arms could be seen through the low serving hatch as she doled the black stew out into the bowls and shouted at the men: 'Come on! Let's have you!'

Roman ducked his head down to show his face through the hatch and said, 'Hello, Olga!'

That was as much as he ever saw of her; he straightened up again quickly so as not to attract attention from the few guards squeezed into corners of the room. As she dumped the food into his bowl they exchanged a few guarded words.

'Any letters from your brother?' she asked him.

'Ah, very bad news, someone tried to kill him on Tuesday. They really mean to do him in.'

'Ah! It's another Time of Troubles!' She shook her head sympathetically as he took his bowl and moved along to squeeze onto a place at the end of a bench.

After the work teams had finished their guzzling and been kicked back out into the cold, the cooks and trusties cleaned the kitchen and Olga returned to the women's quarters, barricaded off behind a barbed-wire fence outside the main prison area, where she lived with two old nurses and the commandant's secretary. Since her husband had left her, and her only son, Anatoly, had been killed in Chechnya, all that was left was her daughter, Vera, in Moscow. She hated the government for what they had done to her son but had had to take this job in a hellhole when her boss at the catering company had told her to.

She was upset now because of the information from Roman. She always had found decisions difficult and now she was torn between two options. She was allowed only ten minutes of phone time a week and her regular slot was not until tomorrow evening, Friday 12 December. She knew that

143

all phone calls from the camp *could* be tapped by the guards, but she also knew that most of the time they didn't bother. So she wondered if she should wait until Friday to call, when they wouldn't bother listening in, or should she say that there was an emergency and risk them taking more interest than usual and probably deciding to listen?

She had no illusions about what they would do to her if they caught her passing on information. As much as she hated Krymov and his whole regime, and wanted to help protect Roman from them, she eventually decided that she could afford to wait twenty-four hours before making the call in greater safety. Nothing would happen to him soon anyway.

Chapter Eighteen

FRIDAY 12 DECEMBER

Olga finally made her move the following evening.

After she had served dinner and cleared up, the bulky old cook wrapped herself up in her heavy coat and several shawls, and slipped out to the phone booths in the hall of the main guard barrack block.

The hallway was old and freezing from the draught under the swing doors. A fug of cigarette smoke hung in the air from the soldiers leaning up against the wall waiting their turn on the phones. With a hundred and ninety guards in the camp and only three phone boxes, there was always a queue for them and people guarded their time slots jealously, banging on the doors to remind others when their time was up.

As she walked past the queue to take her place at the back, several of the younger soldiers leered at her, more out of boredom than lust. Many of them were just conscripts and hated it in the camp as much as the prisoners. She stuck her nose in the air and pulled her shawls tighter around her.

A sign on the wall next to the booths read: 'Ministry of Interior orders: no official information is to be transmitted over these phone lines. All conversations will be monitored for illegal content and severe punishment imposed on transgressors.'

To emphasise the point a guard sat in a booth at the end of the row, with headphones for listening in. As she walked past she glanced in and saw that the bored young private was watching hard-core porn on a small DVD player with headphones on. The official eavesdropping ones were draped unused around his neck. She tutted at him in disgust; he looked up at her with a blank stare and then went back to his film.

When her time came, she marched into a booth and shut the door firmly behind her. She called a number in Moscow; a woman's voice answered casually, 'Hi there.'

'Verouchka?' Olga asked a little hesitantly.

There was a pause. 'Ye-es?'

'How are you?' It was a curt request without any sentiment.

'Very good, Mama.' The voice gained confidence. 'How are you?'

'Ah, you know, not so good, I had some bad news from Pyotr; his brother was nearly killed in an accident recently.'

'Oh, I'm sorry to hear that. Do you know any more about it?'

'No, not much to say really. Anyway, how are the cats?'

They exchanged domestic details in a desultory way for a couple of minutes before Olga hung up and made her way back to her quarters.

In Moscow the woman put the phone down, hastily turned to her laptop and sent an email to an anonymous Hotmail address.

Chapter Nineteen

Planning and training continued at a fast pace at Akerly.

All the men knew that they were going to face a tough assault when they arrived, and the fear focused their minds. Magnus led them out on a five-mile cross-country ski around the estate every morning, followed by a gruelling PT session in the medieval hall led by Yamba.

The skiing used muscles they were not normally conversant with and Yamba's ferocious PT drilling found a lot more. Arkady was the only one who grumbled – as a pilot he felt all this wasn't really his scene – but he got no sympathy from Alex.

'Look, we just don't know what's going to happen when we get out there. If we get shot down in the helicopter on the assault we are going to have to do some serious escape and evasion. It'll be a hundred miles south to the Chinese border through an arctic wasteland with MVD troops in hot pursuit after us on Skidoos, so we're going to need to be fit.'

Arkady backed off after that and got on with his squat thrusts.

The work on developing protection from the ground blizzard made progress. Magnus took a spare tent, cut rectangular sections of the white Gortex and stitched them on the inside with space blankets to create a wind- and cold-proof material. Each of these had four elastic straps, taken off rucksacks, sown into their corners, so that they could be slipped over someone's hands and feet. The person was then fully covered so that when they crawled through the ground blizzard, over the open two hundred metres to the outer perimeter fence, they were well insulated from the killing frostbite risk.

The preparations enabled Alex not to think about Lara. He was careful to avoid seeing her alone again and she too kept herself apart from him and the guys. Both had been unnerved by their rather too candid conversation in the kitchen and realised that that sort of involvement was not going to help them get the job done.

Eventually, everything was ready.

Sergey's Gulfstream G550 flew back in from Moscow to Wolverhampton Halfpenny Green airport, which lay half an hour's flight by helicopter northeast from Akerly. It was an old Second World War RAF base that was now setting itself up as a West Midlands executive airport, and was perfect for a low-profile departure from the country.

The irony of launching a coup in a faraway land from there was not lost on Alex, though. He joked with Colin: 'Well, I don't know if we'll succeed but we'll certainly be the most exciting thing ever to come out of Wolverhampton.'

'Exactly. Better than their fookin' football team, I tell yer.'

Arkady's weapons order was finalised and waiting for them, along with details of the refuelling arrangements in Transdneister.

Magnus was confident that, although they weren't going to win any competitions, they could at least ski at a reasonable pace cross-country. He was looking forward to picking up a new sniper rifle from Arkady's dealer.

They were due to leave on Sunday, but then on Friday lunchtime Lara ran into the kitchen as the rest of them were eating. She looked deadly serious.

'Sergey has just emailed me. They tried to kill Roman earlier this week. He got a message through from the contact in the camp. We don't know when they will try again, but we have to move straight away. Can we leave tomorrow?'

Alex put his fork down and stared at her for a moment.

'Well, we're going to have to, aren't we?'

He stood up, orders quickly coming to mind. 'OK, training cancelled this afternoon. Start packing straight away! Col, sort it out! Arkady, get on the phone to your dealer and see if the order can be brought forward by twenty-four hours. I'll talk to the airport and see if we can revise the flight plan.'

The kitchen door burst open and they ran out: Pete to the barn to recover his FIBUA kit, Magnus to get their skis and arctic kit packed up, and Yamba to help Col.

The training period had been good to get them used to working together and they responded well to the emergency and all plans were successfully brought forward by twenty-four hours.

Chapter Twenty

By eight o'clock on the following morning, they were all packed and loaded up into the helicopter. Lara was going to fly with them to Halfpenny Green and meet a pilot of Sergey's there. He would then fly her back to London in the helicopter whilst the others flew straight on to Siberia in the jet. When they landed at Krasnokamensk a contact of Sergey's was supposed to meet them at the airport. However, Alex still had no idea how reliable that person would be or what sort of reception would await them.

He couldn't help wondering if they would meet the same fate as the Equatorial Guinea coup attempt, when another former public school, British officer, Simon Mann, had been arrested at Harare airport on his way to war. A thirty-four-year sentence in an African hellhole prison had been his reward.

Alex went back into the medieval hall to check that everything was packed and no incriminating evidence had been left behind; operational security was still very much on his mind.

He stood at the far end of the huge stone-flagged room in his arctic warfare kit: white combat trousers and jacket,

151

and white webbing, with his bayonet strapped to his shoulder harness.

He took one last look around the room, glancing up at the portraits. The irony of another Devereux going off to war under the eyes of his ancestors did not escape him. He felt the pressure of them looking down on him.

'Better do a good job, Devereux, or don't bother coming back here.'

'Death or glory, Devereux.'

He nodded to them and bent down to haul his rucksack onto his back.

'Sashenka.'

He turned round. Lara stood at other end of the hall watching, and then walked towards him uncertainly through the streaks of December light coming down from the high windows.

She came up close to him and paused for a moment, looking nervous. 'Please be careful. I don't want you to die. I embrace you.'

She wrapped her arms around him and pressed her head into his shoulder so that her hair caressed his cheek; she exhaled slowly and he felt her breath on his neck.

She stood back, looking pale and all the more beautiful for it, and holding his arm affectionately. 'You are brave, going off there to fight: Sergey just talks about things but you are *doing* something. You are a soldier.'

Alex blanched and stood stock-still with his rucksack balanced awkwardly on his shoulder. His head had been full of last-minute checks and plans, with thoughts of the operation, of doing his duty to his ancestors and his country, when she had caught him off guard. He was staggered by such a gorgeous woman being so Russian, so emotionally direct, with him.

He was too flummoxed to think of anything to say so he just nodded gravely.

Lara took his silence as stoic indifference to danger, which prompted her to feel she had to make some gesture to match his bravery. She looked down, trying to think of something to say or do. Faced with the finality of their departure, their last chance of being alone and the fact that Alex might die, she desperately wanted to give him something as a keepsake. She gritted her teeth in frustration, unable to think of anything to give him; she had no jewellery on, nothing. She looked up at him and saw the bayonet on his webbing shoulder strap.

She pointed her finger at him and said sternly, 'I'm going to give you something now and you're going to bring it back to me.'

She reached out and yanked the bayonet out of its scabbard.

'Hey!' Alex dropped his rucksack in alarm and grabbed her wrist to stop her.

'No!' Her eyes flared up at him.

He looked at her and slowly released her hand.

She flicked her hair round over her shoulder and leaned her head over to one side so that it hung down in a cascade like a sheet of white gold. She then stuck the knife into it at the nape of her neck, pinched a thin lock with the other hand and cut it off with a sharp movement of the blade.

She held up the long strand of hair triumphantly; it shone in the winter sunshine. She stuck the bayonet back in his scabbard, then leaned towards him and twisted the hair onto a strap on his webbing over his heart.

Alex could only watch her as she stood back looking at her handiwork with satisfaction and smoothed it flat with one hand.

'There.' She tried to regain her composure by adopting a brusque tone. 'Now that is mine and I want it back.'

She pointed a warning finger at him again and smiled her electric smile. Before he could respond she kissed him slowly on the lips, looked at him meaningfully and then turned and walked away down the long hall.

Chapter Twenty-One

Alex sat in the front of the helicopter, as Arkady flew it, his head in a daze.

He was aware that he should be fully switched on and anticipating any events that might occur when they arrived at the airport, but he couldn't get his brain to work. It was like a screw not threaded properly; it just kept turning round and round aimlessly, so he just stared at the white fields and roads coursing past underneath them.

Lara sat with the others in the back of the helicopter. They had both returned to quietly ignoring each other in front of the others.

After half an hour they flew over Halfpenny Green airport: a flat field with the snow-shrouded outlines of a few Cessnas and helicopters parked along the edge of the single runway, a small control tower next to it. It was not a busy place at the best of times on a Saturday morning; with the state of the economy and the weather, it was utterly deserted.

Once they landed, Alex came out of his dream; he had to start responding to events. Two large hangars had recently been built at the end of the runway and Arkady landed next to one. Sergey's pilot stepped out of it and walked over to the helicopter. The team pulled their rucksacks, skis, tents and other gear out of the luggage compartment and then stood around as Lara said a muted goodbye.

'See you in Moscow.' She grinned at them all, uncertain if she would.

'Oh, and, Alexander, one last instruction I remembered on the way here.' She handed him a folded piece of notepaper that she had scribbled on during their flight. Alex nodded and her eyes met his for the briefest moment before she hurried away and got back into the helicopter. He stuffed the note into the top pocket of his snow smock and then turned to help the others lug the gear through the side door of the hangar.

The gleaming white Gulfstream G550 was parked inside. It was the intercontinental version with twin Rolls-Royce engines mounted either side of the tail plane and a wider wingspan than normal, giving it a range of 7,800 miles. With a normal seating configuration it could take up to nineteen passengers, but Sergey's version had been modified to include a front kitchen and then a large six-seat cabin with a shower and bedroom in the tail.

Once the gear was stowed onboard, Arkady spoke to the tower, the hangar door motors whirred and the doors rolled back. He powered up and they taxied forward along to the end of the runway. The rest of them settled back into the luxurious white leather chairs.

'Bit plusher than what we usually go to war in, eh?' commented Colin, looking round at the oak and gold-trimmed cabin. In Africa they usually travelled strapped into the draughty, noisy cargo bay of an old Antonov AN-12.

Alex grinned and settled back for the flight. He pulled out a wallet full of the maps and plans of the attack that he wanted to look over and consider further. As he sorted through the papers, he surreptitiously pulled Lara's note out of his top pocket and flicked it open as discreetly as he could.

The Cyrillic handwriting was bold but flowing:

Alexander, one more thing, as it says in *Dr Zhivago* I hope we can find peace in our lives through 'human understanding rendered speechless by emotion.'

He folded the note and slipped it back in his pocket.

'Human understanding rendered speechless by emotion.' What did she mean by that?

Chapter Twenty-Two

SUNDAY 14 DECEMBER

A thin dawn light shone over the deserted airfield at Krasnokamensk as the Gulfstream broke through the clouds and began its final approach.

Arkady was tired from flying, haggling over weapons, loading them and then flying again for the last twenty-four hours.

'Krasnokamensk Tower, this is Flight GX 3974, come in,' he said wearily into his headset.

Alex watched him anxiously from the co-pilot seat. He established contact and identified the purpose of the flight: 'GeoScan geological research team inbound on orders of Governor Shaposhnikov.'

The name carried weight and had worked so far with the various air-traffic control centres in the six time zones they had travelled across. Sergey and Fyodor Mostovskoy had obviously done their homework: their flight plan and purpose were registered and they were waved through.

A sleepy voice from the tower came back: 'Krasnokamensk Tower to Flight GX 3974, you are cleared for landing. Winds are light northerly with some snow drifting on runway, so watch it.'

'Acknowledged.'

Arkady shook his head to clear it and settled down to take them in.

Alex quickly ducked back into the rear cabin.

'OK, everyone, we're going in. Weapons ready but keep them out of sight and stay away from the windows until we've touched base with our contact.'

Yamba, Colin, Magnus and Pete were all wearing full arctic combat gear, complete now with white body armour under their webbing; they all sat and looked back at him with tense faces. Assault rifles and grenade launchers were checked, put on safety and tucked under seats.

Alex picked up his standard-issue Russian army AN-94, cocked it and propped it next to him in the co-pilot's seat. He nodded at Arkady and they sped in towards the runway.

Touchdown was nervy because of the light dusting of snow on the tarmac since the gritters had cleared it. Arkady slammed the engines hard into reverse thrust and Alex flinched at the extra noise and vibration.

It died away and they taxied over to the end of the runway, where three large black hangars were. Arkady kept the engines turning over. They were low on fuel but the plan was that if something didn't look right they would go for a quick take-off and just make it over the border into China, whilst sending out a mayday call saying they had had a navigation failure. They would then have to take their chances with whatever regional airfield they could make it to.

It was far from perfect and Alex just hoped it didn't come to that. With the amount of weapons and ammunition they now had onboard it would be patently obvious to whoever stopped them that they were up to no good, and with the region's most famous resident only fifty miles away it would not be hard to work out what they were doing there.

As they taxied past the control tower, Alex glanced carefully out of the window. An MVD border guard officer was surveying them through binoculars as they passed, but Sergey's Gulfstream was a regular sight at the airport and the flight plan was in order so they didn't get a closer inspection.

Alex and Arkady breathed out once they passed the tower.

Alex unbuckled and ducked back into the cabin. 'OK, everyone, spread out around the aircraft. I want a full three-sixty lookout, report any movement. We should have a single person contact – he's called Bogdan Goncharov.'

The team spread out around the portholes; this was the first concrete test of Sergey's reliability. Arkady taxied forward and swung the aircraft round at the far end of the runway, positioning them for the quick getaway if needed. Everyone waited, eyes flicking around the limited view from their portholes, fingers on the triggers of their weapons.

After five minutes, Alex called back from the cockpit, 'Anybody seen anything?'

A series of, 'No,' and, 'No movement,' came back.

Alex began to get twitchy. Should he call Sergey?

No. There was to be no direct contact. Everything was to be handled through intermediaries until the last possible moment.

Should he get out and have a look around?

He wouldn't be able to see anything that he couldn't already, and the sight of a man in combat gear really *would* prompt a delegation from the control tower. As much as he hated inactivity he would just have to sit and wait this one out until something definite happened.

As usual it was Colin who voiced everyone's thoughts. 'You don't think our Russian friend has fooked us over, do you?'

161

Alex wished he could reply with certainty but the best he could do was, 'We'll just have to wait and see.'

The team sat silent and impotent next to the windows, fingers on triggers. No one said anything but they were all thinking the same thing: Have we just walked into a trap?

Pete shouted: 'Truck approaching from rear, seven o'clock!'

Alex was back there in a flash and they all crowded round the portholes. A large GAZ, six-wheeled truck with huge metal-studded snow tyres was parking up next to the chain-link gate on the airfield perimeter. A man in a heavy blue parka and padded trousers got out of the cab, unlocked the gate, swung it open, drove the truck through and headed towards them.

They watched carefully as the exhausts over the cab belched diesel and the truck picked up speed, swinging across the runway and approaching. Alex couldn't see what was inside the dark green tarpaulin over the high rear section.

The truck swung round and parked alongside them. The high cab door opened and the man jumped down and ran over, his head covered by his hood. He didn't look threatening.

'OK, everyone, stand down. Doesn't look like the border police. I think this might be Bogdan. I'll go and see what he wants. Pete and Magnus, stay inside the door and cover me. Slot him if he tries anything funny.'

The other two nodded and followed Alex with their assault rifles ready; he yanked the large door lever open and swung the steps out and down.

After the long, air-conditioned flight, a warm fug had developed inside the aircraft that was very different from conditions outside. As soon as Alex broke the seal on the door, a freezing blast of air at minus thirty-five degrees C rushed into the cabin.

With such a differential, the first breath Alex took felt like a cold razor slash down his throat. Involuntarily he put his hand over his mouth to try to stop the pain and had to struggle to control his breathing.

A thick-set Russian face peered up at him with ice around the rim of his parka hood.

'You Grekov?' he asked, with an aggressive upwards flick of the chin. He frowned unsympathetically at Alex's reaction to the cold.

'Yes.' Alex forced the words out: 'Who are you?'

'I'm Bogdan. You'd better follow me,' he replied gracelessly. 'We're going over there.' He grunted and jerked his thumb over his shoulder towards the hangar. With that he turned round and climbed back into his cab.

Alex nodded his assent, unimpressed by the reception but with no choice but to co-operate. Bogdan seemed to be on their side – why would the MVD border police go through this façade? If they knew about the plot and wanted to get them now they could just have shot the plane full of holes there and then.

He retracted the steps and Arkady wound up the engines and taxied over to the large hangar with Sergey's mining company logo across the huge sliding doors.

Bogdan stopped alongside it, got out and unlocked a small side entrance. A minute later the doors began to creak open; when the gap was big enough Arkady increased power and eased them through. Once they were inside he shut down the engines and the doors rolled shut behind them.

Bogdan drove over to them on a small, yellow airport tractor and, with Arkady's help, hooked it up to the front wheel and manoeuvred the plane round to face the doors.

He came back over to Alex and grunted, 'When we come back here, we might be leaving in a hurry, yes?'

Alex nodded. They certainly would be.

Arkady switched on the fuel pumps, dragged the heavy hose over and with Yamba's help connected it up to the wing fuel tanks. The huge long-range pods took a long time to fill and again they wanted them to be ready to go straight away when they blasted off on their return leg to Moscow.

As Arkady refuelled, everyone else busied themselves unloading the cargo from the luggage bay under the aircraft. Arkady's arms dealer had surpassed himself – they had enough munitions to fight a small war. Alex hoped it wouldn't come to that but he wanted to be prepared if it did.

The heavy weapons were in large crates: four B8V20 rocket pods with 80mm S-8 rockets and an AGS-30 30mm automatic grenade launcher for the helicopter. Others contained 9M133 Kornet anti-tank guided missiles and RPO Shmel launchers and missiles for taking out the watchtowers. There were also boxes of fragmentation, smoke and phosphorous grenades.

The team's individual AN-94 assault rifles were all fitted with GP-30 underslung grenade launchers. They already had their individual rifles on their backs and magazine bandoliers under their snow smocks, but smaller metal boxes contained thousands of rounds of 5.45mm ammunition as well. Three Kord, 12.7mm heavy machine guns, three PKM 7.62mm general-purpose machine guns with 250 round ammunition boxes and NSPU night sights had also been included, along with command- and squad-level radios.

Pete's special requests for FIBUA equipment had not been ignored. These included two Benelli M4 Super 90, 12 gauge, semi-automatic combat shotguns for blowing the hinges off doors and general close-quarters fighting. A variety of scopes, laser illuminators, night-vision sights, and flashlights had been included for fitting onto these and the other individual weapons.

His prize request were mouseholing charges: MTP-2 delayed-action mines used for blowing holes in walls.

'Doorways – fucking hate 'em,' he had explained. 'When you go through you're on your own, unsupported, sil-houetted, enemy knows where you're gonna come in, easy target – bang. Fucking death funnels. Much better to make your own door and take the bastards by surprise.'

The dinner-plate-sized devices had two kilos of plastic explosive each, and sticky pads that allowed them to adhere to any surface. They were detonated by a simple, red tear-off chemical fuse that could be crimped up to a three-minute delay. Radio detonated versions were also included.

Most of this specialist urban warfare equipment was left onboard the aircraft for use once they got to Moscow.

When the truck was fully loaded, they mounted up and Bogdan got back into the cab. They swung out of the hangar, waited for Arkady to close the doors behind them, and then drove off the airfield to their forward operating base and the next stage of the preparations for the big assault.

Chapter Twenty-Three

Captain Lev Darensky's shoulder muscles were filling up with acid. They seared as if they were cutting their way out of his skin.

He had been in the 'dried crocodile' position for nearly half an hour now – his arms locked in press-up position holding onto the rail at the head of the bed and his feet apart pressed against the rail at its foot.

The individual vertebrae of his neck and back were each made of red-hot iron that had now fused together into a single burning rod. Each tendon stood out on his neck and a fit of trembling ran through his shoulders. He fought against it but the tremors were becoming more and more insistent.

I can't keep this up for much longer but I know what they will do if I fall.

A fresh current of fear pumped through his blood system and steadied the tremor for a minute more. He tried moving his head from side to side to ease the pain. His vision was reduced by the sweat dripping from his fair hair into his eyes, but he could see two of his fellow officers and sergeants either side of him in the same position on the beds in the barrack room, their heads down and teeth clenched against the pain.

'Hey, Darensky! You're a dried crocodile, not a live one! Keep your fucking head down or I'll thrash you so hard you'll forget your name!'

Colonel Karenin's voice sounded like a bull's bellow from the other end of the barrack room. A heavy-set man with a chubby, vodka-ravaged face, he was drunk and looking forward to punishing the first man to drop from his stress position. He sucked his gut in under his combat jacket and squared his shoulders. This was the sort of thing that they had done in the army in his days as a conscript – when the Soviet Union was great.

It was what his old friend Krymov had appointed him to do – to restore the dignity of the armed forces from the snivelling wreck that it had become under Gorbachev and Yeltsin: forced to accept advances by NATO on all fronts, into the Baltic States for God's sake! To sell off its flagship aircraft carrier to the Chinese to become a floating casino. To be reduced under Yeltsin to infighting on the streets of Moscow like a rabble of hooligans. Never would they accept such humiliations again. Never!

And the fight back began here! That was why it was important that these junior officers and NCOs suffered, to make sure that they did the same to the men under them, who would do it to the privates and conscripts under them, who would then do it to the enemies of the Motherland that they were sent against.

This remorseless logic drove him on in his campaign of sadism against the 568th Regiment. He would make them strong, if it killed them.

He felt that his work was all the more important because the 568th had such a vital role in the defence of Moscow. Based twenty miles north of the capital, near Sheremetyevo airport, it was ready for immediate deployment there in case of terrorist attack. Krymov's paranoia also meant that he feared a full-scale foreign airborne assault on the capital, so the regiment was a powerful force equipped with T-90 tanks, anti-aircraft artillery and armoured personnel carriers, all of which were kept at a high state of alert, with a full fuel and weapons load.

That evening, Karenin had got drunk with his three company majors and some sergeants and they had hauled the youngest officers into a barrack away from where the main body of the 568th Regiment was based. He was happy for this to go on all night, as far as he was concerned.

This practice of *dedovschina*, or bullying, was institutionalised in the Russian armed forces. At its worst the process culminated in *opusteet* – 'taking someone down'.

Male rape.

The thought of it excited Colonel Karenin now.

'I've got the antiseptic cream, boys!' he laughed as he paced up and down along the row of beds behind them and waved a tube of the lubricant.

Equally the thought of it revolted Darensky and he pushed his arms out and clenched his vertebrae.

They won't do that to me! No – not that!

Darensky knew he couldn't last much longer. He had fought against the final collapse so long that it had overwhelmed him. The only thing in his consciousness now was pain and he was getting tired of it.

He just wanted it to stop.

Never mind what Karenin did to him, it couldn't be worse than this. His right arm juddered and he didn't try to stop it.

This was it. He was going to fall onto the bed, be dragged away, sodomised and beaten to a pulp.

So what? Here I go.

'Ah!' There was a brief cry and thud from down the room as Lieutenant Panin collapsed onto the bed.

'Ha ha!' Karenin shouted, and ran down the line of beds to see his victim. 'Well, we have a volunteer after all for special duties!' He signalled to the sergeants to drag the man out.

'The rest of you, stand easy!' he laughed, and followed the inert, moaning form as it was dragged past Darensky with its feet trailing on the floor.

Darensky and the other men collapsed on their beds and screamed and writhed as the cramp overcame them.

The morning after, Captain Darensky was summoned to the administration block where they had dragged Panin.

Darensky was a young and lively officer but he moved now like an old man; his neck and shoulders were stiff from the ordeal and he hunched himself up with fear as he walked slowly around the edge of the snowy parade ground to the old, four-storey, concrete building. The square was bounded by several Soviet-era blocks on each side, their grey cement sides streaked a darker grey by rainwater, and hung with icicles now. The shouts and curses of the regimental duty officer echoed off them as he got the men lined up for morning parade.

What have they done to Lieutenant Panin and what will they do to me?

His brother officer hadn't come back last night. Darensky walked reluctantly up the steps from the main parade ground to the glass-panelled door and pressed the buzzer. There was a long pause and then he heard footsteps dragging inside the door and it was yanked open.

Colonel Karenin looked awful after a night's heavy drinking. His grey hair stuck up on one side of his head and his face was creased from where he had passed out asleep on the floor.

170

'Darensky,' he growled, 'get some men ...' He paused 'There's been an accident.' With that, he shuffled off, leaving the door open.

Darensky stood on the threshold for a moment, staring ahead before he returned to the main mess hall, picked three men and came back.

They went inside.

The body of Lieutenant Panin was lying in the hallway against the wall, wrapped in a grey army blanket like an old carpet that was being thrown out. Darensky stumbled in shock but directed the men so that they each took a corner of the blanket and picked him up.

They could then clearly see what had happened.

He was naked and had been beaten until his face was unrecognisable; an entrenching tool handle stuck out from between his buttocks, stained with dried blood.

Colonel Karenin appeared at the end of the corridor and swayed, glowering at them.

'Get it out of here,' he grunted, and gestured to the door.

The four-man squad stumbled down the steps of the command block, trying not to let the body bump against their legs or to look down at the face swollen with purple bruises.

Darensky was stunned. He had joined the army as a young volunteer because he was filled with ideas of doing his duty to the Rodina, the Motherland.

Not for this.

Not for sodomy and murder.

Darensky was from a middle-class family and his parents wanted to buy him the usual doctor's certificate that kept nice boys like him out of the draft. However, the young Lev had craved a challenge and looked forward to the hardships of conscription as a rite of passage into manhood.

He had been a member of Nashi – 'Ours' – the pro-Putin youth movement founded to promote the resurgence in Russian national pride.

Nashi had pumped him full of ideas and he believed the old Orthodox mantra that Moscow was the Third Rome, the seat of faith on Earth and therefore of all righteousness. He knew that Russia was *the* special nation on earth, neither European nor Asian but Russian. He wasn't exactly sure what Russia's message to the world was, only that it had one and that it demanded respect.

But the reality of his time as a conscript had battered that idealism.

He found himself asking: why was it necessary as a recruit to be kicked out of your bed every night and beaten by drunken 'lords' from the different platoons: Recce, Tanks, Artillery, Signals? Whose turn was it tonight?

How much abuse could his frame take?

The black eyes, split lips, bruised ribs, cuts and grazes, broken bones, concussion – he found himself living with the iron taste of blood in his mouth from busted teeth and gums, exhausted by the permanent state of fear.

What was the point of being so starved that you ate tubes of toothpaste for nourishment? Of having no equipment issued so you had to wrap your feet in newspaper instead of socks?

But when he asked those questions, his inner sense of duty had replied that it wasn't the system that was at fault, it was him. It was his own weakness that was the problem. The challenge of maintaining the constitutional order of the Motherland was a tough one and he just wasn't up to it. He should try harder, he could not fail.

This devotion forced him to stay on as a volunteer and propelled him through to the rank of captain. It was at this point, once he was on the inside, he discovered that it was the system that was at fault and not him. He realised that what was happening was not character-building – it was soul-destroying.

It had to stop.

The activism in his character that had fired his nationalism now fired a rebellion. Two months ago he had contacted a journalist to try to get a story run on the reign of terror that Karenin was pursuing in the 568th.

The journalist had told him quietly that there was no way that the story would ever be published with the censorship of the media under Krymov's regime. However, the man had then put him in touch with Sergey Shaposhnikov, who was only too pleased to hear about a potential rebellion in a powerful military force stationed near the capital. Sergey had encouraged Darensky to organise a group of similarly mutinous NCOs and junior officers and to await his instructions as to when to bring the regiment into action.

The only problem was that at the moment the rank and file of the 568th, although they hated Colonel Karenin, were too afraid of him and the system to rebel. As Darensky dragged the body past the regiment on parade that morning, he looked at the lines of men and received only averted eyes and sickened expressions in return. They had no stomach for a fight.

Panin's body bumped against his feet as they walked along and he shifted his grip on the blanket. He felt sick and weak.

He didn't know how he was going to get the regiment to mutiny.

Chapter Twenty-Four

MONDAY 15 DECEMBER

President Krymov was sitting at his desk staring out of the window.

He had taken his glasses off and his thick-set face had a lost expression as he looked across at the other side of the hexagonal courtyard in the middle of the Senate building complex.

He was back at the grindstone, trying to control every aspect of life in Russia, surrounded by the piles of paperwork that made him feel like he was achieving something. He had paused from his deliberation of what to do with a new pipeline proposal and was now thinking about the business with Shaposhnikov last week.

Who was this Devereux man and what is Sergey up to with him?

He was annoyed with Commandant Bolkonsky. Apparently his first attempt to have Raskolnikov killed in an accident had failed and he hadn't heard anything since then. If the man couldn't get it sorted out then he would just have him removed and find someone who could.

Major Batyuk knocked on the huge wood-panelled door and then entered. 'Message just come in to the ops room, sir. Bolkonsky says Raskolnikov will be killed in the sawmill tomorrow.'

Krymov stopped looking out of the window and shot a defensive glare across the large room at him. Well, there was his answer: Bolkonsky was getting on with the job after all.

'Hmm, very good,' he nodded, and Batyuk turned to go.

Krymov chucked his glasses on his desk and folded his hands as another thought came to mind.

'Batyuk?' The tough-looking major paused by the door. 'You know that I care a great deal about Shaposhnikov.' The major looked back at him respectfully but with a lack of animation that made it transparently obvious that he didn't care about Sergey. 'But I want him to learn an important lesson in loyalty.' Krymov paused. 'I'm going to call him.'

He nodded and Batyuk withdrew.

Krymov picked up the phone on his desk and called Sergey's mobile number.

At that time Sergey was in a meeting in his offices in Moscow with some partners in a clothing chain that he was trying to turn around. He had to go through the whole thing pretending that he hadn't just got the email from Alex in Siberia saying that they were launching the raid that night and that therefore he didn't know that a civil war was about to break out.

As usual, when he saw the word '*Vozhd*' light up on his phone, he grabbed it and ran out of the meeting room, back into his private office.

'Hey, Boss, what can I do for you?' he asked cheerfully.

'Shaposhnikov, what are you doing?' Krymov sounded suspicious.

'Oh, you know, a bit of this, a bit of that. I'm trying to sort out a company that sells bras and knickers, if you must know.'

Krymov grunted in amusement. 'Hmm, well, I think I have a little cause for celebration and I want you to come over tonight to get drunk and help me relax in the banya.'

'Well, you know me; I'm always on for a drink, Boss, but …' Sergey said as he desperately looked around his office for inspiration to get him out of this.

Of all the nights to be with Krymov he couldn't afford to tonight, not when the news of the raid hit Moscow. If they got Raskolnikov at six a.m. Krasnokamensk time that would be one a.m. Moscow time. It would take longer than that for the news to be reported but he just could not risk being anywhere near Krymov tonight.

He thought fast. 'I've got a big awards dinner that I'm doing the keynote speech at tonight so I'm afraid that you're going to have to get pissed without me.'

Krymov stood up at his desk, his face flushed red as he bellowed down the line, 'Now listen here, Shaposhnikov! If the President of the Russian Federation requests your presence tonight then you'd better get your fucking arse over here! They're going to kill Raskolnikov tomorrow morning and you need to make sure you raise a glass to it, d'ya hear! Or you may be packing your bags to Siberia as well!'

There was nothing Sergey could do when Krymov was in that sort of mood.

'Boss, Boss, of course, of course. I'll be right there.'

When he hung up, Sergey sat on his desk with his head in his hands.

He had caused the revolution that would start tonight and now it looked like he would cause his own death as well.

Chapter Twenty-Five

Somehow Lara never quite got over seeing the Ostankino tower.

When the car from the TV station dropped her off in the car park in front of it, she walked towards the monolith and had the feeling that the Earth was sure to buckle under its fifty-five thousand tons.

She forced the feeling away, telling herself that she was just terrified because of what was going to happen that night. The raid was all set to take place and she would be playing her key role in events the following morning. In the meantime she had to go through a normal day's work, doing a lunchtime TV slot, whilst pretending that she didn't know that the country was about to be plunged into a murderous civil war.

It wasn't going to be easy.

She swallowed and tried to adopt an unconcerned look as she went up the shallow steps onto the two-hundred-metre wide concrete base of the tower and walked over to reception.

The tower was shaped like a vast sceptre; it loomed over the whole of Moscow; you could see it from across the city on a clear day. The sky was overcast and it was snowing lightly now, so the top of the tower was lost in the clouds, but it was basically just an enormous concrete tube with three wide bands of satellite dishes and radio antennae spaced along its shaft. These transmitted the signals for eleven television stations, twelve radio stations and seventeen satellite TV channels to the Moscow region, and then on to relays across the whole of the rest of Russia.

As Lara got near, she craned her head back and could see, above the bands of transmitters, just under the cloud base, the five floors of offices for the TV and radio stations, complete with the Seventh Heaven restaurant. They bulged out from the tower like a great jewel near the top of the sceptre. It then narrowed in again to a final two hundred-metre spire but this was lost today in the grey murk overhead.

The base of the tower splayed out wide like a funnel, it looked like the bottom of a power station cooling tower and had huge curved arches cut into it. She walked through one of them, up to the four-storey wall of plate glass inside it, and went through a sliding door into the ultramodern reception area. Huge video screens were mounted all around it, displaying live feeds from all twenty-eight TV channels.

It was full of media types coming in and out: the older, grey-haired guys sporting 'liberal dissident chic' with black polo necks and scruffy suit jackets with the sleeves rolled up. The younger, trendier men wore 'media cool': ragged-bottomed jeans and smart blazers, with gelled-up hair and goatee beards. More than half the crowd were sharp-styled media girls with either spiky, asymmetric haircuts and heavy kitsch clothing or just slobby jeans and T-shirts.

Quite a lot of the TV station staff knew that a rebellion was in the offing but none had been told that it would all start that night. Grigory Bezukhov, as director of the station, was in charge of organising everyone when the coup happened. As Lara walked through the turnstiles, she managed to make herself mutter 'Hi' to a few people and exchanged more significant nods with others that she knew were in on the plot.

Somehow she couldn't manage her usual smile to the uniformed porters but scurried past them with her head down instead. The two men exchanged glances and shrugged, as she walked across to the bank of huge lifts. She squeezed into one, careful to keep her eyes averted from anyone else, next to a make-up artist with short, blonde hair scraped down over one eye and a lime-green pashmina draped over her shoulders. The door closed and the express lift catapulted them up 347 metres in less than a minute. She felt her knees buckle slightly under the Gs.

She walked out of the lifts in the central shaft of the tower and into a huge double-height space that spread out like a ninety-degree slice of a pie looking south over the whole of Moscow. The curve of the outside of the slice was one large glass wall; sections of it were closed off to form studios but otherwise the rest of the room was open plan, with a huge newsroom with rows of journalists sitting at desks covered in computers and all the usual paraphernalia of office junk: calendars, family photos, coffee cups. On her right, a glass wall ran along the side of the slice; on the other side of it was a studio that housed the phone bank for the big charity telethons she hosted, with a massive videowall to display the results.

Today, though, she was going to be doing a much more modest lunchtime TV interview with a well-known soap star who had recently come out of rehab and was trying to make a go of things again. The thought of such trivia at a time of crisis irritated her intensely but she forced herself to put her fear on one side and concentrate on the task in hand.

As she walked out of the lift she turned right and glanced up at the rear wall of the director's gallery that overlooked the big telethon studio. She stiffened slightly and then forced herself to relax again. Behind the glass wall she could see that Sergey was up there talking with Grigory. They

181

were standing close to each other with their heads down and arms folded, talking urgently. Grigory wore his trademark rumpled, black Armani suit with his curly black hair splaying out over his heavy-set shoulders. He stroked his stubble nervously and glanced sideways over the newsroom.

Seeing Lara, he touched Sergey's arm to interrupt him and then mouthed, 'See you later,' to her. He tried to smile reassuringly but it didn't work. He looked terrified. Sergey also looked unhappy as he waved to her.

What is Sergey doing here? He isn't supposed to get here until everything starts tomorrow.

Her stomach clenched in anxiety but she did her best to smile back. She had to go on air shortly so there was no time to stop.

She walked round the central lift shaft to the rooms at the other side of the tower, where the make-up studios were located; she felt like asking her make-up artist to slap a wall of it on her so that she could hide her nerves.

Lara smiled as the camera pulled back from her and her guest and the studio lights went down.

She then yanked her earpiece out, quickly unplugged herself from the desk mike and ran out of the studio before she had to make any more small talk with the soap star.

In her anxiety to find Sergey, she busted open doors and pushed past people in corridors. They looked back at the normally poised TV star with astonishment. She hurried up into the gallery where she had last seen him with Grigory. The big director was sitting hunched over a control desk, watching a show go out on the bank of screens in front of him.

When she burst in, he quickly put his headphones on the desk, stood up and ushered her out with a warning finger pressed over his mouth.

'Where is he?' she asked anxiously.

'He's upstairs. He's gone outside to think.' Grigory pointed up to the roof terrace over their heads.

Grigory and Lara hurried down the stairs, back into the newsroom and past the coat racks to collect their heavy parkas. Although it was mid-afternoon it was still minus eight outside and snowing.

They ran up the stairs to the roof of the TV centre. Sergey was alone, leaning against the guardrail, looking at the fading view over Moscow and smoking thoughtfully. From up here the whole of the city was spread out in front of them: the streets of the suburbs and then, in the distance, the floodlit, golden domes of the many churches and cathedrals, and the sinister Gothic skyscrapers of Stalin's Seven Sisters. He looked down at the thousand-foot drop to the car parks in front of him and let go of his cigarette butt. The red dot spun into the void and vanished.

Lara ran over to him and clutched the arm of his coat. 'What's happening? Why are you here now?'

Sergey turned round and grinned nonchalantly. 'I have to go to drink with Krymov tonight. We are celebrating Raskolnikov's death tomorrow.' He said it as if he were just going to a pub that night.

Lara's eyes widened. 'Well, you can't go,' she said simply, as if he were trying to defy a law of nature. 'The raid's happening. You'll be with him when he finds out and he'll kill you. You can't go!' She held out her hands in exasperation.

Sergey gave a comic grimace and shrugged. Then he held up an index finger and declaimed with mock seriousness, 'Yes, and as Gogol says in "St John's Eve", we are not going to a wedding: "a black raven will croak over me instead of a priest; the open plain will be my dwelling, the grey storm clouds will be my roof; an eagle will peck out my eyes; the rains will wash my Cossack bones and the whirlwind will dry them.'"

He grinned and started singing an old folk song: "'Black raven hovering over me, You won't eat my flesh ...'"

Lara shrieked in frustration and clenched her fists but he ignored her and carried on singing.

She looked around her and then hit him with her open palm on the side of his head, then grabbed a fistful of his hair and bent his head down. Her voice was a horribly shrill shriek as she jabbed a finger at him and screamed as if she were admonishing a disobedient child.

'Sergey! You stupid bastard! You're not going mushroom picking! He will *kill* you! Do you want to kill yourself? Do you want that?'

Sergey went limp under her attack and kept his head down. Eventually she let go of his hair and stepped back, breathing hard, her face flushed red with anger.

Sergey straightened up slowly, the side of his face was red from her blow and his hair was askew, but he accepted her violence as a sign of vitality and did not object to it. His earlier bravado had gone, though, and he looked at her meekly, pushing the hair out of his face.

'Lara,' he began imploringly.

She stood back, breathing out into the cold air from her exertion and glowering at him with dangerous eyes. Some of the fear that had built up in her over the last few weeks had been released, though, and she was more able to listen. Grigory stood back from it all, he knew what the two of them were like.

Sergey realised that he had to be more practical. He held the palms of his hands out to her and began in a pacifying tone, 'Krymov has given me a direct order. He already suspects something is up and if I don't appear he'll *know* it is and take action. The whole revolution will be prevented from happening – I *have* to go. If I have to make a blood sacrifice to the Russian nation then I will.'

Lara looked back at him, not giving any sign of acceptance.

'Lara, what is the purpose of living?' He looked at her with an earnest, quizzical expression on his face.

She was caught off guard and frowned. 'What?'

Sergey stretched out a hand. 'Why are we doing all of this?'

'Why are you asking me that now?' Lara was exasperated.

'No, I'm not questioning it. I have been thinking about this for a long time – and this quarrel has crystallised it for me.'

Lara knew there was no point interrupting him until this was over so she watched him warily.

He gained confidence. 'The purpose of living is to go from what we know –' he swept a hand to his right to take in the whole view of Moscow – 'this stuff, this material world – to go from what we know to what we *suspect* we know.' His index finger sprang up alongside his head to indicate an inkling. 'You see, *that* is the issue. The question is not what is out there – the truth is always out there – it is just a question of: do we have the courage, the faith, to believe in it?'

His tone became more conversational. 'You see, that sounds obvious but in practice there is a huge void placed between what we know and what we *suspect* we know. And our challenge is to cross that void, to overcome that uncertainty, to have faith.' His face shone as he built up to a climax. 'That is the only way that we can externalise our vitality, that we can reach that greater vision, that magnificence of soul that is *Russkaya dusha!*'

Lara could not argue against him any more. He had accepted his fate – that he might have to die to save the revolution – and in the face of this magnanimity her worldly concerns seemed petty and inconsequential. She knew he had won.

As ever, in these encounters with Sergey, she was thrown back into herself by his fervour. It had always been like that with him. It was how he had taken her soul in the first place and she began to feel pain again as his words tugged at the scar of that old wound.

Grigory could see that they had come to an accord and that it was time to move them back to more pressing practical matters. He walked towards them and the movement broke the tension.

Grigory was always a very generous character, used to handling sensitive creative egos. 'Sergey, that was great, just beautiful, just beautiful. I loved it. Now, we need to think about when things are going to happen tomorrow.'

Sergey and Lara both nodded.

Grigory continued, 'So, the email from Alex says he thinks he will have completed the raid and taken off from Krasnokamensk at 7.30 a.m. tomorrow. They are five hours ahead of Moscow, and the flight time is also five hours, so they will arrive here at 7.30 a.m. Does that work?'

Presented with a simple practical question, Lara could get going again. 'Yes, we need to make the morning rush-hour news broadcasts. If we can get Raskolnikov into the studio straight away then we can go on air at once – maybe 7.45 a.m.? We have to hit everyone at the beginning of the day or all the media effect of a live broadcast will be lost. We need people going into work talking about it so that they can either come straight out onto the streets or at least spend the rest of the day watching it on TV.'

'Hmm.' Grigory furrowed his brows. 'Right, I will email Alex now and tell him he needs to get that plane in here as fast as he can or we are lost. We can't afford to have our big broadcast go out late.'

He turned to Sergey and laid a hand on his shoulder. 'And, Sergey, you will have to get yourself away from Krymov as fast as you can tonight or you are lost as well.'

Chapter Twenty-Six

Lieutenant-General Fyodor Mostovskoy knew that the attack on the prison camp would start that night but he did not hurry to get to his post at Moscow Air Defence Command.

Fyodor never appeared to get excited about anything.

The expensive call girl that he had just shown out of the door felt chilled by her recent encounter with him. With his thin features, pale skin and hair and lack of animation, it had felt like doing it with a corpse.

Even though this would be the riskiest night of his life, Fyodor had not hesitated from booking her; he never had any problem compartmentalising the different areas of his life.

It was late afternoon, but he took his time, dressing fastidiously in his airforce uniform. Although it might have seemed an odd time to go into work, air defence was a twenty-four-hour business and none of his subordinates questioned him; they were all too terrified of his chilling stare. Fyodor was that unusual creature in the Russian military, a teetotal hard worker, and this contributed to his capacity to unnerve his colleagues.

He did up his tie precisely as he looked out of the window of his apartment off Ulitsa Kosygina at the bleak winter view over the Moskva River. It was dark already and he could see the lights of the waterfront opposite through the gently falling snow. The area was the preserve of top government officials, bankers and businessmen. Fyodor was one of the youngest generals in the airforce and hadn't pushed his way up to the top so fast for nothing; he knew what he wanted and enjoyed the trappings of power. His official driver and limo were ready waiting for him in the basement garage as he walked slowly down the corridor to the lift.

The black Zil swept out onto Leninskiy Prospekt. Fyodor enjoyed the feeling of being screened from view behind the small black curtains as they drove through the frozen Moscow streets. Although his features never showed it, the whole experience of the coup exhilarated him. It was a high-stakes game of poker that he had calculated would make him billions of roubles if his gamble paid off. It would also allow him to take cold and very bitter revenge on that idiot Krymov, who had failed to respect him in the allocation of spoils from the United Aircraft Corporation.

The rush-hour traffic going out of town was light because of the petrol rationing. They headed southwest, over the MKAD ring road towards an area of pine woodland. Passing the turning into the village of Kommunarka, they continued on and then turned right through a band of trees into a fenced-off military installation with a sign that merely read: 'Moscow Military District Depot 5'.

The car pulled up at a guard post with a striped road barrier and his driver passed his ID out, as Fyodor waited dismissively behind his black curtain. They drove through into a large empty factory shed and parked.

When Fyodor got out, his expensive leather shoes clicked on the cold concrete and a small stream of frozen breath followed him like a scarf fluttering in the wind. He walked over to where more armed guards stood by a door and slotted his security tag into the wall. The factory shed was actually just a cover over a low reinforced-concrete bunker to shield it from satellite observation. He walked inside and through more security checkpoints, a metal detector and then had his retina scanned before he finally came into a room with a lift door.

A guard snapped to attention and he entered the lift and settled back to wait for the long descent. Eight floors down, the door opened and he walked out through another security checkpoint into the Moscow Military District strategic command bunker. This was the place that, in the event of a nuclear war, command would initially be handed to. The huge semi-circular room had rings of officers sitting at desks all facing a massive screen with various computer map displays showing the disposition of Russian air, sea and land forces around the world, as well as the last known position of potential enemy units: NATO forces marked in red and Chinese in orange.

It was full of officers from all the services: navy, army, marines, FSB, MVD, GRU and airforce, and had the subdued lighting and feel of a library. People stared at computer screens on their desks or talked quietly on secure phone lines. The main status board updated every five seconds, blinking as it refreshed. He shrugged off his greatcoat and handed it to the pretty female NCO by the coat racks and then walked over to his usual desk in the inner ring in front of the main screen and sat down to await events.

Nothing in his demeanour showed, but Fyodor took a distinct pleasure in knowing that somewhere in Siberia right now a small team of armed men was preparing to shatter the tranquillity around him and that, as a result, enormous amounts of money and sweet revenge would be flooding his way.

Chapter Twenty-Seven

As soon as they had arrived at the deserted geological survey base on Sunday, the team had feverishly set about preparations. If all went well they planned to leave at 22.00 the following night, Monday 15th, and hit the camp early on the Tuesday morning.

The civilian Mi-17-IV medium transport helicopter was waiting for them in a large hangar with a workshop. It was a big aircraft, consisting of a front cockpit with a single large cargo bay behind, capable of carrying up to thirty men. Arkady and Yamba fired up the compressors and got to work on it to adapt it for military operations.

Arkady used the oxyacetylene torch to weld the four 80mm rocket pods they had brought onto pylons on either side of the aircraft. Yamba rigged up a simple firing switch through to the cockpit. It was going to be a crude and inaccurate system – relying on the volume of rockets rather than pinpoint accuracy – but would go some way to make up for the imbalance in troop numbers. The automatic grenade launcher was fixed into the cargo bay next to the rear clamshell doors to give the helicopter a sting in its tail if they needed it.

As they adjusted the helicopter indoors, Colin got to work with the spray gun on the huge Vityaz tracked ATV outside, and Alex was able to get a quick update from Bogdan on local conditions. During this he discovered that the Russian was a former Spetznatz soldier who had been working on Sergey's close protection unit for years and was trusted by him. He was dour and taciturn, and obviously didn't like having to work with foreigners, but once he saw that Alex was purely focused on the job in hand he got stuck in as well.

Alex then got the team organised on their skis and they trekked out two miles into the forest. As they slid along between the silent trees, the cold still made him gasp and the dry snow creaked under their skis. They came to a long break through the trees where they could begin zeroing their weapons.

They set up four logs at the end of the open ground. Alex, Colin, Magnus and Pete then lay prone, squinted along their weapons and began the slow process of firing into the targets, stopping to tweak their sights and then firing again until they were satisfied their iron and laser sights were zeroed. Their 5.45mm AN-94 assault rifles were more complex to use and maintain than the older AK-74s, but had a higher rate of fire at 600 rounds per minute, were more accurate, and packed a greater punch with their GP-30 underslung grenade launchers.

Magnus took twice as long as the others as he had his sniper rifle to take extra time over as well; this would be absolutely crucial to the success of the assault and was now his prized possession.

Arkady's dealer had really come through for them. In a short space of time he had managed to get hold of a much-prized Accuracy International L115A3 long-range rifle. This was the top NATO-issue sniper weapon, firing a 8.59mm bullet, heavier than the 7.62mm round of the old L96, and thus less likely to be deflected by wind over long ranges. With its Schmidt & Bender 5-25x56 PM II LP telescopic sights, an extra night-vision sight attached and suppressors to reduce flash and noise signature, it was going to add a silent and lethal element to the assault.

The plan was for the three-man assault team of Alex, Magnus and Pete to fly fifty miles due north to the prison. Colin and Bogdan would approach the camp at the same time, but overland in the Vityaz ATV.

The fly-by-wire systems in the Mil made single-pilot operation possible for Arkady, but Yamba would still act as his co-pilot and gunner. To make sure that the helicopter couldn't be detected by any radar systems in the area they would fly at treetop level. Alex knew from experience that Arkady took this literally. He had come back from more than a few raids with branches stuck in their landing gear.

To avoid the possibility of any noise detection they would rope down into the woods with their skis ten miles out from the camp. On the way in they would recce two clearings large enough to take the Mil's twenty-one-metre rotors, to act as main and backup extraction points. Co-ordinates for these would then be relayed back to the helicopter by secure burst VHF transmission. Alex wanted extraction to be done well away from the camp. Helicopters were delicate flying machines and he didn't want theirs brought anywhere near a camp full of men with assault rifles and watchtowers with machine guns.

The alterations on the helicopter had taken longer than expected but once they and all other preparations were complete, the team had sat down with Bogdan round a table in the office to finalise details in the early afternoon on Monday, in expectation of leaving at 22.00 that night.

The door banged open and Arkady stomped in, his face

was grim, a cigarette sticking upwards in his mouth as he scowled. He had just been on the internet and held a printout from the Russian Federation Meteorological Office in his hands.

'Hmm, it's not looking good. We have storm coming in tonight from the northeast. That will be real bitch.'

He handed the sheet to Alex. Magnus walked round the table to look over his shoulder. Ignoring the Cyrillic writing, he could see the projected weather maps and they didn't look good.

Alex turned and looked at him, prepared to defer to his arctic expert. 'How long will it take to blow through?'

'Looks like it should go through overnight tonight; it will be quite severe, but fast at least.'

'What are the operational issues?'

The Norwegian gave his characteristic pause and then cleared his throat before answering, 'Well, this type of storm will make conditions very dangerous. Flying the helicopter will be difficult, navigation on the ground will be much harder in a whiteout, and there will be increased frostbite risk. I know we have to be quick but I think we must wait for a day until this blows through. It would be risky to go out in it.'

Alex thought hard. This was what being the commanding officer was all about: balancing the possible threat to Raskolnikov against operational conditions. There was no point in rushing off into a terrible situation and risking everything if it would blow over tonight. Raskolnikov could survive another day in the camp.

Alex nodded and turned to the team. 'OK, then we'll delay departure until 22.00 tomorrow, Tuesday the sixteenth. I'll go and transmit that timing to our Moscow contacts.'

The rest of the team nodded, relieved that they wouldn't

have to face the teeth of the storm. Col sighed. 'Right-oh, well, I'll go and put the kettle on, shall I?'

Alex walked out to the small office down the corridor that had an internet connection to send the details to Sergey and the others. As there was no mobile signal around the base, it was their only contact with the rest of the operation.

Two minutes later the door banged open as he marched back in.

'Right, cancel last orders! Moscow contact reports target will be killed tomorrow morning. We go as soon as it's dark tonight, storm or no storm! Crack on!'

Chapter Twenty-Eight

Roman Raskolnikov was worried.

He was lying on his bunk just under the frosty rafters, in the time before lights out. He had spoken to Olga last Thursday and hadn't seen her since, so he had no idea if she had been able to pass the information on about the attempt to kill him, and if it would do any good if she had. He didn't know what she did with it or who received it, and what they could do for him anyway. It just helped to feel that someone outside this place knew and cared about what was happening to him.

Now, however, Roman felt uncharacteristically depressed by recent events. He had taken Danni's death hard and the river of courage inside him that he had been drawing on for two years seemed to be drying up. As he lay there he had a cold, sick certainty that they were finally going to get him.

All the precautions his supporters had taken to protect him seemed pitiful and pointless. They might want to make his assassination look like an accident for the sake of the press but they could do it whenever they wanted. Whether they used Getmanov or just some guards it didn't seem to matter. Part of him wished that they would just get on with it.

He heard a whispering sound below and someone

muttered: 'Vadim's coming up.' The high stack of four wooden bunks creaked and swayed as Vadim climbed up the ladder.

He was a supporter of Roman's, who worked as an orderly in the hospital block, a frail former nurse and junkie convicted of stealing drugs. As a trustie he was able to move around the camp and do jobs that allowed him to pick up information from overheard conversations. He was also a homosexual and had been abused throughout his life for it; he seemed to favour Roman because he had at least tried to stand against the whole system of oppression in the country.

He didn't sleep in Barrack 9 so Roman wondered what he was doing here now; he hadn't spoken to him in weeks. He raised himself on an elbow and drew his legs back to allow the little man to swing himself onto the foot of his bed.

'Roman,' he said by way of greeting, and nervously put out his hand. They sat next to each other on the bed, hunched down under the ceiling with their heads close together.

'I've been trying to see you for a week now,' Vadim whispered urgently, his eyes popping out of his rat-like face, 'but I couldn't get into your hut until I did someone a favour.' He winced. 'I tried to come and see you as soon as it happened – I mean Danni …' He tailed off and ducked his head before picking up again. 'I was on duty in the infirmary when they brought him in … they were laughing.' He shook his head. 'Said it was planned – to let the stove run out – said they wanted to get rid of him so's they could get at you easier.' He looked down.

Roman looked at him dully. It was bad news heaped on bad news, like a blow falling on a bruise; he hardly even felt it now.

Vadim sobbed as he recalled: 'He knew he was going to

die – the guards told him they'd let the stove go out – so he cut the words "Our last hope!" into his forearm.'

Roman looked at him in horror now, shaken out of his numb state.

Vadim took it as disbelief. 'No – it's true; they knocked out one of his front teeth when they beat him up in the cell and he used it to cut his skin.'

They both paused to contemplate the horror, before Vadim came out with his parting shot, almost an afterthought now.

'Also, today, I was in the guardroom scrubbing the floor when I overheard Kuzembaev saying that they're going to send you to the sawmill tomorrow. He said that orders had come through last week to kill you and that, after they failed with the logging, the commandant just wants to get on with it and make sure they kill you this time.'

Roman was now jolted from grief to fear.

Vadim tried to give a look of support but it ended up looking like pity offered to a condemned man.

When the nurse had swung himself awkwardly back down the ladder, Roman was left in a state of shock. In his mind's eye he could see the spinning blades of the sawmill.

He knew he would not sleep that night but would lie awake trying to fight the challenges of the day to come in advance, wearing himself into exhaustion.

Chapter Twenty-Nine

'OK, let's do noise checks.'

Alex stood back as Pete jumped up and down. Something rattled in one of his webbing pouches and he quickly repacked it so that the spare magazine wouldn't give his position away when he was creeping up close to the enemy.

The assault team were doing a final check of each other's kit in the hangar. Alex wanted to get going as soon as possible before the storm made flying too dangerous, but equally he didn't want to rush off half-cocked.

In Alex's webbing pouches he had everything he needed to live and fight for twenty-four hours: rations packs, field dressings, small stove, fifteen magazines with 450 rounds for his assault rifle, frag and phosphorous grenades plus two smokes if they needed to signal the helicopter or cover a retreat.

A camelback water pouch was slung across his stomach, under his clothing – if it went on his back, as it was supposed to, the water in it would just freeze. His white rucksack rested on top of the line of belt pouches around his waist. It contained an entrenching tool for digging out snow, ten MTP-2 mines with radio detonators, his squad and VHF radios. Strapped onto the side of it was an RPO Shmel fuel-air bomb launcher, which looked like a three-foot green drainpipe with simple fold-out sights and trigger grip. One round was already inserted in it and he carried two more rockets.

He wore a lot of clothing; they knew that the storm was going to be ferocious. Over layers of underwear and socks went padded Gortex salopettes and Thinsolite boots. Similar layers covered his torso and then came his body armour, with a heavy Kevlar plate over his heart. He still had Lara's lock of hair tied on his webbing.

Over this was a three-layered snow smock, consisting of a fleece undergarment, a cotton layer and a Gortex outer shell. On top, Magnus had added a heavy parka with a large fur-trimmed hood. His rucksack, Shmel launcher and spare rounds went outside of all this, with his assault rifle slung across his chest. When it came to the actual assault they would ditch the parka and fight in their smocks in order to be able to get to their webbing equipment quickly.

His hands were covered in silk glove liners, gloves and then a heavy pair of Thinsolite mittens. These were clipped onto the sleeve of his coat so that if he needed to work and fire his rifle he could just shake them off and get firing. Over his face he wore wide snow goggles and a white face mask with eye, mouth and nose holes that covered his whole head to keep the heat in. A throat mike and a headset over one ear allowed quiet radio comms.

Before they had put on all this kit, they spent a lot of time on navigation, compasses and maps: checking distances and directions, estimating speed, rations and water usage. With no moon or stars and a storm whiteout, their GPS and compasses were going to be vital. The large-scale geological maps and satellite photos that they had would be of limited use, as most detailed terrain features would be buried under drifts of snow.

Alex had also run through their 'actions on', such as: 'Actions on getting lost: make for rendezvous at grid ref X.' Other eventualities he planned for were: equipment failures, misread signals, unexpected contact with enemy units, stepping on a mine and casualties in battle.

As ever, when going into combat, this last one ran through his mind like an annoying song that he couldn't get out of his head. His usual litany of injury fears were: losing a limb or being paralysed (his personal horror), being blinded, decapitated or disembowelled. He had seen them all and unwanted images flashed back in his head.

At least on this operation they could get going as soon as they were ready so they didn't have to hang around waiting for a deadline. Alex always found that the worst bit about getting ready for an assault was when he had nothing to do but just sit around and think about what could go wrong.

As soon as the equipment checks were finished the three heavily laden figures trooped outside to the helicopter. Arkady was stalking around next to the cockpit, having a last nervous cigarette. They stamped up the cargo ramp at the back of it with their skis and poles clutched in one hand, and settled onto a metal bench on one side. Yamba was attaching the line that they would rope down from the rear ramp, clipping it onto a hardpoint by the rear door.

Colin and Bogdan followed them into the aircraft to say goodbye.

Alex stood up and turned round to face the whole squad. As the commander this was the final moment when the weight of responsibility for everything that would happen really did bite deep into his shoulders. He was not one for speeches; he knew that they had done everything they could and that the team were all good men.

He kept it short and to the point.

'Right, everyone knows what to do; we just have to get on with it now. We go in, hit them hard – bags of aggression – get our man and get out of there. They won't be expecting us and they won't know what the fuck hit them.'

Chapter Thirty

The storm was picking up as the helicopter lifted off.

Gusts of wind ran before the weather front like eager outriders ahead of the main army, lifting flurries of snow off the tops of pine trees and whipping them into the helicopter windscreen as they flew low overhead.

Arkady switched on the wipers; they were flying straight into the wind and it made a huge howling noise around them. The idea was to drop the assault party ten miles north, and therefore upwind, from the camp, meaning they could approach it with the wind at their backs. Magnus reckoned it would make a significant reduction to their frostbite exposure, to have the brunt of the wind on their rucksacks rather than in their faces.

The aircraft was completely blacked out; Arkady had his flight helmet on with his night-vision goggles down. He had to have the ambient light magnification turned up highest because the low, heavy cloud deck cut out any moon or starlight. He needed all the illumination he could get so that he could fly the aircraft low to the trees to avoid radar detection.

205

Alex sat with the others in the noisy, black cargo bay, shivering with cold. He was used to flying in Africa with the clam-shell doors at the back open, enjoying the cool rush of air through the cabin and the view out of the rear. That same breeze now would kill him.

The wind began throwing the machine around and they had to hang onto the aluminium struts of the cargo bay to stay on the bench. Then the underside of the helicopter crashed through the top branches of a tall larch.

Fuck!

Alex knew Arkady was a good pilot but sometimes his machismo made him take unnecessary risks. Alex stood up and made his way forward, holding onto the cargo straps on the walls. He poked his head through the door into the cabin, where they had the heaters on full blast, and had to clutch the doorframe hard as they lurched in a gust. He recovered and stared out of the front window, but without his NVGs he could see only the ice-rimed edges of the window panels and the lashing snow that the wipers constantly fought to clear.

'Take it easy, huh?' he shouted to Arkady, who grunted in reply.

'How long?' he shouted to Yamba, who checked the GPS on the instrument panel and the map on his knee.

'Five minutes.'

Alex nodded and then stumbled back to the others to get ready to go. After five minutes, Yamba joined them and they stood up and groped their way to the back of the cargo bay, weighed down by their webbing, weapons and rucksacks, and holding their skis and poles tied in a bundle that would hang down from their waists as they lowered themselves.

Arkady had them in a drifting hover as he tried to find a gap in the trees to lower them into.

'LZ!' he shouted through his headset mike to Yamba in the back, who hit the switch to open the rear doors and lower the ramp. Hydraulics whined, a gap opened in the back of the aircraft and immediately the wind burst in, eagerly clawing at the hole as it widened. A large black chasm opened, which howled with wind and snow.

Arkady was now struggling to hold the aircraft in position as the gusts kept shoving it away from the small clearing.

'Make it quick!' he yelled.

Yamba kicked the long coil of rope out of the back; they were all going to go down on just the one line as the wind would tangle up three ropes. It was clipped onto a hardpoint high at the side of the doors so that the men could hold it easily. Pete had volunteered to go first; he lowered his bundle of skis and poles over the edge of the ramp, gave a thumbs up, adjusted his rifle across his chest and then walked backwards into the abyss. The others couldn't see, because his face was obscured by his ice mask, goggles and hood, but he was grinning quietly. Events were beginning to edge over his danger threshold and he was enjoying himself.

He lowered himself down. As Yamba peered out after him, his white form dwindled into the darkness. Alex and then Magnus followed him and, to Yamba, it seemed that a human being could not survive in the thrashing black maelstrom into which they disappeared.

Once they were down, Alex gave a quick double click on his radio transmit button: the rope began to disappear back into the darkness and the noise of the huge aircraft above them drifted away as Arkady moved on to his next objective.

They were now alone.

Even with their NVGs lowered it was hard to see anything because of the amount of snow in the air around them, both falling and being whipped up from the ground; contrast in the subsequent whiteout was limited. The wind raged through the branches of the trees like a maniac, bowing and snapping them.

They hunched together for some shelter and Magnus, as calm as ever, peered at his map in its clear plastic case around his neck and then checked the compass and GPS strapped onto his forearms. To Alex he looked like an alien – the single lens of the NVG stuck out of the funnel of his parka hood like a strange snout. The creature came close and shouted in Alex's ear over the noise, 'We move this way!' He gestured behind him to the south.

Alex slapped his arm to signal a response rather than trying to shout over the wind. They clipped their toes into the ski bindings and Magnus led off, followed by Pete and then Alex.

The Norwegian was never happier than when he had his sniper rifle strapped across his back and was heading out into a storm with his skis on. He set off at a steady pace, poles rising and falling in time with his long, sliding strides. Everything moved in a graceful rhythm, the heel coming away from the ski on each step as he coasted forward. The other two followed with a less relaxed, choppier motion. They had ten miles to cover to the camp.

They should have plenty of time to do all this; Alex was beginning to wonder if he had allowed too much time and set off too early. They couldn't survive out in the open in this weather for long.

The storm was rising. The noise of the wind had become a constant base roar with higher-pitched screams over-laid on it. The blizzard was tearing at any loose clothing, flapping and billowing their parkas, making it look as if they had the outlines of madmen jumping around them.

With the constant buffeting Alex felt it was like trying to move with a snarling snow leopard on his back, bowing him down under its weight, ripping at his clothing with its claws and roaring right in his ear.

Ice particles drummed on the hood of his parka in a continuous barrage and he began to get earache on the left-hand side of his head – the storm was northeasterly, they were heading south and so the left side of his body was more exposed. He was at the back of the group and, even with his rucksack taking the brunt of the wind, the wind chill on his legs, head and left side was down to minus seventy degrees C.

He was a large man, well clothed and burning calories with the skiing, but even with these factors the wind was sucking the heat out of him faster than he could produce it. His core body temperature began to drop.

He could feel the straps of his pack cutting into his shoulders; it was heavy with the weight of the mines and Shmel rockets. His fingers hurt like hell, the cold ache from his left ear had increased and spread across that side of his head, and he forgot to keep flexing his hands on the ski poles to keep their circulation going.

As he got colder and more tired his reactions slowed and he became clumsy. He had a picture of Magnus's effortless gait in his head, which he tried to emulate, but his rhythm began to go and his steps became shorter and less economic. He failed to balance himself when they skied over a tree root and simply flopped over.

His shout of alarm was loud enough to reach Pete, just ahead, who yelled, 'Magnus!'

The leading figure stopped and neatly flicked each ski round in turn with a flowing movement, as elegant as a ballet dancer. Alex floundered in the snow, furious with

209

himself for the fall. The shock of it had woken him up and he shouted at himself in his head: *Fucking hell, Alex! Keep up!*

As Magnus skied back towards him Alex managed to use his poles to lever the weight of himself and his heavy pack back upright. The effort left him feeling weak and giddy, but he was determined not to slow the team down.

'No, I'm fine, I'm fine!' he shouted at Magnus. 'Let's crack on!' He jabbed forward with the handle of his right ski pole.

Magnus looked at him for a moment; he was watching him carefully for the first signs of hypothermia: clumsiness and slurred speech. He knew that the sufferer was often immune to them himself, as his brain functions begin to shut down. However, he didn't want to counteract his commander directly so he leaned close to Alex and shouted over the wind, 'I think you go in the middle now, yes?'

Alex nodded, lumbered in front of Pete and they set off again.

After another five minutes they came to a slight hill and Magnus sidestepped up it. Alex skied up towards him and then, as the incline started, fell over again; Pete only just managed to stop in time.

Alex lay on the snow. It felt comfortable and he had the same pleasant sensation as when falling asleep in a boring meeting. Feelings were moving away from him: the annoying pain of the cold and the bellowing wind were retreating. His vision blurred, and he didn't really care about the mission much, it no longer seemed such a high priority.

Magnus stepped back down the slope and looked at the two of them: Alex on the ground and Pete swaying on his skis. 'OK, now we make the camp!' he shouted at them, and looked around.

'Come! We go over here!' He dragged Alex to his feet and

got him into shelter behind a large pine tree. 'Get some food down him!' he shouted to Pete.

He unclipped his skis, stuck them in the snow and shrugged off his pack to get his entrenching tool out. He cast around him for a minute until he found a large drift of snow packed up against the hill.

He set to work cutting into the side of it to make a snow cave. With his experience and the small spade he quickly cut blocks of compacted snow out, making a narrow entrance passage, and then widened it inside. He made a rectangular chamber just big enough for the three of them and then poked a small air hole through the roof with the end of his ski pole. He dragged Alex in out of the wind, followed by Pete, and then sealed up the entrance with the blocks of snow. Alex was shivering uncontrollably now. He tried to stop it but his body was shaking as if were in the grip of an evil spirit.

Inside it was still minus thirty-five but they were out of the killer wind; it was also pitch black. Magnus switched on a headtorch with a low-wattage LCD light.

He set his hexiburner going on the floor and made an energy drink with melted snow. He then fed them both the hot, sugary liquid and some high-energy rations.

Being out of the wind and taking on a steady flow of warm liquid and calories all meant that Alex's core body temperature rapidly climbed back up and he quickly regained his faculties. He felt tired and weak but was at least alert again.

Having solved the emergency, Magnus could now move on to assessing if there were secondary ones.

He pulled Alex's bulky outer mittens off. 'Hold your fingers out straight,' he said. Alex tried but had difficulty; they had frozen into claws from clutching his ski poles.

Magnus pulled his fingers straight for him, took his outer

gloves off easily and then began peeling off his inner glove liners. His right one came off fine, but as he was pulling away at the left hand one, the thin silk glove stuck on his little finger. It was frozen solid on to it.

Magnus paused, looked at it closely with his torch, made a 'Hmm,' noise and then said, 'OK, we leave it a while.' He turned to Pete and began the same process on him, without any problems.

Alex's hands were red and swollen; as the circulation came back into them he felt a biting pain. He shook them. 'Ah! Hurts like shit!'

Magnus nodded. 'OK, well, this is good. So we are warming up. Let me try the left hand again.'

This time the thin glove liner peeled away from the skin. Magnus peered closely at the hand with his headtorch; the little finger was frozen stiff and was white and waxy in appearance, the skin hard from ice crystals under it.

He manipulated it gently. 'Do you feel this?'

'No.'

The air in the cave had warmed up but was still only minus ten so without internal circulation the finger remained frozen solid.

Magnus frowned. 'OK, so we now have, er, the problem.' He cleared his throat. 'Hmm, you have what you call "wooden finger".'

'That doesn't sound good.'

'No, it's not – the burns are very severe. When the tissue thaws out it will blister and then rot.'

'So what do we do?'

'Well, we cut it off.'

'What?' Alex stared at him. 'Are you joking?' He still felt light-headed from the cold, and Magnus's usual understated tone had confused him.

The Norwegian shook his head and continued, 'No, we will have to amputate it now. It is dead and will have to come off sometime anyway. This is the last chance that we will have to operate on it before the mission gets going and we don't know how long everything in Moscow will take. It could be days before we can operate on it, and if you leave it that long you would risk getting gangrene and septicaemia.'

He looked straight at Alex, who stared back at him, grappling with the dilemma. Magnus's logic was faultless but he was thinking, It's not your fucking finger!

Magnus continued, 'We cut it away and put the field dressing on. No problem.'

Alex remained silent.

He could see what Magnus meant about there being no time to operate once the op was underway, and the idea of septicaemia didn't appeal. He had seen cases in Africa – the rigors it caused were not pleasant and usually fatal.

But still, it was *his* little finger and he suddenly felt very attached to it. Every fibre urged him to just leave it for now. However, one of his traits, both in his personal life and as a commander, was not shirking when it came to making hard decisions.

Alex didn't say anything but slowly drew his bayonet from its scabbard on his shoulder webbing and gave it to Magnus. It was the same blade that Lara had used to cut her hair off; the irony of its different purpose now was not lost on him.

He stretched his hand out.

Magnus hefted the knife. 'I am afraid I have to cut into the living flesh or there is no point in doing it.'

'I'll help you, yeah?' Pete asked Alex, who nodded slowly.

They lay Pete's assault rifle on its side on the floor of the cave; Alex sat down next to it and put his finger on the metal breech casing. Pete kneeled behind him, reached both arms around him and held his hand firmly in place.

Magnus touched the edge of the blade on the skin just below the second joint; Alex felt how cold it was. Every instinct screamed at him to pull his hand away.

Magnus tried to do it quickly before he could register what was happening but the bone was too tough to slice through and he ended up having to saw and hack at it. Alex bellowed with pain and tried to pull his hand away but Pete's grip was too hard. Eventually the bone cracked and the knife sliced through the remaining flesh.

Alex moaned through gritted teeth and clutched his wrist, blood jetted in pulses across the narrow confines of the cave.

Magnus quickly wrapped a pressure dressing over the stump. 'Grip your wrist here,' he instructed calmly to get Alex to reduce the blood flow to his hand. He then set about binding the dressing onto the stump with bandages.

Eventually he had stanched the bleeding and he sat back to admire his handiwork. He nodded with quiet satisfaction. 'Yes, this will do.'

Alex's face was screwed up and his eyes closed as he fought against the pain.

Things were *not* going according to plan.

Chapter Thirty-One

Lara lay in bed in her luxurious flat and wondered what was happening to Alex.

He might have started the attack by now. She knew it was cold, dark and dangerous where he was. Siberia was a frozen hell and the MVD didn't mess about with people who opposed it.

And what was happening to Sergey, drinking with Krymov? The President frightened her – he was a creep and a sadist. She wanted Sergey to be away from him.

She wasn't sure who she was more worried about – Sergey or Alex. The two men were both so different: Sergey loud and manic, Alex quiet and brooding. One had conceived this whole crazy plan and the other was now effecting it.

But they both meant so much to her. Was she a terrible person because she loved them both? That guilty question harried her as much as her concern for them.

She knew she had a big day ahead of her and had tried going to bed early but the thoughts chasing themselves around her head were like a record stuck on one lyric. Eventually they so unsettled her that she sat up and put the light on.

She needed something to take the needle off the record – a short, intense experience to distract her. She pushed aside the covers and walked naked across to the huge bookshelves she had had fitted – following Cicero's dictum that a room without books is like a body without a soul.

She stared up at a row of spines and dragged her fingers lovingly across them, sensing the physicality of the words they contained.

Anton Chekhov, *Selected Short Stories*.

Perfect.

An elegant index finger curled over the top of the book and hooked it down.

She settled back into bed and flicked through the pages.

Two friends once met in a railway station; one was lean and the other was fat. The fat man had just finished dinner at the station; his lips were still buttery and as glossy as ripe cherries.

She never quite knew how Chekhov did it. How he slipped a character under her skin, without her noticing it. However he did it, it worked.

After reading three short stories Lara's eyelids were drooping. She folded the page and put the book in the empty space next to her in the bed. She leaned over it to switch off the light and then lay on her side, pressed her cheek into her pillow, pushed her hand under it and drew her legs up.

She turned her head quickly and kissed her pillow good night, still unsure which name to whisper.

Chapter Thirty-Two

The noise of the storm outside the snow cave had begun to die down.

Alex was feeling more able to function with all the hot drinks and rations inside him and a couple of hours' rest. His finger hurt like hell but it was hardly an incapacitating wound. He wrapped it up well and stuffed his hand back in his mitten.

They still had four miles to go to the camp and then a lot of business to attend to before the prisoners were on parade at 6 a.m. They strapped their kit back on and prepared to go outside. The wind was still strong but without the fury it had had before.

Magnus led off, followed by Alex. They skied hard, conscious that they had lost a lot of time and still had much to do.

On the way in to the camp they went through a logged clearing about two miles out that was large enough for the helicopter to get into. Magnus worked out the eight-figure grid reference on his GPS and they designated it as LZ 2. As they got nearer the camp, the clearings increased and Alex selected another extraction point, called LZ 1. He had to play off the balance between needing to be able to reach the helicopter as fast as possible whilst at the same time not wanting to land it near all the machine guns in the camp. LZ 1 was the nearest he wanted to land. If they lost the chopper then they would be spending a lot of time in MVD prison cells having the shit beaten out of them, and he wasn't keen on that.

In the clearing, Alex got his VHF set out and transmitted both sets of LZ co-ordinates in an encrypted burst to Arkady and then to Colin.

At 4 a.m. they arrived at the camp. The forest edge thinned out as it neared the two-hundred-metre cleared zone around it. They buried their skis and Alex crept forward on his stomach to observe the outer perimeter from under a tree with his binoculars. It was still dark but with night sights he could see enough. The main problem was flurries of snow that swept in overhead from the forest behind him, obscuring his view. In the gaps between them he could make out the watchtowers, single razor-wire fence and some of the support buildings in the outer area behind it.

They were on the north side of the camp that had borne the brunt of the storm, and he could see snowdrifts piled up on the sides of the buildings and a snowmobile antenna poking up out of a drift. A glance at the windows of watchtowers showed them covered over with a rime of ice that the guards had not yet cleared away.

Also, as Magnus had predicted, the ground blizzard was in full swing. The open space in front of him was covered in snowdrifts like the waves of the sea; the wind was whipping ice particles over them, creating the effect of a rapid fog streaming across the ground. With that, the snow flurries and the iced-up windows he doubted the guards could see anything. It was time to find out.

He headed back into the woods and found the others. They all stripped off their outer parkas so that they had just their snow smocks over their webbing. Then they quickly pulled the Gortex camouflage sheets out of their rucksacks and fitted the elastic straps over their hands and feet so that the sheet covered the whole of the back of their bodies and heads. A last check of their radios and rifles, a round of silent, grim nods and they were ready.

Alex used the compass strapped on his left forearm to take a bearing that he could follow to a point exactly between two of the towers and then led the way. They crawled out of the forest in a line behind him so as to minimise the frontal area they presented to the enemy. With the sheets stretched over them, they were just a patch of white on a white background with a white fog blowing over them. He felt sure they wouldn't be detected visually. Their experiments with the space blankets had shown that they couldn't be seen with infrared either.

Moving on elbows and knees across two hundred metres was hard work at the best of times. With his head down under the sheet Alex couldn't see anything, and had to keep checking his compass. The last thing he wanted to do was crawl around in circles under the eyes of the MVD.

After his recent experience he was also very concerned about the frostbite risk. The Gortex sheeting kept most the stinging ice particles off him, he could hear them drumming on it, but some whipped in under it and he could feel his legs and crotch beginning to grow very cold. He increased his pace, huffing and puffing now as he shuffled along. He paused in the dip between two drifts, twisted round and lifted the sheet to peer out and check that the others were still with him. A blast of ice particles hit his face and rattled on his goggles but he saw Magnus and then Pete slip over the crest and crawl down next to him.

He stuck his head under Magnus's sheet and shouted, 'Halfway,' in his ear. He could feel the familiar cold ache setting in on his exposed ankles and calves. He and his men couldn't stay here long. He scuttled over the remaining ground as fast as he could.

When they finally arrived at the perimeter fence there was a drift of snow up against it. Alex wriggled down into the soft upper layers so that he was less exposed to view; the others did the same as they waited for him to cut through. He pulled the wire cutters out of a pocket in his smock and attacked the razor fence. His hands were shaking again with cold but he got both mittens on the long handles and yanked at them hard, wincing at the pain from his missing finger. He was careful to cut only three of the lowest strands once, so that the team could crawl through and then bend the pieces back into place.

They wriggled through one by one and then shuffled over to a gap between two machine sheds just inside the perimeter. Alex felt hugely relieved; they had not been detected and were inside.

It was 4.30 a.m. – they had an hour and half to get their tasks done and be in place for roll call. After a quick round of silent thumbs up and a slap on the back each from Alex, the other two men melted away into the darkness. The lights on the inner perimeter fence illuminated it but everything else was dark. Apart from the guards in the watchtowers overlooking it, the prison was deserted and quiet, the main body of MVD soldiers still in bed in their barracks.

Alex pulled the VHF out of his rucksack and sent a single command word to Arkady. He then packed the set up and slipped around the corner of the shed, his senses coming alive like an animal on the hunt. Objects were sharply defined and the smallest sounds became loud as his adrenalin flowed.

He had a map of the camp in his mind and a list of objectives to achieve. He looked around for the first of these, crouched down and then ran towards it.

Fifteen miles north of the camp in a clearing in the forest, a huge set of helicopter rotors stuck up out of a snowdrift.

The Euromil-17-1V was five metres high from the bottom of its wheels to the top of the rotor shaft, but all but the rotors and the last metre of engine casing were hidden.

After they had dropped the assault team off, Arkady had gone in search of a place to land, lie up and wait until he was contacted again by Alex. He and Yamba had spent the night on the freezing floor of the cargo bay with the VHF set next to their heads.

As soon as the codeword came through, Yamba acknowledged it and shrugged out of his bag.

'OK, my friend, let's go,' he muttered. He connected a large fan heater to a car battery, climbed up the access ladder to the engine compartment over his head and shoved it inside to warm the engines up.

Arkady went through to the cockpit to start pre-flight checks; it was dark because of the snow pressed up against the windows. After ten minutes, when he thought the engines would be warm enough, he pressed the starter motor button and the AI-9V auxiliary power unit whined.

In the darkness above the snowdrift the rotors began to turn slowly.

After he left Alex, Magnus followed his memorised map of the camp and made his way west, keeping in the shadows and scuttling, bent double, between buildings.

He headed for the sawmill complex. Outside this there was a large lumberyard where the logs were brought in and piled up in stacks. No one was at work at this time, but he did a double check around the yard before he clambered up a twenty-foot-high pile of logs. The ends pointed in towards the parade ground.

A thick layer of snow had built up on top of these and he walked carefully through it, balancing on the slippery surface, until he was at the end. Once there, he quickly made a nest in the snow with an insulated groundsheet and lay down so that he was out of sight from anyone below and was not overlooked by a watchtower.

He pulled the rucksack off his back containing his sniper equipment. His L115A3 Long-Range Rifle came out first; he unfolded the stock, screwed the suppressor on the muzzle and balanced it on its bipod in front of him. A box magazine of five 8.59mm rounds was already clipped into it.

Peering down the SIMRAD night filter, which was attached to his normal Schmidt & Bender sights, he could see a ghostly green image of the parade ground platform between the crosshairs. He then pulled out his laser range finder and measured the distance accurately: 400 metres, which was fine – the rifle could go out to 1100 metres.

He set about estimating the windage; he was west of the parade ground now with the wind blowing from the north so there would be some effect on the round. The wind speed was dropping all the time as the storm exhausted itself but he still reckoned it was Force 5, so he clicked the windage drum on the sights up to the appropriate setting and looked back down them at his target. He could adjust it again as the wind dropped.

Having got the rifle ready he pulled his white Gortex sheet over him so he was completely covered, wrapped himself up in the insulated groundsheet and waited.

Pete and Alex were also busy. They both moved quickly and silently between buildings, hurrying to get their jobs done before the guards started rousing the prisoners at 5.30 a.m.

When everything was complete they settled into positions near the inner perimeter wire and waited.

Chapter Thirty-Three

The MVD colonel straightened his peaked cap, brushed his gold epaulettes down on his greatcoat and nodded to his driver sitting across the other side of the cab.

He engaged the tracks and the huge Vityaz ATV lumbered forward through the forest, crushing small trees in its way. It was painted in standard Russian army white camouflage with a large MVD flag flying from the radio antenna. They broke out onto the open ground around the camp and headed for the gate on the north side, snow spewing out from the tracks and the vehicle rising and falling over the undulating snowdrifts like a ship in a heavy sea.

The guard corporal sat up in his watchtower as they emerged and called down to the gate: 'MVD Vityaz approaching. Is anyone expected?'

The sergeant in the hut next to the gate sounded surprised. 'No, get the Kord out.' He pressed a buzzer to the main guardroom. It was just before 6 a.m., when parade started, so most of the shift were busy with that. He would have to use the men in his guardroom here to deal with the arrivals.

The corporal and the two privates with him in the tower swung the Kord 12.7mm heavy machine gun out. The gunner slapped a fresh ammo belt into it, cocked the weapon and aimed it at the ATV.

It was driving slowly and steadily towards them. When it reached the gate it was illuminated by the floodlights under the tower and stopped at the large razor-wire barrier. The sergeant came out of the guardroom next to it and walked forwards, looking at the huge machine suspiciously. Other guards came out and stood around the gate watching uncertainly.

The passenger door in the high cab opened and the MVD colonel clambered down onto the tracks and then jumped onto the snow.

Bogdan and Colin had driven all night across country from Krasnokamensk. The Para had a lot of experience driving tracked Russian vehicles in Africa and the Vityaz had the same steering system.

Likewise, Bogdan had been in the Russian army long enough to be able to do a good impression of an imperious officer.

'Who's in charge here?' he barked at the sergeant on the other side of the wire.

The man shifted the assault rifle on his shoulder nervously. 'I am, sir!' he snapped back.

Bogdan surveyed him disdainfully. 'I'm Colonel Bulgakov of the Interior Ministry Far Eastern Command; I have special information to give to Commandant Bolkonsky in person.'

'What's it about, sir?'

Bogdan kept his voice curt and only just under control. 'It's with regard to a certain prisoner. We have been patrolling the area for a team of saboteurs. This is an official matter.'

The sergeant sounded distrustful but slightly nervous. 'Right, why didn't you radio it in, sir?'

Bogdan exploded, 'If I could have got the clearance to fucking well radio it in, don't you think I would have done? It's an official investigation! Do you think I like riding around in this weather! Just open the fucking gate, Sergeant. Bolkonsky will shoot you if I don't get this information to him now!'

The sergeant paused and then gestured to the guards next to him, who pulled the long metal bar back from across the gates and swung them open.

Bogdan was relieved; he hadn't expected the sergeant to be that difficult and he had only just got away with it. He turned to get back into the cab; as he did so the wind carried gusts of sound from the loudspeaker over the parade ground, blaring out the names and destinations of the work teams for that day.

He climbed back into the cab and shut the door, glancing nervously at Colin, who kept his face straight, engaged the tracks and drove through into the camp.

Chapter Thirty-Four

Roman Raskolnikov woke up and wished he hadn't.

He had been racked all night by fear of his inevitable death in the sawmill that day, but had then drifted off into a deep sleep for half an hour just before the guard banged the metal bar at the end of the hut to wake them up.

He shrugged the old blanket off his head and stuck his head out. His body ached from shivering all night. The guards were going up and down the central aisle between the two rows of towering bunks, shouting and shoving people awake.

Men swore and stumbled around in the dim light looking for their boots under the bottom bunks. Two trusties had the easy work of carrying the huge bucket of nightsoil on a long metal pole. People stood back as they made their way along the aisle.

Shubin, the team leader, was at the bottom of his bunks, shouting: 'Come on, get down here!'

Raskolnikov knew his fate couldn't be avoided. He swung his legs onto the ladder and moved like an automaton down the rungs.

Vadim had obviously told the other politicals what the guards were planning to do and they looked as depressed as he did when they saw him. The nine men of the 33rd work team walked out to roll call as if they were all condemned.

Roman stood to attention, under the arc-lit night, amongst the ranks of black-clad prisoners, waiting to hear what he had imagined hearing so many times before.

The work roster was read out from the platform: 'The following teams are on forest detail: 43rd, 21st ... The following teams are on construction detail: 57th, 65th ... The following teams are on sawmill detail: 9th, 82nd, 57th, 78th –' come on! They were playing with him now – '44th, 56th and 33rd.'

There – they had left it until last, a final sadistic ploy.

That was it then, it was all coming true. He would never see his wife, Ivana, again. Little Masha and Irina would both grow up into beautiful young women without him to look after them.

He couldn't see clearly, because of the lights shining in his face, but he was sure that Commandant Bolkonsky, standing on the platform directly in front of him in his grey greatcoat and peaked cap, was looking at him, gloating over his fate. The commandant clapped his gloved hands and flexed his shoulders in a satisfied way; he had just delivered the orders that had sent Roman to his death. He was the final stage in the system of oppression that Roman had fought against to bring freedom to Russia, and that system had just won.

Bolkonsky looked across at the machine-gunner next to him, with the bipod of his weapon resting on a chest-high wooden frame, and reached out to press the button on the podium for the siren to signal the end of roll call.

A puff of red dust went up off the forehead of the machine-gunner and the soldier fell over backwards. The gun slipped off the wooden frame and clattered onto the planking.

Commandant Bolkonsky's hand stopped in midair. He looked at the soldier on the floor, first with irritation and then alarm as he saw the bullet hole neatly drilled in his forehead.

Heavy cracks and flashes of white light exploded all around the parade ground and the power cut out, plunging the whole camp into darkness.

An MTP-2 mine went off under the main oil tanks and a sheet of orange flame shot up into the dark sky. Burning oil spattered across a wooden barrack hut, which burst into flame.

The large radio mast with the satellite antennas on it went next, a double explosion blew two of its four metal legs out and the whole structure tilted slowly over before crashing down onto the radio hut roof. The generator shed, phone lines, gas tank store and diesel station all blew up one after another.

The sound of a helicopter swirled in from somewhere outside the camp. Arkady and Yamba were both watching carefully through their NVGs in the cockpit and saw the lights cut out, the signal for them to make their first approach.

Keeping in a low hover over the treetops, Arkady used the windspeed antenna, on the outside of the aircraft in front of his window, as a crude aiming device for the 80mm rocket pods mounted on pylons just alongside the cabin; using the helicopter as a standoff artillery platform.

When he was on target he barked, 'Fire now!' to Yamba next to him. The African hit the firing switch and the first 80mm rocket screeched away from the pod by Arkady's right hand, trailing a stream of burning orange propellant sparks.

The orange dart coursed away into the night and exploded on a building behind the target. It was the right height but went wide to the west, so he adjusted the aim and then yelled, 'Fire the pod!' as he swung the aircraft in an arc across the target.

Yamba ripple-fired the remaining nineteen rockets in the pod; they shot out one after another and howled into the target; a series of white explosions stabbed across the side of the helicopter sheds. The two Mil Mi-17s inside were hit repeatedly, their fuel tanks went up and with their aluminium airframe they burned with a brilliant white light.

Arkady quickly threw the aircraft into a sharp bank and retreated back into the woods, circling round to come in and strafe the vehicle sheds, with the trucks and Vityazs, on the other side of the complex in a similar way.

Commandant Bolkonsky dived behind his podium and took cover. The entire camp was blowing up around him. Orange flames and secondary explosions were now the only light source, and thick clouds of oil smoke drifted across the parade ground. Some sort of shoulder-launched rocket was fired from just outside the inner fence and hit the door of the armoury shed by the parade ground.

From where he was, Bolkonsky crept round the edge of the podium and looked at the nine hundred prisoners in front of him. They had initially thrown themselves on the ground as well, along with their guards, but were now beginning to get up and scramble away. Bolkonsky could see that the armoury door had been blown open; if they got in there he would have a war on his hands.

His special prisoner could not be allowed to escape. He had spoken to President Krymov's First Secretary only last week and promised him that Raskolnikov would be killed; he had to get back in charge of the situation and finish the job.

He looked around him and saw the machine gun lying on the floor near him. He wasn't sure where the shot had come from that had hit the gunner and he didn't want to find out, so he reached across, pulled the machine gun behind the podium and then yelled out to the guards in front of him: 'Shoot Raskolnikov! Shoot the bastard!'

He then opened fire on where he thought Raskolnikov had gone to ground. The gun chattered and red tracer lines spat out across the parade ground; most of them went over the prisoners on the floor because, from where he was lying, Bolkonsky couldn't get the gun depressed low enough to hit anyone, but the effect was still great.

The prisoners scrambled and scattered for cover. Many had already attacked the guards, grabbing their rifles and shooting others; firefights and complete carnage broke out in front of him.

Shockwaves made him duck his head as another peal of rockets exploded on the other side of the camp, blowing up more buildings.

From where he lay on top of the log pile, Magnus saw the tracer coming from behind the podium but couldn't see Bolkonsky to shoot him so he concentrated on the guards. A man with a whip coiled at his waist brought his rifle up to his shoulder, swung it in towards Raskolnikov and fired a burst. The rounds kicked up snow amidst a group of men crawling on their stomachs away from Bolkonsky towards the gate. One screamed and sat up as a bullet went through his ankle.

Magnus centred the crosshairs on the guard's chest, to give himself the largest target area, held his breath and slowly squeezed the trigger. The impact of the heavy round sent the rifle flying up out of the guard's hands as he was knocked over backwards. Magnus calmly worked the bolt, chambered another round and looked down his scope for anyone else causing problems.

As soon as he had seen the machine-gunner go down, Alex had hit the switch on his radio detonator to blow the ten mines that he had set around the camp, and Pete had done the same, before also firing a Shmel round in through the inner fence at the armoury.

Alex was in cover near the inner perimeter and as soon as the lights went out he started cutting his way through the three fences to get to Raskolnikov. This took longer than he had expected and so he had only just cut through the final one when he heard Bolkonsky shouting from the podium and then opening fire.

Fuck!

The crazy bastard was about to shoot Roman in front of his eyes. He scrambled through the last fence, swung the Shmel launcher off his back and kneeled in firing position. He quickly pulled out the simple trigger mechanism and sights and focused on the platform. With his NVGs he could see it clearly a hundred yards away and with an area-effect weapon he didn't have to be deadly accurate.

He pulled the trigger, the tube bucked hard against his shoulder, a blast of propellant jettisoned the rocket casing out of the back of it and the fin-stabilised round screeched straight into the wooden stall. In an instant, the primary charge blew up, sending out a cloud of fuelair explosive, which then went off and took out the whole platform in a fireball.

Game over, he thought with grim satisfaction.

He swung the launcher back over his shoulder and ran out into the maelstrom of men in front of him, hunting for Roman. All the figures running around him wore the same black uniforms. A terrified man cannoned into him and turned round. A starved, whiskery face stared at him.

Alex shoved him out of the way.

'Raskolnikov!' he yelled, pushing his way through the crowd towards the area in front of the platform.

'Raskolnikov!'

232

'Over there!'

A small man with a ratty face scuttled past him but then stopped and pointed.

'Raskolnikov!'

A figure on the ground rolled over and looked up at him.

Alex didn't recognise the withered face from the photos of the national football captain, but he saw the number D-504 on his hat. He reached down and grabbed the front of his jacket to pull him to his feet; the frightened eyes widened in alarm.

'Who are you?' the man shouted.

Alex stared at him for a split-second trying to think how much he should say. They could easily be captured at this point and anything he told Roman could be divulged under interrogation.

'We've come to get you out!' he shouted back, and tried to pull him up but Roman grabbed his smock. 'Who are you?' he shouted again.

Alex realised he had to give some reassurance, the guy was in shock. 'Shaposhnikov,' he said more quietly.

Roman frowned as he tried to take it in and let go of Alex. He couldn't think how the billionaire supporter of the government was connected with this mayhem thousands of miles from Moscow, but whatever was happening was undoubtedly better than being murdered in the sawmill.

Alex saw he was mollified for the moment. 'Come on! We've got to get out!'

He dragged him stumbling towards the gap in the fence that he had cut.

Pete barged towards them from the other side of the parade ground, using the butt of his rifle to knock people out of the way. He grabbed Roman's other arm and helped propel him along.

Other prisoners had found the open armoury door now and were passing out assault rifles; the scrappy fighting intensified as convicts scurried around, crouched low in the darkness, firing indiscriminately at anything that moved. Bursts of automatic fire ripped out and stray bullets cracked and zipped all around them.

Alex dragged Roman through the gap in the fence and headed north in the direction where Bogdan and Colin were waiting in the Vityaz. He dragged Roman forward into cover behind the bakery hut. From there he began pairs fire and manoeuvre with Pete.

Alex kneeled low with his AN-94 pressed hard against his cheekbone, scanning for targets behind them. 'Prepare to move!' he barked.

Pete got a firm hold of Roman's coat collar.

'Move!'

The Aussie dashed forward, dragging Roman towards the next piece of cover.

With all the burning buildings around them, there was a lot of illumination now, and the movement attracted the attention of a pair of guards. They were running along the fence with their rifles held across their chests; they stopped and turned their weapons towards Alex.

His eyes zeroed in on them. In his hyped-up state he saw each movement slowed down so he could discern it clearly: the way one of them skidded in the snow slightly as he stopped, how the one on the left was taller and had a more natural shooter's stance as he swung the black gaping hole of his muzzle round.

Alex squinted into the V-shaped backsight next to his eye and lined it up with the sighting ring on the end of the barrel; he centred the aiming point at the bottom of the left-hand soldier's ribcage.

The AN-94 was designed for asymmetric recoil, allowing it to fire two-shot bursts without the hefty kick of a normal assault rifle.

Alex squeezed the trigger, the gun cracked out two rounds but only dug back lightly into his shoulder instead of kicking up, allowing him to traverse instantly to the right, target the next guard and drill another two rounds into him. Both targets went down and stayed there.

'Prepare to move!' Pete shouted from behind him. He was now down on one knee, hunched over the sights of his own AN-94, ready to cover Alex.

'Move!'

Alex got up, sprinted back to where Pete was and they repeated the cycle all the way towards the north gate.

They came to the corner of the final building, where they were supposed to meet the Vityaz with Colin and Bogdan, and flattened themselves in the shadows.

Alex stuck his head round the corner. The Vityaz was there but Bogdan was standing next to it in his colonel's uniform and peaked cap, with three guards with rifles held across their chests questioning him.

He caught an intense question from the sergeant: 'But, sir, *where* is your authorisation?'

'Sergeant, this is an official matter! The place is being attacked by saboteurs, you need to stop fucking around here and get back on the gate!'

Bogdan was sounding tense; this couldn't go on for much longer.

They were fifty yards away. Alex reckoned he could slot the two guards but Bogdan was now standing between him and the sergeant.

The sound of snow being scuffled by footsteps came from behind him. Alex turned round to see that Pete had it covered and had allowed Magnus to slide into the shadows with them, his sniper rifle held in front of him.

'Right, we've got three guards. I can hit two on auto; Magnus, can you take the one Bogdan is talking to? It's fifty yards.'

The Norwegian looked round the corner and saw the face of the sergeant, partially obscured by the back of Bogdan's head.

He turned back to Alex. 'Sure.'

They both crept to the corner and took up firing positions. Magnus kneeled with the barrel of his rifle wedged against the corner of the hut for extra stability and Alex stood, hunched over his sights, above him. The sergeant's head was still half hidden behind Bogdan's.

Alex clicked his rifle's selector onto full auto and took aim. 'After you,' he muttered.

Magnus's rifle coughed and the sergeant's head split in two.

Bogdan ducked and involuntarily threw his hands up around his head at the terrible sight right in front of his face.

Alex pulled the trigger and swept a long burst across the other guards, throwing them back against the machine's tracks.

They ran out from behind the hut and over to Bogdan.

'OK, let's go!' Alex yelled, and pushed Roman up into the high cab. Inside, Col hit the starter and the huge diesel roared into life, belching smoke. He spun one track forward and the other in reverse so the vehicle turned on the spot, churning snow as it went.

By the gate, the remaining guards looked towards them. They had seen their sergeant go behind the machine and then heard shots. Two men began hurrying over towards them.

'Hit the towers!' Alex shouted to Pete. The two towers along the perimeter nearest the north gate overlooked their escape route back into the woods and from there, prison guards would easily be able to fire at them. Alex didn't want to have to have to drive off in the Vityaz with two heavy machine guns chewing it up.

'Right-oh,' said Pete in his laconic way, and they both swung the Shmel launchers off their shoulders. Alex ripped a new round out of its plastic twin pack and shoved it into the tube, before they kneeled either side of the Vityaz and sighted up.

Alex squinted through the simple iron sight and saw the wooden hut on its high legs.

'Fire!' he barked.

The two rockets streaked out in different directions trailing propellant sparks and slammed into their targets. Alex's went slightly high and hit just under the roofline, but both structures exploded with orange fireballs.

'Bonza,' said Pete with a satisfied smile.

Alex grinned back at him. It was always like this when the fighting got going. It wasn't perverted bloodlust, just the high spirits of being caught in a near-death experience.

'Let's go!' he shouted, and Magnus and Pete clambered up into the cab.

'You go!' Bogdan yelled at Alex, insisting, with typical Russian machismo, on being the last in.

Alex wasn't going to have a fight with *him* as well, so he shouldered his weapon and pulled himself up.

The two guards from the gate were in range of them now and opened fire. Bogdan picked up the sergeant's rifle, dropped to one knee and snapped quick bursts back, forcing them to take cover. He turned and grabbed the handles to get up to the cab; Alex reached out to help pull him in.

The 5.45mm high-velocity round went through his chest just under his right collarbone. Alex's head was next to him and he heard the deep thud and clang as the round went through him and hit the cab metalwork.

Bogdan gave a heavy gasp and his grip went slack.

Alex grabbed him under the arms; Col was moving off and he couldn't drop him now.

'Give us a hand!' he yelled, and Magnus quickly moved next to him. Between them they dragged the limp body up into the cab, slammed the door and got on the deck as more rounds smashed the window above them and punched puffs of insulation out of the door over their heads.

'Drive!'

Col floored the accelerators and the huge machine lurched forward, smashing through the side of a storage hut and bringing it crashing down in its wake.

'Get some rounds down!' Alex yelled at Pete, and pointed at the top hatch.

The Aussie shoved it open and jumped up onto the platform between two seats, bracing himself against them as they roared off. He brought his rifle up and fired long suppressive bursts back over the roof at the guards behind them.

The Vityaz lumbered on, gaining speed.

'Fence! Get yer fooking head down!' Colin shouted and Pete ducked inside just in time.

The blunt snout of the machine hit the razor wire and took out a twenty-metre section as if it were peeling cotton threads from their posts. The higher strands above the cab were left in place and swept over it like a lethal cheese cutter.

Pete popped straight back up and continued firing; behind him the orange flames of the burning camp were impressive. He grinned as he admired his handiwork, slapped a fresh magazine into place and opened up again.

Magnus grabbed Alex's rifle and hung out of the side window, putting down more suppressive fire on the guards. Col was doing thirty m.p.h. – maximum cross-country speed – as he charged towards the first LZ extraction point in the forest. The vehicle ploughed across the snow drifts, rearing up like a behemoth on the facing slopes, the front of the tracks clawing at thin air, and then tilting over the crest and crashing down.

Alex was on the floor of the cab, desperately trying to save Bogdan. His body bounced around with the motion but Alex managed to unbutton the heavy greatcoat, uniform jacket and shirt, and push them back off both his shoulders. The Russian was bleeding heavily from a large exit wound.

Fuck, this doesn't look good.

Hot, sticky arterial blood jetted out and covered Alex's face and the front of his jacket. He blinked it aside, reached inside his smock and ripped the field dressing off his webbing strap, put there for exactly this sort of situation.

He pulled the wrapper off and stuck it in the hole; it would soak up a pint of blood. After a minute he shouted, 'Dressing!'

'Here you go!' Col ripped his own one off and chucked it across the cab. Alex tore it open and again stuck it on the wound. He didn't have much hope, though. He reached for Bogdan's pulse on the other side of his throat. It was weakening and his eyes were going hazy, the lids slowly closing like coffins.

'Three snowmobiles, six o'clock! Two blokes on each of them!' Pete yelled down from his vantage point in the hatch.

Fuck.

Decision time.

Should he try to save this probably about-to-die person

or organise defence against the new threat to the rest of the currently alive-and-well team?

Commander's dilemma. This was what he got paid for.

Alex let go of the field dressing, grabbed Col's rifle and leaned out of the other side window.

Bogdan quietly bled to death on the floor of the cab.

Just before they plunged into the forest, Alex got a glimpse of three Skidoo snowmobiles roaring over the snowdrifts towards them. The soldiers mounted behind the drivers were touting PKM light machine guns with 250-round ammo boxes.

He knew those guns could not go anywhere near the helicopter.

The Vityaz continued to plunge deeper into the forest. Col was still driving at full speed in the dark using his NVGs and working the two track-steering levers like a maniac to zigzag them between large trees and crash through the smaller ones. Lower branches scythed over the cab, forcing Pete down from the hatch and dumping their loads of snow on them.

The three Skidoos switched on their headlights, which flickered through the trees, and roared after them. Alex could hear engines snarling as gears changed and spiked rotary tracks bit deep into the snow, propelling them forward. The gunners on the back leaned their machine-gun barrels on the shoulder of the driver and began cracking off bursts of red tracer after them.

They couldn't do much to stop such a large machine, but if they weren't taken out by the time they reached the LZ then they would cause problems when the Mil came in to get them. Alex reached over Bogdan's body for the VHF set and called up Yamba. He had to shout over the noise of the engines.

'Two, this is Baba Yaga. Come in.'

'Baba Yaga, this is Two. Over.'

'Extract at LZ 2! Repeat – extract at LZ 2!'

'Roger, Baba Yaga, will extract at LZ 2. Out.'

He had bought them some room for manoeuvre.

Now, what to do about the Skidoos?

They were not going to be able to take them out from the moving vehicle – the terrain was too rugged and they had no stable firing points.

They were a couple of hundred yards ahead of them; they could just about do it.

Alex shouted, 'Snap ambush! Stop when we're in cover!'

'Right-oh!' Col called back.

He jerked the levers and they headed for a thick stand of pines. Once they were behind it he braked hard; the whole machine dipped forward and bucked on its tracks but kept moving.

'Debus!'

Alex, Magnus and Pete jumped out of the side doors, rolled over in the snow and then got up as Colin roared on in a wide loop to come back to the wood after the ambush.

They waded through deep snow back into the trees and spread out, each pressing their rifles hard against a tree trunk to stabilise their aim and waited.

The Skidoos didn't seem to have noticed their slowing down; Alex could hear their engines roaring and see the flicker of their headlights through the dark trees as they came nearer.

Alex tried to remember how many rounds he had in this magazine – about half full he thought. Fifteen rounds. He had thirteen more magazines in bandoliers but there wasn't time to switch now. He brought the rifle up to his shoulder to fire, hugging the backsight close in against his cheek, feeling the freezing metal stick to his skin.

In an ambush situation like this there was no time for

subtlety and the carefully aimed shots that he would normally have liked. He slid his hand down the casing and flicked the selector on full auto.

They waited until all three machines had burst into view, the blinding headlights making easy targets as they weaved towards them.

Alex squeezed the trigger and the weapon went cyclic, roaring and bucking hard in his hands this time, spitting out rounds at a rate of 600 per minute.

Two seconds and the magazine clicked empty. The other two guys kept up longer bursts.

The snowmobile Alex had targeted gave a surge of revs as the driver collapsed forward and then ploughed into a drift and stopped. The passenger tumbled off the far side.

Alex whipped a fresh mag out from his webbing, yanked the old one off, slapped it into place and cocked the weapon hurriedly. The other two snowmobiles had also been stopped dead; he didn't know where their soldiers were.

Silence settled slowly over the great wood like a cover thrown gently over a bed.

His breathing sounded obscenely loud after all the engine noise and crashing gunfire. He knew now there were at least two enemies out there in the wood.

He suddenly remembered Sergey rambling about dark woods in your head and finding the place of courage where the wolf drank from the river at midnight.

Well, he was in one dark forest now and he'd better find that place fast. He forced himself to be calm and use his fear; it was always there, it was just that over the years he had learned to make it work for him.

He tried to settle his breathing. Better to stay still and listen for them; any movement would just give away his position.

A huge burst of red tracer came out of a drift on his left and slapped into the tree trunk next to him, he felt it judder with the impacts that chewed off chunks of wet, white wood and sprayed them over him.

He threw himself down on the ground.

Fuck.

That was close.

Would have been better to move to a new firing position after all. They had clocked him.

He wriggled back away from the tree. At least the guy had now given his position away for Pete and Magnus to fire at.

There was a flash of brilliant white light behind him and the guy started screaming.

Phosphorous grenade; that'll shut him up.

Alex continued extracting himself rearwards from the danger zone as Pete and Magnus did pairs fire and manoeuvre. An Aussie shout of 'Left flanking!' drifted through the trees to tell him what they were doing.

'Roger!' Alex shouted back.

He'd better go right then.

He got up and stumbled forward into some open ground in front of the pines in a crouch, trying to be as quiet as possible, ever conscious of the two PKMs still out there and pointing at him.

Flashes of red gunfire stabbed out at him from his right. He threw himself down into the snow and could hear Pete and Magnus shouting: 'Prepare to move!' and 'Move!', interspersed with bursts of suppressive fire as they tried to outflank and kill their enemy.

Alex immediately wanted to stick his head up and see what was going on but the old infantry skills mantra came back to him: dash, down, crawl, advance, sights, fire.

He wriggled sideways away from the position where he

had gone to ground so the enemy didn't blow his head off if he just stuck it back up in the same place. Then he shuffled forward to gain some ground and pressurise his opponent. He quickly popped up with his rifle in place, scanning forward over his sights. He was lucky he had bothered with his drills.

The PKM burst of red tracer scythed across his old position from behind a tree on his right, sending up puffs of snow.

The next burst walked its way in towards him.

This is going to get me.

He started running back for cover in his original position in the pine trees, but stumbled over a branch hidden under the snow.

The PKM gunner knew he had him on the run and chased after him across the open ground. He stopped and raised his weapon to his shoulder, all senses fixed on firing at Alex's prone figure.

A noise to his left made him look over his shoulder as the Vityaz burst out of a screen of birch trees and roared over him.

Chapter Thirty-Five

'Where are they?' Yamba barked into his headset in frustration.

Arkady shrugged next to him in the cockpit, and they both continued scanning the ground out of the windscreen.

The Russian scratched his stubbly chin anxiously and grunted. His hands were cold on the controls, despite the heating being on full blast; they had the rear ramp open, ready for the extraction, and the wind howled around the cockpit.

The Mil had been circling for five minutes, burning up precious fuel. Yamba got out of the co-pilot seat and looked out of the side door just behind the cabin, scanning the woods in the grey dawn light for some sign of the Vityaz.

Arkady shouted, 'There! Portside!'

He had seen its broad headlights flick on and off three times. He swooped in low and flared hard over the LZ. As he hovered, the heavy rotors thumped away and blew a blizzard of snow off the ground, exposing the two-foot tree stumps left after logging; there was no way he could land.

Yamba stood at the side door, peering out and shouting directions back over his helmet mike on the intercom. Arkady couldn't make out the ground in the weak dawn light and the mass of snow blasting up around them. It was crucial to be able to hover low enough for the men to climb onboard, but at the same time not hit a stump. The slightest bump would tilt the whole machine, meaning that the rotors would then hit the ground, shredding them and flipping the machine on its back.

'Thirty feet!'

'Twenty feet!'

'Ten!'

'Five!'

'Hold!'

The Vityaz had pulled up on the edge of the clearing and the five remaining men jumped down – four in white combat smocks and one in ragged black prison garb. They stood next to it, shielding their faces from the blast of snow.

Once it was obvious they could go no lower, Yamba waved across to them from the rear ramp and they stumbled forward, clutching their weapons; one hand over their faces against the wind.

Alex clambered up on a stump, pulled Roman up next to him and gave him a leg up to Yamba, who grabbed his jacket and pulled him onboard.

The rest of the team clambered up and lay exhausted on the floor of the cargo bay as Yamba hit the hydraulic switch to close the door.

Chapter Thirty-Six

The helicopter swooped in out of the dark sky over Krasnokamensk airport.

Alex watched the control tower closely from the co-pilot seat, using binoculars to see if the news of the raid had reached the MVD guards there. The mercenaries had blown up the phone lines, radio hut, helicopters and Vityazs at the camp to make sure that it was sealed off from the world. He knew they would have auxiliary radios and generators somewhere but, with the chaos caused by the armed prisoners, it would take them a while to get them working and then raise the airport.

The plan was that they would have bought at least the half-hour it took to fly from the camp to the airport and take off. If they hadn't, and the guards came out shooting, then there would be a hell of a firefight before they managed to take off – if they did at all.

They had fired off all their rockets, their main armament, and then landed quickly en route to detach the pods so they weren't seen by the tower. However, they still had a lot of firepower. Colin and Pete waited with their Shmel launchers ready by the rear door and Yamba had the AGS-30 30mm grenade launcher set up there. If there was any resistance then Arkady would spin the tail round, drop the ramp and they would unload a lot of munitions.

Arkady called up the tower.

'Krasnokamensk Tower, this is GeoScan team, landing for outbound flight to Novosibirsk in Gulfstream G550. Request permission to take off.'

No response.

Alex twisted the magnification slightly to improve the focus; he could see the wide windows on the tower over-looking the runway. The lights were on inside but from this angle above he couldn't see if there was anyone there.

Was this just a sleepy provincial airport at 7 a.m. or a trap?

'Try them again,' he instructed Arkady without taking his binoculars off the tower.

'Krasnokamensk Tower, this is GeoScan team, landing ...'

'GeoScan team, this is Krasnokamensk Tower, you are cleared to take off.' The man sounded groggy as if he had just woken up.

Alex exhaled and then turned round in his seat and shouted through to the cargo bay, 'Stand down!'

Arkady took them in behind the large hangar and they quickly hurried over to the side door.

Stepping inside and seeing the white plane all fuelled up and ready to go was a huge relief. But they weren't out of it yet. Yamba hit the switch on the main door motors and Arkady fired the engines and then taxied them forward.

They strapped themselves into the big white seats for take off.

It was only when they had passed the tower and Arkady eased back on the yoke, the wheels lifted up and they rocketed away skywards that the whole team let out a huge whoop.

In his blood and smoke-stained battle gear, Alex jumped out of his seat and punched the air, yelling with the others. They all danced around the cabin, jumping up and down and shouting.

'Fucking did it!'

'Fook you, yer bastards!' Col jabbed a V-sign back at the airport.

Pete ran into the cockpit and slapped Arkady on the shoulder. The Russian was celebrating with them and trying to fly at the same time.

Pete came back through the galley and found some champagne bottles in a rack, which got sprayed all over Sergey's expensive white carpet, walls and ceiling. Eventually they sank back down into their seats, exhausted.

Roman was still sitting in his filthy black clothes looking shocked but pleased. After two years in hell this was a monumental change for him.

When the assault team had calmed down, Alex was able to stop laughing and actually think straight. He pulled his mobile phone out of his webbing, but had to wait until they flew over Irkutsk until it acquired a signal. First he sent a text to Sergey, Lara and Grigory: 'Baba Yaga is returning with her stupa' – Sergey's idea, as ever: something about the bronze pestle that she flew round Russia in. Alex grimaced and pressed send.

Then his phone bleeped as incoming texts registered. He opened the one from Grigory, which told him to get to Moscow as fast as possible so Raskolnikov could make the morning news programmes. If they landed on schedule at 7.30 a.m. it would be a tight squeeze to make the 7.45 bulletins. Roman would need to be prepared to go on air as soon as he arrived.

Alex sent an acknowledgement and then turned to Roman

to explain what was going on. He took him into the aft section of the aircraft and told him who was behind the raid and what the plan was when they got to Moscow. Roman gaped as he grappled with the enormity of what was being planned for him. Grigory had prepared a pack of cuttings and a briefing paper to bring him up to date on what had happened over the last two years so that he could write his speech.

Before he settled to that, though, Roman disappeared into the shower unit and, for the first time in two years, was able to wash without using freezing cold water out of a concrete trough. He shaved and, looking in the mirror, was horrified by how emaciated his face looked: eye sockets hollowed out and cheekbones sticking up into his skin. He scrubbed the filth out from under his fingernails, trimmed his overgrown, yellowing toenails, and luxuriated in being warm and clean. A fresh suit of clothes was laid out there ready for him and he changed into the dark suit and tie, baggy because of his weight loss. He felt the texture of the cloth of his shirt and suddenly felt the urge to cry at how clean and soft it was after so much dirt and hardship.

Once he was ready, he settled down with a laptop in the rear section. He thought back to his footballing days and planned how he was going to give the greatest team talk of his life.

Alex slipped forward to see Arkady. 'OK, we need to get a move on. Any power you can give it, please do. We need to buy every minute of broadcast time at the start of the day so we can to get the revolution rolling.'

Arkady nodded and shoved the throttles forward.

The assault team expected that they could well be in action in Moscow as well, so they all settled back and began stripping and cleaning their weapons, removing the cordite dust from the working parts that could cause stoppages and cost their lives. Fresh weapons were also prepped from the crates in the back of the aircraft.

Magnus pulled Russian army-pattern helmets out of a box and began trying them on for size. Colin looked across at him and shouted, 'Oi! Magnus, shouldn't you 'av horns on that, like?' He gestured with two hands to indicate Viking horns sticking out of the top of his helmet.

Magnus looked up and nodded quietly. 'Hmm, yes, you're right. I had forgotten them; I think maybe I left them on my longship.'

'Yer silly booger, I'll have to find you another pair now.'

They ate a heavy meal of field rations and caviar and quails' eggs, scrounged from Sergey's fridge, before crashing out asleep on the big chairs. The cabin filled with snores as Arkady sat at the controls, swigged champagne from a bottle and powered them on to Moscow.

Chapter Thirty-Seven

Corporal Lermontov was the only radio operator to have survived the attack on the prison camp unscathed, after the main radio mast had been blown up and collapsed on the radio hut.

The surviving MVD troops had managed to rally themselves and find an auxiliary generator and radio in the wreckage, which they hoped to use to get through to Krasnokamensk airport.

A squad of six men formed a defensive perimeter in the ruins of the radio hut around Lermontov as he fiddled with the old set. Prisoners armed with assault rifles from the armoury and dead guards were still on the loose, and bursts of automatic gunfire were going off all around them. The main generator was still out of action so the only light came from the orange flames of burning wooden barrack buildings nearby. The fires crackled angrily and the smell of smoke drifted everywhere.

Lermontov shook his head to clear it as he switched on the set. He couldn't believe the speed and ferocity of the attack on the camp. Within seconds the whole place had been blown up and set alight.

He slipped the earphones over his head and the set whined

and crackled with static. He twisted the dial, trying to find the right command frequency.

'Krasnokamensk airport, this is Yag 14/10 Penal Colony, come in. Over.'

Nothing.

'Krasnokamensk air—' He had to break off as one of the soldiers behind him ripped off a long burst of fire at a prisoner behind a wall.

He eventually got through to the drowsy officer at the airport.

'We have been attacked by a superior enemy force and they have taken Prisoner Raskolnikov. Over.'

'What?'

'You need to get a message through to MVD command in Moscow immediately. Understood? Over.'

There was a pause before an incredulous voice repeated, 'Understood.'

Chapter Thirty-Eight

Major Batyuk banged on Krymov's bedroom door at his Novo-Ogaryovo residence west of Moscow, and waited.

He knew that the President had been up late drinking with Sergey and would be passed out asleep.

He banged again, louder this time, before walking in and turning the light on.

Krymov rolled over onto his back and put his hand over his face against the light. When he took it away gingerly he squinted like a bleary-eyed pig. He had passed out naked on top of the bed after his drinking session in the banya. Batyuk tried not to look at his lumpy white body.

'Mr President, I am sorry to wake you up but we have had a report from MVD command that Raskolnikov has been freed from prison and is now being flown to Moscow on a private jet.'

Krymov stared at him blankly and then suddenly sat up and looked scared. His face went white and his hands cast about the bed covers beside him.

Batyuk could see that someone needed to take charge of the situation.

'I think we should go to Air Defence Command immediately,' he suggested.

'Hmm …' Krymov seemed to have lost the power of speech and stood up to go.

'You need to get dressed first, Mr President.'

Batyuk stood aside as the major-domo scuttled into the room and dressed Krymov. As he became more conscious, he suddenly turned to Batyuk.

'What about Shaposhnikov?'

Batyuk didn't know about the SVR report from London that Sergey had been linked to Alex's journey to Krasnokamensk, so he just looked back questioningly.

Krymov continued angrily, 'Bring him with us! I want him with us. Go and wake him up *now*!'

Batyuk nodded and ten minutes later the President and Sergey stumbled down the front steps to Krymov's limo. The squads of Echelon 25 troops hurried around them and into their waiting vehicles.

The convoy drivers gunned their engines and swept out down the long driveway. Sergey sat opposite Krymov in the back of the Zil limo; both of them looked ill as the car lurched around the corners.

Krymov was in a state of shock; he had never really been a leader and liked to hide behind bureaucracy to cover it up. Now that he was presented with a shock he had lost his wits. All he felt was scared and he could not formulate a coherent plan of action. Somewhere in his mind he knew that Sergey might have something to do with all this but, at the same time, he regarded the man as his greatest source of comfort and understanding, and this emotion refused to let him see the man clearly for what he might be: a traitor.

Sergey felt sick with alcohol poisoning and fear. He had had to throw himself into his usual clownish routine last night and had drunk more than usual to cover up his worries.

The convoy roared on through the night round the deserted MKAD ring road to the junction with the A-101 southwest of the capital. They turned off left and shortly afterwards drove through the barriers into 'Moscow Military District Depot 5' and got out inside the deserted factory shed. The guards all snapped to attention as the President's entourage marched past them and they plunged eight floors down into the command centre.

It was 3.45 a.m., but luckily Lieutenant-General Mostovskoy was on duty. He walked calmly over to them as they came in, looking smart in his airforce uniform jacket and tie. He was surprised to see Sergey there as well, looking shambolic in his crumpled suit, diamond earring and messed-up hair, but his face betrayed no sign of it.

'Mr President, the situation is under control, we are tracking the terrorists' plane on the radar and we will shoot them down as soon as you give the order.'

Krymov still looked dazed and was relieved to see that someone had got a grip on the situation. He began to recover some of his normal bravado. 'Very good, Mostovskoy. D'ya hear that, Shaposhnikov?'

'Hmm,' Sergey shrugged.

Krymov turned back to Fyodor. 'Well, Mostovskoy, get this sorted out and maybe we can see if we can find a bit more control on the board of UAC for you, eh?'

For once, Fyodor's face flickered slightly.

'Yes, go ahead and blow them out of the sky.' Krymov turned to Sergey. 'Looks like that Raskolnikov bastard's going to kill himself even before Bolkonsky could, eh?' He laughed heartily.

Chapter Thirty-Nine

The red alarm on the wall flashed and the buzzer blared.

Captain Anton Brodsky and his wingman, Lieutenant Denis Chernov, were slumped in armchairs in the crewroom watching a rerun of their favourite Russian cops and robbers show, *The Specials*.

Brodsky was one of the top fighter pilots in the Russian Federation; his reactions were like lightning.

Within a second, he had leaped up, chucked his coffee cup in the bin, grabbed his helmet and was out of the door and running down the corridor, Chernov a couple of yards behind him.

Brodsky slammed open the heavy doors into the huge, underground hangar, and ran over to his large interceptor with Russian Airforce red star markings. The alarm buzzer was going, lights flashed and ground crew hurried across the chamber.

The pilots both bounded up the ladders and jumped into the cockpits of their aircraft. Brodsky didn't like what the Krymov regime had done to the economy and freedom, but, as a pilot, he was able to offset this with the sheer pleasure at the new toy that the increased military spending had given him. Since Krymov had forced the merger of all Russian aircraft manufacturers into the United Aircraft Corporation, the famous fighter aircraft design bureaus of Sukhoi and Mikoyan had come together and, with the extra money, had produced their most radical design ever.

He was now sitting in the cockpit of a brand-new, sixth-generation fighter, the Suk-MiG-41 Berkut, 'Golden Eagle', NATO designation 'Fury'.

It was an improbable-looking aircraft, as if a model aeroplane kit had been wrongly put together by a child. The main wings were mounted right at the tail, instead of in the middle of the fuselage, and pointed forward towards the cockpit instead of sweeping backwards in the usual way. Two small triangular wings, called canards, had then been stuck just under cockpit. They could be tilted quickly back and forth to a maximum angle at which they were flat against the airflow past the aircraft.

The whole thing was totally unstable in flight and would simply fall out of the air if it were not for the eighty onboard computers and automatic flight control system that made constant changes to the wing surfaces. This apparently illogical setup meant that Golden Eagle could achieve mind-bending agility in flight, from lightning-quick turns in any direction to almost being able to hover in midair. Brodsky's favourite trick was pulling a snap loop and then allowing the jet to actually drift backwards through the air for a second before powering it forward again.

The huge, twin AL-41F engines generated twenty-five tons of thrust, a massive amount for a single-seater aircraft, and powered it through its instability by thrust vectoring, using nozzles on the jets that could twist up to thirty degrees in any direction, rather like a duck waggling its tail feathers.

Brodsky wasn't sure what he was going to be shooting down today but he was looking forward to putting all this new technology into action. Sitting in his narrow cockpit, he held his arms up as the ground crew leaned in, connecting up his life-support, comms and G-systems. The suit began pressuring up ready for the massive Gs of take-off.

As he did so, the large covers over the exit ramps from the underground airbase were sliding smoothly back on their hydraulic rams. It was another Krymov regime money-no-object innovation: burying an airbase so it was impervious to first-strike missile attacks from the US. It was built in the wastes near Vologda as part of Northern Air Defence Command, against incursions from over the North Pole.

The planes were launched along underground tunnels with the same catapult turbines used on aircraft carriers. As Brodsky glanced forward through his windscreen now, he still couldn't get over the alarming feeling that he had the same view as a bullet had sitting in the barrel of a gun, except that the barrel looked as if it was blocked by a concrete wall. In fact, what he was looking at was a narrow underground corridor that gradually angled up, like the ski ramps used on carriers, so that it would fling him up into the air.

During his flight, a short runway on the surface, with arrestor wires, would be cleared with a jet engine, to allow the planes to land and then taxi down a ramp back into their subterranean lairs again.

As the technicians continued clipping in his parachute and ejector seat around him, Brodsky leaned forward and ran through his pre-flight checks. He flipped down the visor of his helmet so that he now looked like a bug-eyed alien with his oxygen mask sticking out of it like a proboscis. Inside the visor was a full-colour display that allowed him to see in all weather and at night using remote sensors all around the aircraft. As he moved his head around he could even 'see' through the floor of the cockpit.

Data was already being fed through to the display imposed

on this view from the air controllers at Central Air Defence Command in Moscow. He read the details of what he was going to be hunting that day:

Target: Gulfstream G550
Max speed: 0.8 Mach
Offensive systems: None
Defensive systems: None

The display flicked to a map showing that the target was coming in towards Moscow from the east; it had just passed Perm, so the projected intercept point was marked over the forests leading up to Nizhniy Novgorod. The map showed that once Brodsky was airborne he would accelerate to attack speed of Mach 2.9, 3552 km/h and use his new-generation, forward-looking, pulse-Doppler radar with a phased antenna array to seek out the target. Moscow command would track it and feed him updates all the way into the target.

He wondered briefly who was on the plane – terrorists? At the end of the day, he didn't know and he didn't care, he was just going to obey orders and get a huge kick out of doing it.

The Gulfstream certainly wasn't going to be much of a challenge, though.

'Weapons targeting check,' he barked out to Nadya, the onboard voice-control system, and the computer quickly overlaid various screens on his helmet display: radar, laser range finder and infrared imager.

Once in range, he could either use one of his latest air-to-air Vympel R-45 missiles with passive IR guidance, or just get close and give it a burst with the 30mm cannon. Even in the era of advanced missiles, he still carried an old-fashioned gun, because once you got into the swirling mess of a dogfight, where targets came and went in microseconds, there just wasn't time to prep, target and fire missiles. He would just get in close from behind and see what the air controller told him to do.

Brodsky finished his checks and glanced fifty yards to his left, where Lieutenant Chernov sat in the firing chamber of the other barrel of the underground base. He waved to his wingman, who acknowledged just before the black canopy automatically slid shut over his head, followed by a hiss as it pressured up.

The whole aircraft jolted and Brodsky rocked in his seat as the catapult clamped onto the hardpoints and then dragged him backwards. A shot of adrenalin went into his bloodstream – he never got over this bit.

He eased his throttles forward, building up engine thrust. The jets behind him roared red, flaming anger against the heat shield at the end of the chamber. The aircraft shook as the catapult wire pulled back to its furthest extent and wheels locked into their final slots. The whole machine was now trembling and twitching all around him like a greyhound held tight on its leash. As the forces built up, he felt it must surely snap like a twig bent too hard.

Above him, it was still pitch-black, with a strong north wind blowing snow across the flat arctic wasteland. The two huge covers had pulled back to their fullest extent, exposing the twin muzzles of Krymov's latest air defence toy.

Two flaming bullets spat out of the ground a second after the other. Already doing 300 k.p.h., they kicked in their after-burners and went vertical at a climb rate of 350 metres per second. The enormous thunder of the jets shook the ground but faded rapidly as they disappeared into the howling snow-storm on their deadly mission.

The covers slid silently back into place.

Chapter Forty

'Mr President, you can see the enemy aircraft here in red.'

Fyodor pointed above him at the huge screen that the semi-circular room was focused on. Krymov and Sergey were sitting at the large desk right in front of the screen with all the other banks of computers and technicians radiating out behind them.

'Our two Berkut aircraft are about to intercept the enemy just east of Nizhniy Novgorod up here.'

Krymov stared dully at the twin blue tracks making their way south to intercept the Gulfstream on its way to Moscow.

'I will have Captain Brodsky establish visual identification of the target before we shoot it down, and you can listen in to the radio traffic. I will now take personal command of the intercept process.' With that Fyodor gave a curt nod and walked back behind them to his large desk with an array of computer screens in front of him.

He hit several switches and then, when he spoke into the desk mike, the transmission played over loudspeakers around the room. Krymov grinned and nudged Sergey.

'Captain Brodsky, this is Lieutenant-General Mostovskoy at Air Defence Command. Do you have eyes on the aircraft yet? Over.'

A crackle of static filled the large room.

In the cockpit of his interceptor, Brodsky was howling through the night at 30,000 feet. He clicked the transmit button and his voice boomed out near Moscow. 'Yes, I have a twin-engined jet flare at my twelve o'clock.'

He had approached the Gulfstream from behind so as not to show up on its radar, which wouldn't have been able to make out much of his stealth-engineered profile, anyway. He could see the twin red stabs of the Rolls-Royce jet exhausts above him.

'I have decelerated and am keeping station with the target until further orders. Over.'

'Roger that, Berkut One. That's good, close up now and identify target as white Gulfstream G550. Over.' Fyodor was typing something on his keyboard as he said this.

'Roger. Closing now.'

There was a pause and crackle of static as the huge fighter powered up alongside the slow-moving Gulfstream.

'Roger. I have eyes on. Target aircraft is a white Gulfstream G550.'

There was another pause as Fyodor typed more commands into his system and then said, 'Roger, engage and destroy target with cannon fire. Over.'

'Engaging now.'

A harsh buzzing sound cut into the transmission as the cannon fired.

'Target is hit and breaking up. Over.'

Applause broke out around the room. 'Good work, Captain Brodsky. You have successfully defended the constitutional order of the Motherland. Over and out!' Fyodor added this uncharacteristically flamboyant touch as he signed off and walked over to Krymov, who stood up, shook his hand and then embraced him.

'Mostovskoy, you've done a great job! We got that bastard at last! Ha, ha!' he hooted with relief.

Fyodor smiled his icy grimace. 'Thank you, Mr President, I will see to the dispatch of helicopters to the crash immediately.'

'Yes, but first we're going to get pissed, and after we have seen the pictures, you, Mostovskoy, and you,' he put his arm around Sergey in a gesture that brooked no refusal, 'are going to come with me to carry on getting pissed at the Kremlin!'

Chapter Forty-One

Boris Frolov pulled the dirty VW Transporter pick-up onto the hard shoulder of the A-103 motorway in Moscow and got out. It was snowing and dark.

He walked calmly round to the back of the van, dropped the tailgate, and hopped up onto it. He pulled off the tarpaulin, picked up a jerry can of petrol, unscrewed its lid and poured it liberally over the stack of old car tyres, leaving a little trail of petrol onto the tailgate.

Once it was empty, he tossed the can into the grimy snow-drift on the motorway embankment and jumped down from the back.

A few cars with their headlights blazing hissed passed him through the slush, heading out of town on his, south, side of the road, along the Shchelkovskoye Shosse, A-103, to Balashika. He looked at the heavier flow of traffic on the opposite carriageway from him; he was seven miles to the east of the centre of Moscow and the early morning rush hour was getting going: hundreds of commuters who were rich enough to still drive into work, despite all the petrol rationing. Frolov hated the Krymov regime, which favoured those rich bastards and neglected the poor.

269

Well, they'd certainly wish they hadn't driven into Moscow today.

He pulled out his mobile phone and sent a text message. He calmly lit a cigarette, took a couple of slow drags and then tossed it into the back of the truck before walking away. The flame whooshed across the tyres and a thick pall of black smoke began to billow over the motorway.

Two miles further west towards the centre of town, Mikhail Nikitin got the text message and signalled to the men dressed as police officers in the two Lada police cars behind his.

They took off their caps, ducked inside their vehicles and switched on their sirens. The howl and flashing lights of the three cars allowed them to pull out into the traffic on the motorway and quickly spread across the three lanes. Once in line abreast, they began slowing down gradually until they had brought the traffic to a standstill a mile back from where the van was now burning furiously on the hard shoulder.

As the traffic ground to a halt behind them, people shouted and banged their steering wheels in frustration at the thought of missed meetings and wasted time.

'What are the fucking police doing stopping the traffic like this?'

Once the cars were stationary the six men dressed as police officers switched off their sirens and blocked the gaps between the cars.

A truck's airbrakes hissed and the cab dipped as it jerked to a halt. The bearded trucker in a checked shirt jumped down and ran over to them.

'Hey, officer, what's happening?'

Nikitin looked at him unsympathetically. 'Got a big pile-up ahead,' he said, and jerked his thumb.

There was a bright flash and a second later they heard the boom as the van's diesel tank exploded.

'Look at that, eh?' He turned round and gestured at the filthy black smoke plume they could see in the orange street-lights, spreading towards them. 'Really big crash, apparently, it'll be a while before they—'

His words cut off as a large white shape smashed through the air over their heads and roared down the motorway. The slipstream ripped off his cap and everyone dived for cover.

Arkady struggled to get the Gulfstream lined up on the motorway.

The controls shook in his hands and he fought the rudder hard. He was wrestling with the steering yoke, trying to slot the aircraft into the narrow trench between the row of street-lights in the central reservation to his right and the trees and pylons on the embankment to his left.

He had calculated that the wingspan could just fit into the narrow three-lane tunnel but he hadn't counted on the northerly crosswind and they kept sideslipping south in the breeze, towards the roadside.

He was so low that snow and ice were ripped up off the verge, the road surface and the central reservation by the slip-stream and whorled up under each wing in a vortex curl.

He lowered the flaps to reduce the airspeed.

An electricity pylon stretched across the road up ahead. Arkady threw the throttles forward again and hauled back on the yoke. They just made it over – the slipstream ripped the cables off their brackets and they cracked and whipped after the plane in showers of blue sparks.

He settled the plane back down into the trench and then suddenly veered the left wing up over a stand of pine trees on the verge. The Gulfstream burst through the cloud of black smoke from the burning van on the side of the road.

People in cars driving on the other carriageway gawped up in horror through their windscreens as the struggling jet screamed down past them. The slipstream sucked cars in towards it; they veered across the road and the tarpaulin sides of trucks ripped off.

Inside the jet, Alex, Pete, Magnus and the others were thrown around like rag dolls by the roaring, slewing and lurching motion.

Arkady wrestled with a steering yoke, which seemed to be possessed by a demon, trying to veer them off to the side to smash them against the steel streetlights. They had to land soon or a gust would get them eventually.

In an obstacle-free stretch, Arkady got the flaps down hard and brought the nose up. Airspeed dropped away fast and he managed to get the rear wheels to touch down on the slushy road surface and tried applying the brakes. He was too busy fighting to keep the plane on the straight and narrow, but Alex looked ahead and saw a road bridge coming up. He could see two things at a glance: that the solid cement pillars were narrower than the wingspan of the aircraft and that there wasn't enough distance to take off again before they reached it.

Alex knew that they had to just go for the dead centre of the gap under the bridge. If they hit it off-centre then the impact would spin them off to one side and either smash them into the central traffic lights or flip them off up the embankment.

'Go for the centre! Go for the centre!' he shouted to Arkady over the noise, and stabbed his hand forward.

The Russian looked up, saw the gap, frowned and then set his face hard. The nose wheel touched down and he threw in maximum reverse thrust; the plane juddered furiously and balked, veering more wildly from side to side.

Alex glanced at the airspeed indicator: seventy m.p.h.

Fuck – we're not going to stop in time.

The reverse thrust was making them too erratic on the

slippery road surface; Arkady darted a hand off the yoke and cut the reverse throttle. The plane stopped veering around as much but accelerated away again towards the bridge.

To Alex it looked like the most massive structure on earth: two solid chunks of grimy, pebbledash concrete, one in the middle and one on the side of the road.

Their poor, frail plane was about to smash into it. Arkady fought to get them centred in the channel between the bastions. Alex turned in his seat and shouted into the cabin behind: 'Brace!'

They hit the bridge.

An explosive screech.

The wings sheared off.

The fuel tanks ripped in half and a great cloud of Avtar whipped back down the fuselage.

It hit the hot jet exhausts.

A fireball exploded around the aircraft.

It scorched the paint off, melted the surface of the Perspex cabin windows and whirled behind them in a torrent of fire.

The shock of the impact jumped through the airframe. Bodies knocked forwards in their seats against straps.

They had hit dead centre and stayed on the road.

Their speed cut away in a horrid lurch. Arkady pulled himself back upright from over the yoke and hit the brakes again. With much reduced momentum the crippled aircraft creaked and ground to a standstill.

The outside aft section was black and smoking, the wings reduced to stubs ending in twisted metal.

Inside the aircraft, the rear cabin was in disarray, gear strewn everywhere. Champagne bottles, trays and rucksacks had all been flung against the front of the cabin and crashed down in a tangle on the floor.

Alex threw off his shoulder straps and dived back through the galley.

'Out, out, out!'

He had no idea if a secondary fire was going to break out. The rest of the team were struggling out of their seats.

Roman was hard hit, slumped forward in his straps, gasping for air. Yamba pulled him upright, unstrapped him and got him on his feet.

Seeing everyone was moving, Alex turned back, ripped open the door exit lever and shoved it out with his shoulder. The steps unfolded and banged down hard on the concrete.

He staggered down them and it was good to reach the bottom and feel the hard concrete under his boots and the cold wind fresh on his face.

Across the road, the traffic had slowed to a crawl as people stared out of their windows at the extraordinary sight of a half-burned jet sitting in the middle of the road. Behind it was a long scorched streak on the concrete that steamed from the melted snow.

Alex waved at a good-looking woman in a Mercedes and then ran back up the steps. Inside he could hear Colin in Tasmanian Devil mode shouting: 'Get yer kit! Let's go!'

The others needed little prompting. Yamba and Magnus were quickly down the steps after him and formed a human chain to ferry their gear out onto the road: rucksacks, crates of equipment, weapons and ammunition all passed down and then more came as the luggage bay under the aircraft was unloaded.

Alex got his Moscow map out and walked back behind the aircraft to look at the burned road signs on the bridge to try to work out where they were. As he walked back he smiled at the thought of how they had got through the Moscow air defences.

The two Suk-MiG-41s had caught them over the forests a couple of hours east from Moscow. The pilot of the lead one had flown up close to get a visual ID on the Gulfstream.

Alex looked out of the side window of the cockpit and saw the enormous fighter suddenly loom up out of the night. As their jet laboured along on full throttle, the Berkut seemed to hang effortlessly in midair. Alex could see the canard wings just under the cockpit fluttering slightly, as quick as a bird's wing, constantly adjusting to keep the fighter stable. The cockpit canopy was black and as sleek as a hawk's head. He couldn't see what the pilot inside was doing.

Captain Brodsky had his thumb on the 30mm cannon button. He was looking forward to blowing these terrorists out of the air. Moscow Command was being pedantic as usual and insisted on him getting in close and doing a visual ID. He pulled alongside and looked to his right; the lights were on in the Gulfstream cockpit.

What was inside surprised him. The man in the co-pilot seat wore a blue Russian Airforce uniform jacket and an airforce officer's peaked cap.

The guy seemed relaxed, not in the least bit perturbed at having a state-of-the-art fighter about to blow him out of the night sky. He smiled and waved across at Brodsky and mouthed: '*Priyvet!*' in greeting.

Brodsky ignored him and kept station as he talked to Central Air Command in Moscow on his radio.

As he was doing this, a message flashed across the display screen on the inside of his helmet visor. The red text was preceded by the correct command codes and could only have come from the Head of Air Defence Command. The message read:

TRAINING EXERCISE ONLY.
REPEAT.
TRAINING EXERCISE ONLY FOR
MOSCOW CENTRAL COMMAND.
DO NOT ATTACK GULFSTREAM.
FIRE BURST NEXT TO AIRCRAFT AND
REPORT THAT IT HAS BEEN HIT.
ACKNOWLEDGE ORDER NOW.

Brodsky looked at it indignantly and read it again.

A fucking training exercise! Unbelievable, just when he was getting hyped up for his first kill.

His commander was obviously getting very agitated. Another message flashed up: 'ACKNOWLEDGE ORDER NOW!'

Reluctantly, Brodsky hit the acknowledge key and then, with a sour expression on his face, said, 'Firing now,' and fired a long burst from his cannon past the nose of the Gulfstream. The airframe juddered and the deadly red tracers streamed harmlessly off into the night.

The man in the cockpit clenched his fist and pumped it and then grinned and gave him a thumbs up.

Cocky bastard.

Alex had then seen the huge fighter simply flip over onto its left-hand side and disappear in an instant.

Arkady followed the plan and took the Gulfstream down in a steep dive to a prearranged site in the forest where a white airforce Sukhoi training jet had just been crashed, the pilot having safely ejected.

The whole thing had worked very smoothly. When the airforce search-and-rescue helicopter had located the site half an hour later it was able to film and beam back images of a crash site complete with broken-off trees, a still burning white jet fuselage and wreckage scattered over a wide area.

The Gulfstream had swooped down low until it was under the radar and then levelled off and continued on its way to Moscow; Fyodor had arranged safe passage for it through the remaining air defences with his supporters in the airforce.

All in all, Alex was very pleased with the way it had gone. Trying to land at one of the conventional airports in Moscow would have been suicide for them. He had got the idea of the motorway landing from Switzerland, where he knew that, in the absence of much flat land, in time of war they requisitioned motorways for use by the airforce.

Planning the landing zone had taken a long time. Fyodor's experienced pilots had scoured the maps of Moscow motorways to find a suitable runway and then driven up and down the A-103 with a mental picture of the stopping distance of a Gulfstream in their heads, trying to find the necessary straight piece of road. That bit hadn't worked so well, but at least they were here in one piece.

'Alex, get back here!' Colin shouted at him from the plane and he ran back over to it. 'We've got company up ahead!'

Alex saw two helicopters skimming in low over the motorway towards them.

The two small aircraft flared hard and dropped onto the motorway in front of the crashed jet.

Alex waved to them as they landed. The pilots worked for Sergey.

He turned to his right-hand man. 'Right, Col, get the weapons and the rest of the gear in that one, I'll take Roman now.'

He glanced at his watch anxiously: 7.35 a.m.

They had only ten minutes to get Roman across town and on air.

Roman had been shaken up by the crash but Pete manhandled him firmly down the steps and then, with Alex, bundled him over to the first helicopter, opened the door and pushed him inside.

Alex and Pete both had their assault rifles across their chests as they settled into their seats, the aircraft's engines roared and it tilted and quickly swooped away east towards Ostankino.

Chapter Forty-Two

Grigory stood up in front of the assembled journalists and technical staff in the Ostankino tower to break the news of the coming revolution.

They had all gathered together in the big newsroom, standing and sitting amongst the rows of desks. Grigory and Lara climbed up onto a table in front of them. The room buzzed with anxious chatter and people looked around with worried expressions.

'OK, people!' Grigory clapped his hands together and held his arms up for silence. He had on his black suit and a white button-down shirt, and was unshaven as usual. Lara stood next to him, looking uncharacteristically formal in a fitted, dark blue skirt suit. She had her arms crossed over her stomach and stared down at her feet. She was sick with tension and thinking about Sergey.

'Right, I have a big announcement for you. Some of you may have guessed what is going to happen.'

Those in the know swallowed hard: the revolution that they had thought about for so long was really happening. No longer would it just be fighting talk over a glass of wine at home – they were really going to go head to head with

279

the might of the Russian state and try to do what no one had achieved since the Bolsheviks in 1917.

Grigory was a popular MD at work and he in turn cared about his staff. He looked out over them now and wondered – Could they really do this?

They didn't look like a band of crack revolutionaries. Scruffy, intellectual and cool – yes, but definitely not hardened fighters. He looked down in front of him and saw Nikolai, an anaemic script editor, staring up at him expectantly through his large black-rimmed glasses.

He was going to have to make this good.

'Now, you all know what the Krymov regime has done to human rights in this country – the reopening of the Gulags and the disappearances. You know how many journalists have been harassed and murdered over the years.'

There were nods around the room; their profession had been heavily targeted by the regime. In addition to notorious cases like Anna Politkovskaya, over sixty others had been murdered.

'You know also how the regime has damaged the economy with inflation and petrol rationing in a country with the second largest oil reserves in the world.'

Again people shook their heads at the situation.

'And how, with his energy blockade of the UK, Krymov has taken us into a virtual Third World War with the West. This has to stop!' Grigory said emphatically.

There were shouts of encouragement from around the room and a smattering of applause.

'Well, today will go down in history as the day of the second Russian Revolution! The day when the ordinary people of Russia get to determine the course of her future! We will do what the first Decembrists could not achieve all those years ago; we will build a free and democratic Russia!'

Many more clapped and shouted.

'Today, we will have, very shortly, returning to us after two years in a labour camp, the leader of the United Civil Opposition! Our last hope! Roman Raskolnikov!' He punched the air.

Everybody burst out clapping and cheering now.

'He will be here in a few minutes and,' he threw an arm around Lara, who had rallied under the influence of his rhetoric and managed to smile shyly, 'our very own Lara Mikhailovna Maslova will front his broadcast to the nation, calling for the people and the army to come out onto the streets!' He raised the fist of his free hand.

Chapter Forty-Three

The helicopter skimmed over the dark roofs and orange streetlights of the Moscow suburbs, heading for Ostankino.

Alex was up front next to Sergey's company pilot while Roman and Pete were in the back.

In a couple of minutes they would be at the Ostankino tower for Roman's revolutionary broadcast, but Alex could only think of one thing: he was going to see Lara again.

Throughout the whole raid he had been too focused on the job in hand, but now that he had a free moment the thought of her streamed back into his consciousness like a floodtide. He looked down at the front of his arctic combat smock. The white material was stained brown with Bogdan's blood. He reached a hand in under it and felt his webbing shoulder strap.

It was still there. The long lock of her hair felt silky smooth to his touch. He had done what she wanted and brought it back safely to her.

The pilot was gaining altitude now as they approached the tower. They rose up and up until the city streetlights dwindled vertiginously below them. Ahead, Alex could see the black bulk of the tower looming over the city, with lines of red aircraft warning lights running up its length.

They flew level with the roof of the TV station, just underneath the cloud base, and went into a hover. The pilot was wary of the gusts of wind whipping around the tower and sideslipped gradually over the guardrail and onto the flat roof. Alex could see a little group of people standing inside the glass doors at the top of the staircase.

The two skids bumped down and the pilot cut the rotors. As they wound down, Alex and Pete leaped out with their assault rifles held upright in one hand, and helped Roman down.

The wind billowed around them and flapped his dark suit and tie. The group inside the doors burst out and ran over to them. Several were United Civil Opposition members who were in tears to see their party leader again. They cried and hugged Roman as Grigory stood back, smiled and watched, as solid and reassuring as ever.

Lara stood next to him in her heavy coat with the hood framing her face. Alex glimpsed her behind the others and began to walk over to her. Grigory intercepted him with a smile, shook his hand and then thumped him on the shoulder. 'Very well done, Major Devereux!'

Alex lowered his assault rifle and let it hang at his side on its sling. He grinned back. 'It was the least I could do,' His eyes flicked on to Lara.

Grigory saw he wanted to talk to her alone so he smiled, 'You did great!' and moved on to welcome Roman.

Lara pushed the hood back off her head, her blonde hair streaming out behind her. She looked uncertain as she saw Alex approach, her head tilted back and her lips parted in a slightly suspicious pout.

After all the tension and danger in getting through the raid and back to Moscow he felt as if she was his reward. For a moment he couldn't think what to say.

'I brought it back,' he said at last, and held up the lock of her hair.

She smiled, but her thoughts seemed to be somewhere else and she twisted her head away and tapped the front of his combat smock to admonish him lightly. She then turned back and saw what she had just touched and appeared shocked. 'Is that your blood?'

Alex was confused. 'No, it's someone else's,' he said blankly as he looked down at her, trying to work out what game they were playing now.

Her eyes travelled over him. His face was still covered in camouflage cream streaks and cuts and bruises from the storm and the assault.

She noticed that his left hand was bandaged and held it up. 'What did you do?'

'Someone cut my finger off.'

She frowned at him questioningly, but then answered the question on his mind. 'Sergey just texted me. He's with Fyodor and Krymov in a car on their way back to the Kremlin.' She paused to see if Alex understood her.

He nodded, feeling overwhelmed with disappointment at Lara's taciturn reception of him, but knowing that he couldn't let it show. Of course she would be concerned about Sergey.

'I have to do the broadcast now but as soon as Krymov sees that Raskolnikov is in Moscow he will know it is because Fyodor and Sergey have betrayed him.'

Alex looked grim as he fought hard to be fair to her; he also knew that they had to be practical as well.

He said quietly, 'We can't stop now. We have to go on.'

She looked up at him, her blue eyes wide with pain. 'Even though I will cause Sergey's death?'

He looked straight back at her. 'Even though you will cause Sergey's death.'

She gave a sob and pressed her face against his bloodied chest, her voice muffled. 'He has my soul.'

Despite everything Alex felt compelled to embrace and hold her. For a long moment they stood completely still.

Lara breathed and sighed deeply against him before she pushed herself away and wiped the tears from her eyes. She looked up at him helplessly and kissed him quickly on the mouth before she broke away and walked purposefully over to Roman.

Alex looked away at the vast city panorama stretched out around the tower. The lights of Moscow glowered back at him from the darkness. He felt more dazed and confused than ever before.

Chapter Forty-Four

After he texted Lara, Sergey slid his phone back into his suit pocket before Krymov noticed; they were in the back of the Zil with Fyodor, driving through Red Square and about to enter the Kremlin.

He glanced nervously at his watch. It was 7.25 a.m. The plane would be landing in five minutes and the broadcast would be at 7.45 a.m.

He had twenty minutes of his life remaining.

After the faked shooting down of the plane during the night, Fyodor had insisted they wait for the search-and-rescue helicopters to find the 'wreckage' and beam pictures back to Air Command. Krymov had called for vodka for everyone at the command and had gone round slapping backs and congratulating people. Fyodor had hoped that during the delay Krymov would get tired and give up on his idea of dragging them back to the Kremlin.

Instead he just got more drunk and more elated by the apparent crushing of the coup attempt, and the sight of the scattered white pieces of plane wreckage merely increased his enthusiasm. 'Ha! We made a right fucking mess of them, didn't we!' he gloated as the pictures came in.

So, he was now continuing with his original plan to go

to the Kremlin, steamrollering Sergey's complaints about having a business meeting that morning. Sergey was trying to maintain his usual mask of bonhomie but it was hard to do when he knew he was about to die. At least Fyodor could just maintain his usual mask of icy calm.

Krymov was beginning to notice Sergey's lack of animation. 'Hey, Shaposhnikov, what's up with you? You missing Raskolnikov or something?'

'No, Boss, just tired, that's all.'

Krymov grunted, annoyed that Sergey wasn't joining in his fun.

The convoy swept across Red Square, past Lenin's Mausoleum and drove through the massive gates of the Saviour's Tower. Once inside it, the black Zil slowed to make a sharp right turn and drove along the inside of the main wall of the citadel.

They drew up at the apex of the triangular-shaped Senate Building where Krymov's office was. It was ornate and classical, painted pale yellow with white cornices, dusted now with snow, and with a Russian tricolour drooping from a pole above the entrance.

Krymov pulled Sergey out of the car – 'Come on, you lazy bastard!' – and then ran up the steps and through the impressive large double doors.

The group walked through the grand entrance hall, trailed by Batyuk and a squad of six guards with rifles. The sound of their boots echoed as they walked under the huge dome.

Krymov was in an inspired mood and paused to look up at the beautifully painted cupola, which was just trapping the first gleams of wintry morning light. He clapped his hands – 'Come on!' – and urged them out the other side and down the steps into the central hexagonal courtyard, lined by impressive four-storey classical façades painted yellow and trimmed in white. The whole thing was covered in a field of snow now but the straight path across it had already been swept clear.

Sergey lagged behind again as they walked across, and Krymov dropped back alongside him and poked him in the ribs. 'Hey! I said come on!'

Sergey shrugged; in the face of death he just couldn't maintain the front any more. He grunted disconsolately.

Krymov wasn't taking that as an answer and barged into him; Sergey stumbled over the lip of the path and fell on the snow.

'Ha, ha!' Krymov roared with laughter, glad to have got back to their usual level.

Sergey floundered around on all fours with his back to Krymov, scraping a snowball together, then suddenly stood up, turned and threw it at the President. It hit him in the chest and sprayed up over his face.

Batyuk had his pistol out of his hip holster in a flash and the other Echelon 25 men were already hunched over their rifles, Sergey in their sights.

Fyodor stepped away in alarm and looked at Krymov, expecting an explosion of anger – but this was exactly the sort of horseplay he had been looking for.

Batyuk waved the guards off; they lowered their rifles slowly as Krymov scraped the snow off his face. 'Son of a bitch! Ha!'

He marched onto the snow, scraped a ball together and hurled it back at Sergey, who ducked and the two then began running around each other, alternately flinging snowballs.

Fyodor stood aside, watching with a tense, disdainful expression on his face. How could Shaposhnikov play around at a time like this?

He pulled up the elegantly tailored sleeve of his greatcoat and looked at his watch: 7.35 a.m.

The plane had landed. Ten minutes to live.

Chapter Forty-Five

The excited group of supporters on the roof of the Ostankino tower hustled Roman away and down the staircase.

Grigory and his young female assistant hung back. The big director walked over to where Alex was standing, looking lost after his talk with Lara, and put a hand on his shoulder.

'Alexander, thank you for bringing Roman back to us. I really think he will do it.' Grigory was feeling pumped up on the rhetoric of his own speech to the staff. 'Now that I have seen him again after all this time – it's just so good to remember what a presence he has, how much he means to us – I am sure that we can do this thing peacefully now. As soon as he goes on air, I just know that the surprise will bring the people out onto the streets. The government will collapse. It'll have to.'

Alex looked at him and nodded. In his experience these things were rarely that simple, but he was glad that Grigory was feeling so positive.

He evidently had something else he wanted to say.

'Look, Alex, I don't want to sound ungrateful, but from now on I think we can let the military side of things take a back seat?' He raised his eyebrow questioningly.

Alex nodded. 'Sure.' He was happy not to fight if he didn't have to.

'We have to be very careful from the media presentation point of view when the cameras are on downstairs. We've got a big crowd of United Civil Opposition people in here already and we're going to have several cameras roving around getting the general positive atmosphere. I can't afford to have them picking up any of your guys. Foreign soldiers in Russia would *really* damage our credibility.'

Alex nodded. He knew how prickly the Russians were about foreigners on their soil, having been invaded and trashed by just about every single European and Asian country in the course of their history.

'So, I'm afraid, when the guys arrive in the second heli-copter I'd like you to leave the weapons and ammunition onboard and all go with Natalya.' He gestured to his assist-ant, who smiled. 'She'll take you to a conference room away from everyone and you can watch it all there on TV.' He paused, seeming to remember something, and then grinned and slapped Alex's shoulder. 'The revolution will be both live and televised!' he beamed. 'I'd better go and sort out the broadcast.' He paused, then: 'Alex, I'm sorry to do this to you, but you understand?'

'Sure, I'm English – I'm all about modesty.' He managed a grin.

'OK. *Vive la Revolution*!' Grigory gave a clenched fist salute to Alex before disappearing down the stairs.

Natalya smiled nervously at him and waited at a distance.

Alex turned as Pete sauntered over with his hands folded on his rifle across his chest. The long-haired Australian flicked his head after Grigory. 'What was all that about?'

Alex looked out over Moscow. 'Well, he says he thinks that he won't need our services any more and that we should stay out of sight, which I'm happy to do. But somehow I just don't believe it's going to be that straightforward.'

Chapter Forty-Six

Krymov ran at Sergey, tackled his legs, upended him on the ground and then bent over and stuffed snow down the collar of his coat.

Sergey bellowed, scuttled around and grabbed Krymov's legs so he too fell over.

Batyuk and the bodyguards twitched and hovered, drawing nearer to the pair as they wrestled with each other. Eventually Krymov got on top of Sergey, scraped up snow and stuffed it in his face.

'Ah!'

Sergey gave a sudden shout of pain and clutched his eye; Krymov stopped and looked down at him.

Sergey screwed his face up and put his hands over his right eye. 'Ah, fuck, you put grit in my eye, you cunt!' he gasped.

Krymov laughed victoriously and stood up, breathing hard after the unaccustomed exertion. Sergey rolled onto his knees and then stood up slowly, still clutching his eye. 'Fuck, that hurts!'

Krymov embraced him in mock sympathy. 'Ah, there, there, Serezhenka!'

Sergey pulled away from him. 'Ah, piss off! I'm going to the shithouse to get it out.' He limped off across the courtyard towards a small service door in the façade opposite.

Krymov giggled and flapped a hand after him. 'Ah, you fucking poof!'

He bent over, wheezing for breath, and then flopped down onto the ground and rolled on his back laughing.

Fyodor had been standing aside during the fight, looking at his watch anxiously and praying for Sergey to stop pissing around and get out of there. Now, though, he saw the method in the madness.

'I'll go and give him a hand.'

Krymov grunted weakly, still getting his breath back. The airforce general hurried after Sergey whilst the bodyguards continued to hover nervously around the President.

Once inside the service door, Sergey ducked round the corner of the corridor. It was a backstairs route for servants through the maze of the old palace.

Fyodor came in a moment later and called anxiously, 'Sergey?'

'Here.' He stuck his head out from round the corner and Fyodor hurried over to him.

'What time is it?'

Fyodor looked at his watch. 'It's 7.39. They'll be on air in a couple of minutes. We have to get the fuck out of here!' It was the first time Sergey had ever seen him display so much emotion.

'I know! How?' Sergey stared back at him.

Fyodor thought hard. 'OK,' he nodded, 'OK, let's try it. Come on.'

He ran off along the corridor; as a Kremlin insider he knew the layout of the building well. The rough-flagged passage went along the western edge of the Senate building complex. They headed south, ducking around the twists and turns of the low passageway as it wove under, alongside and behind the grand staterooms it served.

Eventually, at the southern end of the building, they came to a set of stairs leading down, which used to go to a coal cellar.

Fyodor stopped at the top of them and turned to Sergey. 'I don't know if this is going to work but we don't have any choice.'

Sergey nodded, not sure what was happening but trusting that Fyodor knew what he was doing.

Chapter Forty-Seven

Alex sat down at the head of the small conference room table and looked at his team seated around it.

Arkady, Pete, Yamba, Magnus and Colin: still all in their arctic warfare kit, weapons piled casually on the table in front of them, faces streaked with camouflage cream, clothes ripped and smudged, and all smelling of smoke. Tough, lined, intelligent faces looked back at him.

'Gentlemen, we have made it to Moscow,' he gestured around him and grinned, 'and our employers say that we are now surplus to requirements.' He shrugged. 'Personally, I don't believe that –' there were nods of agreement – 'but the point is that you now have a decision to make.' He paused and looked at them. 'You have now fulfilled the main part of your mission brief and earned the bulk of your pay. If you want to get out now, I will be happy to see that it is transferred into your accounts. If you want to continue, then, under the terms of your contracts, the bonus payments will apply. But if it does all take off from here then it is going to take off big and will involve some *serious* warfare.'

There were slow nods of understanding. The basic payment was a substantial amount of money that would buy them each a large home very easily, but Alex wasn't going to try to railroad them in any direction. That just wasn't the way the team worked together on these decisions.

'However, for my part, I will be staying on to see this thing through to the end. What do you think?' He glanced around them with an expectant look.

Pete had been hunched over the table with his chin held in one hand and an intense, evaluating look on his face. Some of his long brown locks had escaped and hung down around the black stubble of his heavy jaw line. He leaned back in his chair, pushed it away from the table, folded his arms across his chest and shrugged. 'Yeah, why not, eh?' He looked round at the others for their reaction.

The older men were taking longer to think it over.

Col was usually the most outspoken amongst them, but he had his lips pressed tight together as he weighed up the factors on his mind. He was thinking about what he knew of the realities of heavy fighting – the injuries and deaths that he had seen many times – and balancing them against the bitty life he led back home, the fact that, when it came down to it, he wasn't really doing it for the money. He was doing it for the professional pride, which was the main thing that he ended up justifying his life with. Like the others in the group, he detested heroic statements as being antithetical to the grim reality of their trade. They all knew that what counted was what you did, not what fine words you came out with.

He scowled, looked down and scratched the grey stubble on the back of his balding head. He said unenthusiastically, 'Yeah, well, suppose it might be a bit of a laff, eh?'

Alex nodded; he didn't need any more words than that to guarantee Col's commitment.

Yamba's stern face turned into a frown as he mimicked his friend's words in a deadpan voice. '"A bit of a laff, eh?"

What kind of an expression is that to use at a time like this?' He looked at Col in angry disbelief.

Col's expression became surly and he shrugged.

Yamba appeared exasperated. 'I mean, we're in the middle of a bloody revolution, man. Can't you find something more epic to say than that?'

Col switched to looking at the ceiling and around the corners of the room, deliberately avoiding his question.

The Angolan looked at Alex and held his hands out to him, asking for his intervention. 'I mean, bloody hell, what kind of idiots do you have to employ, Alex?'

Alex shrugged nonchalantly, contributing to the farce.

Yamba scoffed. 'I have to work with these intellectual pygmies.' He flipped his hand in disgust at Col.

Col took the bait now and sat forward, pointing a warning finger at Yamba. 'I'll give *you* fooking pygmies!'

Yamba pointed back at him. 'Ah! And now you are being *racist* as well!'

'You're the one what's got a problem with pygmies, mate. I *fooking* love them, me!' Col pointed at himself laughing.

Yamba waved a dismissive hand back at him. 'Buffoon!'

'Sh'up!'

They both sat back in their chairs with their arms folded and expressions of mock disgust on their faces as they looked up at the ceiling.

Alex, Arkady and Pete couldn't help shaking with laughter as the exchange went on. Magnus found it particularly amusing and was quietly crying with suppressed sniggers, as the two became more and more insulting.

After they all got their breath back and the laughter died away there wasn't much that the remaining members could say in response to Alex's questioning look.

Yamba just shrugged and nodded. Magnus gave it more

consideration and then said quietly, in the clipped tones of his mother tongue: '*Ja, vi må gjøre det,*' and nodded. 'Yes, we must do that.'

Arkady had been in a quandary because it was the future of his home country that was at stake here. But given the others' commitment, he could not back down now so he grinned his gold-toothed smile and said, 'Yes, for the Motherland, heh?'

Chapter Forty-Eight

The President of the Motherland lay on his back in the snow, drunk and grinning happily.

Major Batyuk wished he would get up, but stood at a respectful distance beside the other six guards.

The President's Communication Secretary, Captain Bunin, opened a window from the press office, on the second floor of the building opposite them, the floor below the President's office, and leaned out.

He was highly agitated and shouted across the courtyard, 'Mr President, there's a report just come in! A Gulfstream jet has landed on the A-103 motorway on the eastbound carriageway to Balashika. Two helicopters have landed at the site and then taken off from there to Ostankino.'

Krymov sat up in alarm and twisted round to see Bunin. 'What?'

'A white Gulfstream jet …'

Krymov ignored the rest and turned back round to look at Batyuk. His expression of euphoria was replaced by one of astonishment as he tried to grapple with what had happened; he couldn't make sense of it.

Batyuk could, though. His face went red with rage and his ear stump flamed angrily. He looked murderously at Krymov and said through gritted teeth, 'I'll kill them.'

Krymov just nodded in his dazed state.

'You and you, go with the President,' he detailed two guards. 'Mr President, please move to your office immediately. The rest of you come with me.' With that he led the four élite soldiers with rifles across the courtyard at a run towards the door where Sergey and Fyodor had disappeared a minute ago.

He busted open the door and charged down the corridor to where it split. He paused and looked around him to try to work out which way they had gone. He looked down at the floor; there were traces of water. It must have come from the snow stuffed down Sergey's back and from their shoes.

'Come on! Shoot on sight!' he shouted to the soldiers, and drew his own pistol. He led off along the servants' corridor to the south; he had an idea in his mind where they were headed. The soldiers pelted along, their boots reverberating on the stone flags, and then hurtled down the small stairs to the old coal store.

As head of presidential security, Batyuk knew that the Kremlin was riddled with underground tunnels; the walled citadel covered sixty-eight acres and included four palaces, four cathedrals and numerous barracks and offices of state. Over the centuries numerous tunnels had been dug to allow tsars, bishops, mistresses and ministers to move between them in secret. The one he thought that Fyodor and Sergey would try to escape along now had been built on Stalin's orders in the Great Patriotic War. It connected the network to the nearest Metro stations, allowing people to be moved in and out in secret and to avoid German bombing raids.

Batyuk ran down the stairs and then ducked into a small archway at the bottom, which gave into a dimly lit tunnel, just wide enough for a man to fit. It sloped downwards and he had to bend his head to avoid a light on the ceiling.

He held up his hand to stop the others behind him and paused to listen; he knew that a hundred metres west of the Senate Building, where it was under open ground, the tunnel split into four, three of which went to different areas of the Kremlin and one that linked into the Metro network. He also knew that there was a guard posted at the interchange. He could hear voices ahead. It was them.

'Come on!' he shouted, and ran forward.

Chapter Forty-Nine

Fyodor led Sergey down the stairs and into the tunnel.

He ran forward, but after fifty metres he stopped and straightened his immaculate blue airforce greatcoat and adjusted his peaked officer's cap. Sergey brushed the snow out of his hair and off the collar of his rumpled suit and coat.

The officer turned on Sergey with calculating eyes. With his shaggy thatch and diamond earring he still looked shambolic, but he was a famous person in Russia so that might help.

He turned and walked off with his hands clasped behind his back, at the steady pace that befitted a general in command of events.

After another fifty metres they came to a four-way split in the tunnel. A small circular concrete chamber had been dug out, with a higher ceiling, and a young MVD private sat at a desk in the middle of it under a light reading a book, his AN-94 rifle propped next to him and a sign hanging over the tunnel behind him saying: 'Metro'.

Fyodor fixed him with a cold stare as he advanced into the room. The private looked up, saw who it was, sprang to attention and saluted. 'General Mostovskoy!'

The general didn't say anything, but continued his dead-eyed stare as he pulled his official pass out of his breast pocket and proffered it.

The soldier glanced at it. 'Thank you, sir!'

He finally noticed Sergey and recognised him as well. 'Ah, Mr Shaposhnikov, do you have a pass as well, sir?' he asked nervously.

'Er, I did, but ...' Sergey made a show of tapping the pockets of his jacket and coat '... I seem to have left it somewhere. Don't worry, President Krymov will vouch for me.' He grinned as if it were a trifling matter.

'I'm very sorry, sir, but regulations state that no one without a pass can use the tunnel network. I'm sorry but you'll have to return the way you came and use another route.' He held out an arm to indicate the way back to the Senate Building.

'Private.' Fyodor's voice was cold enough to lower the temperature ten degrees. 'Come here.' He beckoned the man out from behind his desk so that he was standing in front of them and was about to give him a lengthy dressing-down when the noise of footsteps came down the tunnel from the Senate Building.

The steps paused and then clattered towards them.

Sergey butted in between the two of them. 'Look, son.' He winked, put an arm around the soldier's back and turned him away from Fyodor. 'I know what army pay is like. I'll make it worth your while.' He leaned his head conspiratorially towards him and then brought his knee up hard into the man's groin. The soldier collapsed on the floor, writhing for breath.

'Let's go!' Sergey shouted, and ran round the desk.

Fyodor followed, grabbing the rifle from behind it and, with expert precision, clicked off the safety, flicked it on to auto, and fired the whole thirty-round mag back down the tunnel at Batyuk. The gunfire was explosive in the confined space and red tracers snapped out in the dim light.

There were shouts and cries from their pursuers, and a second later a torrent of gunfire poured back out at them. Bullets blew chunks of concrete off the walls as they ricocheted around the circular chamber, but Fyodor had already dropped the rifle and run after Sergey.

They pelted along the narrow tunnel. It sloped steeply downhill three hundred metres west until it had run under both the citadel walls and the deep outer moat. A long burst of automatic gunfire came from behind them and the bullets cracked and pinged off the walls but the downhill slope kept them out of a direct line of fire.

Batyuk and the remaining uninjured guard inched their way into the tunnel, and then, hearing rapid footsteps, ran after their quarry with rifles held in front of them.

Sergey hit the heavy metal door at the end of the tunnel and heaved at the lever to open it. It moved up and unbolted the door; he swung it open and stepped out into a small closet with brooms and mops lining its walls. Fyodor rushed into it after him and swung the door closed; they couldn't lock it from their side.

'Come on!' he panted, and opened the normal wooden door out of the cleaners' closet. He and Sergey stepped out into a wide, brightly lit Metro hallway packed with morning rush-hour commuters hurrying in different directions. They were in the middle of the huge Metro interchange near the Kremlin where the four stations of Arbatskaya, Borovitskaya, Aleksandrovskiy Sad and Bibliotheca imeni Lenina all intersected.

'This way!' Fyodor pointed up at a grey Line 9 sign, the way north to Ostankino. Nobody gave them a second glance as they were swallowed up in the crowd.

Ten seconds later, when Major Batyuk and the remaining soldier burst out of the door with their rifles raised, people stopped and stared in alarm. Batyuk looked back at them angrily but he knew that he had lost his quarry. He pushed the soldier back through the door and slammed it behind him.

Chapter Fifty

Grigory quickly slid into his chair at the mixing desk in the dimly lit director's gallery overlooking Studio 2 and put his headset on. The team around him were right in the middle of the final preparations for Roman's broadcast.

The room hummed with activity and with terse instructions going back and forth from controllers to technicians in Studio 2 and in the production rooms of all the different TV and radio stations on the five floors of the tower.

Assistants darted behind the line of controllers sitting at the long mixing desk. It was covered in dials and sliders, and in front of it was a bank of screens showing all the different shots from the studio cameras and from the five camera crews spread out around Moscow, ready to catch the public's reaction to the speech.

Next to Grigory was Ilya Witte, who would be directing the cameras on the actual live show. He was busy moving the two joysticks in front of him for the remote-controlled cameras they had set up in Studio 2, checking that they all moved correctly and that he would get the shots he wanted. Further along from him the sound engineer was talking to the technician on the studio floor as he fitted Roman and Lara's mikes and tested them. Grigory glanced through the window under the bank of screens and could see them now standing at the front of the studio, looking tense. The floor manager was bustling around them checking his clipboard and directing people. In his headset Grigory could hear Ilya calmly counting back to everyone: 'On air in one minute.'

The vision mixer next to him was running through the graphics package they had made to front the programme. It had to be eye-catching but also authoritative. After many changes, he was finally happy with it and now had his finger over the play button, ready for when the presenters of the morning TV shows cut off their usual performances and handed over to him.

All eleven terrestrial stations and the seventeen satellite channels that broadcast from the Ostankino tower would carry the programme live, and further along the desk the sound engineer was checking his connections to the twelve radio stations that also transmitted from there.

Grigory quickly brought the microphone on his headset down to his mouth and punched in the dial numbers to Captain Lev Darensky's mobile in the 568th barracks, twenty miles north of him. They had spoken earlier that day and Darensky had been briefed to get the regiment into the canteen and get the TV turned up loud.

Those soldiers were the key to the whole revolution. If they didn't come out in support and bring their tanks down to defend the tower then it was open to a counterattack from Krymov. The one big advantage they had over the President was control of the airwaves, but if they lost the tower, then they lost that, and the revolution would be finished.

Darensky's voice sounded nervous as he answered his mobile. 'Grigory?'

'Yeah, it's me. We're on in one minute. Are your guys watching?'

'Yes, they're all here.' Darensky sounded nervous. 'I told them there was an important announcement this morning.'

'Good, well, there certainly will be! Good luck!'

Grigory hung up and punched in another speed dial to Gerry Kramer, the newsdesk editor at CNN in Moscow. They were old friends but he hadn't said anything to him about the coup yet.

'Hey, buddy?' The American sounded as chipper as ever.

'Gerry, whatever you're showing now, stop it, get a translator on line and take this feed from me.'

'Say what?'

Grigory paused; he couldn't believe he was actually going to say this. 'There's going to be a revolution.'

There was silence on the other end.

'I'll take it.'

Grigory hit the button and then dialled his counterparts at BBC World News, France 24 and Al Jazeera.

Ilya continued his countback to the floor manager standing in front of Lara: 'Forty seconds to on air.'

She was standing on a dais at the front of the studio in the full glare of the lights. A large crowd stood around in front of her, waiting to play their part.

Studio 2 was the biggest the station had, and the back wall of it was double-height plate glass that followed the curve of the outside of the tower. They had decided that it was important to be able to show people that Roman really was out of prison and back in Moscow, broadcasting live from Ostankino, and that the best way of doing this was with a huge panoramic view of the city behind him. A thin dawn light was filtering through the snow clouds now, but the floodlights on the cathedrals and landmarks were still on and anyone could see that it was the capital.

The sound technician finished clipping the talkback earpiece onto her collar and then quickly stood back to see that the wire behind her ear didn't show. He did one more check on the radio mike and handed it to her.

Lara was glad she had something to clutch onto. She felt sick with fear about Sergey, knowing that in doing what she was about to do right now she would be contributing to his death. Half of her wanted to just run off stage, burst into tears and switch off the whole of the world.

The other half of her knew that she had to do this *for* Sergey. It was his whole vision of *Russkaya dusha* – insanely maddening as she found it – that had propelled her to love him so much in the first place. This broadcast for her then would be both an ode of love and a funeral oration in one.

She quickly smoothed the jacket of her blue skirt suit down. She wasn't used to looking so formal and felt constrained by it. The jacket felt tight across her shoulders, but she had decided after discussion with Grigory that she needed to try to look more authoritative than she usually did.

She smiled nervously at Roman across the studio from her and he nodded calmly back. He was standing behind a podium in his dark suit and tie, smoothing the pages of his speech in front of him and gathering himself for his big moment. He flexed his shoulders and thought about all the other spotlight occasions he had been in, the big international matches when he had been the centre of attention and about to play his heart out on the pitch. The fear he felt now was just the same, he just had to make it work for him. He ran through his first lines in his head again and then cleared his mind and waited for Lara's handover.

On the lectern in front of him was the Russian emblem of state, the double-headed eagle. Two Russian tricolour flags stood behind him, furled on poles, just as if he were a president making an important announcement. They had all agreed that Russians were conservative people who respected strong authority so the whole tone of the broadcast had to be sombre and dignified.

The only radical touch was the new flag they had constructed that was stretched out fully between the two Russian tricolours. It was light blue with a black double-headed eagle in the middle of it; Roman would explain its significance later.

'Thirty seconds to on air.'

Lara shielded her eyes against the lights and looked in front of her at the crowd of three hundred United Civil Opposition supporters, who had been summoned by a simple email network. It was important to give the impression of popular support at the beginning to get the whole revolution moving.

'Twenty seconds to on air.'

'Cut from other channels. Run graphics.' Ilya's voice sounded calm and reassuring in her ear.

Everywhere across Moscow and the whole of Russia now people looked at their TV and radio sets in astonishment as their usual news, music, lifestyle, business and shopping channels all suddenly cut off and handed over to her feed, the graphics package ran and a voice announced: 'Good morning, Russia and welcome to a new day.'

Lara now knew that she had the attention of the best part of one hundred and forty million people in Russia and that all the main international news channels were also carrying her broadcast live.

In the conference room on the floor below, Alex and the rest of the team sat hunched around a TV mounted on the wall as the baffled presenter on the BBC News channel responded to the shouting of her director in her ear and handed over to Lara's feed. 'We've got news of something big coming in now from Moscow …'

'Ten seconds to on air.'

Lara felt sick and weak.

How could she do this? Her body was about to snap and shatter into a thousand pieces right there on air as the tension built up in her.

The floor manager in front of her was holding up the five fingers of his right hand next to the remote camera with the red light on and her autocue rolling up over it.

He counted out loud, 'Seven, six,' and then cut off to allow silence before her cue from the gallery; she watched each of his fingers fold into the palm of his hand. It made a fist and then his index finger shot out and pointed at her.

She remembered the feel of Sergey's words in her ear when they were together – as soft as snowflakes falling on water – and she suddenly felt beautiful.

She took a deep breath, pulled herself up and looked straight at the camera, her wide blue eyes positive and smiling. 'Good morning, Russia and welcome to a new day.'

Chapter Fifty-One

Sergey tried to avoid anyone's gaze as the Line 9 train ground into Chekovskaya station.

He was standing hunched in the corner of the carriage with his back to it and his head stuck in a copy of a free newspaper he had picked off the floor. At least his scruffy coat made him anonymous from behind.

Fyodor's uniform was a lot more obvious so he was sitting on the shelf seat, wedged right in the corner, with Sergey standing in front of him. They were both terrified of being stopped by a guard or policeman.

The other passengers, though, were not paying any attention. For them it was just another Tuesday morning journey to work. Things weren't great at the moment: inflation eating away at their wages, and the petrol rationing was just ridiculous. No one could believe it when it was introduced; the state control of media had been so tight up to the point that foreign oil company staff were withdrawn and the refineries stopped working, that it came as a complete surprise. OMON riot police had then harshly suppressed the protests, but enough word of them had got out onto the street for that to add to the disillusionment with the government. People were beginning to realise the value of what they had given up in the good economic times under Putin when he had stripped away constitutional freedoms. Now that times were hard they had no choice but to obey a government that they despised.

They were a mixed crowd: businessmen, shop workers, students and a few tourists; all in various stages of early morning daze, thinking about what they had to do today or trying not to.

Svetlana Glazkova was an intense, nineteen-year-old student of political science at Moscow University, heading off for a lecture. She was a news junkie, had her earphones on and was watching the internet broadcasts on a portable DVD player that her parents had brought her.

When her usual programme was interrupted and cut through to the intro graphics from Ostankino, she frowned and tapped the small unit. It stayed on channel and then Lara Maslova came on.

What's *she* doing?

Lara might be the people's favourite, but Svetlana didn't regard her as a serious newscaster.

She was announcing a big new day for Russia. A new government was coming? What the hell was she talking about?

Roman Raskolnikov had been freed from prison and was back in Moscow!

This was serious.

Svetlana realised that something very big was going on and that she had to share it. She jumped up, ripped her headset out of the jack and turned the volume on the small speakers up to maximum.

'Hey, what are you doing?' the old lady next to her asked. 'That's too loud!'

'Everybody, shut up!' Svetlana yelled down the carriage.

People looked up from their newspapers and conversations.

'Raskolnikov has been freed from prison and is back in Moscow – he's about to do a live broadcast. Just listen!'

She ran into the middle of the carriage and held the TV up for people to see.

'Raskolnikov?' A murmur went up and down the carriage and people gathered round the TV.

Sergey and Fyodor cringed in their corner, while trying to listen at the same time.

Chapter Fifty-Two

Lara kept her intro short, her delivery was modest and to the point. In the gallery, Grigory couldn't help a moment of professional awareness of the added impact that this would have on ordinary people who were used to her being a lot more bubbly.

They cut to a brief underlay, where she did the voiceover as the screen showed highlights of Roman's sporting career: all his amazing goals, him lifting trophies in front of cheering crowds and of course the 'Our last hope!' moment against Germany.

'And, so, ladies and gentlemen, in this Time of Troubles, a new saviour has flown in to be with us this morning. Will you please welcome … Roman Raskolnikov!'

Ilya cut the cameras over to Roman as the crowd of supporters in front of him cheered and waved their blue flags. Grigory nodded to Ilya from down the control desk. It really did look like a rally for an established political party.

Roman was famous for his tell-it-like-it-is style, so he didn't go for flights of rhetoric. The very fact that he was standing in front of people was enough of a shock for them. His face told his story as much as any words could: people could see what two years in the camps must have been like from his weight loss and the frostbite burns on his cheekbones.

He outlined the problems that the country was facing

first, putting forward a lot of facts that the government had suppressed about how and why things had gone so badly wrong, how the *siloviki* control of companies had ruined their competitiveness and driven out foreign investment. Then he turned to the loss of political freedom that people were only now beginning to regret.

He began his finale, and became more high-flown. 'The last Tsarina once said "Russia loves and needs the feel of the whip", and we must address this addiction to authoritarianism in our nature.'

There were some shouts of agreement from the audience at this.

'We must address our paranoia about foreign enemies that becomes a self-fulfilling prophecy. But I tell you now that our greatest threats are not external but internal! I am standing here before you now, a prisoner just freed from our country's most shameful secret, the new Gulag system that the government has hidden from you. I worked there as a slave under that Russian whip, but now I am free, and I have to ask you today to face up to a question about the nature of our beloved Motherland!'

He paused and looked long and hard at the camera in front of him.

'And we must face this question,' he pronounced each of the next words slowly, 'is Russia a slave country?'

There were shouts of 'No!' from the crowd.

'Then if she is not a slave country, she must be prepared to stand up for her freedom. For too long we have had governments that have not matched the spirit of the Russian people. Governments that have lied to us, cheated us and oppressed us!'

The crowd was wild now, shouting, waving their flags and cheering.

Roman's earnest face filled the screens across the country as he shouted, 'Is the Russian soul a slave soul?' He banged the podium insistently. 'No! No! No! It's a *free* soul! So I call on you now to demonstrate on the streets! I announce to you now a new Revolution! I want you to join the Blue Revolution!' He pointed a finger at the stunned viewers across the country. 'We have chosen this colour from our national flag.' He turned, grabbed the corner of one of the furled tricolours and pulled it out so he could point dramatically at the different colours. 'Not for us the Communist Reds or the Tsarist Whites! Not to be the left, not to be the right, but to be the centre of the flag!'

He gripped the central blue stripe and held it up over his head.

'To be the voice of the ordinary, decent people of Russia, who for too long have been caught up by the whims of the extremes. I call on you now to come out onto the streets and let us make a peaceful protest on a scale that this terrible government cannot ignore! The people's will cannot be ignored. Let us express our souls! Let us be free!'

Chapter Fifty-Three

In the Metro carriage complete silence reigned as people stared at the screen.

It really was Roman Raskolnikov.

The face was more worn, the voice was older and rougher, but it had the same lilting Volga accent, and he was the same man they had known and respected for so many years, telling them things about themselves that they knew but did not realise that they knew.

All across Moscow, cars had pulled over on the side of the road, mothers on the school run shut their children up to listen, people over the breakfast table were left staring at each other. In shops and factories, workers and customers had looked up as the usual muzak and phone-in chatter had cut out and then they heard this extraordinary blast of rhetoric.

In the 568th Regiment's huge canteen, the soldiers had been lazing in their chairs over breakfast, when Darensky had jumped up onto the table under the TV set on the wall and shouted, 'Right, shut up! Listen in! There's an important announcement on the telly.'

He jumped down and turned the volume up to max with the remote. It was a good time for the broadcast as the CO, Colonel Karenin, and the officers loyal to him had had another big drinking session last night and weren't out of their beds yet. He had got the junior officers and NCOs who supported him together and he returned to their table to watch.

Would the men come out in support of the revolution or would he be shot for mutiny?

He would find out soon enough.

'Fuck off, mate,' muttered Sergeant Platonov at him under his breath to the younger Private Novikov next to him. He was sick to death of the whole officer corps in the regiment; they were all arseholes, as far as he was concerned, driving the whole unit into the ground with their implementation of Colonel Karenin's sadistic regime.

Private Novikov nodded. Like most of the men he was depressed and terrified by Karenin's reign of fear. All he wanted to do was to serve his time and get the fuck out of the army as fast as he could; he was not looking to be a hero.

The show on the TV was a brightly coloured, high-energy, knockabout breakfast programme that the lads used as a sugar-rush to wake them up in the morning. A pop video was playing when, in the middle of it, the shot cut back to the studio; the normally hyper young male and female presenters suddenly looked worried as they listened to instructions in their earpieces.

The lad with spiky hair did the best he could to convey an air of gravitas: 'Well, folks, we've got a bit of a weird one for you here. We're gonna have to say ciao for now 'cos there's something really big going on …'

His voice trailed off, he looked in confusion at his floor manager, and then the screen blinked and cut to some graphics.

The men in the canteen frowned and paid more attention. Lara came on screen and a cheer went up. ''Ello, love!',

'Awright, darling!', 'Fucking love 'er! Look at those tits!', 'What's she looking all posh for?'

Darensky looked on in horror; this was not the reaction that he had hoped for.

The men settled down once Lara mentioned Raskolnikov. He was hugely popular amongst working-class Russians, and his trial and imprisonment had been bitterly resented, but people had just had to shrug and say, 'What can you do?'

Now he was back on the screen in front of them and the men craned forward to hear him.

Darensky watched the broadcast but also kept flicking his eyes to the men to see how they were taking it. Some of what Roman said about the state of the economy struck home. There were nods about the petrol rationing and a few 'Yeahs' about the price rises, but a lot of the more soaring stuff about freedom and the Russian soul just met with blank faces.

As an earnest student of politics, Darensky found it inspiring and was aglow with fervour by the end. He hit the mute button on the remote and jumped up onto the table under the TV. This was his great revolutionary moment and he threw his arms open to the men in front of him.

'Right, lads. Well, there you go! Wow! That was really Raskolnikov and he really socked it to them, didn't he? I want us to get the tanks and APCs out and go down to Ostankino right now to support him!' He punched the air with his fist. 'We've suffered here enough from that bastard Karenin, but if we join with them now we can get rid of him! Really change the country; make it a better place!'

He looked at them expectantly but met with rows of blank faces.

They were ground down and, as Russians, the idea of joyous optimism for a better future just wasn't part of their psyche. Nothing that he had said had set light to their imagination and a stunned silence prevailed.

Sergeant Platonov broke it by scraping his chair back on the concrete floor; he was a heavy-set man from a coal mining family in the Donetzk area, who had joined the army as the only way out.

He shrugged and said, 'I agree with Raskolnikov. Krymov has done a shit job with the economy. It's stupid that people don't have jobs. But Krymov will never fall – he's too strong. You can't overthrow the government. Besides, Karenin would kill us.'

He shrugged again and sat down; there were nods of agreement around the tables as a consensus was reached. The men quietly began picking up their bowls and walking over to the food counter.

The temporary spell from Raskolnikov's broadcast was broken and, as the soldiers moved past Darensky, they avoided his gaze. He felt suddenly ridiculous, standing up there on the table. He climbed down and walked back over to the group of junior officers, who looked at him equally disconsolately.

In a short while, Karenin would get out of bed, his orderly would tell him what had happened and they would be arrested, beaten and shot for mutiny.

But worst of all, Darensky knew he had failed. He had let the revolution down. The key to it, the Ostankino tower and the control of the airwaves that went with it, was now wide open to attack from troops loyal to Krymov. No matter how many ordinary people came out onto the streets, without regular army support, they wouldn't be able to stop the OMON and the MVD.

Chapter Fifty-Four

As the crowd's rapturous applause rang out, Lara walked across the stage to Roman, kissed him on the cheek and then embraced him. An even louder cheer went up and the crowd started chanting: 'Our last hope! Our last hope!'

The pair of them then held hands and walked down the steps into the sea of blue flags and applauding supporters; UCO party activists struggled to clear a path for them as they were mobbed.

In the gallery Grigory smiled as he looked on. From a media point of view it was stunning. Lara looked amazing; the flipside of her inner sadness was that when she did turn on her smile it was dazzling. Her star quality shone a light around her and the combination of this beautiful national icon holding hands with the grizzled national hero was irresistible.

Grigory looked at Ilya standing next to him in the gallery, smiled, punched his fists in the air and then embraced him; they both knew they had done a great job.

After a round of whooping and hugs amongst the production team, Grigory quickly slotted back into the desk and checked the feeds from the five news crews they had out around Moscow to catch public reactions.

He punched the connection to his reporter on Ulitsa

Arbat, the big pedestrianised shopping street a few blocks west of the Kremlin.

'Stepan, get me some reactions! I need interviews.'

The camera feed showed huddles of people beginning to form in front of a TV shop where the owner had turned up the sound on all the sets in the window and opened the doors. A crowd of people were gathering around it to watch the coverage from Ostankino and begin to discuss what had happened.

'OK, OK,' Stepan shouted back, and hurried over to the crowd with his cameraman. He grabbed the elbow of a middle-aged businessman at the back of the crowd and turned him round to face the camera. 'Sir, can I just have a quick word with you, please, for your reaction to what has happened this morning?'

The man didn't look straight at the camera but stared around at the street behind it. He looked nervous and confused.

'Er, well, I … you know, it's good, I suppose. Yes, I think these things need to be said.'

'What do you think you'll do now, sir?'

'Er, I don't know. I have to think, but maybe … I have to call my wife,' he said, and walked away.

Ilya cut away as more reactions came in from across the city in Pushinskaya Ploshchad. A middle-aged woman shopper was more forthright, jabbing her finger at the camera: 'Yes, those bastards needed to hear that.' She jerked her head south towards the Kremlin, then pushed past the interviewer towards the Metro station but then turned back and waved her fist at the camera. 'I'm off to Ostankino to support Raskolnikov,' she shouted. 'He needs our support!'

Two grinning youths jumped up and down behind her

and started chanting and pointing at the camera, 'Ras-kol-*ni*-kov! Ras-kol-*ni*-kov!'

All over the city the cameras showed groups of people forming on the snowy streets and then crowds gathering in squares and at intersections. UCO supporters had been secretly supplied with Blue Revolution flags and were walking around, handing them out to people. The fluttering blue banners began to sprout like a strange crop of winter flowers across Moscow.

The police were completely uncertain what to do about it all. The political command structure was paralysed by the broadcast. Everyone in authority was sitting on the fence, stunned and waiting to see which way things would go.

UCO supporters sensed this and took advantage. One TV crew filmed a police car as it drove slowly past a crowd that had gathered outside a shopping centre in the north of the city near Ostankino. The officers deliberately ignored the people and a UCO supporter ran up behind the car and stuck a blue flag into the lights and siren bar on its roof. The crowd cheered and flashed victory signs as it unwittingly drove off flying the flag down the street.

Grigory smiled as he watched all this. He stood up and thumped Ilya on the shoulder. 'Well, it looks like we've got popular support, anyway. I'll give Darensky a call; see how he got on. Ilya, take control, will you?' He walked back to his seat and punched the speed dial on the desk to the 568th.

Lara and Roman were still on the floor of the studio. The catering department had laid out a large banquet at the back of it, and bottles of champagne popped open. Everybody wanted to talk to Roman and he smiled and waved around him, a glass of champagne in his hand.

Ilya kept the mix of positive images flowing, cutting backwards and forwards from the studio party to street scenes, to highlights from the speech. Roman would be doing a serious interview with a heavyweight political commentator shortly and then a press conference was being arranged for domestic and foreign correspondents after that.

He was happily directing these shots when Grigory tapped him on the shoulder and jerked a thumb towards the small director's office just off the main gallery. They squeezed into it. As Grigory shut the door, he looked tense.

'The 568th aren't coming. We're on our own; it's just us against Krymov now.'

Chapter Fifty-Five

Major Batyuk ran back into the press office, breathing hard, just as Roman's broadcast was ending.

Krymov was sitting at one end of the large open-plan office in the Senate Building, in front of a huge TV screen that was now on mute, showing scenes of Lara and Roman celebrating with their supporters.

Captain Bunin and other nervous press aides and guards stood in a semi-circle behind him, tensed in anticipation of a presidential rage.

'Mr President, are you OK?' Batyuk was the only one who dared approach him.

Krymov seemed to have lost the power of speech and just sat and stared out of the window at the courtyard where he had been play-fighting with Sergey a few minutes ago. He was still drunk.

'He betrayed me like Prince Kurbsky,' he said in a small voice.

After that thought his emotions reached a critical mass and he exploded, standing up and shouting, 'That mother-fucker betrayed me! They both betrayed me! The Russian state will not accept such disrespect! *I* am the master here!'

People shrank further away from him with each outburst.

'Get on the phone to the OMON, the MVD, the airforce.

I want that fucking tower wiped off the map! We're going to bomb those fucking bastards into dust!'

Aides began scuttling around him.

'Mr President, I must request that we move to the strategic command bunker immediately,' insisted Batyuk.

Krymov was instantly emphatic, his face blotched red and his jowls shaking with fury. 'No! This is not a nuclear war, Batyuk, if you hadn't noticed; it's a civil war! The Russian head of state has been in the Kremlin for nine hundred years. If I leave the Kremlin, I leave office. We will fight this war from my press office here. We're in the Kremlin, for God's sake – who is going to get us here? Now stop fucking nannying me!'

Batyuk had to accept his reasoning; the Kremlin was about as safe a place as the President could be in a time of crisis.

His mind flicked on and he looked at Krymov sharply. 'Mr President, do you have the mobile numbers for Shaposhnikov and Mostovskoy?'

Krymov looked taken aback but then patted his jacket pockets and pulled his mobile out; he liked to be in direct contact with all his important men so he could harangue them at any moment.

'Yes?' He looked questioningly at Batyuk.

'Good. Let me have them and I will get a trace on their location through the network providers. We also need to get Line 9 stopped before they get up to Ostankino. I'll see to that and get a police blockade on the main roads there.'

Krymov looked pleased at his dynamism; it was why he trusted his security chief so much.

An aide approached him timidly and he spun round, glaring at the man. 'Sir, I'm sorry but Airforce Headquarters are not responding to my calls. I can't understand it, we just can't get through at all.'

'That son of a bitch Mostovskoy! He's got the whole lot of them in with him!'

'OMON commander, sir!' Bunin proffered a phone to the President.

Krymov grabbed it and barked, 'Yes, Melekhov! Now look, I can't bomb these fuckers off the planet but I want you to get all your men up to Ostankino and do the next best thing! I want no mercy for them!'

Chapter Fifty-Six

'We know no mercy and ask for none' was the motto of the Special Purpose Police Squad, the OMON.

Riot police were rarely loved by the people of any country; and the OMON were no exception. Indeed, they had established a reputation for brutality above and beyond the call of duty that made them universally loathed in Russia.

Their recent excesses against petrol rioters had not been broadcast on the media but everyone in Moscow knew that half a dozen demonstrators had been beaten to death in the disturbances. After this, Krymov had ordered a strengthened force of OMON troops to be kept on standby in central Moscow.

So, as soon as Colonel Melekhov was off the phone, he was able to get his men organised fast. They poured out of their barracks in their distinctive blue and black camouflage pattern uniforms with the Cyrillic letters ОМОН on the front and back, wearing their black riot helmets and carrying shields, truncheons, tear gas grenade launchers and assault rifles. A few minutes later a convoy of fifteen huge GAZ lorries and five BTR-80 armoured personnel carriers drove out of the metal gates in the grey slab-like block of the Lubyanka and headed along Ulitsa Bol Lubyanka over Sadovoye Kol'tso, the inner Moscow ring road, and then due north on Prospekt Mira, the dual carriageway up to Ostankino.

'The OMON are coming,' Grigory grabbed Lara's arm and whispered urgently in her ear, as she was laughing with someone in the after-broadcast party. The studio was still packed and buzzing with the positive atmosphere of the rally.

Lara stiffened and went pale as she looked back at him.

'Someone saw them leaving their barracks in Lubyanka and called in on their mobile.' He was running a text banner across the bottom of the screen, asking people to call the telethon studio with information on government troop movements.

'Come on,' he said. 'Let's go and talk to Ilya.'

Raskolnikov was in the middle of his serious interview with the political correspondent, and Ilya was supervising the camera shots. He handed over to an assistant as Grigory came in and the three of them crowded into the small office at the end of the gallery.

'What are we going to do?' Ilya said with a worried frown. 'They'll kill us.'

Grigory nodded tensely. 'We just have to rely on weight of numbers and peaceful protest. There's a lot of people down there.' He gestured down the base of the tower where a large crowd of supporters had gathered. 'Krymov will know that the whole thing will be broadcast on TV in Russia and abroad, and that everyone is now watching, so they can't get too heavy-handed with us or it will backfire against them. We'll just have to make sure that we have a lot of crews out there covering it and hope that the crowds can block the roads. It's our only protection. But we have to keep it peaceful or we'll lose the moral high ground and give them an excuse for violence.'

Ilya and Lara nodded.

'I'll call the crews in town now and tell them to get their arses back here fast,' Ilya said, and turned to go back into the gallery.

'I'm going out there with a crew now,' Lara said, and made to follow him.

Both Grigory and Ilya stopped and looked at her.

Grigory tried to reason with her. 'Lara, there's going to be a riot out there. You—'

'Don't fucking give me that!' she snapped back. 'If this whole thing goes down, *I* go down!'

She turned to Ilya. 'Get me Anton as my cameraman. Tell him to get his stuff together and I'll see him in reception in two minutes. I'm going to change.' She pushed past him.

Since the broadcast had gone out, a crowd of two thousand had gathered around the base of the TV tower, despite Krymov's attempts to stop them getting there. Metro Line 9 had been quickly closed and police units had attempted to stop the crowds on the approach roads running through north Moscow. Despite the rumours of these cordons that had spread through the crowds in town, a lot of people had just ignored them and the police, in the general atmosphere of chaos that reigned, had been unable to stop them. The fleet of vehicles that had driven the five miles from the centre of town were now parked haphazardly along the roads leading up to the tower.

A few minutes later Roman and Grigory stood up on a table that had been dragged out of the foyer at the base of the tower and put at the top of the shallow flight of steps leading up to the plate-glass wall. Lara had changed into jeans and her parka, and stood next to them with two other TV crews.

The crowd milling around in front of them was hugely mixed: some were seasoned UCO members but many were

337

newcomers to political protest, having been inspired by Roman's broadcast, or simply pushed over the edge by economic conditions. They included labourers from a nearby construction site still with their hard hats on, smart office workers from the centre of town, bearded old men, babushkas with shopping bags and youths from the nearby suburban housing estates in hoodies. Blue Revolution flags with eagles on them and blue scarves were being handed out, and a sea of them was waving in front of the steps.

Roman had cut short his interview and postponed his press conference to stand on the table in front of them. Many of the journalists were gathered around the table with Dictaphones out, and several foreign TV crews had arrived. Grigory held up a megaphone next to Roman as he spoke into the mike, feedback crackled, and people who had been jostling and milling around in front of the steps turned to see what the noise was.

'OK, everybody,' more feedback whined, 'can you hear me?'

A cheer went up from the crowd and blue flags waved; they were in high spirits after his speech and buoyed up by the presence of so many other supporters.

The loudhailer stabilised and Roman turned on his best captain's voice: 'Well, I want to thank you all for coming up here to support the Blue Revolution!' Another cheer went up. 'Just look at how many of us there are! Now, we know that the government is sending the OMON up ...' A huge chorus of booing and jeering broke out and a group of UCO supporters began chanting: 'Down with fascists! Down with fascists!'

Roman had to pause before they settled down and he could speak again. 'We have to stop them getting to the tower but we *have* to use only peaceful protest!' He paused to let that sink in. 'If we start any violence then it will give them an excuse to attack us. We have the media here –' he turned and gestured to the three Russian camera crews and four other foreign crews standing on the steps near the table – 'So, Krymov knows that the eyes of the world are on him and he won't dare try anything too heavy-handed. So, what I want you all to do in a minute is to go across the park,' he pointed behind him to the east, to the large area of open ground on the other side of the tower, 'and I want you to go onto Ulitsa Akademika Korolyova and to block the road. We have to hold them there or else they'll get to the tower. Can you do that for me?'

'Yes!' a ragged cheer went up.

'OK, let's go over to the road then!'

Roman was about to jump off the table and lead the way when Grigory grabbed his arm. 'Roman, you can't go! You're our king; if we lose you we lose the game!'

Roman stopped and looked at him. He was used to leading his team from the centre forward position, not the dressing room, but he could see the sense of what Grigory was saying.

'OK, I'll go and then I'll come back.'

Grigory knew that was the best he was going to get. 'OK, let's go.'

He helped Roman down and, with the TV crews filming them, they led the crowd round the tower and across the snowy open ground.

The TV tower was on the western side of a plot of land of about half a kilometre square, with the main road, Ulitsa Akademika Korolyova, running east–west along the northern edge of it. The OMON would be coming from the eastern end of this, so the builders and young men enthusiastically ran the five hundred metres over to the northeast corner of the plot, through a line of trees, across a car park and out onto the main road. This was a wide, tree-lined boulevard, with a large central reservation with a few trees spaced along it.

In the director's gallery, Ilya watched the feeds coming back in from his three crews on the ground and the one that he had put up on the roof of the TV station, three hundred and fifty metres up, where they had a bird's-eye view of the whole process. They fed back pictures of the crowd fanning out around the tower base and moving across the snowfield to the road.

Other people had heard the call to block the street and ran off to get their vehicles. Two bus drivers had ordered their passengers off their bright yellow municipal bendy-buses and then driven both of them up to Ostankino. When they drove these down the two carriageways of the road and then swung them round to block it there was huge cheering from the crowds. Only a small gap was left for people to squeeze through in the overlap between the buses on the central reservation.

Other people were inspired by their action to drive their own cars into the gaps left by the buses on the verges of the road. They then jumped out and called on the crowd to turn them on their side. Men and women all gathered round and began bouncing an old Volga sedan until they rocked it over onto its side to the accompaniment of a huge cheer.

The barricade now effectively blocked the boulevard because its northern end stopped at the edge of the Ostanskiy Prud, a large ornamental lake right next to the road, and its southern end ran into some woods, where people parked their cars between the trees, and which then ended in a large office block complex.

Despite what Roman had said about peaceful protest, some of the crowd had other ideas. Quite a few of them had been in the petrol riots and wanted revenge on the OMON. Others were just hyped-up, bored suburban youths who fancied the idea of a good scrap. Some had brought Molotov cocktails in rucksacks and others paused on the way through the trees to rip large branches off or began digging paving slabs up from under the snow and smashing them into pieces.

Alex and the rest of the team, in the conference room at the top of the tower, hunched round their TV set and watched all these preparations anxiously. Alex stiffened when Ilya cut to a shot of Lara with a microphone standing in the middle of the road out in front of the buses, talking to Anton, her cameraman.

'So, citizens of Russia, you can see the preparations that are going on here at Ostankino to defend the Blue Revolution from attack by the OMON,' she jerked her thumb behind her at the crowds milling around the buses, 'who will shortly be coming from down the road over there.' She pointed back behind Anton. 'We hope that the will of the people will be respected and that the fascist forces will not resort to violence.'

'Hmm.' Colin made a doubtful noise and folded his arms. Alex shot an irritated glance across at him.

The soldiers of the 568th Regiment also watched the developments closely in their canteen. In the continued absence of Colonel Karenin, a confused atmosphere prevailed at the base. Men had wandered away from the canteen after Darensky had failed to rally them, but instead of going to their normal duties they hung around on the parade square in groups, smoking and discussing what had happened. When the shout went round that Lara was back on telly and that a riot was likely the canteen packed out again quickly. Men crammed into seats in front of the TV and moved tables in a circle behind them so they could stand on them and see what was happening. Darensky and his junior officers were torn between running away before Karenin arrived and staying on to see if they did actually still have a chance. In the end they crammed into the canteen with the others.

'Fucking OMON cunts,' said Sergeant Platonov, as he sat in the front row of chairs in front of the TV. He chucked his cigarette butt on the floor and ground it out. Apart from the usual reasons for disliking riot police, there was a lot of inter-service rivalry in the Russian army, and the OMON were hated by the regular forces, who saw them as jumped-up policemen who thought they were hard because they could beat up civilians.

Colonel Melekhov was riding in his command APC at the front of the OMON column and led them west, off the Prospekt Mira dual carriageway, and onto Ulitsa Akademika Korolyova. As he drove down the straight boulevard he could see immediately that it was blocked off by the two yellow buses, overturned cars and a large crowd of people in front of it.

The BTR-80 he was in was an army-green-coloured vehicle, nearly eight metres long, with four massive, all-terrain tyres along each side and an armoured front that sloped down, under the vehicle. It carried a crew of three – him as commander, a driver and a gunner for the 14.5mm KPVT heavy machine gun in the small turret on the top of it. In the armoured compartment at the back of the vehicle was a squad of seven soldiers, including his two signallers.

Melekhov was a stern-faced man in his forties with an OMON black beret on his head bearing its badge of a brutal bison head on a Russian tricolour. He stood up out of the commander's hatch at the front and spoke into his headset mike to the rest of the column on their radio net. 'Right, halt here!' They were a hundred metres from the line of barricades.

As soon as the OMON halted, a chorus of whistling and jeering poured out of the crowd, filling the street in front of the buses; activists had climbed up on top of them and were waving Blue Revolution flags. Some of the teenagers even ran towards the OMON; they rolled snowballs and pitched them into the air but they fell short of the commander.

Grigory was in the crowd and shouted into his loudhailer, 'Peaceful protest only!' but his voice was drowned out by the jeering. Roman had slipped back into the safety of the tower.

'I want the APCs across the road alongside me! All troops debus!' Melekhov shouted.

The huge diesel engines of the four other BTR-80s snouted and their gears ground as their drivers manoeuvred them awkwardly back and forth to get out of the convoy and drive up alongside their commander. They all poured twin spouts of grey diesel fumes into the cold morning air as they approached and formed a revving armoured phalanx across the road, three to the south of the central reservation and two on the northern carriageway.

Officers and NCOs shouted and yelled and got the three hundred men in riot gear formed up into two ranks with long riot shields in front of the vehicles. Walkie-talkie radios crackled and garbled as orders went back and forth from Melekhov in his command APC. Behind the lines of shields came the APCs with squads in between them equipped with tear gas grenade launchers and rifles.

When they were ready, Melekhov keyed the mike on the powerful loudspeakers mounted on the front of his APC and his metallic-edged voice boomed out over the crowd. 'You are an illegal gathering against the constitutional order of the Motherland! You must disperse now!'

A howl of abuse went up from the crowd around the

barricade. Groups on different sides of the road started chanting: 'Shame on you! Shame on you!'

The noise was deafening.

'Advance!' Melekhov jabbed his hand forward and the riot shield wall walked slowly towards the crowd, with the APCs advancing behind them.

Lara was in front of the buses with her cameraman next to her. She was carried away by the chanting and roaring of the crowd; she couldn't believe, with such a press of people around her, that anything could stop them.

She was breathless and flushed as she turned to Anton and the red light went on on top of the camera. She was being jostled constantly by people pressing against her and had to shout over the noise. 'We're here, in front of the barricade across the street, and you can see the OMON line behind me.'

Anton raised the camera above his head and focused in on the menacing metal wall of APCs and riot shields coming towards them.

'There's a lot of people who have come out to defend the revolution here.' Someone barged into her and she had to stop to get her balance back. 'I'm sure we'll succeed!' she said, almost laughing with the exhilaration of the crowd. A chant of 'Motherland or death!' started around her and everyone took it up, shaking their fists at the soldiers in unison and cutting off any further commentary.

Anton kept the camera above his head as the wall of shields crashed into the crowd. Pushing and jostling between people at the front of the crowd became scuffling and fighting as riot policemen leaned in around their shields and aimed blows with heavy truncheons. Men hit back with branches, planks from park benches and tyre irons. Heads split, fists flew, blood flowed and men grappled with the edge of shields trying to get at the OMON behind them.

Chunks of paving slabs flew in from the sides of the road and clattered down on helmets and the metal tops of the APCs. Grigory was still out in front of the buses as well and desperately shouting into his loudhailer, 'No violence! Just block the way! No violence!' but he was jostled until he dropped the megaphone.

A petrol bomb sailed over the crowd and smashed on the front of an APC, spraying burning gobbets over the men next to it, who danced around to avoid them. A volley of tear gas canisters banged out from the squads behind the shield wall. They landed over the other side of the buses, flashed orange as their bursting charges went off and spun around in the snow, spewing out white gas. As soon as they landed, eager hands picked them up and flung them back over so they started causing more problems for the OMON. Riot police gagged and choked, and ran off to get away from the gas.

A woman next to Lara punched her fist in the air and shouted at them, 'Shame! Shame! God's shame on you!' as the hail of petrol bombs increased and splashes of fire splattered down inside the police lines, which began to waver. The crowd was whipped up into a fury now, and men in the front row ripped into the shield wall, grabbing any baton that came out at them, pulling the man out and punching their way into the line.

In the 568th Regiment's canteen the men were absolutely rapt. The three cameras positioned in the crowd gave them an insider's view on a full-scale riot.

'Go on, give 'em a kicking,' muttered Sergeant Platonov, and the men sitting hunched forward in the prime seats around him smirked.

'That's a proper fucking punch-up,' said one.

Alex was less pleased. He looked across at Col with pursed lips. 'This is going to get messy.'

345

In the Kremlin communications office, Krymov sat and watched the same pictures with growing horror. There was a battle of wills going on between the regime and the protestors, and he could see the lines of police breaking and men slipping and sliding on the snow as they were forced back.

'Bunin, get me a line to Melekhov now!'

His communications officer hastily punched into the OMON command net and ran over with a desk mike on a long lead.

Krymov grabbed it and keyed the mike. 'Melekhov! Can you hear me?'

The OMON commander had ducked down behind the metal hatch cover in front of him, away from the shower of stones coming in. He had to press his earpiece to his head to hear Krymov over the noise of the crowd. 'Yes, sir!'

'I want those fuckers dead! Do you hear me? Shoot those bitches! Shoot them all!' He waved his fist in a repeated stabbing motion to emphasise his words. 'If I don't hear gunfire now, I'll have *you* shot! D'ya hear, Melekhov?'

'Yes, sir!' Melekhov was surrounded by chaos and was losing control. The crowd facing him was too big for the number of men he had, and were buoyed up by a passionate belief in what they were defending. But he had been given a direct order by the head of state and implemented it.

'Rifle squads!' he shouted into his mike over the open net to the commanders of the squads between the APCs. He stood up in his command hatch and waved his arm indiscriminately forward at the crowd. 'Get on the APCs and open fire! Live ammunition! Just kill the fuckers!'

The squad commanders thought they hadn't heard the order clearly on their walkie-talkies to start with, but as their commander repeated it and they could see him waving frantically, they got the message.

'Mount up, open fire!'

Riflemen clambered up the stirrup steps between the huge wheels onto the tops of the five-foot-high APCs, from where they had a clear field of fire down into the crowd. Even then the men paused and looked at their commander again.

Did he really mean this?

'I said, open fire!' Melekhov screamed over the net, and waved his fist forward again.

In the crowd, Lara and Anton had managed to work their way to the back next to the narrow gap between the buses, and away from the fighting at the frontline. They found a space against the yellow side of the bus and paused for breath as Anton swung the camera off his shoulder and changed the battery quickly.

A childish popping sound like a domestic fireworks display in a neighbour's garden came faintly over the noise of the shouting and fighting. It sounded innocuous and Lara ignored it and continued waiting impatiently for Anton to finish changing the battery so they could film again.

Anton had spent a lot of time filming in Chechnya and other war zones; he looked up at Lara, his face tense and white.

'Shit!'

'What?'

'They're firing!'

'Eh?'

'They're firing! Fuck, let's go!' He slammed the battery in place, shouldered the camera, grabbed Lara's arm and dragged her through the gap between the buses.

The crowd stood still at first, not realising what was happening. Then, as people looked up and saw the troops on top of the APCs hunched over their rifles and cracking bursts of fire directly down into the crowd, they understood.

High-velocity bullets fired at close range smashed into the ranks of people and tore through flesh and bone with dull thumping sounds. Figures jerked and flayed backwards but couldn't fall because of the press. People screamed and shouted in utter terror at their imminent death. After a confused pause of a few seconds, the crowd now reacted as one, like a shoal of fish. Utter pandemonium now broke out and they fled in panic, leaving bodies flapping in the snow, streaked red with their blood.

The two camera crews on the sides of the road had turned and fled round the ends of the barricade. Their camera shots just showed a scramble of feet in the snow as the cameramen ran for their lives with their cameras down at their sides.

Back in the gallery, Ilya fed the scenes out live but couldn't tell what was happening. At the same time he shouted into his headset, 'Lara! Lara! Are you there? Are you there? What's happening? Are they firing over the crowd? What's happening?'

Anton dragged her round to the sheltered side of one of the buses. She ran through the open side door and up the steps into it, so that she was now able to stand and look out over the crowd through the side window.

'Anton! Come on!' she screamed back at him and he followed her up into the bus. 'Are we getting this? Are we live?'

'Yes! We're live! We're live!' He brought the camera up on his shoulder, got his eye on the screen and focused on her.

Ilya's voice shouted into her earpiece again, 'What's happening? Are they firing into the air? You're live now!'

Millions of people around the world watched in horror as Lara stood up in front of the window in full view of the APCs with her back to them and her strained face looking at the camera. 'No! They're not firing in the air! They're firing into the *crowd*! Look!'

She half turned and pointed. Anton's camera shot steadied and clearly showed the soldiers standing on the APCs firing indiscriminately down onto the crowd.

The whole bus window went white and shattered as a burst of bullets swept across it. Lara screamed and ducked down, the camera shot went to the floor of the bus as gunfire poured in over their heads.

The mike still picked up muffled sounds – 'Let's go!' – followed by the sight of Anton's feet sprinting and snow spraying up around the lens as he ran with it at his side. They fled for their lives with the rest of the crowd streaming back through the gap between the two buses.

Krymov was still shouting in Melekhov's earpiece, 'That's it! Get the fuckers! Look at 'em run! Now get through those fucking buses!'

'Clear the way in front!' Melekhov shouted into the loud-speakers on his APC to the riot troops still in front of the line of army vehicles. They turned, ducked back under the gunfire and ran behind them.

The crowd had scattered to the sides of the road or crammed back through the gap so that there were now only a pile of bodies in front of the APC.

'Delta Two! Break through the gap! Go over the bodies!' Melekhov yelled across to the carrier next to him. The troops on top of the carrier stopped firing and dropped down into the hatches as it backed up noisily and then paused as it was aimed at a bus.

The driver revved as hard as he could, the massive diesel roared and then he let in the clutch and it charged forward, the all-terrain tyres grinding over bodies in its way. The armoured snout, backed by fourteen tons of metal, smashed into the back section of one articulated bus and shovelled it aside, knocking people flying who were sheltering behind it.

The driver backed up again and took another charge, which bent the rear section completely aside. Metal shrieked as the carrier broke through the gap and its green snout burst out on the other side.

'Follow them through! Follow them through!' Melekhov yelled, and the other carriers grunted forward and through the gap.

Krymov was now ecstatic and jumped out of his chair in the press office.

He keyed the mike again. 'That's it, teach those fuckers a lesson! I want you to make an example of them that they won't forget! Keep firing!'

'Keep firing!' Melekhov relayed on to his men.

Lara and Anton had fled with the crowd and were running back in terror through the screen of trees to the open ground around the tower. The five carriers broke out and charged through the trees after them, their huge tyres churning up the snow and their exhausts bellowing enthusiastically. Troops stood up in the hatches and shot randomly at people running around them. Bodies twisted and spun as rounds slammed into them, injured people cried out to those running past, red streaks spattered on the snow.

Ilya quickly cut to the crew filming on the top of the TV tower. From above, the crowd could be seen fanning out from the northeast corner of the square of flat land, running back to the tower with the five carriers now driving slowly amongst them to allow their crews better aimed shots.

People around the world continued to watch, transfixed with horror, as he cut back to the shaky camera shot of Anton's feet, accompanied by the sound of his puffing breathing. Twice he stepped over dead bodies, then carried on running.

'Here! Here!' He grabbed Lara and they dived into cover

behind a solid concrete park bench. They huddled up against the back of it, sheltering from the slaughter going on all around them.

'We've got to do this. Come on!' Anton lay on his side a few feet away from the bench and twisted the camera round so he could get a shot of Lara with her head down behind the bench. She was breathing hard and was scared out of her wits.

'We're live!'

She looked straight at the camera, tears in her eyes and her face contorted in desperation. 'Please! Please! I appeal to you, men of the 568th Regiment! Please, in the name of God!'

Her voice rose to a shriek as a burst of gunfire blew chunks of concrete off the back of the bench and showered her in dust and splinters, she was sobbing hysterically now and ducked her head, tears pouring down her face. 'Please help us!'

The microphone picked up the growling sound of a carrier's engine as it approached out of shot behind the bench. As the men on top got a better angle over the bench they first saw Anton lying on the ground and poured fire at him. The shot of Lara shook and the mike picked up the thumps as the rounds raked across his chest. Lara screamed, the camera dropped out of his lifeless hands into the snow and the screen went black.

Chapter Fifty-Seven

The men of the 568th Regiment couldn't believe what they were seeing. Their favourite feminine icon was being shot to pieces in front of their eyes.

Sergeant Platonov muttered in disbelief, 'Those cunts are gonna to kill 'er.'

Standing behind his chair, Private Novikov had tears in his eyes and said in a small voice, 'They can't do that ...'

The men were also overcome, not with revolutionary fervour this time, but with simple protective anger. Where Darensky's previous rhetoric had failed to connect with their Russian psyche, this footage now exploded it.

The doors of the canteen burst open and the solid mass of the regiment poured out and ran across the parade ground to the vehicle park.

Colonel Karenin looked at them groggily through the windows of the administration block as he was getting up and wondered what the hell was going on.

The men scrambled up onto their green, camouflage-painted T-90 main battle tanks, Tunguska anti-aircraft vehicles and BMP-3 armoured personnel carriers. Hatches flipped open and they wriggled down into cramped driving and command positions. Infantry squads grabbed rifles, flakjackets and helmets, and, buckling them on, ran over to the back of the APCs as the two armoured doors at the back swung open and they crammed into their seats inside. Engines burst into life and roared.

Darensky strapped his padded commander's helmet on and punched through to the regiment radio net. 'All units, follow my lead!'

Crisp barks of 'Roger that!' came in from the commanders of the eleven other T-90 tanks, three Tunguskas and the ten BMP-3s.

Darensky traversed the turret of his tank as he led the way out of the vehicle park and the long barrel of the 125mm main armament swung round.

'Load HE-FRAG!' he barked on his headset to his gunner, on the right-hand side of the turret next to him.

'HE-FRAG, loaded!' the gunner called back as he selected the correct ammunition on the auto-loader carousel and it rammed the high-explosive fragmentation round into the breech.

Forty-seven tonnes of heavy metal thundered forward, kicking two arcs of snow out from behind its tracks, and then jerked right, round the corner of a barrack block onto the parade square. On the way out to the main gate, the tank passed the grey concrete administration block, where Karenin and his remaining loyal officers watched them from the first-floor windows.

Darensky spotted them. 'One hundred metres, our nine o'clock, first-floor window to right of main entrance, one round HE-FRAG. Fire now!'

'Firing!'

The gun muzzle boomed a tongue of propellant fire and smoke and the breech clanged back next to him as the auto-loader spat the cartridge out. He felt the tank rock back on its suspension under him and then flow on again.

The round smashed into the old concrete building and exploded inside in a flash of orange and a burst of dust.

The tanks behind him all swung their guns round as they followed his example and round after round crashed into the side of the building as the regiment delivered its contemptuous farewell salute to its former commanding officer.

Tanks and APCs tore past the burning building and out of the gates of the base onto the A-104 Dmitrovskoye Shosse. Cars and trucks swerved into the middle lane as the long stream of armoured vehicles poured out and headed south to Ostankino.

Chapter Fifty-Eight

Lara cringed behind the bench, looking at Anton's dead body stretched out in the snow in front of her.

She could hear the heavy growl of the APC approaching and feel the vibrations of its engine through the ground. Any second now it would pass the bench and she would then be exposed, targeted and shot dead by the soldiers standing on top of it.

She was too terrified to move, though. She had made her appeal to the regiment but it was too late now for them to do anything. This was it: she really was about to die. She hugged her knees to her chest and sobbed as she stared at Anton's body.

All sound stopped.

The colour orange moved across her vision.

A heavy blow hit the side of her head, making it ring.

Pieces of metal spun over her head and some hit Anton's body, jerking it obscenely.

She couldn't breathe.

She fell forward on her hands and knees, trying to make sense of what was happening.

'She's moving. I think she's OK.'

'Fuck, that was close,' Alex said with relief and then shouted, 'Reload!'

Col heaved another three-foot-long green Kornet missile tube into place on top of its tripod launcher. They were on the top of the TV station with the launcher set up on a table that they had dragged over to the guardrail.

When they had first seen Lara's footage of the soldiers firing at her on the bus Alex had shouted, 'Let's go!' and they had run up onto the roof, pulled their weapons out of the second helicopter that was still parked there and quickly set them up.

Alex continued the missile bombardment now.

He hunched over the table, pressed up against the eyepiece at the bottom of the tripod. He spun the two small dials and the baleful glass eye of the optical tracking unit, under the missile, rotated round until another APC was in the crosshairs of his sights.

'Firing now!'

Col stood clear of the backblast.

The thick tube flashed and spat out a missile almost too fast to see. The semi-automatic command-to-line-of-sight laser beamriding guidance kept the dart on target. It slammed into the thin top armour of the carrier with an instant bright orange flash followed by a slower burst cloud of diesel flames, snow and debris. Gravity filtered the pieces so that the heavier bits of metal crashed down first in a large circle around the vehicle. The explosion of the two shaped-charge warheads in the missile made the fourteen tonne carrier bounce off the ground and then stop dead.

Pete and Yamba had each set up a Kord 12.7mm heavy machine gun with its muzzle poking through the railings and its bipod mount resting on the floor so they could depress the gun far enough to hit the targets below them. Accurate five-round bursts banged out at the other three carriers, knocking men off the top and forcing the others back down into the hatches.

Under this onslaught, the APC drivers increased speed and spun round in a wide circle heading back for the trees and then the road. Alex slotted another Kornet missile into the engine compartment of a third carrier as it ran away. It burned fiercely with the other two.

Colonel Melekhov had survived, though, and decided that his force needed to get out of the area; he pulled his trucks back down the boulevard and then south along Prospekt Mira.

Alex looked down on the carnage on the white field below him. The three burning wrecks of the carriers sent ugly black drifts of smoke over it but he could still see fifty or sixty bodies strewn on the ground in a fan shape starting back at the road block. He didn't know how many other dead were piled up there.

Lara stood up from behind the bench, her ears still ringing from the nearby explosion of the Kornet that had taken out the carrier. She looked at its blackened, burning hulk and stumbled away through the snow, along with Grigory and the crowd of other shocked survivors, towards the tower.

Chapter Fifty-Nine

In the Kremlin press office, Krymov also looked at the TV screen in shock. The camera crew on the roof had the perfect vantage point to film the rout of the OMON forces.

Major Batyuk, Captain Bunin and the other press aides looked on with worried expressions. The whole thing looked awful from a media point of view. There had certainly been violence from the demonstrators but the cold-blooded hunting down of them in broad daylight had been filmed in detail and transmitted around the world.

Krymov wasn't thinking about that, though, he was thinking of the military situation; that had been a disaster as well.

He spoke quietly: 'Batyuk, I want regular forces up there now. Whatever we've got in town, I want it up there now: tanks, artillery, whatever.'

Batyuk's shaved head nodded. 'I'll see what we've got.'

Some quick communications work assembled a force of MVD and regular army troops in trucks, BTR-80s and BMP-3 tracked carriers. Krymov appointed Colonel Vronsky in command.

Vronsky had seen what the Kornet missile launcher had done to the first attack and so led his forces up a back road to the tower, staying in built-up areas to keep them out of line of sight of its lethal gaze. As the column of vehicles crossed a railway a kilometre south of the tower, the troops debussed and the APCs rumbled off the road and along the side of the railway so that they were sheltered by the steep embankment. After a few hundred metres the line of them growled their way up it, through an industrial estate with gravel bunkers for railway ballast, and then on to an area of woodland. This ran north to the back of an office block that was just fifty metres directly across the side road from the main entrance to the tower.

The squads debussed from their carriers and crept in slowly towards it.

Chapter Sixty

Alex, Lara, Grigory and Roman were all hunched round a table in the telethon room in Ostankino, looking at the huge videowall on the side of the studio. It showed a map of Moscow that was being used by the graphics technicians to plot the movement of government troops coming towards them as supporters reported them in on their mobiles.

Lara had quickly grabbed a plastic cup of sweet tea from a vending machine and hugged it to her with one hand as she bolstered herself with a chocolate bar with the other. Both she and Grigory still looked shaken after their experience outside the tower. The snowfield was now covered in ambulance crews and medics carrying the wounded off to hospital. The bodies of the dead had to be left.

Grigory felt he had to say something to Alex. 'Well, we tried the peaceful route.' He gave a grim shrug.

Alex nodded. 'We had to. But from the reports coming in it looks like they want a real war this time.' He indicated the screen and the symbols of troops and carriers approaching them.

Roman said slowly, 'I think they mean to kill us. Krymov isn't messing around. This really is a fight to the death for him and we have to play by his rules now. Alex, you're the one with the military experience – can you defend us?'

Alex rubbed his mouth ruefully and thought about the situation in the tower, the men and weapons at his disposal and his own chances of getting out alive. They didn't look good.

'Well, I'd better bloody well try, hadn't I?' he said, and raised an eyebrow.

Lara looked at him thoughtfully across the table. They hadn't heard anything from Sergey since the broadcast and she presumed he was under arrest or dead. In the absence of his huge personality, and in her shaken-up state, she found herself gravitating back to the Englishman.

Everybody was conscious of Sergey's absence but there was nothing they could do about it. Lara had called his mobile but it was switched off, and there was so much else going on around them that they tried to force it from their minds.

'Let's get on with it then!' Grigory said.

He and Alex quickly set about organising what defences they could muster against the new threat. A lot of the crowd had fled in terror but several hundred diehards had stayed on and were packed into the huge foyer downstairs and around the steps leading up to it.

Grigory got them and his staff organised into gangs to carry desks and sofas out of the TV offices, into the lifts and down to the foyer where they piled up the furniture as a barricade across the doors.

They had been able to collect six functioning assault rifles and some spare magazines off the dead OMON soldiers, and these were handed out to six volunteers who had done military service. Alex looked at them warily. They weren't going to tip the balance in his favour but, given their desperate situation, he was open to all offers.

After a quick consultation with the team he decided to put most of their heavy weaponry up on the top of the TV station, partly because of the all-round view it gave of the approaches to the tower but also because at such a height it was hard for attacking forces to elevate their weapons enough to fire at them. Infantry could raise their rifles but it would be difficult for vehicle or tripod-mounted heavy weapons to get that high.

Despite their much smaller numbers – Alex estimated the attackers, from the reports of the numbers of vehicles, at about three hundred – they might have some chance of holding them off until ... he wasn't sure. They just didn't have any alternative at the moment.

Lara and the other TV crews would be at large as before, but the massacre had deterred any more people from coming out and there was nothing that the international community could do for them now. Consequently, they got all their supporters up from the lifts to the TV station and sheltered them in the offices on the north side of the tower, away from the troops approaching from the south.

Alex also took his newly raised force of six volunteers and set up firing positions for them in two huge loop windows near the base of the tower. These were directly above the massive arch over the main entrance, on the equivalent of the fifth floor. He put three men in each window along with a supply of fragmentation grenades. Their rifle fire would be of limited accuracy and use when the enemy were approaching so he told them to keep their heads down and out of sight until he called them on the walkie-talkie from the roof.

The team grimly set about preparing for the coming battle. They moved the Kornet launcher round to the west of the tower where it overlooked the direction of the enemy approach. They had only four missiles left, which weren't going to win the war on their own though they could certainly help.

Alex asked Grigory for something to cut away the metal railing around the edge of the roof and his maintenance man came up with an angle grinder from his workshop. He quickly cut four sections out of the fence. As the last section gave way, Alex watched the metal bend out over the three-hundred-and-fifty-metre drop and finally tumble away into the air. They all stood and watched it slowly somersaulting down until it smashed abruptly into the ground. Alex didn't like having to stand in front of the abyss without the rail but it did mean that Pete and Yamba could set up their two Kord heavy machine guns with their bipods resting right on the edge so that they could kneel and point the barrels down at targets approaching the base of the tower. Arkady also dragged the AGS-30 grenade launcher out of the helicopter; even though he wasn't flying he was determined to play his part.

Magnus readied his sniper rifle to pick off commanders and other high-value targets that showed themselves. He stood next to the parapet and his lined face looked out over Moscow to the south.

During all this, Pete ran out of the foyer and set up some MTP-2 mines on tripwires in places the enemy was likely to use around the office block across the road from the main entrance.

Their three Shmel launchers and two PKM light machine guns were also loaded and would do against trucks and groups of infantry. After that it would be down to their assault rifles, and after that they would probably all be dead.

'There they are.' Col looked down from the parapet with his binoculars into the gravel yard along the side of the railway line, a kilometre south. They could just see the top of a BTR-80 moving behind a pile of gravel and then glimpsed it as it passed by a gap between two large conveyor belt machines.

He watched it go by but then shouted to Alex, 'Hey, BMP-3 coming up!' He had seen the distinctive small turret moving behind the gravel and it would pass the narrow gap in a moment.

'Let's get it!' Alex had the Kornet set up ready and quickly twirled the dials to zero his sight in on the five-foot gap between the machines. He could see Interior Ministry troops filing past it in their blue-grey parkas, green flak jackets, helmets and rifles. One of them glanced nervously up at the tower, not realising that he was being watched by such a deadly gaze.

What worried Alex most about the attacking force were the three BMP-3s that had been reported. These were shaped like large tanks and carried a squad of seven infantry, but also had a small turret on them, which, despite its size, contained a horrific amount of weaponry. He couldn't work out how the Russian engineers had packed it all in. Apart from a 30mm cannon and a 7.62mm machine gun, there was also the main armament of a 100mm gun. This could fire normal high-explosive rounds but, most crucially, could also spit out Stabber 9M117 anti-tank guided missiles, and he knew that these certainly could hit the top of the tower. They needed to get the three machines before they brought their weapons into action.

He saw the green bow of the vehicle emerge from behind one of the conveyor belts; it was moving at walking pace, keeping step with the infantry around it. He centred the crosshairs of the laser guidance device on it and called, 'Firing now!' so that no one got caught by the backblast.

The fat tube above his head on the tripod boomed. The missile kicked out straight ahead but then quickly angled sharply down to follow its guidance beam as Alex kept the laser on the side of the carrier. A soldier behind the BMP looked round and saw it coming, his eyes widening in horror as the dart hurtled down at him.

The missile hit the thin side armour. The first warhead blew a hole in it, allowing the second charge to pass through into the interior of the vehicle and explode.

Alex looked up from the launcher at the large cloud of debris rippling up from the industrial estate. His gaze met Col's gimlet eyes and they both nodded grimly. This was not going to be pretty.

After that, Colonel Vronsky ordered red smoke grenades thrown out to cover the gap from the missile launcher's sight. He quickened the pace of his advance, spreading his infantry screen out through the wood. They used the cover of the trees to set up machine-gun firing points, angling the muzzles up by resting them on low branches or the shoulders of other men. Other soldiers tilted their heads back and aimed through the sights of rocket-propelled grenade launchers.

Five of the BTR-80 APCs were detailed to find points under trees several hundred metres back from the tower so that they could bring their 14.5mm main armament into play. Their turrets allowed the gun to elevate sixty degrees and from that far back they could hit the top of the tower. The range was quite long – about seven hundred metres – so the fire wasn't accurate, but none the less a wall of lead blasted up at the defenders. The burning tracer rounds in it made it look like a dense red spider's web stretched out of the wood up to the TV station.

Alex and the others winced as the bullets cracked over their heads and blew chunks off the concrete spire that soared up behind them in the middle of the roof terrace. Other bullets went low and smashed the windows out on the offices below them; panes of glass slipped out and spun off into the void before crashing down around the entrance.

RPGs screamed overhead, exploding on the spire and spraying out metal shards.

The southern and western sides of the station were being plastered with fire. Pete and Yamba banged a few rounds out in response with their heavy machine guns but there were just too many firing points to aim at: more than twenty flashes of light spread out amongst the trees, jabbering lead up at them. The weight of incoming fire meant that they had to duck down to minimise their exposure over the edge of the roof. However, a few heavy-calibre rounds then smashed through the ceiling below them and punched out some of the roof by their feet as well.

'Shit!' Alex yelped and jumped further back from the edge as a big 14.5mm bullet blew a hole the size of a fist in the floor by his right knee.

Col and Magnus managed to crawl up to the lip of the roof, despite the bullets slamming in around them, with their Shmel launchers, and put two rounds into the trees that exploded with large fireballs and snuffed out a couple of machine-gun squads each.

However, the two remaining BMP-3s had got into cover behind buildings and now darted forward and launched guided missiles at the top of the tower.

Magnus spotted the white flash of a launch – 'Missile!' – and they all threw themselves back away from the edge. The Stabber ploughed into the floor below them, exploded on the ceiling and blew a five-foot square chunk out of the roof. Debris sprayed out and splinters of metal pinged off the huge concrete spire.

Winning firefights was all about getting a heavy weight of suppressive fire in, which forced the enemy to keep their heads down. Alex could see that they were losing this battle and that he had to do something to change the direction of play.

'Right! Everybody off the roof and spread out in the offices below! Pete, Arkady and Yamba, you're one floor down! Col, me and Magnus, two down! Don't show yourselves and only fire on my command!'

They all grabbed their weapons and ran down the stairs, relieved to be away from the lethal metal gale blowing over the edge of the roof.

By the time they had set up firing positions and radioed in to Alex on their headsets, the attackers had moved through the trees up to the two-storey office block fifty metres across from the entrance to the tower. A couple of Pete's tripwire mines banged out but officers' shouts and threats drove the advance on. They set up firing points and a torrent of gunfire poured through the archway and into the plate-glass foyer wall; the whole thing shattered and collapsed like a glass waterfall. Bullets whined off the metal turnstiles and hammered into the concrete back wall, sending sprays of dust out over the whole large space. The furniture barricade began to be shredded, RPGs smashed into it, blowing tables and desks across the foyer.

When they were all in place, Alex gave the order and they popped up in their new office positions and were able to get a few seconds of fire down on the attackers before the machine-gun onslaught shifted from the roof and blew the windows out in the floors they were on, driving them back inside the station. Alex managed to take out a BTR-80 with another Kornet, but he knew it wasn't going to change anything. He sprinted back away from the windows, deeper into the building, lugging the heavy launcher with Colin. They stopped in a corridor, breathing hard, and then both got knocked over by the blast of a guided missile hitting the office they had just been in.

Alex had splinters of glass sticking out of the side of his

face so that blood ran down and dripped off his chin. He coughed and choked on the dust whorling around.

'Shit.' He winced as he moved his hand to check his face and accidentally jabbed a shard further in.

Col leaned over, carefully pulling all the bits out. He held up a large piece in front of his face. 'There goes your modelling career, mate.'

'Thanks.'

Alex levered himself onto his feet and tried to think what he was going to do next. Whenever they tried to fire they just attracted a wall of lead. They were running out of options, and soon the attackers would charge the main entrance and get into the tower. There was no way they would fight their way up three hundred metres of stairwells; all they needed to do was to get into the basement and switch off the huge generators down there and the Blue Revolution would be off air and effectively dead. Just as his team would be if they were captured. Alex had no illusions about what Krymov would do to them as foreign mercenaries. He thought about Sergey, the madman who had got him into this whole thing. He was probably dead already. Well, they would be joining him soon.

Alex poked his head round the corner of a window in the bottom floor of the TV station that hadn't been shot up yet. He waited for the first troops to break cover from the office building and then yelled into his walkie-talkie to the volunteers stationed above the entrance, 'Now!'

The six guys had each prepped two grenades and lobbed them out of the loophole window at the troops. They then ran for their lives along the corridor away from the windows as the twelve grenades went off outside and the full weight of attacking fire came smashing back in where they had been. Two guided missiles slammed into the thick concrete and blew in the wall, sending dust and fragments down the corridor after them.

After that Colonel Vronsky brought up a BTR to lead the assault into the lobby. It growled up next to the office block as the attackers reloaded and readied themselves for the final push. The smoke grenade launchers on the front of the APC banged and a fan of six grenades shot out. Soldiers lobbed more out into the open. The grenades spun around in the snow, spraying out oily fumes that dispersed into a thick red smoke screen over the open ground leading up to the foyer. Shouts and whistles sounded and a hurricane of gunfire opened up on the entrance, the loopholes over it and any other potential point of return fire.

Alex peered carefully down through a hole blown by an RPG explosion in the wall of an office. This was it: the final assault, and he had run out of options. There was nothing he could do to stop it now.

All the attacking soldiers were focused on this final push, firing at points in front of them, and didn't notice two civilians running along the front of the office block, right across their line of fire. Where streaks of red machine-gun tracers spat out of ground-floor windows they just ducked their heads down and ran under them. They got as close to the tower as they could and then kneeled down between two windows, breathing hard in the swirling red smoke all around them and eyeing the fifty-metre gap to the foyer: it was filled with smoke and machine-gun fire.

Sergey stood up to run and looked back at Fyodor, his face distorted in desperation.

'Come on, we can make it. Let's go!'

Fyodor stared back at him. His eyes narrowed and flicked out to his right, over the hellish no man's land, and then back to Sergey, calculating the risks. He nodded and Sergey turned to run.

As he burst out away from the building something made him glance to the right to check that Fyodor was with him. He saw the impassive face standing still by the wall looking at him and then it turned and disappeared back into the swirling red mist.

Sergey was already out in the open; he was fully committed. He threw his arms out, shouted, '*Russkaya dusha!*' and ran for his life.

The attacking soldiers were hunched over their sights, focused on hitting the foyer, the loopholes or the TV station above. The appearance of a single, screaming, unarmed madman running at full speed across in front of them took them by surprise.

'What the fuck … ?'

'Is he ours?'

Fire slackened off as confused faces flicked towards commanders.

Before they had time to even answer the questions, the figure disappeared into the red fog, charged in through the shattered lobby, vaulted over the furniture barricade and disappeared.

Colonel Vronsky saw the madman's dash and ordered renewed effort. 'Keep going!'

The eight-wheeled BTR-80 charged forward through the smoke, leaving red whorls in its wake. Its engine roared as it drove up the shallow flight of steps to the foyer and smashed into the remains of the furniture barricade. Files of troops ran forward on either side of it, rifles and RPGs held ready. They flattened themselves against the tower base and prepared to make the final dash through into the basement to get at the generators.

Having cleared a way through the barricade, the BTR reversed out and the soldiers around it threw a shower of fragmentation grenades into the room, which exploded, sending out bursts of metal splinters.

The BTR also exploded and blew over onto its side. The deep thumps and shockwaves of more explosions came from the direction of the office block. Tracer rounds started streaking in at the assault troops from the north of the tower. Men about to run into it were dashed against the wall and spun round. The others threw themselves on the ground.

Shouts came from confused men: 'What the fuck is going on? Which fucking idiots are firing at us?'

Soldiers crawled away into cover behind the burning BTR. Engines roared in the red fog around them and more gunfire crashed out. Guided missiles streaked in from the south of the tower as well. They were taking hits from both directions now. A BMP-3 on the edge of the woods took a missile and exploded with a deep boom.

A huge metal monster burst through the smoke in front of the foyer, smashed into the back of the burning BTR and spun it out of the way. The big gun traversed round towards the office block and fired with a white flash that swirled the fog violently.

The assault troops broke and ran as the tanks and BMP-3s of the 568th chased them back into the woods, chainguns spitting out defiance at them.

Chapter Sixty-One

Alex led the team out of the lift and into the shattered foyer.

They moved carefully with their weapons held ready. They still couldn't believe that the 568th had arrived and they were actually alive.

Like the others, Alex's face was caked with blood and dust from the missile explosions. Their eyes flicked round the lobby, taking in the devastation. As they stepped slowly forward their boots crackled on a carpet of broken glass. Every wall and surface was pockmarked with bullet and RPG holes and stank of cordite. A red fog swirled around in patches on the floor, stirred by the gentle wind coming in where the glass wall had been shot out.

They moved forward and took up defensive positions behind the bits of furniture still scattered around. They could hear the 568th troops still out in hot pursuit in the woods. The black hulk of the BTR burned on the steps in front of them and bodies were strewn across the open ground to the office block, which was also now on fire from all the tank rounds and missiles that had hit it.

'Foyer is clear. You can come down,' Alex said into his walkie-talkie. Another lift shaft hummed as Lara, Roman and Grigory descended. They too walked out in stunned silence as they surveyed the devastation.

Something rattled across the hall and five assault rifles swung round at it. Sergey pushed the bullet-riddled door from the stairs open and it fell off its hinges.

Lara shrieked and rushed over to him, throwing her arms around him. 'Sergey! Sergey!'

Chaos broke out as everyone forgot their imminent demise and ran over.

'What the fuck happened to you?' Roman demanded delightedly.

Sergey was grinning from ear to ear and was only too pleased to tell a good tale. 'They chucked us off the Metro at Tsvetnoy Bulvar so we decided to walk here, but then someone in the crowd said there was a police cordon. Fyodor wanted to play it safe and take it slowly so we had to stop to buy some new coats and hats.' He held out his cheap parka; he had lost the hat in his mad dash. 'Then we hid in a public toilet until I made him carry on. We walked through a back route, around all the housing estates and then over the railway line.'

'Where's Fyodor?' Grigory asked with a concerned look.

Sergey looked confused. 'Well, he was right here,' he gestured to his side with both hands, 'and then I went to run in here. I looked back, but he had stopped.' He paused and looked shocked. 'Then he just turned and went ...'

The others looked at him, trying to work out what had happened.

Lara's mood turned icy. 'I think our gallant general probably looked at the situation here and decided that his best interests lay elsewhere.'

The others looked down at the ground, but from what they knew of Fyodor's motivation for the coup, they could see that it made sense.

Sergey, typically, was the least affected by it. 'Hey, but we are alive!' he shouted.

Other staff were coming down out of the lifts now, looking at their smashed building. UCO supporters were less bothered about the damage and ran out of the lifts with blue flags flying, down the steps outside and over to the 568th soldiers, who were returning.

Tanks, APCs and Tunguska anti-aircraft vehicles rumbled back in from the woods. Captain Darensky stood in the turret of his huge T-90 tank, grinning, and ordered his troops to take up 360-degree defensive positions around the tower.

Blue Revolution supporters jumped up and down on top of the tanks, waving blue flags for the cameras, and the media girls went mad kissing soldiers. A huge cheer went up from the troops as Lara did a lap of honour round the base, stopping continually to kiss her fans.

Chapter Sixty-Two

On CNN, General Fyodor Mostovskoy sat next to President Krymov in the Kremlin press office as if they were, and had never been anything but, close allies.

Sergey was incensed. 'That fucking son of a bitch traitor! How the fuck can he just sit there next to Krymov! We only just betrayed him!'

'Sergey, darling, will you shut up, please? I'm trying to listen!' Lara snapped, reached for the remote and turned the volume up louder on the large TV in a conference room.

The Kremlin press room was buzzing with chatter between correspondents from all the foreign and domestic media as they speculated about what might be said. Journalists moved around in front of Mostovskoy, hunched down on the floor shifting their microphones about amongst the mass of them on the table, like a large flower arrangement, or trying to slot small tape recorders into it. Captain Bunin shepherded them out of the way, trying to get the press conference going as fast as possible.

The CNN Moscow editor, Gerry Kramer, standing at the back of the room, managed to squeeze in a quick broadcast to his anchor before they got going. 'Well, Mike, this is the latest in an extraordinary morning here in Moscow. We can hardly believe that it was only a few hours ago that Roman

Raskolnikov flew back into the capital in such a dramatic fashion. Since then there has been an alternative government announced at the Ostankino tower, an appalling massacre to rival Bloody Sunday, a huge gun battle and now this. One of the original plotters has realigned himself with the Krymov regime. We have no idea what is going on here, and it's not often you'll hear me say that, Mike.'

There was a loud cough from the front and Captain Bunin spoke to quieten down the feverish journalistic babble. Lara and everyone were watching CNN on a satellite feed – they weren't relaying it on from Ostankino on the terrestrial network for obvious reasons. That meant that Russians without a satellite dish couldn't see it but enough had dishes that the coverage could still deal a serious blow to the support for the revolution, depending on what Fyodor said. They all waited anxiously to hear.

'Please, ladies and gentlemen, Lieutenant-General of the Airforce Mostovskoy will now address the press conference.'

Fyodor didn't bat an eyelid. He was sitting behind a desk dressed once again in his full airforce uniform and acted as if he had never had any notion of disloyalty to the regime. Krymov sat next to him with his arms folded across his chest and his chin in the air, with the look of a man who was master in his own house again.

'Mr President, people of Russia, ladies and gentlemen of the press, I have called this press conference because I wish to make plain to you what I have learned from my penetration of the foreign coup attempt this morning. It was important for an agent of the Russian government to shadow the plotters in order to determine the full extent of their connections with foreign governments.'

'Head-fucker!' shouted Sergey in outrage, before Lara slapped him to shut him up again.

'This "Blue Revolution",' he uttered the words with icy contempt, 'is exactly the same as the Orange Revolution, the Rose Revolution, the Tulip Revolution and all the other criminal movements inspired by fascist governments. As Russians we must be on our guard against these foreign saboteurs. We have been infiltrated!' Fyodor let slip a rare flash of anger.

Next to him Krymov shifted in his seat, nodded and muttered, 'Fascists.'

'Through my work inside the coup, I have been able to confirm to our air units, who had been misled by them, that the real reason for the plot is to allow the fascist agent Shaposhnikov to take over control of all areas of the United Aircraft Corporation whilst extending his grasp of the media that has distorted and misrepresented so much freedom in Russia.

'If anyone questions this information then I am happy to provide them with the name of a well-known British mercenary commander hired by the British government to organise this coup in retaliation for Russia's entirely justified withdrawal of its energy services to that country, following their unjustified aggression against the peace-loving people of Russia.'

Alex froze. He could imagine Harrington, the PM and the Cobra committee watching this in their bunker under Downing Street.

Oh fuck, this is heading towards World War Three. We have just started a fight with a nuclear-tipped psychopath who now has concrete proof that Brits are involved.

Alex knew that no matter how 'deniable' Harrington claimed he was, at the end of the day he and Colin were former British army officers and that was enough in any ordinary Russian's mind, let alone Krymov's, to label the whole coup a foreign-backed plot.

He had to hand it to Mostovskoy, though; his volte-face was unbelievable, performed without a hint of irony. It was vintage Soviet era stuff – claim that black is white and just stonewall any naysayers.

After Fyodor had finished reading his prepared statement, Krymov took over the mike, and leaned forward, jabbing his finger at the journalists.

'You lot need a lesson in journalism! You see, now you have clear evidence of everything I have been saying to you for years. I wasn't making it up! These foreign bastards have strangled our economy. I call on all free Russian people to refute the efforts of Shaposhnikov, who has been behind this campaign of corruption and gangsterisation. Through his greed he has been responsible for driving out our valued foreign partners in the petrol refineries. I say to TNK-BP, Total and ExxonMobil and all other foreign investors that once we have crushed this unacceptable face of Russian capitalism then they will be able to operate in Russia again, free from the scourge of the harassment that Shaposhnikov has led. And we will crush them! Now that the airforce has been set right about the truth of this foreign plot they are once again in their true role of defenders of the Motherland. Yes, now they have learned who their boss is, and I have already issued tactical orders to them, so those sons of bitches in Ostankino will also be learning a lesson today.' He couldn't help grinning here. 'Yes, they're going to be meeting a *real* father-figure.' He gave an odd laugh.

Bunin brought the conference to a rapid end, sensing that Krymov might be about to go off on one of his rants. 'Ladies and gentlemen of the press, thank you for your time this morning and I would urge you to remain here in the Kremlin press centre, where we will be able to keep you updated with the rapid progress of the President's reassertion of control. Thank you very much.'

Krymov and Fyodor stood up and walked out of the door at the back of the room and up the stairs to the President's office.

The journalists stood up and either got on the phone to their editors or began doing live broadcasts standing away from the rest of the crowd. The room was full and they were all clearly there to stay.

Sergey continued to watch the screen in disbelief as Lara hit mute. He shook his head, muttering, 'Fucking traitor,' and then looked at her.

She was furious at Fyodor, but also more aware than Sergey of the irony of what he was saying, having himself just betrayed the government.

The evil shape of a Mil Mi-24 gunship roared past right outside the window and everyone ducked; its heavy rotors thumped the air in the room.

'Let's get up top, use the Kords on it!' Alex shouted to the team.

They ran for their weapons and lugged the two heavy machine guns upstairs. The Mil Mi-24 was one helicopter he was very afraid of and he wished he had something more serious than just machine guns; its titanium rotors and armoured body were designed to withstand 12.7mm hits.

As the six members of the team ran up the stairs to the roof, Alex keyed the mike on his headset and called Captain Darensky, who was in charge of the 568th defence ring around the tower, over the local command net they had agreed. He shouted as he ran: 'Darensky! We have a Mil Mi-24 overhead! Can you hit it? Over.'

What he wanted to say was, 'How the fuck did you let that get near the tower?' but it was too late for that.

Darensky's voice crackled back to him. 'Negative! Major Devereux, aircraft is a friendly! Major Oleg Levin has defected

383

from the airforce and flown it from Torzhok.' Alex knew that was the main Russian airforce helicopter base a hundred miles northwest of Moscow. 'He requested permission to land on the roof and I gave it.'

Great, thanks for telling me, Alex thought, but said, 'OK, we'll go and see what he wants.'

'Stand down!' he called to the others, who were lugging the heavy guns ahead of him on the stairs. 'Apparently, he's a friendly, defecting to our side.'

Despite this report, they were still very careful, creeping up the stairs with rifles held ready. The Mil was sideslipping in to land, blowing a gale of snow across the roof. The Russian airforce nicknamed it the Krokodil and Alex could see why: it was a very long aircraft with a green and brown camouflage-speckled body, ending in a snout-like cockpit with a bulging double canopy; the Gatling gun and re-fuelling probe stuck out under this like jagged canines from a jaw.

It landed and settled onto its three wheels, winding its rotors down. The fearsome array of armaments, in the nose and on its short wings, was pointing directly at Alex, standing inside the doors at the top of the stairs. As Major Levin moved his head in the cockpit, looking around him to see if anyone else was coming, the 12.7mm, six-barrelled gun under the nose followed sensors in his helmet to stay on his line of sight, making it twitch as if it were alive. As Alex opened the door and walked out it flicked over to point straight at him.

Well, he'd better be on our side or I am mincemeat, Alex thought as he walked towards the double cockpit.

Levin saw him and waved, though, popped the cockpit and swung his leg out as it hummed open above him. He held up a hand, uncertain of his reception.

Alex waved back, walked over and shook hands. The short Russian in a green flightsuit climbed down from the large aircraft and removed his helmet, revealing cropped black hair and a rounded face.

They shook hands and, despite a naturally serious disposition, Levin couldn't help smiling with relief that he had made the risky transfer between the two sides.

Alex led him down to the conference room and Roman, Sergey and the others questioned him.

'Why have you joined us?' asked Roman, smiling but reserving his judgement on the newcomer.

'Mr Raskolnikov, you need to know that the tower is about to be attacked. The other officers in my squadron are meeting to discuss the situation in Torzhok now. Both General Mostovskoy and the commander-in-chief of the airforce, General Korshunov, have ordered us to change sides and support Krymov now.' He became suddenly angry. 'But after I saw those fuckers shooting people this morning, I said to myself, "Never! Never will I take an order from this government again!"'

He paused to control himself and carried on, 'I don't know whether they'll agree but I think that in the end they will follow the chain of command because at least that way their arses will be covered.' He shrugged. 'We initially thought you guys were going to win but after Mostovskoy defected, nobody knows what the hell is going on so they'll just take the safest route for now and say they were obeying orders.'

Roman looked at Sergey, who pursed his lips but said nothing. He then nodded to Levin, convinced by the sincerity of the anger he showed about the OMON massacre that his defection was genuine.

'OK ... and if they do attack? What will happen?' Roman glanced across at Alex as well, who had been trying to work it out. A Mil Mi-24 was a flying tank with a huge amount of firepower and the idea of a squadron of them attacking worried him greatly.

Levin continued, 'Well, the orders were to attack and knock out any anti-aircraft capability that you have, especially the three Tunguskas. I'm not exactly sure why they want to degrade your anti-aircraft defences, presumably because they have something else lined up. I heard from our squadron signals officer that he had been liaising with Engels airforce base and the only unit based there is the 121st Guards Heavy Bomber Regiment. They fly White Swans.'

He looked round at the group with a regretful expression at having delivered such bad news. The Tu-160 Tupolev bomber was famous in Russia, as both the heaviest and fastest bomber in the world, capable of carrying forty tonnes of bombs at over Mach 2. The huge, swept-wing aircraft got its nickname because it looked as graceful as Concorde and was painted white to reflect the flash of the atomic weapons it drops.

'The base is four hundred miles southeast of Moscow but they could be here in half an hour if their officers agree to back Krymov.' Levin fell silent.

The others were looking at him with wary, calculating stares as they tried to figure out what their next move should be.

Sergey nodded and then spoke with quiet intensity: 'That's what Krymov meant.' The others looked round at him. 'When he said we will be going to meet a real father-figure, in the press conference.'

Major Levin looked at him with a startled expression.

Sergey nodded back at him. 'Yes, I think he would use it. Go on.' He gestured to Levin to explain.

The small major looked round at the others and then spoke

386

guardedly. 'The Father of All Bombs is a fuelair device they developed in response to the American MOAB – the Mother of All Bombs. The Americans used it to blow up the whole Tora Bora mountain in Afghanistan. The Russian version is even more effective. It's the most powerful subatomic munition in the world; it weighs seven tonnes but yields the equivalent of forty-four tonnes of TNT. It's dropped by a White Swan and it's stored at Engels.'

He fell silent again.

Sergey continued in a grim voice, 'Yes, Krymov is capable of using it. He always used to talk about the FOAB. It was his favourite defence project.'

In his mind's eye Sergey was replaying the film he had seen of it being tested on the accommodation blocks of an old army base in the desert in Kazakhstan. The enormous bomb was dropped from eight thousand feet and fell slowly on three huge parachutes as sprayers underneath it dispersed a large cloud of liquid explosive into the air. When a volume several hundred feet wide was filled with explosive, a simple lighter on the bomb clicked and all the air vaporised. Filmed from a distance of over a mile there had been a huge flash of flame as the explosive cloud had detonated. An instant blast wave showed up as a distortion of the air that flashed out across the plain, but the explosion also caused a vacuum and then overpressure as air rushed in to fill it. Footage of the aftermath had showed whole, six-storey blocks of flats levelled as if by the sweep of an enormous hand.

Grigory had seen the footage on national TV as well. He shook his head. 'He wouldn't use that in the middle of a city? I mean, the destruction, the civilian casualties, would be enormous.'

Sergey sighed as he thought about what he knew of Krymov's

vindictive temperament. 'He's not bringing a bomber up for a Christmas firework display,' he told Grigory.

Lara was shocked by the scale of the violence they faced. 'Well, can we defend against it?'

Alex shrugged. 'They have to drop it from eight thousand feet because the parachutes mean it is unguided, so that's certainly in range of the Tunguskas' missiles. We just have to hope they stay in action and can keep it off.'

Sergey was looking at him askance. 'No, Alex, we must have something more than that. Our whole strategy cannot be to simply sit back and hope they don't blow us to fuck!'

He became more heated. 'The situation at the moment is very finely balanced and we need to take the initiative.' He gestured at Major Levin. 'Look, Alexander, you heard what Levin said, how they are all sitting around watching it all on TV. People are selfish; they are not committed to either side at the moment; their main concern right now is simply to make sure that they are on the winning side.'

Alex nodded. He knew Sergey was right. They needed to keep up the Revolution's momentum or Krymov would either bomb them or just strangle them slowly.

Sergey was getting more enthusiastic as an idea formed in his mind. 'No, what we need is a big gesture, a big display of strength. This is a media war and we have to *show* that we hold the symbols of power, even if we don't hold them in reality.'

Alex had a feeling where this was going.

'No – we have to go for their jugular!' Sergey continued. 'The only way is take the Mil and go for the Kremlin!'

Everybody stared at him, grappling with the audacity of his plan. Sergey was just getting going, though.

'We know that Krymov is in his office and that all the press are downstairs in the press room. We will land there, kill Krymov and then do a broadcast from inside the Kremlin! The Senate building is recognised as the seat of power in Russia. If we are broadcasting from there then everyone will know that we have won and that the Krymov government must have fallen.'

He looked round at them, excited by his idea.

Nobody said anything; it was just too much to take in in one go. They realised it would probably be their only hope but no one wanted to take responsibility for condoning it by speaking.

Sergey realised he needed to be more practical to get a response from them. 'I will go as cameraman. I know how to use one and I know the layout of the Senate building and Krymov's routines.'

He looked imploringly at Alex. 'Alexander, I need you and your men to do it. I can't rely on Russian troops to kill their own commander-in-chief.'

The tall major folded his arms and took a deep breath. He looked at Sergey and then round the circle at his team: Col, Yamba, Pete, Arkady and Magnus. They all looked back at him pensively. When he had offered them the chance to go home earlier that day, they had all said they were willing to stay to the bitter end, and their loyalty to the team meant that they stuck by their word now.

Alex thought through the practical details rapidly. Technically it was possible. The Mil Mi-24 was unique amongst helicopter gunships in that it was both a flying tank and an armoured personnel carrier, with enough room to fit a squad of eight men in the troop bay and with enough power to carry a full weapon load at the same time.

He needed more details, though, before he could answer. He looked at Sergey. 'What are the defences inside the Senate like?'

Sergey looked uncertain. 'Well, I don't know for sure. There's always Batyuk and quite a lot of Echelon 25 guys around, and the main body of MVD Kremlin guards are stationed just across in the Arsenal building.'

Alex nodded; it didn't sound good but then neither did the alternatives. And he was a risk-taker at heart.

He looked at Sergey and nodded slowly.

With Sergey, Alex and his whole team onboard, Lara couldn't stay out of it. She announced defiantly, 'Right, I will do the broadcast! We can't afford to let Roman go, so people will need to see the other symbol of the Revolution there, and that's me! This is *my* Revolution and I'm not going to miss out on it.' She glared around her, defying anyone to refuse her.

No one did; they needed all the commitment they could get right now.

'Right, Roman, you stay here,' Sergey said, 'and, Grigory, you too. Supervise the broadcast and don't you fucking lose my feed or I'll kill you.'

They began to break up but then Sergey thought of something else and clapped his hands to regain their attention. He looked serious. 'Yes, and one other thing: we don't tell anyone in the station that they are going to be bombed, otherwise no one will stay and we will all be lost. I will tell Darensky so he knows he has to keep his Tunguskas intact, but otherwise we don't tell a soul!'

He glared round at them, pointing a warning finger. 'OK, everybody understand?'

There was a round of silent nods as they absorbed the duplicity they were visiting on their comrades.

Chapter Sixty-Three

Four hundred miles to the south of Moscow, on the desolate, windswept steppe, lay Engels airforce base.

The site was enormous, with a three-and-a-half-kilometre-long runway built to take the world's heaviest bombers. It was covered in snow and a keen wind whipped across the humped outlines of the fifteen huge, reinforced concrete hangars. Inside each hardened nest lay a White Swan.

Deep under the frozen base in a munitions bunker, a winch whirred and a large dull green cylinder rose upwards. Cyrillic stencillings on it designated it as: 'Russian Airforce, Munition Number 1'.

In a cavernous hangar nearby, Major Rostov and his crew – co-pilot, navigator and weapons system operator – walked in through a side door in their green flightsuits with their white helmets under their arms.

Rostov never got over the excitement of seeing his beautiful white plane, with its variable wings swept back now against the body, a high tail plane and elegant, clean lines. It looked very similar in size and shape to Concorde but with a much more deadly payload.

He walked underneath it and quickly inspected the intakes on the four Kuznetsov NK-321 afterburning, turbofan engines, the most powerful ever fitted to a combat aircraft.

Rostov was an intelligent man and had been concerned by the contradictory orders issued over the course of that morning. Initially, Colonel-General of the Airforce Korshunov had sent orders from Airforce Command that no action was to be taken when the coup had broken out.

Then, later on, they all saw Lieutenant-General Mostovskoy's press conference on CNN. It seemed very odd that he had been involved in the plot in the first place – it didn't make sense – but then he was so composed and convincing when he explained that he had been a double agent all along and had exposed the rebels' foreign backers that they believed him. How else could one explain the fact that he looked so at home sitting next to the President? Rostov then saw that the whole thing was actually a very clever trick on the rebels. Maybe Krymov wasn't such an idiot as everyone said.

If there were foreigners involved in the coup, then they had to be wiped out, even if that meant blowing up a famous Moscow landmark. They had started the game and they knew the rules.

Rostov was a fiercely cheerful man with a loud laugh. His role as a nuclear bomber pilot involved him being able to follow orders that would cause him to kill a million people and he took a fierce professional pride in not questioning them; he was part of a very efficient machine and he would play his role. He knew what the blast radius of the FOAB was and that it would destroy many of the tower blocks near the TV station that were packed full of civilians. However, just as he didn't get lily-livered about dropping nukes, so he wasn't going to about this bombing mission. He had received his orders from the chain of command and that was all he needed.

He finished his pre-flight inspection of the outside of his beautiful aircraft and led his crew proudly up the ladder to the cockpit.

On the Torzhok airforce base, a hundred miles to the north-west of Moscow, more preparations for the final assault on the tower were underway.

Pilots and crew ran out from the crewroom to where their twelve Mil Mi-24 gunships sat in hardened concrete pens.

Colonel Turgenev knew it would be a tough job to locate and destroy the three Tunguska anti-aircraft vehicles around the tower, to allow the White Swan to make its bombing run. With their mixture of cannon and missiles they had a high aircraft kill ratio and a fearsome reputation.

However, he looked with pride at his own deadly machine. The mixed load of rockets and missiles on the wing pylons and the gun under the nose all gave it a jagged, aggressive profile. His ground crew were busy around it, completing fuelling, checking the guided missiles and rocket pods and loading long belts of Gatling gun ammunition.

When he and his co-pilot closed their double armoured glass canopies, he hit the starter and the deafening roar of the twin Isotov turbines began winding up. The five-bladed rotor turned slowly and was then lost in a whirr. The aircraft shifted on its three wheels, straining to get off the ground.

He radio checked with the other eleven machines in the squadron and then, as one, they all rose up out of their pens, like a flock of evil-minded birds, and banked south towards Moscow.

On top of the Ostankino tower, another Mil Mi-24 was preparing for launch.

Major Levin sat in the pilot's seat with Arkady down in front of him as co-pilot and weapons systems operator.

Alex and the rest of the team were standing next to the aircraft doing last-minute equipment checks. They were all in full FIBUA battle kit: flakjackets, helmets, Wiley-X blast-resistant goggles and webbing filled with grenades. Winning at FIBUA is all about weight of firepower so Alex, Col, Yamba, Magnus and Pete were all armed with 7.62mm PKM light machine guns, with spare 250-round ammo boxes in their rucksacks, plus a Shmel launcher carried by Yamba. Any remaining room was stuffed with MTP-2 mines for mouseholing their way through walls if they needed to.

Alex carried the radio on his back to maintain communications with the helicopter, as well as Grigory and Ilya in the director's gallery as they waited for the precious satellite dish feed from Sergey with his broadcast of Lara.

He was feeling drained after all he had been through in the past thirty-six hours: the prison camp raid, the firefight around the tower, and the wounds on the side of his face and his hand hurt like hell. He looked around at the rest of the team. They were equally battered: green combat jackets stained with smoke, blood and dirt, their faces covered in stubble and cuts, and their eyes red-rimmed.

He glanced across at Sergey and Lara, who were standing apart, talking quietly with their heads close together. They were both wearing blue TV flakjackets over their parkas; Sergey held his bulky camera in one hand and had the satellite uplink in a rucksack.

Despite everything that was going on, Alex couldn't help feeling a twinge of jealousy. He suppressed it angrily. How the hell could he be feeling that at a time like this?

He looked at his watch; it was only just before lunchtime – what else could happen today?

He took one last look out over Moscow before they boarded. Dark snow clouds brooded low over the city. In the distance he could just make out the pointed towers of the Kremlin citadel. He forced himself to look away and get psyched up for the mission.

'OK, everyone, let's go!' he yelled.

They all packed into the back-to-back benches inside the Mil. The troop bay smelled of sweat and machine grease. Alex slid the armoured side door shut and sat back on the bench. Levin increased the revs and the rotors whirred above them.

I am setting off on a mission to attack the Kremlin, what the hell am I doing?

He couldn't see anything outside because of the armoured cocoon he was now in, but he felt the whole body lift and tilt as they sideslipped off the roof and over the void.

They dropped away sickeningly and swooped down to rooftop level on their run in to the target.

Chapter Sixty-Four

Captain Lev Darensky stood on the TV station roof and watched the helicopter depart.

Alex had taken him aside and explained that the station was going to be targeted with the FOAB and that he had to keep that secret whilst at the same time making sure that his three Tunguska anti-aircraft vehicles were not destroyed.

Even though he was a junior officer he had now become the *Kombat* – the regimental field commander in charge of four hundred men. His signaller was standing next to him with his radio backpack, waiting to relay any commands on to the men of the 568th. Some men might have been daunted by the task but Darensky was a visionary figure and felt that his hour had come.

In a minute, he would take the elevator down to his T-90 command tank on the ground, but he wanted a last look out over the field of the coming battle to review his troops. Next to him on the roof were three two-man teams with shoulder-launched 9K38 Igla surface-to-air missiles. They had only limited range so they wouldn't be able to reach the White Swan at 8,000 feet, but the tower gave them a great firing platform against low-flying helicopters.

He looked down and watched one of his three

Tunguskas moving north across the open ground around the tower. The vehicle had the tracked body of a tank with a wide turret, painted in a black and green camouflage pattern. However, instead of a single main gun, it had a six-foot-long, 30mm anti-aircraft cannon and four long black tubes for 9M311 surface-to-air missiles mounted on either side of the turret. A small radar dish rotated rapidly on the back of the turret, anxiously scanning for incoming aircraft.

He had allocated positions for the three vehicles at equal distances around a defensive perimeter a kilometre out from the tower. His eleven other T-90 tanks and ten BMP-3 tracked fighting vehicles were also spread out along this defensive line. Unit commanders had picked out the approach routes to the tower, found ambush sites and dug in around them. The troops were dotted between offices and apartment blocks in the surrounding area, and, where possible, were hidden behind buildings or snowdrifts.

Darensky had split the defences into four companies covering four sectors: northern was spread out amongst an area of woodland to the northwest and then across to a housing estate with four huge tower blocks to the northeast. Eastern sector covered the main approach road, where the massacre by the buses had happened this morning, as well as an area of lower-rise flats. Western sector was based in some light industrial and factory blocks and, finally, southern sector, under Sergeant Platonov, was spread out along the main railway embankment.

All the men of the 568th knew that this was their final battle. The Krymov regime wouldn't let them live if they lost; their backs were well and truly against the wall so they went about their preparations with a grim determination.

Sergeant Platonov looked down the line of his men

digging into the snow along the railway embankment and shouted, 'Might as well go down fighting, lads! Give 'em a proper fight!'

A mile to the south of Platonov's men, Colonels Vronsky and Melekhov were meeting in a warehouse, finalising the assault plans for their mixed force of five hundred OMON and MVD troops with BTR-80 APCs in support, the ones that had survived the two routs that morning.

They scrutinised the map on a packing crate in front of them, trying to work out how they could put pressure on the defenders to allow the Mil gunships to single out and destroy the Tunguskas. Given the amount of firepower they had flying in to help them, they might even be able to capture the tower before the White Swan arrived. They would have to see how it went.

Their soldiers were already advancing cautiously towards the TV station. They were all clad in heavy winter clothing and laden with body armour, webbing, helmets, rifles, grenades, knives, entrenching tools, RPGs and spare rounds, flamethrower packs and radios.

Squads of soldiers advanced, huddled along walls, sensing potential threats in every direction, halting before each corner to peer nervously around it. Each one could be a deathtrap, and when they had to cross open ground they did so frantic-ally, sprinting with arms and legs pumping, equipment banging and flapping around them. As they got nearer the tower they dropped onto their stomachs and wriggled forward into firing positions, peering over snow mounds and around fences.

Colonel Turgenev's gunships approached the tower with equal caution.

The twelve Mil Mi-24s spread out in a circle around it to

probe the defences. As they got near Ostankino they dropped right down on the deck, using every scrap of cover to shield their approach to within two kilometres.

With their wheels retracted, the huge machines skimmed along roads a few feet off the ground, hopping over terrified car drivers, their powerful downdraft shoving vehicles sideways as they roared over them.

Two of the aircraft approaching from the north slowly slid in amongst the tower blocks like a pair of sharks, and hovered there waiting for the attack to commence. Terrified people looked out of the windows of their flats and saw, twenty feet away, the pilots' heads turning as they checked the buildings around them and then used their infrared and optical sensors to identify targets on the defensive perimeter.

When they had all picked out heat signatures that seemed to indicate tank engine exhausts or troop concentrations, they radioed in to Colonel Turgenev, who then barked out over the RT net: 'Launch missiles!' and all twelve gunships rose up from cover, fired off a volley of 9K114 Shturm air-to-surface anti-tank missiles and then accelerated to attack speed.

Inside the three Tunguska vehicles, the radar operators hunched over their glowing orange screens and watched the line sweeping rapidly round the centre point as the scanner above them turned and tracked the incoming helicopters. It was hard to pick them out amongst all the ground clutter; they appeared and disappeared rapidly behind buildings, popped over the top of them and then sank back behind others.

The operators designated targets on the screen and linked them into the gun and missile guidance computers. Outside each vehicle, on each side of their turrets, the two long black missile launchers raised themselves up from their horizontal positions and twitched across the sky like the eager snouts of two gundogs following a bird.

When the Mils emerged from cover to launch their salvo, the Tunguskas at last had clear targets as well, and the missile duel began. Their missiles kicked out of their tubes with a bright flash and a cascade of propellant fire before vanishing into the distance with frightening speed.

One of the pilots hovering between the tower blocks glimpsed a black streak coming towards him just before it turned and slammed into the engine exhaust outlet below his helicopter's rotors. The nine-kilo high-explosive warhead detonated and blew the whole rotor unit off. It spun away and crashed into the flats next to it whilst the body of the aircraft dropped down like a stone.

The other Mils swarmed in regardless, howling along at two hundred k.p.h. At closer range the Tunguskas' guns came into play. The two long barrels followed their radar guidance and fired out bursts at five thousand rounds per minute with an unearthly roar that sent twin streams of red tracer up into the air, whilst the recoil pushed each thirty-four-ton vehicle back on its tracks. Two enormous gouts of black exhaust smoke poured up from the gun barrels like twin horns and a solid stream of spent shell cases poured out of the side of each gun.

A Mil on the northern front went head to head with a Tunguska, firing its rocket pods at it. A series of explosions on the ground got nearer the vehicle as it sought to knock out the aircraft with a constant barrage of 30mm cannon fire. The guns twitched with computer-guided intensity as they followed every jink and swerve of the helicopter, in a desperate battle to kill or be killed.

A line of five 30mm cannon shells punched through the titanium body armour and hit its fuel tanks, exploding it in an aerial fireball. But as the Tunguska was occupied with this battle another helicopter targeted it and punched out its remaining Shturm missile.

The radar operator spotted the launch and screamed, 'Reverse!' to the driver next to him. He threw the tracks into gear and charged backwards but the missile smashed into the front of the turret and the high-explosive warhead exploded. Bits of the radar scanner, missile tubes, guns and crew blew up in a cloud of debris.

Private Novikov was dug into a pile of salt sand used for gritting roads on the central reservation of the main approach route along the Ulitsa Akademika Korolyova boulevard.

He was lying prone on the ground and his balls were freezing as he squinted along the sights of his Kord heavy machine gun on a bipod mount. His squad were dug into foxholes in the verges, two hundred metres in front of the smashed-up yellow buses from that morning's massacre. Bodies were still lying around them in the snow.

The battle between the helicopters and the Tunguskas was going on over his head; missiles streaked in over him and streams of 30mm tracers roared back out; the air was heavy with the smell of their burning.

He was concentrating on the troops and APCs advancing down the road in front of him. He could see soldiers running between buildings laden with equipment. Two had just lugged a heavy machine gun on a tripod behind a bus shelter, and others scurried forward, bent double with Shmel tubes strapped on their backs that waggled as they ran.

The corporal in charge of the squad judged they were now in range, stuck his head out of his foxhole and yelled, 'Right, that's about far enough for them! Open fire!'

Novikov squinted along his gun, and squeezed the trigger. The Kord jumped with a heavy thock-thock-thock of propellant explosions, accompanied by the jangling of the metal cartridge belt as it fed through the breech. Long .50 bullets spat out down the boulevard, smashed through the bus shelter and hit the machine-gun team behind it. A stream of hot cartridge cases spewed out of the ejection port on the right-hand side and melted into the snow with a faint hiss. All around Novikov, firing broke out as his squad targeted the enemy. Fire soon came back in at them as well, with bullets cracking just overhead.

Enemy troops began pushing in on all four sectors. To the north, the sound of firing echoed off the high-rise blocks of flats, as defenders poured fire down and a guided missile slammed back into the buildings in return. Debris and glass blasted out and rained down in an umbrella pattern over the street below, smashing car roofs and windscreens, and setting off their alarms.

On the southern sector, Sergeant Platonov was kneeling on one knee in the middle of his men, as they fired their machine guns around him. He had the radio receiver pressed hard against his head and was shouting over the racket of chattering and banging guns.

'Darensky! Darensky! I need armour support here! Enemy helicopters and APCs have pushed us off the embankment. They've crossed the bridge and are advancing up Novomoskovskaya Ulitsa.' He glanced to his side down the small street running north between blocks of flats. It was packed with cars abandoned by the people who had flooded up to the TV station that morning. He could see a BMP-3 manoeuvring on the other side of the cars, firing its 30mm cannon over the top of them at his position.

In the commander's hatch of his tank near the tower, Darensky shouted back, 'OK, I'll send armour!'

He called in his last remaining mobile reserve of two T-90

tanks. They pulled out of their hides in the woods and roared south over the snowfield and down the narrow street, using old-fashioned cavalry shock tactics. Despite being completely blocked with cars, parked nose to tail, the two forty-seven-ton monsters simply increased speed and their tracks effortlessly rose up over the first cars and then flowed over the rest, crushing them into a splintering mass of glass and metal. They both advanced on top of this carpet, their tracks tearing chunks off the roofs and spewing them behind, as their gun barrels swung and belched out rounds, blowing up the BMP-3. Their machine guns chattered, scattering the enemy troops.

The noise of battle engulfed the whole of northern Moscow. The crackle of small-arms fire, the boom and thump of tank guns, exploding shells and the scream of missiles overhead, mixed with the constant clatter of helicopter rotors reverberating off buildings, made it impossible for the defenders to tell where the next gunship would pop up from to unleash its deadly load. Their constant attacks began to get the upper hand and enemy troops pushed in all around the perimeter.

In the middle of it all, the young Darensky sat in his tank with his radio helmet on his head, listening to the increasingly desperate voices coming in over the net.

He was trying to follow the rapid flow of the battle, directing reserves to where the enemy threatened to break through the perimeter.

Platonov, on the southern sector, was taking the brunt of it all. Darensky managed to get through to him again.

'Platonov, give me a sitrep now!'

The radio hissed and then Platonov's shout came back to him, edged with hysteria and with the roar of gunfire in the background.

'We've got three gunships on us now! They've hit the tanks! They've just hit the Tunguska. It's on fire! We're taking hits!'

A loud explosion cut him off and then there was just an empty hiss.

'Platonov! Platonov!'

Darensky's head sank down and he rested his forehead against the top of the armoured hatch flipped open in front of him.

He had only one Tunguska left and the White Swan was on its way.

Major Rostov pushed the throttles forward and felt himself shoved back into his seat of the Tupolev bomber as the four huge turbofans roared behind him.

He was sitting in the tiny cockpit perched on top of the fully fuelled and armed plane. He had personally supervised the winching of the huge bomb up into the bomb bay with powerful hydraulic jacks. The weapon was an ugly, eleven-foot-long, fat cylinder, a bit like an old-fashioned diving bell. It had been raised slowly into place until the clamps clicked and locked it in. Technicians armed the firing bolts and it was now hanging ready for him to press the release button.

Crammed in next to him was his co-pilot, with his navigator and weapons system operator behind him. As Rostov pulled the yoke back and took them up off the runway, they were all busy with their jobs. The tactical computer had uploaded all the target information: weather conditions, atmospheric readings from the met centre, the wind speed and direction over target.

The weapons system operator was busy running this data through his computer to calculate the right bomb launch trajectory and detonation height. The FOAB was a difficult weapon to drop and the whole crew were focused on getting it right.

Rostov ran through the mission timings in his mind. The four hundred miles to the target was just a short hop for his intercontinental bomber, with its full range of eleven thousand miles. Although his maximum speed was Mach 2.05, he needed to wait for the all clear on the anti-aircraft defences before he went in on his final bomb run. This would be sent through by General Korshunov as soon as he got word from the helicopter attack force. In the meantime they would cruise in at just under the speed of sound.

'Estimated flight time, thirty minutes,' his navigator called from over his shoulder.

Rostov keyed the mike on his radio and called through to General Korshunov in the command bunker near Moscow.

Korshunov was standing next to a conference table in front of the huge display screen. A group of senior air-force officers were standing around it, watching different screens on the wall that showed feeds from all the main TV channels.

A signals officer called across to him, 'Major Rostov, sir!'

'Put him through,' Korshunov nodded, and the sound came through on speakers set into the desk.

'General Korshunov, we have just taken off and will be over the target in approximately thirty minutes. We are standing by for your instructions.'

Korshunov leaned forward and pressed the transmit button on the desk mike. 'Very good, Rostov. I'll tell you as soon as I get any news.'

He clicked the desk mike off and looked around at the other officers. They nodded and went back to staring at the screens.

Everyone was on edge and Korshunov's nerves were shot.

He couldn't believe it when Mostovskoy had called up and said he was switching sides, but then Krymov had come on the phone and assured him that the airforce had made its point and that he had learned the error of his ways and they would get full control of United Aircraft Corporation.

He didn't quite know what to believe, but when he had seen Mostovskoy's performance on TV, with his damning accusation of foreign involvement, then he had realised that the balance of events had tipped back towards Krymov and that he had to go with him for now.

He had duly given the orders for the attack helicopters to launch from Torzhok and the Tupolev was now on its way. He hoped that Colonel Turgenev's squadron would be able to destroy the last of the three Tunguskas, to allow the bomber in to settle the situation once and for all.

He flicked his eyes over the TV feeds in front of him, searching for any new developments. The situation was very fluid and he was prepared to change sides at short notice, but right now it looked like the Blue Revolution was well and truly over.

Colonel Turgenev was certainly doing his best to finish it off. He still had eight helicopters remaining.

'Go for the tower!' he shouted over the radio.

With the defenders on the ground hard-pressed, he seized his chance to get in close. A Mil broke cover over the top of an office block and streaked in fast.

'Helicopter inbound from the east!'

'Firing!'

The shout went up from one of the missile teams stationed on the roof. A soldier leaned over the railing and fired an Igla missile down at the intruder, but it spat out a burst of defensive flares as it approached. The bright sparks shot out and hissed in the snow and the missile's infrared seeker ploughed into one of them instead and blew a large crater in the ground.

The helicopter fired its rocket pod at the satellite dishes on the trunk of the tower. Explosions bloomed from its concrete side and a shower of debris blew out from it. From a distance it seemed to move in slow motion as the heavier pieces travelled out further in a gently arcing downward trajectory. Huge chunks of concrete then smashed down on cars parked near it, caving in their roofs. A twenty-foot satellite dish also sailed down and smashed into the ground.

Darensky's tank was parked under the trees to the south of the tower and he now spun his turret round to the north to wait for any other attacks. Another Mil swept in over the trees to the west. He couldn't react fast enough to stop it hitting the tower with another rocket salvo, but he tracked onto it as it swept past the tower and over the clear ground around it.

The laser designator on the 125mm gun put a red dot on the side door of the helicopter and banged a high-explosive round through the side armour. It exploded inside and blew the aircraft to pieces twenty feet off the ground. Burning chunks of machinery and a fireball of fuel scattered across the snow, hissing and tumbling over it.

Having seen the Igla missile launch from the tower roof, Colonel Turgenev's next tactic was to pull a Mil out of the fighting and load it up with troops.

The pilot then swung round to the west of the battlefield and sank down right to ground level so that he could creep in behind the elevated monorail that ran east–west from the Metro line.

With great agility he kept inches away from the massive concrete pylons supporting the twenty-foot-high railway.

The soldiers on the roof heard the rotor noise, though, and fired three Iglas at it, but the aircraft threw out a spray of burning flares that foxed them.

The helicopter pressed on undeterred. It hopped up over the top of the monorail, shot across the open ground to the base of tower, right under the Igla gunners as they frantically tried to reload their launchers.

It then went into a straight vertical climb, rising three hundred and fifty metres in a matter of seconds. It shot past the TV station with its rotors a metre away from the office windows, smashing them in and blasting a gale inside that scattered papers everywhere. Staff sheltering in the offices screamed and ran at the sight of the menacing machine feet away from them.

It then rose up suddenly over the lip of the roof. Some soldiers managed to raise their rifles and crack a few bursts at it but they pinged harmlessly off the armoured glass of the cockpit.

The Mil responded with the withering fiery breath of its Gatling gun that swept all the defenders away; their bodies smashed against the railings or knocked over it to tumble like strange leaves down to the ground. It circled the whole roof until all the defending soldiers were dead.

It then hovered over the roof, the side door slid open and eight heavily armed soldiers jumped down with rifles at the ready. They ran across to the stairwell and quickly pitched grenades down the stairs.

They exploded and staff ran in panic across the open-plan office. The six men with rifles from the morning's gun battle ran over and took up positions behind desks. They shot the first soldier who came down but others got into cover and a firefight broke out across the room.

The helicopter then took off again from the roof and

dropped down over the windows of the floor below. It began a slow rotation around the offices, smashing the windows with its downdraft and firing into them with its Gatling gun. The torrent of metal poured in, smashed computers to pieces and blew desks and chairs across the room.

Grigory was in a director's gallery on the floor below. He looked at Ilya and they both glanced nervously at the explosions and gunfire above them and ducked under the control desk.

Grigory's mobile rang; he pulled it out and checked the caller. It was Sergey; he hit answer. 'Yes?'

There was a loud rattle of gunfire from the other end with Sergey's voice shouting, 'Grigory! Are you getting my feed? Are you getting this? I've got the satellite dish going!'

'Hang on!' Grigory reached up over the desk and punched the feed through to a screen above him.

A darkened picture of the inside of a corridor showed up, billowing with smoke from an MTP-2 explosion.

'Yes, I'm getting it!'

Grigory flinched back under the desk as he heard the helicopter drop down and begin to shoot up the floor he was on. It rotated past the studio and bullets smashed through the back of the gallery and hit the videowall in the telethon studio, which exploded in a shower of sparks.

Sergey could hear the firing. 'What's going on there?' he yelled.

'We've got enemy troops landed on the roof. There's fighting on the floor above me and there's a gunship shooting us up!'

'What?'

A bullet went through the control desk in front of Grigory and the screens above it went black.

'Shit!' he shouted.

'What?' Sergey yelled back over the noise of more gunfire. 'We just got hit! We've lost your feed!'

One of volunteer soldiers on the floor above saw the helicopter drop down and, as the other five men battled against the enemy soldiers, he grabbed an RPG launcher and ran down another set of stairs.

Ducking down behind desks, he scuttled across the office and then sprinted along the central corridor around the concrete tower core. He took up a firing position behind a photocopier, kneeling on one knee and waited for the helicopter to rotate round to him.

He saw the nose of the beast swing into view and squeezed the trigger. The armour-piercing dart leaped away and smashed through the heavy cockpit glass, went through the pilot and exploded against the metal plate behind him, throwing his body forward onto the stick and driving the machine into the building.

The five main rotors clipped the window frames and then shredded off in a horrid grating crash against a steel girder. The last one bent round it and for a second the whole eleven-tonne weight hung on the side of the building. The rotor then snapped and the machine dropped silently down the side of the tower, smashed into the sloped base and exploded. Wreckage and a cloud of burning fuel scattered out over the ground.

Darensky watched the explosion from his tank to the south of the tower.

The situation was now desperate. They were under pressure on all fronts, the tower had enemy soldiers inside it and he only had one Tunguska left.

He decided to pull his troops back to reduce the length of the defensive perimeter.

He keyed the mike on his command radio. 'All stations fall back! Fall back to the tower!'

Units began disengaging and running to the main entrance. Some took up positions around it; others packed into the elevators and shot up to the floors above. They spread out around the office windows, whilst a squad took on the government soldiers on the top floor.

As Krymov's forces closed in they began firing at the tower, lobbing shells and missiles in at it, aiming for the satellite dishes. A BMP-3 got in range and fired its 100mm main armament. The round smashed into a dish and blew it off the side. It whirled down with a tangle of wires attached to the back of it.

The 568th troops fired back from the tower with RPGs and machine guns, sending streams of bright tracer out over the surrounding area.

The whole tower was lit up by the flashes of explosions against the grim December sky like a strange Christmas tree looming over Moscow, with red ribbons of tracer draping out from it like tinsel.

The incoming fire was getting more and more intense. Grigory took a decision and keyed the mike on the internal Tannoy. 'All staff evacuate the offices! Everyone into the stairwells!'

Two hundred staff and supporters ran into the emergency stairs on the inside of the concrete tube of the tower, protected by its thick outer walls.

So many people packed into the narrow wells made for a claustrophobic scene. Air quality deteriorated rapidly as they huddled together and listened to the explosions and gunfire outside. Occasionally the whole building shook as a missile hit. Dust scattered over them and people coughed and screamed.

Grigory remained in the gallery with Ilya, as he struggled to fix the desk with two technicians. He was desperate to get it ready for when Sergey finally managed to set up his big broadcast. If it was still out of action then the whole Kremlin raid would have been in vain. He thought about the gunfire in the background of Sergey's phone call and wondered what the hell was going on down there. It couldn't be any worse than what was happening here but at least they were still just in the game.

He heard a heavy explosion from somewhere outside the tower.

The radio connection on the desk speaker barked: 'Grigory, Grigory!' It was Darensky.

Grigory punched the transmit button. 'Yes!'

'They just got the last Tunguska!'

'Fuck!'

Grigory banged the desk and Ilya looked up at him in surprise.

The tower was now defenceless against the White Swan.

The Blue Revolution really was over.

Chapter Sixty-Five

Arkady and Major Levin flew the Mil in low over Red Square.

The multi-coloured domes of St Basil's Cathedral flashed past on the left, then Lenin's Mausoleum and they were over the high, red brick wall between the Senate Tower and St Nicholas Tower. They immediately dropped down and skimmed along the ground in the fifty-metre-wide gap between the long neo-classical façade of the Arsenal building and the side of the Senate. The whole Senate building was a triangle pointing east, and this western side was its long base running north–south.

The Mil drew level with the southern end of the building a hundred yards along from the President's office and went into a hover. The body then spun rapidly and pointed the full array of its armament at the south end of the Senate building's long façade.

Arkady centred the electronic targeting ring, on his heads-up display, on the ground floor and triggered one of the 80mm rocket pods. The airframe juddered as they roared away one after the other, on ripple fire, and crashed into the ground floor. The repeated onslaught blew out the wall so that the rest continued exploding inside, knocking out structural walls and bringing the three upper floors of that part of the complex crashing down.

Major Levin had to pull back rapidly on the stick as he saw the upper floors begin to go, to avoid the bursting landslide of dust and stone blocks that exploded out from the building and across to the Arsenal fifty metres away, smashing the windows.

The tunnel that Fyodor and Sergey had used to escape from the Senate that morning was now buried under tons of rubble.

No one could escape from the building now.

The helicopter swung round to face the next potential problem. The Arsenal building was where the MVD Kremlin guards were housed. Sergey wasn't sure how many there were but guessed it would be a couple of hundred troops.

Levin pivoted the nose across the whole two-hundred-metre-long frontage as Arkady strafed it with the Gatling gun, smashing out the windows, and then put a rocket through the main door in the middle of it.

When the Mil had first arrived, Krymov had been raising another toast of vodka to Fyodor.

'And here's to your aplomb!'

He was still light-headed and excited at how well the press conference had gone, how his peasant cunning had skilfully been able to turn all his enemy's strengths to his own advantage: their use of foreign support, the way he had blamed the economic problems on Sergey, how he had ended up lecturing all those foreign press bastards and getting the last word on them! It really had been a very satisfying experience.

The sudden roar of the Mil outside cut roughly across these celebrations. Major Batyuk ran in through the double doors with three Echelon 25 men with rifles.

He nodded cursorily to the President, strode across to the windows and looked out just as Arkady unleashed his rocket volley into the Senate.

The whole building shook as the series of explosions hammered home and the floors then collapsed with the rumble of an earthquake.

Batyuk didn't hesitate. 'Mr President, we need to leave immediately.'

Krymov was shaken by the blasts but was still full enough of himself to demur. 'Ah, Batyuk! Calm down, just get out there with a squad and sort them out. They're not coming in here.'

The large body of the Mil moved over the dome on top of his office and the heavy rotors shook plaster dust out of the ceiling and then smashed the skylights in above them.

The helicopter landed on the Senate roof and the side door slid open. The assault team jumped out onto the flat surface, followed by Lara and Sergey with the bulky TV camera on his shoulder.

Alex and Col ran over to one of the skylights down into the President's office as the other three soldiers each dropped to one knee and took up security positions. They both pulled frag grenades out, slipped the tape off the spoons, pulled the pins out and dropped four down through the skylights.

They exploded, smashing the windows out, knocking over chairs and setting fire to the long curtains and carpet with burning fragments. A rope dropped down, along with a long burst of suppressive PKM fire angled at the wooden door, but Batyuk had already evacuated Krymov and Mostovskoy.

Arkady took off as soon as he saw the team disappear down into the skylight. His job now was to fly around the triangular Senate building, preventing any reinforcements from getting across the open ground to it. The helicopter was titanium-armoured and easily capable of withstanding any small-arms fire aimed at it, and it was unlikely that anyone had any heavy weapons; no one expected to be using them right in the seat of government.

Smoke began billowing in the President's office, but the men dropping rapidly down the rope had SureFire torches on rails on top of their PKM light machine guns, and the intense beams of light flicked around in the murk, sweeping all angles of the room.

Alex's Wiley-X eyeguards meant he was unaffected by the smoke and could glance round at the smashed portraits and pictures on the wall.

They had got into the Kremlin, but now he needed to keep the momentum going and find and kill Krymov. He got the team lined up in a stack ready to go through the door; each one was a potential deathtrap. He nodded to Magnus, who put a long burst through it and then yanked it open and the stack scuttled through fast, torches out and probing the landing outside. Lara and Sergey followed behind.

Alex peered over the banister, down the richly decorated stairwell, trying to see if someone was down there.

Col was next to him. 'How many doors?'

'Two.'

'I'll watch right, you watch left, got it?'

'Got it.'

They crept down the stairs in silence except for the occasional scrape of broken glass underfoot from a smashed skylight above them. The team flowed smoothly after them, using the hand signals and drills they had practised in Akerly, covering all the angles, each member leapfrogging forward under cover from the next.

Downstairs in the press office carnage reigned. People were shouting and screaming after the huge explosions at the end of the building and then the roar of the helicopter and grenades exploding over their heads. Correspondents huddled under tables as they broadcast live.

Gerry Kramer on CNN was talking in an urgent whisper to his anchorman: 'Mike, we just don't know what the hell is going on here now. The President and General Mostovskoy just ran through here with some guards and now—'

A burst of machine-gun fire through the door cut him off.

Pete's heavy boot kicked it open and five heavily armed men burst in, clad in helmets and goggles and rapidly flicking the muzzles of their machine guns around the room, searching for targets.

'Everybody on the floor now!' Alex yelled at them in Russian.

They swept the room and then exited through an open door leading into a corridor running north.

Lara and Sergey ran through after them. Sergey was loving it. His plan was working. This was exactly the sort of coverage he wanted going out on all the foreign channels. He pulled a Blue Revolution flag out of his coat and waved it around at the cameras shouting, 'The Blue Revolution lives! We'll get that Krymov fucker!'

He ran out after the rest of the team into a corridor with a closed door at the end and crouched down at the back of the stack that Alex had lined up along the wall. Alex was at the front with Pete across the corridor and Yamba at the back of the line in reserve in case Plan A didn't work.

Alex nodded to Pete, who stepped up and gave the door a massive kick. It shook but didn't open.

'Shit!'

Pete hit the deck as a burst of fire from inside shredded the door and bullets smashed into the walls over their heads.

'Yamba!'

The Angolan bent down on one knee and triggered the

419

Shmel launcher held against his shoulder. The fuelair bomb punched through the door, hit the wall on the other side of the room and exploded in a fireball, blowing the windows out into the central courtyard.

'Let's go!' Alex had to shout after the deafening explosion.

This time, Pete's boot smashed the door off its frame and they charged in. Smashed tables and chairs were blown over against the walls and burning fiercely.

With the lights blown out, the white beams of their gun torches jerked around in the darkness searching for targets. They scanned over two bodies burning on the floor with stinking smoke billowing out from them.

Shouts of 'Clear! Clear!' came in from all corners.

Alex wanted to press the advantage and pointed Col at a door opposite: 'Sustained fire!'

A long peal of gunfire reverberated in the enclosed space and stitched a hole through the scorched door. Col then moved quickly aside as Magnus stepped forward and pitched a grenade through it.

There was the heavy crack of an explosion and a scream. 'Again!'

Another grenade went in and the blast splintered the doorframe.

'Let's go!'

Magnus stepped forward and booted it; the hinges came off and it fell in. The stack streamed through.

The room was full of plaster dust and smoke. The only thing Alex could see was the brightly lit muzzle of his gun through the grey swirl, swinging left and right, seeking some solid form.

'See anything?'

'No!'

He was breathing heavily and felt the dust clog in his throat.

'Just stay still! Wait!'

The dust gradually settled.

He saw the bodies of two civilian office workers stretched out on the floor. *Fuck.*

'Come on, let's go!' Command gave a harder edge to his voice.

His breathing was breathing quick and shallow; he swallowed hard to clear the dust from his throat and spat it out.

They moved on through the rooms and corridors, repeating the clearance procedure in each one.

'Clear! Clear!'

They were flowing forward smoothly, but Alex knew they were falling further and further behind Krymov as Batyuk hurried him away.

They reached a dangerous point where the main corridor ran on ahead north, but a door branched off it to the right, east along the other side of the triangle, which formed the northern edge of the central courtyard.

Sergey stepped forward. 'Krymov will have gone through there to get to the main entrance. It's his only way out.' He nodded to his right at the huge entrance dome across the courtyard at the apex of the triangle.

The door was an obvious ambush point; Alex eyed it nervously.

'OK, let's mousehole it! Pete – get a charge!'

The Australian whipped his rucksack off his back and pulled out the black, dinner-plate-sized mine.

He quickly ripped the plastic cover off the sticky pad, crept forward to the wall next to the door and pressed it onto the plaster. The others watched from back down the corridor as he crimped the detonator cord to a minute length and then ripped off the red firing tape that set the chemical fuse burning. He dropped the strip of red tape on the floor and ran back towards them.

In the time he had been doing this, Sergey had quickly pulled the folding satellite dish out of his rucksack, pointed it out of a window and called Grigory on his phone. He was speaking to him as the two kilos of C4 blew a cloud of red sparks and dust back down the corridor and more gunfire broke out as Alex led the team on.

'Go!'

The stack moved forward to the hole in the wall, large enough for a man to duck through. They poured into the room next to the door and then lobbed grenades down the corridor from there.

The different angle of attack worked and the two soldiers waiting down the corridor were caught by their blasts.

The delay was still too much, though, and Alex could envisage Krymov getting to the end of the long side of the building and slipping out of the main entrance whilst the Mil was flying around the other side of the building. He needed something to stop him getting away.

'Wait!' He held up a hand and the team paused in the corridor, each soldier taking a knee facing out in all-round defence. Alex pulled the receiver from the radio on his back.

'Arkady!'

'Yes?' His voice sounded calm and precise against the whirr of the rotor blades as he flew along the side of the Arsenal over the bodies of three MVD men who had tried to get between the two buildings. He was taking hits from a hail of rifle fire but it pinged off the canopy next to his head.

'I need an airstrike on the east end of the north side of the courtyard. We've got to stop Krymov getting out!'

'Roger that, airstrike, east end of north side of central courtyard.'

Arkady glanced quickly at the Arsenal building; the Gatling gun in the nose twitched over and fired a long suppressive burst at it to make them keep their heads down. Then Levin eased back on the stick and they rose up and swung back over the Senate building to come in at the courtyard from the south.

They hovered low over the roof again and Arkady sighted the heads-up display targeting ring on the end of the building before pressing the fire button and repeating the ripple fire process with the pod of rockets on the other wing.

Again he carefully blew the outer wall open and then shot out the inner walls. The whole building collapsed with a similarly spectacular explosion of debris across the courtyard. Windows smashed all around it, fire broke out from a punctured gas main and flames began pouring up into the sky, sending a pall of smoke out over the Kremlin.

Sergey peered out of a window across the courtyard at the destruction and nodded approvingly. He turned to Alex and shouted to him over the racket of the helicopter.

'They'll have to go down to the servants' corridor on the ground floor and try to run across the courtyard; it's their only way out now. You've got to pin them in there and get me time to do the broadcast with Lara.'

Alex knew that trying to win a head-on firefight to kill Krymov would be tough; the broadcast was equally important. If they could just pen Krymov in, that would have to do for now.

'OK!' he shouted in agreement, and they ran back into the west side of the building. From there they could fire at the whole façade of the northern side of the courtyard and keep Krymov pinned down. The far end of the façade was burning fiercely from the airstrike. He moved the team down into an office on the first floor and they took up firing positions at the windows.

Major Batyuk realised he was now trapped and needed to

fight his way across the open courtyard to get out of the main door and escape, but in order to do that he had to win the firefight against Alex's men. He had been able to get to an internal armoury and gather ten men from around the building. Their machine guns appeared from the windows along the façade and bursts of fire began spitting across at the office where Alex was positioned, the sound echoing off the high sides of the buildings. Under this covering fire, two men tried running out across the snow to the other side. Long bursts from the assault team's PKMs cut both of them down.

A static firefight developed with both sides trying to get in a superior weight of fire to force the enemy's head down. Alex, Yamba, Colin, Magnus and Pete were all on their PKMs, crouching at the windows, looking out at the enemy firing positions and trying to hit them when they stuck their heads out of the windows.

An insane cacophony of gunfire developed, with the solid roar of the machine guns pouring rounds out and the cracking and banging of bullets coming in through the windows, smashing into the walls opposite and blowing chunks of plaster and dust everywhere. A carpet of spent brass cartridges piled up on the floor next to each man as their guns spewed hot cases from their ejection ports. They smoked in the cold air and blue-grey smoke drifted up from them.

Someone opposite them had found some heavier weaponry. Alex saw the distinctive square flash-suppressor on the muzzle of a Kord poke out of a window and then the heavy rounds banged out, smashing into the stone outer wall and beginning to chew holes through it.

On the floor above them, in the press office, the braver cameramen had crawled from under their tables and pointed their cameras out of the windows to film the streams of tracer zipping back and forth across the courtyard.

424

Sergey crawled across the floor of the office and set up the satellite dish pointing back out of the window. He pulled his phone out and got through to Grigory. He had to yell at the top of his voice.

'Are you getting this?'

Grigory was in similar dire straits, crouched under the desk as Ilya and the technicians ripped out circuits and tried patching wires across it.

'No – we're still not live on you! We've taken hits! We've got enemy soldiers upstairs! And Sergey,' he paused before giving him the really bad news, 'we've just lost our last Tunguska! Sergey, you've got to do something fast or we are all going to get bombed to fuck!'

Sergey was shocked to hear his normally calm station chief sounding hysterical.

He thought fast. 'Look, never mind my feed, can you just relay the foreign channels? They're all here – are they filming?'

Grigory reached up and punched the right buttons on the console. CNN's feed of the firefight suddenly cut in over the looped tape that he had been broadcasting.

'OK, we're relaying CNN live now! You're on air.' He looked at the pictures of the gun battle. 'What the fuck is happening there? Are you winning?'

Sergey paused as he tried to sound confident. 'Look, don't worry, I'll sort something out here. We'll win, don't worry! Just stick with the CNN relay for the moment.'

He pressed the end button on his phone and tried to think what he was going to do.

In the Air Command bunker, General Korshunov looked up in alarm as the new pictures from CNN came through on the big wall screen in front of him.

The White Swan was four minutes from its final bombing run.

What the hell was going on in the Kremlin? Which side was winning? Was he supposed to abort the bomb run or let Ostankino have it, as Krymov had made him swear he would do?

His hand hovered over the desk mike as he wondered whether to patch through to Major Rostov and call off his mission.

In the Senate building, Alex could tell they were losing the balance of the firefight. The volume of incoming was beginning to dominate their outgoing fire; his men had to pull away from their firing positions at the windows for longer as bullets ripped through them.

He heard Arkady shouting in his earpiece from the helicopter, 'Alex! Alex, I can't hold these guys back for much longer; I'm getting low on ammunition. Several large groups are trying to cross over to you from the Arsenal! There's a squad just got in through the south end of the building. You definitely have four enemy approaching from behind your position.'

Sergey was up against the wall next to Alex and saw him press the earpiece against his head and then acknowledge grimly. Alex looked at him with a worried expression and then shouted, 'There's a squad just got in the south end, coming from behind us.' He jerked his thumb back the way they had come.

Sergey nodded blankly. He could feel the momentum draining away. The position was deteriorating rapidly: they were running low on ammunition, there was an enemy squad behind them and they were losing the firefight. He looked around the shattered room. Lara was crouched down along the far wall with her hands over her head from the blasts of plaster and ricochets over her.

Magnus moved back to fire out of the window again, was hit in the head and snapped back away from the wall.

Yamba looked down at him lying on the floor with blood pouring from under the rim of his holed helmet.

'He's hit, he's hit!'

Lara crawled on hands and knees to Magnus's body as it convulsed on the floor. She pulled his helmet off; there was a large hole in the back of his head with white skull and brain showing amidst a mess of blood and hair.

She cried out and tried pressing the bone back in place. Alex scrambled over next to her, took one look at the gaping hole and shouted to her, 'He's gone, he's gone! Leave him!'

He moved back to the window, gripped the stock of his PKM harder, drilling his anger out with a long burst at the enemy.

Sergey dragged Lara away from Magnus. He hugged her as she shuddered against him, each movement jolting his soul. He had got her into this and now she was in pain and probably going to die a violent death. He pulled her hurriedly out of the room into the corridor behind it.

Away from the noise of the firing he could hear a roaring sound overhead as if the fabric of the sky was being torn slowly open. Rostov had dropped the White Swan down to a lower altitude. To increase the psychological terror of any defenders left around the tower, he kicked in his afterburners. Each of his four Kuznetsov turbofans shot huge red streaks of burning jet fuel out behind and pushed the aircraft through Mach 1. As he broke the sound barrier, an enormous sonic boom crashed out over Moscow, like a thunderclap heralding *Götterdämmerung*. Despite its large size, the Swan was a very manoeuvrable aircraft and he flicked it over on its side to bank away and circle the tower.

Sergey heard the boom and realised what it meant. He knew from his earlier conversation with Grigory that they had lost the last Tunguska and that the tower was defenceless, the bombing run with the FOAB was about to begin and hundreds of people in and around the tower were about to die.

His bold plan to attack the Kremlin was collapsing around him. He looked down at Lara, hunched up in his arms. In the middle of all the mayhem around him, he had a sudden moment of clarity and felt again how much he loved her. What a ridiculous man he had been not to see that before.

She was going to die soon if he didn't do something fast. He looked out over her head, thinking hard.

A moment later, Alex ducked back from the window to reload and glimpsed Sergey run back into the room to where his camera and rucksack with the mines and grenades in it were piled.

Alex ignored him, fitted the new magazine in with a satisfying snick and stood up to fire another burst. When he looked back, Sergey wasn't there.

Where the fuck has he gone?

'RPG!' Yamba yelled as a man stepped quickly out into the courtyard, sighted his launcher and fired.

The wall along from Alex exploded inwards. Pete took the brunt of the blast at waist height, just under the line of his flakjacket. He was blown back across the room, his stomach and pelvis ripped open by shrapnel. Guts and a blood slick spilled out around him on the floor.

Col shouted, 'Oh fook! No!'

He put his gun down and kneeled over Pete with his hands raised, looking helplessly at the mess of blood, guts and smashed bone.

Alex glanced out of the corner of the window; more men were appearing in the courtyard as their fire slackened off. With Col off his weapon, they were down to two guns from five. The enemy were getting a better angle on them and Krymov would soon be able to slip across when they were completely pinned down.

'Col! I need you!'

Alex looked at Pete; he had seen enough battle damage in African wars and knew he was gone. He switched into command mode. 'Col! Get on that gun now! Leave him!'

Col stood up slowly, forcing himself away from his comrade.

Alex turned back to the window and then Sergey re-appeared, scuttled over to him and shouted, 'Cease fire!'

'What?'

'Cease fire!'

The weight of incoming fire from the enemy slackened off, and Col and Yamba both looked out from their windows to see what was going on.

Sergey shouted at them as well: 'Cease fire! Cease fire!'

Alex looked at him, startled by the sudden silence. 'What are you doing?'

'Don't worry, I have the solution to all your problems!' Sergey gave one of his manic grins. 'Just follow me, come on!'

He waved them towards the door back to the corridor.

Alex knew that their situation was desperate. Two of his men now lay dead on the floor and they were going to be overwhelmed soon. The cessation of incoming fire, however Sergey had achieved it, was an enormous relief. In the end he didn't have any choice but to go along with him. He waved Col and Yamba over.

They all carried their machine guns and followed Sergey and Lara as he led them out of the room. They followed him out and down a backstairs to the ground floor, from where a narrow passageway ran along to a small door opening onto the courtyard.

Sergey paused at the bottom of the stairs and pulled the flakjacket off that he had been wearing over his parka. He then began to walk towards the door to the outside.

'Sergey, don't!' Lara shouted. 'They'll kill you!'

She pushed past Alex and ran down the stairs. Sergey walked back towards her, came close, pressed one hand against her cheek and smiled. 'Look, you'll see. I've solved everything.' He kissed her on both cheeks. 'You're going to be OK now.'

She looked back at him with tears rolling down her cheeks. She couldn't understand what he had done but was temporarily silenced by his affection.

He walked back towards the door.

'Sergey, what have you done?' she called to him, a strange calm in her voice.

He turned and smiled back at her. 'Ah, now you will see my magic.' He waved his mobile phone at her. 'Come on! Follow me.' He opened the door and walked out a few feet into the snowy yard.

Alex tensed, expecting a burst of gunfire, but none came. He ran forward with Col to cover him, their weapons pointed out from the doorway as Sergey stood out in the open in front of them.

A door opened to their left, fifty metres away along the north wall of the courtyard, and Major Batyuk stepped out, looking at them warily over the sights of his assault rifle. He kept the gun trained on Sergey as he carefully stepped sideways into the open.

Sergey turned and gestured back to them to come outside. 'Come on, come out. We're all friends now.'

Three more soldiers followed Batyuk out onto the snow.

Lara came to the door and looked out. 'Sergey, what is happening?'

A horrifying idea was forming in her mind.

'Did you call Krymov?' she said.

Sergey just turned and grinned back at her.

Krymov and Fyodor stepped out of the door across the courtyard, both in long military overcoats. Alex and Col moved out of the doorway and swung their PKMs onto them immediately, but Sergey shouted, 'No!' and spread his arms out in front of them.

He spoke more gently, pleading with them now. 'Don't worry, I've solved everything. It's all going to be all right. Just put your guns down and come out here.'

'What!'

Alex looked at him as if he were mad. After such a vicious firefight he could not accept that they were not going to be shot at.

Sergey sighed at Alex's intransigence and spoke to him as if he were explaining to an idiot. 'I've done a deal with Krymov.' He held his phone up again. 'Alex, the Blue Revolution is over. You've got no choice, Krymov has won and you have lost. I've got immunity, but I don't know what they'll do to you when they get you into the Lubyanka.' He jerked his head back at the infamous FSB prison a few blocks to the east of the Kremlin.

Lara stared at him in disbelief.

Alex looked at Sergey and raged inside.

The fucker had betrayed them just as Fyodor had done. He must have seen how easily Krymov had accepted the airforce chief back and guessed that if he would do that for Fyodor he would easily do it for his darling Sergey. All his

431

doubts about Sergey's sanity when he first met him rushed back. What had seemed amusing eccentricities now stood out as the hallmarks of a traitor.

His face tightened with rage, 'You fucking ...' he said quietly, raising his machine gun.

'Uh-uh.' Sergey wagged a contemptuous finger at him as Batyuk and the other three men swung their rifles up to cover him. Alex could see that in his exposed position he would be dead if he laid a finger on Sergey.

He forced himself not to move and looked back at the Russian, thinking hard. There was no way out. He was under the enemy's guns and more troops were coming up behind them. He had trusted Sergey and been comprehensively betrayed.

He felt most responsible for his men. He looked at Col, next to him in the open, and then back at Yamba, who was with Lara in the doorway.

Sergey had outmanoeuvred them and there was nothing that Alex could do about it now. He slowly bent down, put his machine gun on the floor and motioned the others to do likewise. He stood up feeling weak and defenceless and stared threateningly back at Sergey.

Col and Yamba put their guns down and Sergey grinned. 'There, we're all friends now.'

He turned his back on them and opened his arms in a bear hug towards Krymov as if the two were going off for a drinking session. Across the courtyard, Krymov returned the gesture. He was feeling victorious and jubilant after Sergey had called him and promised to betray all the members of his team and hand them over to him.

Two floors above them in the press room the journalists were all leaning out of the windows now that the firing had stopped, and their cameramen jostled for positions.

Gerry Kramer was flabbergasted as he stood on a chair looking over the backs of the cameramen, out of the window. He commentated live on the scene in the courtyard.

'We just *cannot* understand what is going on here. The firing has stopped and now the well-known billionaire, Sergey Shaposhnikov, seems to be about to speak to President Krymov.'

In Air Command Headquarters, General Korshunov saw the pictures on the big screen, grabbed the desk mike and patched through to Rostov as he lined up on the tower for his final bomb run. 'Major Rostov, delay the bomb run! I want you to circle the target and await my orders!'

What the hell was going on in the Kremlin?

Lara was not feeling so equivocal. She ran out of the doorway and, as Sergey stood with her back to her and his arms open to Krymov, she hit him around the head. She tried to shout at him but was too angry to form words. His words to her had always been so special and now he had betrayed them and thus everything that was dear in existence.

She screamed at him and kicked him. He doubled up and she clenched her fists in rage and battered him around the head.

Finally she managed to shriek, 'You talk … !' and then her anger cut her off. She hit him again and then opened one hand and slashed him across the face with her nails.

He clutched his eyes with one hand and she grabbed hold of a handful of his yellow hair, pulled his head down and began kicking him. Words began to form, and she shouted each one out of her like a disease she wanted to expel.

'You traitor! You just talk!'

Alex stared at her attacking Sergey, shocked by the ferocity of her assault; her sophisticated façade had shattered, making her anger all the more frightening. Alex was mad with Sergey but what he was seeing was too visceral, too raw to watch.

He stepped towards her from behind, grabbed her elbows and pulled her off Sergey, who was on his knees, blood dripping onto the snow from the three slashes across his eyes and nose.

Lara shouted but Alex held her firm. Her anger had spent itself and she went limp in his arms.

Sergey stood up slowly and painfully, wincing from her blows. He stared back at her with a look that combined contradictory emotions: anger smouldered alongside helpless devotion. Alex stared at him and saw the raw pink flesh of his soul exposed and bleeding.

He took a last lingering look at the woman whom Alex was holding and turned slowly away. He straightened up and put his hands inside the chest pockets of his parka. He fumbled with something and then pulled them out again, looked across at where Krymov was standing waiting for him, shocked but sympathetic after the battering his old friend had just received. Sergey opened his arms again before walking towards him.

As he dropped his hands back to his sides, Alex saw a piece of red tape fall to the ground. He didn't recognise it at first; he was so confused and shaken by his anger and the emotion he felt for Lara as she leaned her back against him for support. He looked at the red tape, half his brain saying that it was something that he should take note of and the other half not responding.

Lara was crying quietly and also took a while to recognise the tape for what it was. She realised she had seen Pete tear a similar one off the MTP-2 time-delay mouseholing charge.

She stared at it in shock as she registered what Sergey was doing.

She screamed out at him again, 'No! Sergey, no!'

She threw herself down from Alex's grip onto her knees and begged him, 'Sergey, please! You'll kill me, you have my soul!'

But he was fixed on his task. He had realised in the middle of the firefight that he needed to do something to save her and now that he had committed to it he had passed into a realm of peace. In his mind he had already crossed the void between what he knew, and what he suspected he knew, and now he just needed to walk across the courtyard.

Sergey turned round in mid-stride and walked backwards for a moment, facing Lara with his arms open. Despite the blood on his face and the pain in his heart, he grinned and held up his index finger to admonish her jokingly, '*Russia* has your soul!'

He turned back, walked up to Krymov and embraced him.

Chapter Sixty-Six

The world's media had a grandstand view of the courtyard from the press room.

Gerry Kramer was standing on tiptoe on a chair peering over the backs of the camera crews leaning out of the windows: 'Shaposhnikov is moving across the square to Krymov. He's embracing the President ...'

His hand went to his mouth.

The entire press corps stared in silence.

There was a long pause before Kramer began to articulate again. 'Oh my God,' he mumbled through his hand, 'Oh shit. Oh shit.

'Mike, I'm sorry, this is terrible. There's been an explosion. There are bodies – I can see at least four bodies – I can't see who they are but one of the bodies must be the President. The President must be dead; no one could have survived that.

'There's a woman running over to them. It's Lara Maslova! She's a TV personality here; she was doing the broadcasts this morning. She is crying and screaming, she's on her knees. There are three soldiers coming up behind her – we don't know who they are.'

Alex stood behind her, staring, his machine gun hung from his right hand with its muzzle pointing down, while Lara looked at the mess of her lover, red on the white snow.

She stood up and turned away from it, blindly seeking anything to take the pain away, crying out and throwing herself onto Alex.

He held her with his left arm as she sobbed into him. He looked at the carnage over her shoulder: there was hardly anything left of either Sergey or Krymov. Batyuk had been standing behind the President and had lost most of one side of his body. Fyodor had also been too near and had taken a large piece of shrapnel in the middle of his forehead; he was still just alive, twitching and bleeding heavily on the snow.

The other Echelon 25 men were either injured or too concussed by the blast to do anything. Alex stared at the horrific scene in front of him, the anger he had felt a minute ago against Sergey draining into an uncomprehending horror.

His instinct for command kept him going through it. He keyed the mike on his headset and said wearily: 'Arkady, we need extraction. Central courtyard. Now.'

'Roger, coming over now.'

The huge Mil thudded up into sight and loomed across the courtyard, blowing a storm of snow over him. He stood with his eyes closed, welcoming its cold blast – wishing it would wipe away the horror in front of him.

He felt he ought to return for the dead bodies of his two comrades but he knew that an enemy force was approaching from behind. They wouldn't know what had just happened in the courtyard, so he didn't want to go back into the building and add to the body count.

Lara had gone into shock, clutching Alex tightly. He handed his weapon to Colin and scooped her up in his arms, cradling her to his chest and ducking down as they ran in through the snowstorm towards the helicopter. Yamba dragged the troop bay door open, Alex stepped up inside and sat down on the hard midline bench with the girl still held against him. Yamba slammed the door and there was finally something between him and the awfulness outside.

Major Levin went through transition quickly, lifting them up abruptly, spinning round and then powering away from the Kremlin in a tight turn, heading out north over Red Square. Col and Yamba sank back into the bench, exhausted as they came down off the huge adrenalin high.

Alex undid the straps on his helmet and pushed it off his head, it clanged on the floor. He ran his hand through his hair and looked down at Lara. She was crying quietly against him still.

'I were sure we was fooking gone then,' Col said in a shaky voice as he clutched the barrel of his machine gun between his legs. Yamba nodded wearily in acknowledgement. Alex nodded as well; he couldn't believe they had got out of that insane firefight alive.

'Hey, it's all fucked up out here! You should see it!' Arkady shouted in English on the intercom.

Yamba looked at Alex, who flicked his head towards the door; he stood up and hauled it open. They were flying at five hundred feet and as they squinted against the blast of cold air they could see that northern Moscow had been turned into an apocalypse by the battle around the tower.

Blocks of flats were on fire from missile strikes, sending up huge plumes of smoke visible from miles away. Streets were littered with the debris of war – rubble and glass blown out of buildings, smashed and burning cars, bodies spread-eagled in the snow, knocked-out tanks burning with their gun barrels twisted up at the sky. The trees along the middle of the main approach boulevard were on fire from a flamethrower hit.

A helicopter had crashed into an apartment block and exploded, splitting the building open, so that its innards spewed out: girders, sofas, kitchen units and bathrooms all hung out

439

of the wreckage. Everywhere there were smashed windows and buildings spattered with shrapnel from explosions.

Colonels Vronsky and Melekhov had called off their assault on the tower when they heard the news from the Kremlin. With their commander-in-chief dead they were waiting to hear what happened next. General Korshunov had also ordered the White Swan to return to its nest far to the south. It had roared away with a final contemptuous sonic boom that had shaken the capital again.

Arkady radioed ahead. 'Darensky, you still alive?'

'Yes, still alive,' came the exhausted reply.

'OK, we're coming back in. Don't shoot us down!'

'Roger, all units are stood down.'

As they drew nearer they could see that the Ostankino tower looked a mess. It was cratered with shell and missile strikes, satellite dishes dangled down from cables and the offices at the top were on fire on the east side, sending out a thick stream of black smoke.

Levin took them in low over the open ground around the tower. As they skimmed in, they could see it was littered with dead bodies, crashed helicopters and knocked-out armoured vehicles. Machine-gun ammunition crackled as it cooked off inside a burning tank.

They rose up past the offices; Alex craned his neck and could see all the windows smashed or shot out, and the bodies of dead defenders inside.

They touched down on the roof terrace and Raskolnikov and Grigory ran out from the stairs towards them. Levin shut the motors down as Alex and the others stepped out gingerly and looked at the bodies strewn across the roof.

They ducked through the rotor wash. Grigory ran over to Lara and clutched her to him, rocking her gently as they both mourned the loss of Sergey.

Chapter Sixty-Seven

Later that afternoon the crowds came back out onto the streets of Moscow.

Young men, housewives and office workers chanted and waved victory signs at the camera crews roving amongst them. Blue Revolution flags, which had been hidden after the morning's massacre, came out again and jubilantly thrashed back and forth overhead.

The openness was possible because Raskolnikov had been in phone contact with General Korshunov and other leading members of the Krymov regime and agreed a truce to allow time for negotiations on forming a new government.

When the news of this went out on all channels, world leaders began giving their reactions to the day's extraordinary events. Moscow was three hours ahead of London, so the Prime Minister had been dragged out of bed in the very early morning when the fighting started and rushed to the underground COBRA committee room for an emergency session. The other senior members of the intelligence services, army, air force and navy had all straggled in, looking dishevelled. They had gone straight into a secure videoconference with the American President, who was sitting in his pyjamas at his desk in the White House.

Ever since Harrington had been instructed to brief Alex

on the mission, the government had not known what he was doing and had tried to maintain the pretence that they had nothing to do with him. During those two weeks, the energy crisis in the UK had got worse and worse, with more deaths and more misery, and the pressure had mounted on the Prime Minister to do something. So, when the news had come through that Alex had got Raskolnikov out and he then did his TV broadcast, the PM was ecstatic, punching the air and slapping backs in the COBRA room. The plan had been an incredible risk to take and it had looked like it was going to pay off smoothly.

However, when Krymov had then mounted his counter-attack and the terrible battles had begun around Ostankino, the PM had looked very grave indeed. Maybe he was going to be responsible for the biggest-ever foreign policy disaster in the UK's history. The committee had sat in utter silence, glued to the coverage of the events as the battle had swung back and forth. Alex bursting into the press room in the Kremlin and shouting at the journalists to get down had been a very tense moment. Harrington had sat bolt upright on the sofa in his house in Hampshire and gone white.

Finally, it had all ended in the appalling scene in the court-yard. They had won but no one felt able to celebrate the terrible and very public demise of their opponent.

The PM then gave a hastily convened press conference at Number Ten. None of the previous dramas showed on his face as he stood up in front of the cameras. He always was the consummate politician. Instead he put on his most sombre expression, leaned forward over the lectern to the microphone and said in a very grave tone, 'The government of the United Kingdom is very saddened by the tragic events that we have all witnessed unfolding in Moscow this morning. Obviously, we had our differences with President Krymov, but I and my Cabinet would like to extend our heartfelt condolences to the government and people of Russia for the violent death of their President.' He glanced around at the Defence Minister and Home Secretary standing on either side of him, who nodded soberly.

'In terms of events going forwards, we appeal to both sides in the fighting to seek a negotiated solution to the conflict and the government of the United Kingdom stands ready to lend whatever assistance we can to help resolve the dispute.'

Alex watched the broadcast in the conference room in the Ostankino tower. Standing in the middle of the shattered battlefield he could not but feel contempt for the cynicism of the man who had sent him out to cause all of this mayhem and Krymov's death, which he was now so publicly regretting. He glanced round at Yamba, who rolled his eyes.

Grigory came into the conference room with a smile on his face. 'OK, so we have good news. They put the fire out,' he jerked his thumb back east where the 568th soldiers had been labouring with fire hoses, 'and Raskolnikov has negotiated for you to go home.'

'What about the bodies?' Alex had stipulated their return.

Grigory nodded grimly. 'Levin is going in the Mil to get them now. Then he's taking you all on to Sheremetyevo and we are going to get you out of the country as fast as we can before the government decides it does actually want to go after you.'

Alex looked at him and nodded. It was as good a deal as they were going to get. He was exhausted and felt drained and saddened by the deaths of his two men. The team had done the job, but a mortality rate of a third was not something any commander could feel proud of.

When they heard Levin's helicopter return from its grim

second mission to the Kremlin, they gathered their weapons and packs and headed up the stairs to the roof for the last time. As it landed and wound down its rotors, soldiers from the 568th slid the side door open and stepped out. Alex could see the outlines of Pete and Magnus's bodies under grey army blankets on two stretchers in the troop bay.

Arkady climbed out of the co-pilot cockpit and came over to them where they had gathered by the railing looking out over Moscow. He lit up a Prima and offered one to Col. The two of them smoked as they all stood silently along the rail, looking out at the plumes of smoke still rising over the capital from burning buildings.

Raskolnikov, Grigory and Lara came up the stairs and walked over to them. The four survivors looked battered and grizzled: faces covered in cuts and bruises, clothes in bloodstains and dust, and all stinking of smoke and cordite.

Raskolnikov stepped forward and embraced Alex, then stood back and looked at him sternly. 'Alexander Nikolaivich, the Russian people will never know of your sacrifices and those of your men, but we do, and we will never forget them.'

Alex merely nodded and said, 'Thank you.' Saying anything else would just sound pompous, and that wasn't what Pete and Magnus had been about.

He found it a lot harder to know what to do when Lara stepped towards him. This was their big goodbye; he doubted he would ever see her again, but there were too many people around to get emotional.

He stared at her and could see she was trying hard not to cry. Her huge blue eyes looked up at him but he could only glower back. She reached out and touched the lock of her hair still tied to the webbing over his heart. It was clotted with dried blood and dust.

She forced herself to be brave and said, 'Keep it. It's for you, Sashenka.'

He looked at her straight and nodded.

That second's eye contact said everything; words would just have got in the way.

The line from *Dr Zhivago* that she had written in her note came back to him. It had puzzled him at the time but now he understood it: 'human understanding rendered speechless by emotion'.

Chapter Sixty-Eight

TUESDAY 23 DECEMBER

Alex stepped up to the small gate in the high wall and knocked carefully.

He looked round at Col, Yamba and Arkady and shrugged. They were standing behind him on the busy street wondering what would happen next. It was a week after they had flown out of Moscow, and they were entering Buckingham Palace via a door at the back of the large palace grounds.

Alex had no idea what was going to happen inside. He had done several stints of ceremonial duty at BP as a junior Household Cavalry officer in the past, so he knew that the Queen was away at Sandringham in Norfolk, where she traditionally spent the Christmas break, and that the palace shut down in her absence. Harrington had phoned him to say that some recognition would be made of their efforts but he had sounded uncomfortable and had not given any further details.

The surviving members of the team were all dressed in their best suits and had been bewildered by the news that they were going to the palace. However, any feelings of celebration had been muted by the knowledge of the two other gatherings that were taking place on the same day in different parts of the world.

Their thoughts were with the small family group huddled together in a dusty cemetery on the outskirts of Dagaragu in Northern Territory. The Bridges family were a tough lot but Pete's father couldn't help crying when the shattered body of his son had been returned in its refrigerated steel coffin, with no explanation as to where and why his boy had been killed.

Magnus's father had died years ago, so only his sister was there to put her arm around his mother in the tiny Church of Norway graveyard, on the north shore looking out over Sognefjorden. A cold wind whipped snow around them from the mountains behind the white timber church. Mrs Løndahl was a formidable woman, but she had not expected to outlive her son. She cried as Magnus was lowered into a hole cut out of the frozen ground. She too would never know what had happened to him; his body had been returned with a brief government death certificate.

The group of men who did know their story would never speak about it.

The garden gate in the palace wall opened. Harrington's large reddened face peered nervously out as he ushered them through and then hurriedly shut the door.

'This way, Devereux.' He sounded resentful, barely acknowledging Alex and not even deigning to look at the rest of his team. He pulled the scarf tighter around his overcoat collar and turned and led them through the snow-covered gardens towards the distant palace.

The whole place was deserted. Harrington led them along the winding path through the bare trees to the south end of the enormous rear façade and in through a side door. Alex's mind was whirring, trying to work out where they were going. They paused in an ornate antechamber next to a huge wooden door. It was cold in the room, despite the fact that the energy blockade had been lifted a week ago; with the monarch away, no one had turned the heating on.

Four sheets of white paper were laid out on a polished desk at one side, each with a pen on it. Alex took in the British Army crest at the top of each page.

'Right, all of you, sign here,' Harrington said gruffly to them and pointed at the papers. 'You'll be discharged immediately afterwards, so don't get any ideas.' He glared at Alex, obviously mindful of the last time he had signed an official document in front of him.

They all dutifully scratched their names on the sheets. Harrington looked on in thinly veiled disgust and then checked each one carefully.

He grunted, straightened up and looked them each carefully in the eye. 'You will behave with the highest decorum and *never*,' he held up a warning index finger, 'speak of this!'

He turned, straightened his shoulders and opened the double doors with a flourish.

They followed his marching figure into the vast ballroom, towards its far end, where a small woman stood on a dais. She was wrapped up in an overcoat against the cold and flanked by two Gurkha orderly officers, her equerry and the Defence Secretary. As a woman who had stayed in London throughout the Blitz, she understood a thing or two about a national crisis, and she had not hung about when the time came to honour the men who had resolved it.

Harrington stamped to attention a few feet from the dais and saluted. Alex was startled but forced himself to do likewise. As each of the others realised who was in the room they all came to attention in a line along the steps.

The equerry was in shooting clothes and pulled a piece of paper out of the pocket of his Barbour. Despite the necessary precautions to conceal the monarch's return to the

449

capital, he sounded suitably official as he read out the list: 'Major Alexander Devereux, The Household Cavalry, for outstanding leadership and bravery under fire, the Victoria Cross.'

Alex marched forward like an automaton and stood stiffly to attention as she pinned the small grey cross onto his suit breast.

'Regimental Sergeant-Major Yamba Douala, 32 Battalion, South African Defence Force, the Conspicuous Gallantry Cross, for outstanding bravery under fire.'

Yamba towered over her but kept his hard eyes fixed on the red drapes behind, before executing a sharp right turn and marching away as Col stepped forward.

'Regimental Sergeant-Major Colin Thwaites, Second Battalion, The Parachute Regiment, the Conspicuous Gallantry Cross, for outstanding bravery under fire.'

Finally, Arkady stomped forward in an ill-fitting suit, 'Captain Arkady Voloshin, Armed Forces of the Russian Federation, the Distinguished Flying Cross, for courage whilst flying in the face of the enemy.'

The irony of this last award was not lost on Arkady, but he kept his face rigid.

When he had returned to the line, the onlookers gave a polite round of applause, and, after a quiet nod of her head, the sovereign withdrew.

Harrington was obviously relieved that the highly irregular ceremony was over and led them out to the antechamber where an unseen hand had removed the original sheets and laid out four discharge papers that they duly signed.

He then led them out of the palace and through the snow-covered gardens to the back gate. He unlocked it and then looked at Alex in a grudging way and offered his hand.

'Well done, Devereux, good work. I hope I never see you again.'

Alex looked straight at him for a moment, then shook his hand and said in a polite voice, 'Thank you very much. I hope I never see you again either.'

They walked out and Harrington shut the gate firmly behind them.

The four men emerged onto the south end of Grosvenor Place and stood awkwardly on the pavement. Crowds of last-minute Christmas shoppers pushed past them and the traffic roared through the slush on the road. After the energy blockade had been lifted the country was rushing to catch up with all the usual mundane aspects of the season.

The men were bewildered by the sudden change of pace. Alex looked round at them and tried to think what to do next.

'Pub?'

They nodded and he searched his memories of pubcrawls from his times on ceremonial duty. That felt like a long time ago now. Some forgotten instinct led him across the road, then left into the quiet, residential Lower Belgrave Street and straight to the Plumbers Arms. It was a traditional boozer and, mid-afternoon, was deserted. Alex ordered four pints of bitter and they retreated to an alcove.

When he had finally sat down and drunk half a pint in one long pull, Colin felt able to speak.

'Flippin' 'eck,' he muttered and stared off into the distance along with the others. 'That were really her, weren't i'?'

Yamba nodded thoughtfully. 'She is very small,' he said.

Alex pulled the black case from his pocket and flipped it open to look at the small grey medal with its crimson ribbon.

The VC.

He was in a state of shock, but was still aware that sadness also sat next to them in the alcove. He put the medal away again and looked round at the others. He raised his glass. 'Here's to them.'

They nodded and drank, thinking of the other two.

They quickly finished their drinks, stood up and walked out onto the street. True to form, they kept it short: smiles, handshakes and muttered goodbyes. They split up and headed off into the Christmas crowds.

It had started snowing again. Alex turned up the collar of his overcoat and walked away.

Author's Note

December was written as fiction based on real events. However, during the process of writing it, real events began to resemble fiction. When the credit crunch hit, popular protests broke out in Russia alongside the worst energy blockade on Europe yet.

Most of those financial problems have now passed. However, this also means that we are back to business as usual in terms of Russia's approach to foreign affairs, after a brief period of trying to be nice to the West during the winter of 2008 and first half of 2009. Some of this was in response to the new Obama administration and its attempt to 'hit the reset button'. However, it was also because the Russians feared that the rouble might collapse and that they would need all the friends at the IMF and the World Bank that they could get.

Now that this threat has retreated, and the Russian government is feeling more bullish again, it has returned to its old habits: launching large military exercises near Georgia, breaking off negotiations to join the WTO and entering a customs union with Belarus and Kazakhstan instead. They have also failed to reach an agreement with Ukraine on gas prices, which means that repeated gas blockades are likely.

So what are my own views on Putin's government? Well,

they are probably more balanced than the story might suggest. The Kremlin did a much better job at macro-economic management over the last ten years than the British government, i.e. instead of running up large debts, it fixed the roof while the sun was shining in the boom years and put aside $600 billion worth of foreign currency reserves that were then used to manage the decline of the rouble, preventing another 1998 debt default and insulating the Russian people from a painful economic shock. Putin has also brought political stability to Russia (at a democratic price) and is a lot more competent than his buffoonish predecessor, Yeltsin. In terms of what actually matters to ordinary people in Russia this is very important – you can't eat votes.

It is a great tragedy that Russia and the West have often had such hostile relations, especially now when Russia needs Europe as an energy market as much as we need them as a supplier. There are also so many other issues that would benefit from mutual cooperation such as Iranian and North Korean nuclear ambitions.

In many ways this standoff has been a war of mutual misunderstanding. Part of what I am trying to do in this book is to bridge this gap a little by explaining why Russians are so paranoid – they have been invaded and trashed by every European and Asian power. Apart from this, Russia is a proud nation and its fall from superpower status was painful. The 1990s were a time of utter chaos and collapse in Russia when the West largely thought, 'Job done,' and forgot about the country.

I am not saying that this means that the Russians should be given carte blanche to bully their neighbours but I do think that the US needs to be more cognisant of Russia's historical spheres of interest before it starts encouraging

Ukraine and Georgia into NATO. Would they accept Russian tanks stationed on the Mexican or Canadian border? Both countries are defence liabilities rather than defence assets and both are very internally divided about whether they actually want to join NATO. The organisation that should lead European expansion eastwards is the EU not NATO.

In terms of the veracity of *December*, the book is fiction and so some of it is obviously exaggerated for effect. However, everything I have written about Russian history is factually accurate, as are most of the arguments I put forward about the current problems of its economy and politics. Petrol rationing has not happened, although it did cause riots in similarly oil-rich Iran when it was introduced. I have also exaggerated the UK's dependence on direct Russian gas imports but the point still remains that many of our partners in NATO and the EU are heavily dependent on them and that the Russians regularly use gas blockades on Eastern Europe as a foreign policy weapon. What is an issue for our partners will become an issue for us.

Some of the real-life background to events in the book are given below.

The Blue Revolution

This is based on the 2004 Orange Revolution in Ukraine and all the other colour revolutions that happened after it: Rose, Tulip, Green etc. The Orange Revolution was Putin's worst nightmare come true in Russia's backyard – a western-backed uprising against a corrupt government.

YaG – 14/10 penal colony

This prison exists but is actually in the town of Krasnokamensk rather than outside it. The reason I got the idea for *December* was that I saw an article in *The Times* that mentioned that this prison was also used to incarcerate the members of the Decembrist uprising in 1825, which appealed to my sense of historical continuity.

The conditions described in the prison all come from Solzhenitsyn's unbeatable classic *One Day in the Life of Ivan Denisovich*. This in turn was based on his eight years in the camps. Despite having fought through the Eastern Front campaign as an artillery officer, he was sentenced after it for describing Stalin as 'the man with the moustache' in a letter home.

Fighting in Moscow and around the Ostankino TV tower
A lot of the ideas for the fighting in Moscow come from real events. There was a KGB coup in 1991 against Gorbachev, which Yeltsin was able to break by doing a speech on top of a tank and then managing to get it onto the news.

The real inspiration for the Moscow battle scenes came from the later conflict in 1993 when several hundred people were killed, much of it around the Ostankino TV tower. Tanks shelled the White House, the presidential palace, and burnt it down.

For further information on geographical context and literary references within *December*, please visit www.jamessteel.info.

JS
London
2009

Acknowledgements

Firstly, I am indebted to my agent Judith Murdoch for all her help and support over the years, without which this book would not have happened.

Also, a big thank you to my editor, Maxine Hitchcock, for her patience and creative insight, as well as the production and marketing team at HarperCollins, and Camilla Ferrier at the Marsh Agency.

In researching this novel I would like to acknowledge the help of the following British Army officers: Captain Charles MacDonald (Household Cavalry Division), Captain Patrick Trueman (Royal Scots Dragoon Guards) and Major Mark Richardson (Royal Logistics Corps).

With regards to the Russian language and social content, I would like to thank Margarita Nikolaeva and Katya Grigoruk. I was also greatly helped by the GB-Russia Society, Pushkin House, the Royal Institute of International Affairs at Chatham House, and the London School of Economics Russian lecture programme. Also, a huge thanks to Robert Chandler of Queen Mary College, University of London, for his comments and the inspiration provided by his beautiful translation of Vasily Grossman's epic, *Life and Fate*.

Particular books and newspapers that I wish to acknowledge include:

- Anna Politkovskaya: *Putin's Russia* – for her description of army mutinies
- Arkady Babchenko: *One Soldier's War* - about the brutal reality of being a conscript in the Russian army
- Alena V. Ledeneva: *How Russia Really Works* – for her coverage of "informal practices" in Russia
- Victoria E. Bonnell, Ann Cooper & Gregory Freidin: *Russia at the Barricades* – for descriptions of civil unrest in Moscow
- Orlando Figes: *Natasha's Dance. A Cultural History of Russia*
- Alexander Litvinenko & Yuri Felshtinsky: *Blowing Up Russia*
- Peter Julicher: Renegades, *Rebels and Rogues Under the Tsars*
- David Bellavia: *House to House* - on the reality of modern urban warfare
- *The Times*
- *The New Yorker*
- *The Economist*
- *The Moscow Times*

Finally, for proof reading and suggestions I am indebted to Ashley House and Patrick White.

This book is inspired by and dedicated to all Russian writers and I have used their names and the names of characters from their books in tribute to them, full details are on my website. I am in awe of their Romantic compassion for creation and humanity that led them to write so beautifully.

London, 2009.